They seek it here, they seek it there

They seek that statue everywhere

Real or myth, who can tell

That damned elusive bird from hell.

Books by Alex Willis

Non-Fiction

Step by Step Guitar Making 1st and 2nd editions

Standalone fiction

The Penitent Heart

The Falcon, The Search for Horus.

The Road Home

Buchanan Series

Book 1   The Bodies in the Marina

Book 2   The Laminated man

Book 3   The Mystery of Cabin 312

Book 4   The Reluctant Jockey

Book 5   The Missing Heiress

Book 6   The Jockey's Wife

Book 7   Death on the Cart

THE FALCON

The Search for Horus

First published in Great Britain by Mount Pleasant Press 2014.
This edition published by Mount Pleasant Publishing 2020

ISBN 978-1-913471-04-0

Text set in Garamond 12 point.

Cover photo and layout © Alex Willis 2016

I stand in the rain and hide my tears. © Alex Willis 2016

Foreword

There is story, written many years ago, about a solid gold, jewel encrusted, black enamelled Falcon statue. According to this story, it was gifted to the King of Spain by the Knights Templar. This story truly is a magnificent creation of fiction by the great American writer Dashiell Hammett. But as can be in life, truth is sometimes stranger than fiction.

There was indeed a falcon bird gifted to the King of Spain by the Knights Templar, but not a bird as described above. No sir, it was not a statue, but a real live falcon bird. The gift dutifully recorded in the annals of the Knights Templar.

But let me introduce you to the real story. A tale far beyond anything that than can be imagined with mortal minds. The real falcon statue was carved many millennia ago by Egyptian temple artisans from a block of pure black marble. It was created to ensnare the very soul of the powerful sun god, Horus. Down through the ages, those who briefly possessed this treasure have worked great evil. Ever since the day of its creation, brave men and women have sought it out to destroy it, and the power it wields.

Prof. Caspar Guttmann III

This book is dedicated to the memory of my father,
Alexander Nairn Willis Snr. 1920 - 2013

1

Death in the Night

I heard the thud and cursed Dizzy's cheap heart. I'd worked till gone one in the morning doing the set-up on his bass guitar, and now I was going to have to shell out for a new string at the least. *Don't change the strings,* he'd said, *they're new three gigs ago,* he'd said. Three months of hard gigging more likely.

He'd dropped the guitar off late Saturday – no, it was just into Sunday morning, and said he'd pick it up on the way through to the Newhaven ferry on the Monday morning. If he hadn't been a friend, I'd have told him where he could have shoved his guitar.

I looked at the digits on the bedside clock: three-thirty. At least there would be plenty of time to replace the offending strings and get back to bed before the inevitable whirlwind that was Dizzy showed up.

I turned on the bunk light, threw back the blankets, and swivelled out of bed, watching not to bump my head on the side deck. Living and working on a restored World War 2 tugboat had its good points and of course inevitable drawbacks. Having a bunk that was partially under the side deck was one of those drawbacks. I felt for the floor with the toes of my outstretched leg and managed to avoid the empty Jack Daniels' bottle. Fred, my friendly bartender at Lion's, had always maintained they made them that way so as not to roll off the chest when you were on your back.

My head ached: too much stress. Without turning on the companionway lights I groped my way through to the workshop and almost tripped over the body. I turned on the workshop light

1

and saw the body had a neat hole in the forehead where the bullet had entered; the mess of blood, bone, and brains told me where it had exited.

I stood and looked at it for a moment, willing myself not to bend down and seek for signs of life. *Don't touch anything*, a voice screamed in my head; not touching was the mantra of the TV detectives. Good advice I thought, as I climbed the companionway steps into the main saloon that was my living room for the phone.

I poured a coffee, stuck it in the microwave, and watched the cup go in circles and wondered if cups got dizzy going round in the microwave? Dumb thought, I needed more sleep.

Cup in hand I exited the saloon, stood on the side deck and waited for the police. There were two of them.

'DS Street,' the female officer said, showing me her warrant card. 'DC Hunter,' she nodded towards the partner.

I let them in and told them where to find the body. They were back up in the main saloon in five.

'You called in the report, sir?' she asked.

'Yeah, about half an hour ago. I told the operator I'd heard a noise and found a body in my workshop.'

'Did you touch anything?'

I shook my head and almost said do I look like I was born yesterday? 'No, Sergeant, I didn't touch anything.'

'Could we go back to the beginning, sir? As best as you can, could you tell us exactly what you heard?'

I told them what I'd heard, but got the impression they weren't very impressed with my ability to remember what I heard while sleeping.

'Do you recognise him, sir?'

I nodded, headache level two. 'He was in earlier in the day, said he was looking for a guitar.'

'Was he alone?'

'I didn't see anyone else. I don't get many customers off the street. Most of my customers call and make an appointment.'

'Did he buy one?'

'No.'

'Do you think he was looking to buy, or just casing the shop?'

'I showed him the guitars I had for sale, but he gave me the impression he was looking for something very specific.'

'Why do you think that?'

'The first thing he did when I handed him a guitar was to look at the label. Next he'd strum a couple of chords then hand the guitar back.'

'So you think he was after a specific guitar?'

'Not sure,' I replied, falling against the edge of the table.

'Are you all right, sir? Would you like to sit down?'

'Need sleep and coffee, either order will do,' I replied, wishing the acrobat in my head would stop bouncing on the trampoline and doing cartwheels. 'The cafetière's on the counter, cup in sink,' I said, and pointed to the microwave.

The DS nodded to the constable, who obligingly poured me a cup and microwaved it for me.

'Black all right, sir?'

I nodded carefully. The coffee tasted good, my head started to clear and I waited for the questions to continue. But before the DS could resume, we were interrupted by the arrival of the coroner, the Crime Scene Investigation team, and the press.

'Stephen', said the DS, 'get the CSI's started. I'll continue with Mr – er – can we confirm your name, please?'

'It's Nevis, Jack Nevis.'

'Thank you, Mr Nevis.'

'Will do, Jill,' said the DC.

'You two more than partners?' I asked, as the CSI team, dressed in white overalls, went below.

She smiled. 'Yes, we're engaged. This is our first case together.'

'How's that?'

3

'How's what?'

'Working together as soon-to-be husband and wife. You're a sergeant and he's only a constable?'

'Mr Nevis, we're professionals. The job comes first and besides, if you didn't realise, marriage is also a partnership.'

'Bit different for you – working a case in a marina?'

'No, not really, police work is the same no matter where we do it – though we've had other cases in the marina. Could we get back to what you were saying about the deceased?'

'Yes, I definitely got the impression he was looking for a specific guitar.'

'What gave you that impression?'

'To guitar players, a new guitar is eye candy. The first thing they do after picking it up is to hold it by the neck and look at the label to see if it's one they recognise. Next they spin it round while looking at their reflection in the finish. Finally they try playing it, but not till they have fiddled with the tuners.'

'And did he?'

'Most guitar players need a tuner to set the pitch.'

'Sorry, sir, you've lost me on that?'

'Before the days of electronics, musicians would have used a tuning fork, now most use an electronic tuner. It's a small device that clips to the head of the guitar and, as the musician tightens the strings, the pitch is displayed on the screen of the tuner. He didn't need one, he was pitch-perfect.'

'Did he play any of the guitars?'

'Not much, I think he was more used to electric guitars.'

'What made you think that?'

'Classical guitar trained musicians play with their thumb resting on the back of the neck; he wrapped his hand around the neck with his thumb on the edge of the fretboard, like he was choking a snake.'

'Do you think he looked at the classical guitars as a distraction while seeing what electric guitars you had?'

'Who knows?' I said, shaking my head and realising the acrobat had finished his tea-break and returned to his trampoline. 'It's beyond me. I do set-ups for lots of professional musicians and sometimes have valuable guitars here.'

'So he could have been after one of those?'

'Yes, I suppose he could have, but I knew he wasn't serious, you get to know after a while. Hang on, my head, I need something stronger than coffee, back in a moment.'

I stepped down into my cabin and the bathroom. I reached for the aspirin bottle, downed a double dose with a mouthful of tap water, then returned to the main saloon and the sergeant.

'Feeling better, Mr Nevis?'

I grimaced and gently nodded.

'You were saying why you didn't think the deceased was serious about buying a guitar?'

'The excuses, I've heard enough to fill a book.'

'Like what?'

'Well, Sergeant, they always start enthusing about how great the guitar is, then they'll say something like: "Pity, just bought a new one last week" or "Already have twelve, need to sell one to make space". Or the real killer is: "Got to check with the wife, be right back" and I never see them again.'

'So I suppose he was one of those?'

'It's possible, but I guess we'll never know.'

By then she'd run out of questions or interest in guitars, so I asked her about the other case she'd investigated in the marina.

'Created quite a stir in the press. Maybe you've read about it?'

I shook my head. 'I've only been down here a few years.'

'It was in the spring, surprised you didn't read about it in the papers.'

'I was probably too busy working to notice.'

'All told there were four deaths, three of them here in the marina. In fact, the last death was the killer himself, sort of a case of poetic justice my boss said.'

We were disturbed by the departing CSI's. The DS went ashore and briefed the reporters then climbed back on board.

'We done, Jill?' asked the constable.'

'Are the CSI's finished?'

'Yes, just left, also the coroner wants to remove the body.'

'Okay, tell them they can have it.'

'Will do, be right back.'

I watched as one of the coroner's assistants carried a body-bag below.

'Case of déjà vu, Jill?' said the constable.

'Yes. I was just talking about the last case we had in the marina.'

'Yeah, that was a tough one, but we got there in the end.'

'Oh, before we go, sir. Is there anything missing?' the DS asked, as the poor unfortunate night-time visitor was unceremoniously carried up in the body-bag.

'I haven't had time to look yet, been stuck up here with you, answering questions.'

'Would you do that now, please?' she asked, with that tired voice all policemen do when they've watched too many TV detective stories.

I followed them below and rooted around the workshop, realising the aspirin had thankfully finally kicked in. I waited for the endorphin effect. I found I'd left the top off of one of the glue bottles and my workshop was in a mess – not of my own doing of course. Other than that, all seemed to be in order.

'Do you own a gun, sir?' the constable asked.

I shook my head: no pain. 'No, of course not. Why would you think that?'

'Just checking, Mr Nevis. With this being an old tugboat, maybe while doing repairs you found a pistol hidden somewhere and decided to keep it as a souvenir? It does happen?'

'Nonsense, Constable, the *Osprey* isn't the *SS Great Eastern*, no secret compartments with guns, or more dead bodies. The only dead body here was on my workshop floor.' Then I thought of the guitar I'd found entombed in the false locker at the rear of the *Osprey*. The revelation must have shown on my face.

'All the same, we'll have the specialist search team do a quick sweep of the seabed around your boat, just in case the killer decided to dump their weapon. You are sure about not finding a gun, Mr Nevis?' the constable repeated.

My mind drifted to the story about the two riveters' skeletons discovered between the hulls of the *SS Great Eastern* when it was scrapped. What had they thought when they realised they were entombed between the two steel hulls? I imagined them crawling back and forth in the dark, starving, and desperately trying to be heard above the noise of construction. Had they lived long enough to feel the movement as the ship went to sea, eventually dying of hunger or suffocation? I shivered at the thought.

'No, Constable, definitely no guns, though I did find a guitar concealed behind the panelling in one of the cupboards. At first I thought it was just a cheap classical guitar, no value to anyone.'

'At first, sir?'

'Yes, when I removed it from its case I thought it looked like most classical guitars made in the early 40's.'

'And what made you change your mind?'

'Look for yourself,' I said, reaching over for the guitar I'd found. I lifted it from its hanger and passed it to the constable. I don't know why I was surprised when he tried to play a couple of chords. He gave up as the strings were crap, but he did know how to hold a guitar and his fingering was fine.

'I see you know how to play guitar, Constable.'

'Just some basic stuff, would never make a career out of it,' he replied, passing the guitar back to me. 'What wood is it?'

'I think it might be Brazilian rosewood.'

'Nice, wish I could afford one like it.'

I hung it back up on its hanger.

♦

By the time the police, the coroner – who'd made a decent job of cleaning up the cranial detritus – and the press had left, I'd just enough time to clean up the chaos of spilled tools and wood before Dizzy flew in for his guitar.

I told him about the shooting.

'My guitar, man? Any damage – bullet holes?'

I shook my head. He looked disappointed. I told him what had happened and that his guitar was safe, still hanging from its hanger at the end of the workshop.

'How about blood, any on my guitar? Brains even?'

'Doubt it, have a look,' I said, handing him his guitar.

He took it by its neck and held it up like a chicken he was inspecting for dinner. He studied the head, then the body. 'There – see? Look, blood spatters.'

'Where? Let me see.'

'There,' he said excitedly, 'just below the end of the fretboard. You can see them on the chrome of the pickups.' He was as wound-up as a child on Christmas morning.

'What's so special about a few splatters of blood? Here, I'll clean them off for you,' I said, reaching for the guitar.

'No, don't do that, man. Blood on the pickups adds a bit of mystique. I've always wondered what to call this guitar, now I know.'

'And just what will you call this guitar?'

'Baskerville. You know, like the beast in the Sherlock Holmes story. Got to think up some serious riffs for it, maybe write a song about it'.

'Dizzy, you are the limit,' I said, laughing for the first and only time that day.

♦

By eight-thirty I'd eaten breakfast and lost count of how many cups of coffee I'd drunk. By mid-morning I could feel the after effects of the lost sleep fighting with the caffeine, but at least I'd managed to put my workshop back in order. That was when I noticed that the classical guitars had suffered in the night's mayhem.

In fact, all four of the classical guitars had been damaged. All of them had the strings stretched, two had damage to their sound holes – just like someone had tried to reach inside but their hands were too big and they'd managed to break the wood on the edges. I was particularly annoyed about the damage to the one I been preparing to restore. Of all the guitars I had in my collection for restoration, this one showed the most promise. I'd finally decided that the darkened wood of the body was Brazilian rosewood, so it had a certain intrinsic value. And being old meant that it could be sold without requiring a CITES certificate.

I'd found it in its case, concealed behind a false panel in the aft cabin. I'd chosen the aft cabin for my bedroom as it was a less useful space for a workshop. I'd been renovating the cabin, pulling down some old shelving and a cupboard, when part of the panelling just fell off. As I'd told the police, the guitar, in its case, had been concealed behind a panel in the back of one of the lockers. Just like someone didn't want it to be found.

I'd hung the guitar up on one of the hangers in the workshop meaning to get round-to-it one day. It was in the worst condition of all my *get to one day* guitars. The bridge was loose, as was the fretboard at the body, and the head veneer looked like someone had used it to shovel coal. One of the tuner buttons was missing and the strings when plucked could only give out a piteous plink.

I placed a thick quilted pad on the bench, carefully placed the guitar on top, and got out my inspection mirror to have a look inside. Thankfully the bracing all seemed to be intact, and best of all, there were no visible splits in the soundboard. That's when I noticed the small piece of rolled-up paper stuck to the soundboard at the end block. I teased it out and looked at it. I was excited: it was the bottom half of the original label.

Idiot, I said to myself. Why hadn't I noticed it before? The body shape, sound-hole rosette, the head carving, all shouted Torres. I looked again at the label; I could just make out two rows of writing: *Ano de 1880, Guitara num 19 2e epoca.*

I grabbed my copy of Romanillos' book on Torres, and frantically thumbed through to the index. There was no number nineteen listed for his second age of guitar making. It was like one of those Antiques Roadshow moments, when the unsuspecting owner is told they have in their possession an unknown Fabergé egg. I was in possession of an, up till now, unknown Torres. An instrument that was very valuable, though not quite in the same league as a Fabergé egg or Stradivarius violin, but valuable nonetheless.

I took the guitar and went back up into the saloon for more coffee. Of course, I told myself, it could be a copy of a Torres, there were plenty of them. I'd even made one myself. It was just like a Stradivarius story.

How many people, when looking at the interior of the violin they'd found in a dusty second-hand shop, thought they'd discovered one of his lost instruments, only to be told by the local music store it was probably just a student model made by some young, hopeful, apprentice luthier. If the guitar was an original I could arrange for the *Osprey* to be dry-docked, get the rusted rivets replaced and once and for all be done with the leak that had plagued me since day one of owning the boat.

I knew of only one local expert on Torres and dug out her email address. I emailed her some sample photos with the guitar's dimensions and waited.

Most likely a missing Torres, was her reply, *would suggest you contact Romanillos to be sure, but bring it by and I'll have a look.* I replied thanks, said time permitting I'd drop by later in the day, and sat down at my desk to decide what to do next. Usually I would just tart up used guitars and flog them at the Sidmouth or Towersey folk festivals, but not now – I had a responsibility to history. Out went my ideas of a quick and simple repair; this called for museum-quality restoration.

I took the guitar back down to the workshop and laid it on the pad on the workbench. I had intended to start work on it, but the bloodstains on the floor sent me back up to the saloon for something stronger than coffee to take my mind off of the morning's shenanigans.

Before I got the bottle open, the phone rang; it was the reporter who'd been here earlier.

'Was there any identification on the dead man?' he asked.

I gave him the DS's phone number and told him to call her.

'How about what was stolen?' he asked.

'Nothing,' I answered, wishing he'd just go away.

'So you'd nothing of value in the workshop?'

I thought of the Torres; it was more valuable from its position in musical history than financial. 'No.'

'You do know it has history, don't you?' he continued.

'Yes, of course I do. It was one he made during his second epoch, how did you find out?' I answered, wondering how he'd known about the Torres.

'Second epoch? Listen, I've no idea what you're talking about. I'm talking about that tub you live on."

The tub he was talking about was my home, last boat on the end of G dock.

'What do you mean, it has history?'

'That's for me to know. Knowledge means money. Be seeing you.' And he hung up.

It wasn't till after I'd also hung up I wondered why he assumed something had been stolen.

2

Nancy

I'd just sat back in my chair, kicked off my shoes, and poured myself another stiff shot of Jack Daniels, when the police returned. I let them in and waited.

'You say you didn't know the dead man, yet phone records show he'd called your shop on several occasions during the last two weeks.'

'Sergeant, I get lots of phone calls, these days mostly PPI calls. If I'm busy I just let them go to the answering machine.'

'And when do you listen to these calls?'

'When I remember to.'

'And have you remembered to listen to them during the last two weeks?'

I looked at her, thought for a moment, then answered, 'You know, Sergeant, I don't believe I have.'

'Would you mind doing it now, sir?'

I took a sip of bourbon, put down the glass, and went over to the answering machine. There were fifteen calls waiting.

'You want me to listen to them, Sergeant?'

'That would be the idea, Mr Nevis.'

As I suspected, ten of them included the usual combination of silent and recorded messages about my supposed unclaimed PPI. One was from Dave at Luthier's Supply to say the gold tuners had arrived and did I want them posted. Three of them were from – the sergeant surmised – the stiff they'd removed from the workshop floor, and the last two of them from a female wanting me to teach her how to make a guitar.

'Can we take this, sir?' the sergeant asked, reaching for the tape in the machine. 'You can write down the details of the last two calls first, wouldn't want you to lose business.'

I grabbed the pen on the side table and wrote down the last caller's details.

'If you think of anything else, please give us a call. You have my number,' the sergeant said as I closed the door on them.

They were back two hours later.

'Found out his name, Sergeant?'

'Max Fleishman,' replied the constable.

I shook my head and wondered why that name should sound familiar.

'I thought you said you didn't know him?' asked the constable. 'Looks like you've heard the name before.'

'No, it just sounds familiar. Find out anything about him?"

The constable looked at the sergeant.

'He's an American, according to the driving licence in his wallet,' she answered.

'Know anything more?' I asked.

'We've been able to find out he was working as a private investigator. We're waiting for more information from his office in San Francisco.'

'What would a San Francisco private investigator be doing in my boat at three in the morning?'

'That's what we hoped you could tell us, sir. Are you sure there's nothing of value kept here in your workshop? Something that might have come to light since we were last here?'

I told them about the Torres.

'What sort of value are we looking at?' she asked.

'Not enough to kill for, Sergeant. On a good day you might be able to buy a used Rolls Royce with the proceeds of the sale.'

'Not millions, or hundreds of thousands, then?'

I shook my head. They looked disappointed. 'Besides the thief could never sell it.'

'Why?'

'Because it would be too well known.'

'I'm afraid that's not necessarily so. A great deal of petty stealing consists of the opportune thief breaking in to someone's house, grabbing what's to hand, then scarpering down to their nearest fence and selling their ill-gotten goods for pennies in the pound.'

'You've got a point there.'

'Can you think of any reason at all why he'd break in, if it wasn't to steal a guitar?'

'No Sergeant, I can't, and besides all my customers announce themselves before arriving. They don't have to break in.'

'How many keys do you have to your front door, sir?'

'Wondering how he got in, Sergeant? There are two: one on my key ring and the spare's kept in the drawer in the galley.'

'Would you check and see if the spare's still where you keep it, please?'

I liked her; she was polite. I wandered back to the galley and pulled out the cutlery drawer and looked for the tell-tale piece of masking tape on the outside of the drawer back. It was still there. I poured myself a look-warm coffee and returned to the saloon. 'Spare's still where I left it, Sergeant.'

'This Torres guitar, sir. Could there be something else of value about it?'

'Like what, Sergeant?'

'You tell me, sir. You're the musician.'

'Sergeant, I repair and build, I don't play – much is the pity. As for intrinsic value of the guitar, I suppose if Segovia had played it at a special concert that might add a bit of value, but not enough to kill someone for.'

'And you only heard one shot, sir?'

'Yes, Sergeant, that's what woke me up.'

'How about doors closing or running footsteps?'

I'd wondered about that myself. The gunshot had woken me almost immediately. I hadn't heard the door close or the sounds of running on the dock. If the shooter had followed the dead man down the dock, he must have been particularly light on his feet. But how did he get in – unless the dead man had deliberately left the door ajar?

I shook my head. 'Sorry, Sergeant, nothing. I don't suppose he could have shot himself?'

'No gun, Mr Nevis. Initial inspection by forensics say he was shot by a 9 mm pistol from close range. They think he may have been fired on through one of your windows, or should I say, ports?'

That made sense, I thought, then realised something didn't add up. The ports on the dock side were always kept closed on account of the possibility that someone could climb on the side deck, reach through and pinch some of my tools. It was only the ports on the water side that I kept open. 'Sergeant, if anyone had been walking on the side deck, I'm sure I would have heard them. So unless someone's learnt to walk on water, I doubt that would be possible.

'Did you have a late night, Mr Nevis?'

'Hmm, got to bed about one o'clock.'

'Have a night-cap to help you sleep?'

'Are you insinuating I was drunk, Sergeant?'

'No, just wondering how deeply you were sleeping.'

'Yes, I did have a night-cap, but I wasn't drunk. I didn't hear anyone on the dock, let alone shoot through the port.'

'It's the only possible way he could have been shot, Mr Nevis. Unless, of course, you shot him?'

I liked that! 'Very funny, Sergeant. I've already told you I don't possess a gun. But I've just had a thought.'

'Go ahead.'

'Did any of your team look for anything that might have been put in the door to keep it from shutting?'

'What do you mean, Mr Nevis?'

'The outside door is self-closing. It's possible the shooter followed the dead man down the dock, then on board. But if the dead man had let the door close behind him, the shooter couldn't have followed him inside. So I was wondering if anything was found? For instance, was it on the latch, making it easy for him to make a quick getaway?'

She turned to the constable and asked, 'Was anything found?'

He shook his head. 'I don't think the CSI's looked up here.'

I walked over to the door and looked at the lock: no sign of any tampering.

'So he had nothing to do with music then?' I asked.

'Looks that way – for now, Mr Nevis.'

'I wonder if he was looking for a stolen guitar, him being a private detective?' I said.

'Would he have reason for that, sir?'

I did a mental inventory of all the instruments I had in the workshop but nothing came to mind. Then I thought of the Torres again. Nah, it had been hidden behind the panel in the cupboard for years. I'd only discovered its presence a few weeks prior, so how the hell would a San Francisco PI know about it? 'No, sorry, Sergeant, all my guitars have provenance, no orphans here.'

'How can you be so sure about that, sir?' asked the constable.

'Just about all guitars have serial numbers, so it's easy to look up the net and see if anyone has reported an instrument stolen. Though that doesn't stop unscrupulous people from altering the numbers and then reselling the instrument.'

'Does that happen often?' the DS asked.

'Not too often, just enough to make any buyer be wary. For instance, with Fender guitars being so popular with musicians, sometimes unscrupulous sellers will make up a fake and try to pass it off as an original.'

'How do they do that?'

'They order standard parts and dress them up to look like the real thing, even going as far as stamping fake serial numbers from the early models on the neck. I once heard of a forger who managed to get photos of a very early guitar and spent a few days chipping and sanding the lacquer to make the guitar look like one owned by a famous musician.'

'And none of your guitars have suspicious serial numbers?'

I shook my head. 'Nothing doing, Constable, they're all legitimate.'

'Oh, before we go, could we have your postal address?'

'It's Jack Nevis, Dock G10, Sovereign Marina, Eastbourne, East Sussex, BN23 5BJ.'

'Thank you, Mr Nevis. We'll be in touch if we need to ask any more questions.'

For the third time that day I listened to the sounds of departing footsteps on the dock.

My coffee had gone cold and the ice in my glass had melted so I ignored the cold coffee and poured myself a fresh bourbon and climbed up into what was once the wheelhouse. Garboard the cat was meowing to get in; I pulled the door back and let him in. He lay his customary mouse on the deck in front of me, signifying he wanted feeding. I'd no idea if he had ever had a proper name; Jake in the boatyard said one of the old shipwright's had called him Garboard, no idea why. Garboard appeared the day after I tied up the *Osprey.*'

Garboard was a feral cat, preferring to live alone, I suppose we had that in common. As far as I knew, I was the only person who fed him, or was able to pick him up without being mauled. Judith in the fish and chip shop had tried once; she had the scars on her face for months. He definitely was a one-man cat. Why he never ate the mice he delivered I could never figure out.

When I remodelled the tug I'd left the wheelhouse pretty much intact. Access to it was from the main saloon, up a narrow set of steps. On either side of the steps in the wheelhouse were L-shaped settees, just big enough for two people to sit close together. In the middle of the wheelhouse was the captain's chair, in front, the enclosed binnacle and the huge teak and polished brass wheel. I slumped back into the captain's chair and stared out of the window.

I sipped on my bourbon and watched the yard crane lower a large orange and black lifeboat into the water. There was a roar when the engines started, then idled, as the dock hands pulled it back and tied it to the holding dock. Once more I thought of the Torres; the label just had to be original. I suppose the guitar could have been stolen at some point and hidden behind the panel till the hue and cry died down. But that didn't make any sense. I figured it had been hidden for at least seventy plus years, and in 1944 wouldn't have had any special value. At least that was my reasoning based on the newspapers stuffed inside the guitar case. 1944, that was the date on the headline. Pity it was all in French, and my French only went as far as asking for a ham sandwich and beer.

My peace was disturbed by the sounds of another set of footsteps on the dock; well not the actual sound of footsteps, it was the creaking sound the dock lines made as someone walked down the dock. These sounds were different from any I'd heard in a long time.

There were only three regulars on my dock and each had a particular pattern to their footsteps. Dan, at six foot plus, had a long stride and subsequently a heavy, regular pattern of footsteps. Mr Gross, being considerably shorter at five foot four, walked with a rapid staccato step, and his wife, though slightly taller, being very light on her feet hardly made any impression on the dock and subsequent creaking of the dock lines. Could she have shot the detective? I shook my head at the idea and laughed. Timid Mrs Gross shoot anyone? No way.

The sound of creaking dock lines rose and I knew it was for me. I swirled the amber liquid and threw the remains back in one gulp. The footsteps persisted and I resigned myself to another interruption. I stood up, looked through the window and down at the dock. I watched as a young woman, carrying a guitar case, approached. I let her climb on board and ring the bell before I put the glass down, and slid the wheelhouse door back.

'Can I help?'

'Oh – you startled me! Didn't see you up there.'

'Sorry, didn't mean to startle you.'

'It's my guitar. I called a couple of times, and left messages.'

I nodded. 'Yeah, been busy, just now got round to listening to them. You said something about making guitars?'

'Yes, but first I need some advice on whether my grandfather's guitar is worth repairing.'

'Hang on, I'll be right down.'

I slid the door closed, stared at my empty glass sitting on the binnacle, wondered how it got empty, then made my way down to the saloon and what passed for the front door. She was still smiling when I opened it.

She was almost as tall as me in her calf-length leather boots and faded blue jeans. Her face, framed in bobbed blonde hair, had the most intense emerald-green eyes I'd ever seen, and below, a smile that could quench the fire of any angry dragon.

'Come in.'

'Thanks.'

'Is this your father's guitar – excuse me, your grandfather's guitar?' I asked, as I reached for the battered case.

She smiled at my mistake. 'Yes, this is my father's, father's, guitar.'

I liked her. She was making fun of me, but in a nice sort of way. Why were my hands trembling?

'Yes, it's been in the attic for years. I was having a clean-out and came across it. Do you think you can do anything with it?'

With that smile, how could I refuse?

'Let's go down to the workshop, the lighting is better there.''

She followed, her boots clip-clopping on the stairs.

I hung the Torres up on its hook and took her guitar case and placed it on the bench.

To me the opening of a guitar case for the first time is always a treat. Especially since this case was old, and had stickers from airlines long since flown over the horizon of history. It definitely showed signs of much use; the clasps were rusty and stiff and the hinges loose.

'This is where you live?' she interrupted, while looking around the workshop.

'Yes.'

'Wow, how cute.'

'You should have seen it when I bought it.'

'That bad, huh?"

'It had no doors and the inside looked like a pigeon loft that hadn't been cleaned in years. I've got some photos somewhere.'

'Bet that ponged a bit! I'd like to see those photos, sometime.'

'Thought you're here about your grandfather's guitar?'

'Oh, yes, so I am, silly me.'

She smiled again, little dimples appeared in her cheeks, and her eyes lit up and sparkled like two emeralds in the sun.

I opened the lid. I wasn't disappointed; the guitar was a Fleta. At least that was what the rosette and label told me, but once again there were many copies of these as well. I carefully lifted the guitar out of the case and held it out of the way of the rusty clasps.

'I don't know your name.'

'It's Nancy. What's yours?'

'My what?'

'Your name. You do have one, don't you?'

'Sorry, should have said. It's Jack. Could you hold the guitar for a moment and I'll clear the bench?'

I passed her the guitar, and once again was taken by the emerald-green eyes and the smile. I shook my head to concentrate, placed the guitar case on one of the side-benches, and straightened out the bench pad. She passed the guitar back and I held it up to get a good look at it. At first sight it looked like it only required a good clean and a new set of strings.

'Can you do anything with it?'

I tried to strum a chord and realised, like the Torres, it also needed new strings. It also needed some work on the frets – a couple of them were loose. Also, the tuners were stiff from non-use. 'I'll have to inspect it in more detail first. How about you leave it with me, and I'll give you a call in a couple of days?'

I saw a shadow of disappointment move across her face and she shook her head. 'No, I can't do that. I'm going away, not sure when I'll be back.'

I looked at the workshop clock: five-fifteen. 'It'll cost you, I charge extra for on-the-spot repairs at this time of day.'

'How much?'

'On top of the cost of repairs – settle for the price of a takeaway.'

'On top of the repairs?'

'It's you that's in a hurry, it's almost dinner time, and there's at least a couple of hours' work needed on the guitar. You order the takeaway and I'll fix up your grandfather's guitar while you wait. That's the deal.'

'Just a couple of hours?' she said, as she looked at her watch. 'The kids are with my sister; they're having an extended sleepover. She twitched her nose. 'That'll work, but first I'll need to call my sister and let her know where I am.'

I waited for her to make the call and talk to her sister.

'So, you want me to order a takeaway?' she said hanging up the call.

'Unless you fancy cooking us a meal. You can cook, can't you?'

'Where's the kitchen?'

'It's called the galley, and you've already passed it. Back up the steps and into the saloon, it's on your left at the top. Lift the mahogany counter-top, the hob's underneath.'

21

'Be right back.'

As I was taking a closer look at her guitar she called down, 'How about a stir fry? You've got a bunch of vegetables that need cooking. Do you have any chicken breasts?'

'Have a look in the freezer. If there are any you'll need to defrost them.'

I started to remove the strings and stopped. She was singing; she was in her element. I'd forgotten what it was like to have the sound of a female in the home. When Katie was alive – oh Lord, why? Why did she have to die? My hands started to shake and tears filled my eyes. I thought I was over her loss. I put down my tools, closed my eyes, and listened to the words of the song drift down into the workshop.

> I watched you go, dressed for the fight
> into the night sky, and out of sight
> They swore you'd return, but not that way
> Draped with a flag, you passed my way.
>
> When the gentle breath of spring, warms the winter air
> I'd hold you in my arms, and dream without a care.

I couldn't focus. I sat back on the workshop stool, kept my eyes closed tight and listened to her sing, and thought about Katie and the children I'd never see again this side of eternity.

♦

The clatter of pots and pans, and sound of dishes being placed on the table told me dinner was close.

'Dinner's ready, come and get it!' she shouted with enthusiasm.

'Be right there,' I called back. I wiped the tears from my eyes and climbed the stairs. She'd prepared a chicken stir-fry, complete with rice. She'd even managed to find a bottle of white wine I'd forgotten about.

'Dinner is served. How's the guitar?'

'Ah – er – yes, the guitar, it's going to take a bit longer than I first thought, might have to re-seat a few of the frets.'

'Is that a problem?'

'Not really, just need to push them back in and apply a couple of drops of glue. Would be helpful if you gave me a hand.'

'Will I get a discount for helping?'

'Cheeky monkey! I'll have a word with the accounts department,' I replied, and took a mouthful of food. I liked it, much better than anything I'd made recently. 'How many children do you have?' I asked, between bites.

'Three.'

'Really? What are their names?'

'Stephen is nine, the twins, Stephanie and Sandra, are coming up for eight. How about you? Are you married, have any children?'

'My wife and three children died in a car crash on the M1 five years ago. We'd been returning home to Garforth from a birthday party for Tina, she was our youngest.'

'I'm so sorry! How awful for you. And here's me going on about my three.'

'No, honestly, it's fine, I've learned to live with the loss.' *Liar, liar, pants on fire*, I said to myself. 'What about your children's father? Won't he be wondering where you've got to?'

She grimaced and shook her head. 'Their father was killed in Afghanistan. My second husband abandoned us just after we were married. Went to Saudi Arabia to work on the oil fields and never came back. Tried to find him, his company forwarded my messages but said he'd left and gone to live in Germany.'

'That's a crap attitude! Left you in the lurch with three children to raise?'

'I got over it. So how did you end up living down here, in Eastbourne, in the marina?'

'After the accident, I decided I needed a complete change. I'd been making and repairing guitars as a hobby since high school, and thought I was now experienced enough to go pro. The house had too many memories and I didn't fancy living over a shop. So when the money for the sale of the house came through I started to look for alternative living and working accommodation.'

'In the Midlands?'

I nodded. 'At first I looked at converted farmyard workshops and decided they were too far out of the way for customers to get to me. Next I looked at factory units with much the same conclusion. It wasn't till I was on my third pint in my local, that a magazine article caught my eye.'

'Must have been really special, especially after three pints.'

'Very funny. It wasn't what you're inferring, it was a period piece in the county magazine about bargees and how they managed to work, live, and even raise families while working on the canals.'

'That sounds like fun. So what'd you do?'

'I wasn't much interested in the travelling part, more interested in living on the water and yet still being somewhere my customers could get their instruments to me.'

'That makes sense. Can I have some more wine, please?'

I poured the last of the bottle into our glasses and realised it was getting dark. I reached up and switched on the ceiling light and as I did so I saw something in her face that set my pulse racing. I knew at that moment she was someone I could learn to love. Love at first sight? Don't be daft, Jack, you're just hung over and lonely.

'What? Why are you looking at me like that? Do I have food on my face?' she asked, dabbing at her face with a napkin.

Relieved I didn't need to explain myself, I replied, 'You got it, bit of sauce on your upper lip.'

'Thanks. You were saying?'

'I had previously decided I wanted to relocate so I had the whole country to choose from. This wasn't as easy a choice as I had first thought. Most canals and places to tie up are now recreational and frown on someone running a business that competes for space with the leisure tourists and canal-bank fishermen.'

'So what did you do?'

'I gravitated away from the canal barge idea and settled on the *Osprey*. You're currently dining on her. She's a 1930's tugboat and was home to a group of Sea Scouts for many years. Then, when she was deemed too expensive to maintain, she subsequently fell into disrepair and was sold.'

'Must be exciting to live and work so close to the water?'

I'd completely forgotten about the events of the night. It must have shown on my face, because she asked, 'What's wrong? You look like you've seen a ghost.'

'Exciting is not quite how I'd describe it. Someone was shot and killed in the workshop during the night.'

She must have thought I was joking, as she then asked, 'Didn't pay their bill on time?'

'If only it was a joke."

'What happened, then? Someone really died – here on the boat?'

'I was woken by a loud noise, came through into the workshop, and found a dead body lying on the workshop floor. Police think maybe he was after a guitar I'd found hidden behind a panel in a cupboard.'

'And you can't figure out why?'

That was when I remembered the French newspaper. 'Don't suppose you can read French, can you?'

'*Oui, mon ami, mais certainment. Pourquois?*'

'Wait right here, I'll be back.' I made a beeline for the workshop and the newspaper I'd found stuffed in the guitar case with the Torres. I glanced at the paper and realised it wasn't much of a paper, only three double sheets. By the time I'd returned to the galley she'd cleared the table, stacked the dirty dishes on the counter, and put the kettle on.

'I'm not sure why these pages of newspaper were stuffed in the case with the guitar. It's French – could you have a look and read it to me? Maybe there's something in one of the articles that will explain why it and the guitar were incarcerated in the cupboard.'

'Let's have a look,' she said eagerly, as I passed her the paper. 'Kettle's on by the way, I like my coffee black.'

Just who was she? Brings me a guitar for repair, now I'm being bossed around in my own home. I decided I didn't mind.

'Well, anything?'

'If you would tell me what I'm supposed to be looking for, maybe I could find it. Just what am I looking for?'

'Anything to do with music – guitars in particular, I suppose.'

The kettle started whistling so I left her to her perusal of the paper while I poured the boiling water into the cafetière and waited for the grounds to infuse. 'Want a biscuit to go with your coffee?'

'What? Er – yes, thanks.'

I put the cafetière on a tray along with two mugs and the biscuit barrel and carried them over to the table. I resisted my desire to sit down close beside her and chose instead the seat opposite. Her hair shone like gold candyfloss. I was hooked and just needed to be landed.

'Anything?'

'Appears to be a local newspaper from the town of St Nazaire. Mostly local stuff, editor's obviously not happy with the town being overrun by German soldiers and Nazis. Though he is quite guarded in what he says, mostly attributes his comments to overheard conversations in cafés. There's a column written by the area commandant, requiring all men between seventeen and thirty-five to report to their local police station for air-raid duties. Also, there's an article about the impending visit of the area Gruppenführer.'

'What's one of them, when they're in town?'

'Gestapo chief – and this one's very influential, according to the article.'

'Does it say why he's in town?'

'Something to do with a British warship stuck in the main entrance to the harbour, blocking access to the inner harbour. Apparently a team of British commandos sailed it up the channel and rammed it straight into the main lock gate, then blew it up. According to the newspaper it's causing havoc for the German navy.'

'Nothing about guitars, music shops, bands, even?'

'No, but – wait a minute – this might be of interest. Says here that a local landowner, the Count de Brissac, was arrested by the Gestapo for hoarding art treasures, and that the artwork had now been commandeered for Hitler's Reich Museum. Not only did he have paintings of great value, he also had a collection of rare violins and other musical instruments. Could that be where your guitar came from?"

'Beats me, I'm only interested in how it got on to the tug.'

'What's its history?'

I looked at the clock and said, 'It's getting a bit late?'

'Darn, just when things are getting interesting.'

'And we haven't fixed your guitar yet either. If – if, nah, that wouldn't work.'

'What wouldn't work?'

I could see by the look in her face that I was at a crossroads. I could say good night, come back tomorrow and your guitar will be ready; or I could say what I was about to say. 'You could call your sister and say you're helping me with your guitar and since it will be late, you will be staying here overnight. You could use my cabin and I'd bunk down here in the saloon. That way you could finish translating the paper for me, and I could complete the repairs to your guitar. Just for tonight, all above board. There's a lock on the cabin door, only got one key.'

'Just for tonight, then. I've got work in the morning, Stephen and the girls have school first thing in the morning.'

'Yes – of course, that's what I meant. Great, er – I'll get started.'

'I'll call my sister and let her know what's happening.'

♦

I reheated a coffee in the microwave, went down to the workshop, and left her to get on with the newspaper. The repair to her guitar was quite straightforward, and I even managed to reseat the loose frets myself. I cleaned and oiled the fretboard, fitted a new set of strings, did an initial tune-up, oiled the hinges and clasps on the case, and returned to the main saloon. I was pleased with myself. It was only ten-fifteen.

'Your guitar is ready, just waiting for the oil on the fretboard to dry. How are you getting on with the newspaper?'

'Mostly done. There's a diatribe from the commandant about what will happen to anyone who is harbouring British commandos. Also the results of a football match between the local garrison and the town's team, but nothing more about musical instruments.'

That was more or less what I'd expected and assumed the newspaper was there just to pad the guitar while in its case.

'So, Jack, what's the history on the boat? Why do you think an unknown Torres guitar was stuffed in a case with a World War 2 French newspaper?'

That was the second time someone had mentioned the boat's history today. But more importantly, how did she know about the Torres? I hadn't said anything to her about the guitar being a Torres, I'd only said there was a guitar in the case. The newspaper reporter didn't know, and as far as I could remember I'd only told the police.

'All I know is it was used by the Sea Scouts till the cost of keeping it afloat got too much for them. I bought it a few years ago and had it towed along the coast to this marina. It desperately needs dry-docking.'

'What's dry-docking?'

'Basically it's a narrow dock with a watertight gate at one end. The boat sails in, is tied up and the gate closed. Next the water is pumped out and the boat is sitting on dry ground.'

'And your boat needs that done why?'

'There's a bad spot on the hull under the waterline that needs some of the rivets replacing, they're rusted badly and constantly leak.'

'So why don't you have the work done?'

'Last time I checked, the cost to use a dock big enough to hold the *Osprey* was over two thousand pounds a week, and that doesn't include all the repairs.'

'Oh! That makes my car service sound cheap.'

'In the meantime I make sure the bilge pump keeps on pumping. But I don't mind telling you, though, it took quite a bit of wrangling to be allowed to have it tied up in the marina, and to be allowed to live and work on board. I wouldn't change it for any palace.'

'You're quite a romantic, aren't you?'

'Don't know about that, just like the peace and quiet of boat life.'

'And that's all you know about the boat?'

'Yes.'

'Do you have a computer?'

'Yes, couldn't exist without it. Why?'

'Where is it?'

'In the workshop, it's a laptop. I use it to keep records while working on guitars. When I need internet I go up into the wheelhouse.'

'Why's that?'

'No signal, the steel decks and bulkheads cause havoc with the WIFI signal, the router is in the wheelhouse

3

The Mystery Revealed

'So this is where you found the body?' she asked, pointing to the stain on the workshop floor.

'The very same, I was going to bleach it, but just can't quite get round to it.'

'I wouldn't – adds a bit of mystique to the boat's history.'

'I'll think about it; the laptop's over here,' I said, pointing to a small desk covered in books and guitar magazines.

'How do you manage to get anything done with this chaos?' she asked.

That caught me off guard, then I saw the smile and realised she was just trying to wind me up.

'Maid's day off.'

I picked up the books and returned them to the bookshelf. 'Here,' I said, passing her a stack of magazines, 'they go over there on the shelf by the steps.'

She reached out to take the magazines, and for just a moment, a fleeting glance, our eyes met. It took all the will power I had not to drop the magazines on the floor and take her in my arms. Don't be daft, Jack, I said to myself, you've only just met her, and look at her ring finger, she's a married woman.

'The top shelf, please,' I indicated, turning away to hide the embarrassment that must have been showing.

I took a deep breath and looked back; she was still standing there, holding the magazines, just smiling.

'Were you going to add something?' she asked, cocking her head.

'Er – the laptop – the battery's charged, we won't need the cable.' I picked it up and shoved it under my arm.

She put the magazines on the shelf and followed me up the stairs to the wheelhouse.

'That's better,' she said, sitting on the settee and leaning back. She pulled off her boots and tucked her legs up under her. 'Do you have a blanket? It's chilly up here.'

'Be right back,' I replied, and headed for the aft cabin for the throw blanket I kept for cold nights.

'Do I need a password?' she asked, tucking the blanket around her knees.

'No, just go for it.'

I watched as her fingers flew over the keyboard and wondered, if the computer were alive, what it would think of being pushed like this? She certainly was very adept at typing.

'Not much on your boat,' she said, in a disappointed tone. 'All I can find is a reference to the sale by the Sea Scouts and a newspaper article in the *Seaford Times* about someone breaking in and vandalising the interior.'

> Last night, Sussex Police, responding to a call from a worried member of the public, were called to Denton Island to attend a possible break-in to the former Sea Scout boat, the *Osprey*, formerly known as the *Kestrel*. The police reported that the vessel had suffered from severe damage to the interior. They surmised it was likely someone had been in the process of stripping copper wiring but was disturbed.

I obviously knew about the sale, but nothing about the break-in. I got up from the captain's chair, sat down beside her and tried to concentrate. I looked over her shoulder at the screen as she read and wished I knew the name of her perfume. I'd buy some and spray it all over the boat.

I never knew about the vandalism. When I bought the *Osprey* the interior was intact and it wasn't called the *Kestrel*. I was fighting the urge to put my arm around her, so got up from the seat and wandered over to the window and gazed out at the harbour lights.

'Did you buy the *Osprey* from the Sea Scouts?' she asked.

'No, I bought it from a broker; I just assumed the Sea Scouts were the previous owners and I didn't know about its previous name.'

'What do the registration papers say?'

'Not much. I seem to remember filling out a form and sending it and the registration documents off with a cheque to somewhere in Wales.'

'Where are the documents now?'

'Gone – well as good as. A few months ago I was having a sort-out inside the boat. I put the box with the folder containing all the paperwork out on the deck while I moved things around inside. It wasn't till I started to put everything back that I noticed the wind had blown the folder with all the documents into the harbour. I managed to recover them, but they were illegible. Never quite got round to applying for replacements.'

'What about the maker's plaque? What does that say?'

This caught my attention. 'I've no idea what you're talking about.'

'All boats have a plaque, usually brass, fixed somewhere on them. It tells when and where it was built, along with its name. Where's the *Osprey's* plaque?'

I'd no idea about brass plaques; to me they were the things you saw on the wall outside fancy offices, not on rusty old tubs like the *Osprey*. I shrugged and said, 'Beats me. I've never seen one and I've been over most of the interior with a paintbrush. If there was one, I would have seen it.'

'What about the engine room, been down there lately?'

I shook my head. 'The last time was to clean out the bilge so the bilge pump would work properly, didn't notice any fancy brass plaque.'

'Typical man, can't see the nose in front of his face.'

I waited for the smile – I wasn't disappointed.

'Where's the engine room?'

'Under the saloon floor, you get to it from the workshop. The hatch is on the left of the steps.'

'Let's go,' she said, throwing the blanket back and reaching for her boots.

I turned the catches, pulled the hatch open and reached inside to turn on the lights. Though the engine hadn't been run in years the engine room smelled of stale diesel and bilge water. I climbed down the short flight of steps and stood on the metal grating that surrounded the giant English Electric diesel engine and waited for her to climb down beside me.

'Where should we be looking?' she asked.

'I don't know – it's your idea, remember?'

'But it's your boat.'

'Point taken. It's unlikely to be on the engine, that's not original. Probably on one of the bulkheads.'

'Do you have a torch?'

'Wait a minute; I've got a couple in the workshop.' The desire to wrap my arm around her and pull her close was almost overwhelming. I resisted and headed for the workshop.

I returned with the brightest LED torch I had and handed it to her. 'See anything?' I asked, as she shone the torch over the bulkhead.

'Over there – see that rectangular patch?'

All I saw was the outline of something fixed to the bulkhead and covered with umpteen years of paint. I climbed over the engine and up to what she was sure was the maker's plaque. I shone the torch on it and couldn't discern anything. 'Just looks like a plate that's been fixed to the bulkhead.'

'Welded or riveted?'

I looked again at it and saw four dimples, one on each corner. 'Looks like it's a plate that's been riveted on.'

'That's going to be it! Can you make out anything?' she said, her voice quivering with excitement.

'The only way anyone is going to do that is to remove many layers of paint; it's so thick it will take a chisel to get it off.'

'No, can't do that, you'll damage the writing. Do you have any paint stripper?'

I climbed back into the workshop and went over to the maintenance locker, returning with stripper, brush and a couple of old shirts to wipe up the mess. By the third application it was becoming clear this was the maker's original brass plate. It took two more applications before we could make out the writing. I cleaned the last of the sludge from the plaque and shone the torch on it: SS *Kestrel*, built 1935, Kerr and Ross, Port Glasgow. That was a surprise for me, and a delight for Nancy.

Armed with the new information, we ascended to the wheelhouse. I grabbed another bottle of wine and our glasses. Nancy made herself comfortable on the settee and set to work, tracing the history of the *Osprey*. For a fleeting moment I wondered if I should now be calling her the *Kestrel*; but no matter what Nancy tried she couldn't find anything about its past. Apparently the shipbuilder's office was bombed during the war and the paper records were destroyed in the ensuing fire.

'Well, you tried,' I said.

'Sorry, I thought we were on to something. But at least you now know what the *Osprey* was originally called, and where and when she was built.'

'Thanks for trying.' I said, picking up the bottle. 'Another glass?'

'Why not? Oh, is my guitar ready?'

I'd completely forgotten it was sitting on the bench in the workshop. 'Be right back.'

I made sure the guitar was in tune and returned to the saloon. I handed her the guitar and sat down to watch. She fiddled with the tuners, strummed a couple of chords, sang that song, and declared her guitar fixed.

4

A letter from the past

I didn't sleep well, kept re-dreaming a dream where Katie and Nancy were fighting over cooking bacon and eggs, and the cooker timer kept ringing. I should have known better than to mix wine and bourbon.

At seven o'clock I knocked on the cabin door and called her name. 'Nancy, it's time to get up if you're going to be on time for your children.' No answer. I tried the door and found it wasn't locked. I turned the handle, gently pushed the door open a bit and peeked around it. The bed was empty. I called her name again. Maybe she was in the toilet? Still no answer. I entered the cabin and saw her clothes were missing. She was gone. But the strangest thing of all, Garboard was curled up on the bunk beside the pillow.

I went back up into the saloon and called the number she'd left on my answering machine. *Sorry, the number you are calling is not in service at this time* was the automated reply from the phone company. I climbed down into the workshop. Where the Torres should be hanging, was her grandfather's guitar, the Fleta copy.

I picked up the DS's card and dialled her number. I was about to hang up when she answered.

'DS Street.'

'Sergeant Street, it's Jack Nevis. Not sure if it's important, but I've had a most bizarre experience. Any chance you could stop by?'

They arrived twenty minute later, I offered them coffee.

'No thanks, Mr Nevis, we're quite busy today. You said something about a bizarre experience?'

I told them about Nancy showing up not long after they left, about her grandfather's guitar and about her strange desire to help

35

me find out the history of the *Osprey*. Then I added the weird bit about waking up this morning, finding her gone and the telephone number she'd given me being out of order.

'Mr Nevis, I'm afraid if you're hoping we will go and get the money for the guitar repair for you, it's not what we do.'

'No, sorry, you've misunderstood me. Don't you see how bizarre it is?'

'No, sir, we don't. Would you explain, please?'

'Yesterday morning I woke to find a dead man on the floor in my workshop, then I discover that a guitar I found sealed in a secret compartment is possibly part of looted Nazi art trove. To top it off, this woman shows up with an equally valuable guitar she wants me to repair. She gets me to tell her about the history of this boat, swaps my recently discovered guitar for hers, then disappears. Don't you think that's a bit bizarre?'

'Mr Nevis, this Nancy – did you spend the evening together, share a bottle of wine over a home-cooked meal, and then when you woke this morning found she was gone?'

'It was two bottles, actually, and yes, that's what I just told you.'

'And you think it's odd that she's gone?'

Shit, what was I saying? I was acting like a lovesick teenager who'd just had his first date and got the cold shoulder the next morning. True I liked her, she was fun to be around, and that smile – that smile and those lovely emerald eyes!

'Mr Nevis, is there anything else that you want to add?'

'We need to find her, and my guitar, Sergeant. I think she's in big trouble.'

'*We*, Mr Nevis? Do you know anything about her? Where she lives for instance, or even her full name?'

'No, I don't know where she lives, that's why I'm asking you for help.'

'And her full name?'

'She only said her name was Nancy; she never told me her full name.'

'No surname?'

'No, just Nancy. She did say she had three children and her husband abandoned her soon after they were married.'

'There's not much we can do without a surname, Mr Nevis.'

'How about fingerprints? I've got a wine glass that she was drinking from, it should still have her prints on it.'

'I suppose we could run it through the system.'

I climbed the steps to the wheelhouse and the detritus of last night. I gingerly picked up the wineglass by its stem and returned with it to the saloon. I handed the glass to the constable who carefully slid it into an evidence bag.

'Depending on what we find we'll get back to you, Mr Nevis. But you must realise that we are involved in a murder investigation and that takes priority over everything.'

'That's all right Sergeant. I just thought – well, we got on together and then she – she's just disappeared. I'm worried about her.'

'I understand, Mr Nevis. If we find anything we'll let you know. Now about your boat – I might be able to help you with that. I know someone who's involved with boats and he has connections in Scotland on the river Clyde. I'll give him a call from the office and get back to you if that helps.'

I gave her what details I had and decided, no matter what I did that day, I needed to eat. So I locked up and walked over to the Harvester and a late breakfast.

I was chasing the end of a sausage round my plate when the sergeant called.

'Mr Nevis, it's Sergeant Street. I've had a word with my friend and he says he'll call you if he can find out anything about your boat.'

'Thanks. Any word on Nancy?'

'Er – not at the moment, we're still looking for her.'

'So you know who she is?'

'Yes, we've identified her.'

37

'So who is she? Where does she live?'

'Mr Nevis, when I say we've found her, I mean we know where she lives, but she wasn't there when we visited.'

'And you can't tell me where she lives?'

'Mr Nevis, it's a delicate situation. How do we know you have her best interests at heart? Would that make sense to you?'

'No, not really. Are you implying she's in danger from me?'

'I'm sorry, I can't give you any more than that just now. Call the number I gave you. And Mr Nevis, be careful, there are things going on and, should they get out of control, a lot of people could get hurt.'

The world is full of conspiracy theories I thought, mostly tosh and wild imagination. I finished breakfast and returned to the *Osprey*. I headed for the workshop and decided I'd better get to work on the guitars that were waiting to be repaired. I placed one on the bench, removed the strings, tuners and saddle and was about to start on the fretboard when the phone rang. I grabbed my mobile: no one. Then I realised the ringing was coming from my cabin so I walked through and searched, finding the phone under the duvet; it was Nancy's, a Samsung, just like mine.

'Hello, who is this?'

'Sarah, Nancy's sister. Who are you? Where's Nancy?'

'Jack. She's not here, she's left her phone behind.'

'Are you the guy who's fixing her guitar?'

'Yes. You have her children?'

'Yeah, they're here with me but they want their mum.'

'Didn't she come to see them this morning?'

'No, haven't seen her since last night.'

'Where does she live?'

'She's got a house in Westham, just up the road from the castle. I tried to call her but there's no answer.'

'She gave me her number, but it doesn't work.'

'What did she give you?'

I read off the number and Sarah laughed.

'She's dyslexic. She's reversed the last two digits: should be eight nine, not nine eight.'

'Thanks. If she does show up, would you let her know I've got her phone?'

'Okay,' bye.'

I stuffed her phone in my pocket and went back to work on the other guitars that were waiting to be repaired. I was interrupted once again by a loud ringing.

'Jack Nevis. Nancy?' Then I realised it was my own phone I'd picked up.

'No, Mr Nevis, it's Nathan Greyspear. I've got some information on your tugboat. Would it be convenient for me to drop by, in say – twenty minutes?'

'Yes, fine.'

'Great, which dock are you on?'

'G10.'

'Good, be right over.'

♦

His right over was ten minutes and a forty-foot runabout with two growling inboards. I helped him tie it up beside the *Osprey* and climb on board. He was a fit man, in his early fifties I figured.

'Nathan Greyspear,' he said, almost crushing my hand. Another name I couldn't quite identify till I saw the maker's name on the side of his boat. There were many of them in the harbour. I wondered if he was associated with the company.

'Welcome aboard, Nathan. Shall we go inside?'

'After you.'

'Can I get you something to drink?'

'Coffee, black no sugar.'

I made fresh coffee for us and passed him a mug. 'Biscuit?'

'No thanks, coffee's fine.'

'You said you'd found out something about the *Osprey*?'

He handed me a couple of sheets of A4 paper. 'Mr Nevis – '

'Call me Jack, everyone does.'

'Well, Jack, apparently you own a piece of Clydeside history. My yard manager asked around and found one of the tug's former crew members – he's getting on in years, but his memory is still intact. Apparently, the boat you call the *Osprey* was originally called the *Kestrel*.'

I looked at the first page and read what I already knew about her being built and launched in 1935, yard number 534, at the Kerr and Ross yard in Port Glasgow. What I didn't know was that in April 1939 the then owner of the yard, Sir Archibald McLeish, dispatched the tug to Monte Carlo to bring back his private yacht, whose engine had broken down, to her home port on the river Clyde. Apparently, due to the disintegrating peace in Europe, he was concerned that it would end up being appropriated into Hitler's war machine, which at that time was sitting on the border between France and Germany.

According to the report everything went well till they had to put into the port of St Nazaire for coal for the tug's boiler. This was in late May, just a few days after Hitler had commenced his invasion of France.

All would have gone well, and they should have been on their way if it were not for the fact that coal was in short supply. By the time the tug's coal bunker had been filled, France had signed the amnesty with Germany and the *Kestrel* ended up being impounded for the duration of the war.

The report went on to say a story went around the yard that, in February 1944, some enterprising Gestapo chief, acting on orders from Reischmarschall Göering, had filled the tug with looted art treasures and gold. The *Kestrel* had sailed up the river Loire to Orleans, where the treasure was to be transferred to a private train destined for Berlin. The report emphasised this had never been confirmed and was just another World War 2 story about gold and art treasures.

The thought of a hoard of gold secreted on the *Osprey* intrigued me. Where hadn't I looked while restoring the interior? Then I thought about the Torres that had been hidden on board since 1944. Why not gold?

'Thinking about the gold?' asked Greyspear.

I smiled and shook my head. 'If there's any on board I never found it and I've been through every nook and cranny on this boat. If there was any, I'd have found it by now.'

'Was the report what you were expecting?'

'I'd no idea what to expect, though it does answer a few questions, but in turn creates new ones.'

'For instance?'

'For instance, where was she from 1944 till I bought her from the Sea Scouts? I know she had been rotting, tied up in Newhaven for about fifteen years – that takes her back to about 1998. How many years did the Sea Scouts have her, and who owned her before that?'

He shook his head. 'I'm sorry, I can't help you there.'

'That's okay, I couldn't have found out what I have without your help.'

'You could try the broker who sold you the boat.'

'I'll do just that. Thanks for the information on the *Osprey*, or should I be calling her the *Kestrel*?'

'No problem, glad to be of some help.'

I waited till he'd started the engines before casting him off. I watched his boat motor across the harbour and wondered if he was any relation to the Greyspear who ran the Greyspear Yacht Company.

I went back indoors and, looking at the clock on the wall, saw there was still time to call the broker – assuming he closed at five.

I poured myself a drink, and dialled his number. I was in luck, he was in, and remembered the sale of the *Osprey*.

'If you hang on a minute, I'll go and check our records. Might have some information for you.'

He returned five minutes later with an apology. 'I'm awfully sorry, Mr Nevis. We had a burglary last week and for no understandable reason someone went through our records and the information on the sale of your boat is missing.'

'That all?'

'Yes, just don't understand kids these days.'

'Did you report it to the police?'

'Wasn't any reason to, nothing else was missing.'

'Do you know anything about the person who handled the sale for the Sea Scouts?' I asked.

'You're in luck there, I do. Have his card somewhere in my desk drawer – ah, here it is – got a pencil?'

When don't I? I thought. 'Go ahead, I'm ready.'

It was a local Eastbourne number. I dialled and waited; the answering machine kicked in on the fourth ring. I left a message and returned to the workshop, life goes on regardless and there were still guitars to repair.

I'd just started a strip-down on a Fender Strat, when my phone rang.

'Nevis Guitars. How can I help?'

'Ah – Mr Nevis, it's Joyce Cornfield. You left a message, something about a boat?'

'Yes, I was looking for Mr Cornfield, the broker said he handled the sale of my boat on behalf of the Sea Scouts. Could I have a word with him?'

'I'm afraid not at the moment. He's in hospital – was knocked down by a car a week ago.'

'I'm sorry to hear that, Mrs Cornfield.'

'It's not as bad as it could have been, he's recovering in the DGH.'

'How is he doing?'

'They say there is no permanent damage, some internal bruising, and the worst is he's broken his right arm just above the elbow.'

'No driving for him for a while, then?'

'Nothing new there. He got an eye infection last summer, his right eye, and though the infection cleared up he says he can't see well enough to drive.'

'Well, at least we have a good bus service in Eastbourne. How long do you think he'll be in the DGH?'

'The doctor says he should be able to come home in a couple of days.'

'Would it be possible for me to visit him in hospital?'

'Oh, I'm sure he wouldn't mind. He's in the Hailsham ward; visiting hours are between ten and four-thirty.'

I said thanks, hung up, grabbed my car keys and drove to the DGH. I stopped on the way at Sainsbury's and purchased a copy of *Yachting Monthly* and a bunch of grapes. It took me a few minutes to navigate through the corridors and staircases to get to the Hailsham ward.

I found him sitting up in bed staring across the ward at the rain being driven against the windows.

'Mr Cornfield?'

'You must be Mr Nevis; my wife said you'd called and might visit.'

'I thought you might be bored, so I brought you something to read,' I said, passing him the grapes and magazine.

'Thanks,' he replied, placing the yachting magazine on top of a stack of DIY magazines. He smiled and shook his head slowly, 'My wife – ever hopeful I'll turn in to a Nick Knowles and refurbish the house, and me not knowing which end of a hammer to hold.'

Poor man, I thought. Trapped in a never-ending story of not being able to be the man his wife married.

'Mr Cornfield, I came to ask you if you had any information on my old tug boat?'

'The *Osprey*, you mean?'

'Yes.'

43

'You need to ask the broker, I passed him all the documentation before the sale.'

I shook my head. 'He can't; someone broke in and stole the file, nothing else.'

'That doesn't make much sense. Only the file, you say?'

I nodded.

He looked up into the corner of the ward as if to see if the stolen papers were pinned to the ceiling. 'Let me see now – from what I remember, the Sea Scouts bought the tug back in 1982 for one pound from the Royal Navy. It was destined to be scrapped. Sometime in the mid-sixties, I think, the navy overhauled it and had a used diesel engine fitted. The old boiler had rusted out and would have cost too much to be repaired and recertified. They used it as a harbour tug to pull barges and small ships between Portsmouth and Chatham, and that's, I'm sorry to say, all I can remember.'

I thanked him, wished him a speedy recovery, and started for the door.

'Oh, hang on,' he said, 'wait a minute. There was a chap, he apparently worked on the *Osprey* while she was in the navy. He showed up at the sale, seem to remember him saying he used to help with the maintenance. Don't even know if he's still alive. Anderson – CPO Anderson – he was called. Think his first name was Dave or was it Darrel? You could try the phone book, if not, check through the Royal Naval Association.'

I thanked him again, and returned home to the telephone directory app on my mobile. There were eighty-three Andersons, with seventeen of them being D Anderson. There were five Deborahs, and two Doreens. That left ten numbers to call. I got him just after D Anderson's Groceries.

'Yes, I remember the *Kestrel*,' he shouted, 'must have been the Sea Scouts who renamed her *Osprey*. Hang on, let me put my hearing aids in.'

While I waited for him to find his hearing aids I wondered just where this trail was going and if he could add anything to what I already knew. He was back in seven minutes, 'What did you say your name was?'

'Jack, Jack Nevis.'

'Well, Jack, she was a fine vessel, never let us down.'

'You worked on her while in the navy?'

'Yes, as a deckhand; used to run between Portsmouth and Chatham.'

'Can you tell me where she was prior to the navy owning her?'

'Not sure. I seem to remember a story about some army engineering officers finding her tied up and derelict in Orleans in France sometime in 1945. They got her running and sailed her back to the UK. The navy commandeered her in 1946 and replaced the steam turbine with a diesel, that's really all I can remember.'

I thanked him and hung up. I now knew the outline of the history of the *Osprey,* but not why she should have recently attracted so much attention. She had been built and launched in 1935, used on the Clyde till 1939. when dispatched to bring Sir Archibald's private yacht back home from Monte Carlo. Being short on fuel they'd put in to St Nazaire harbour for coal for the boiler but, due to a shortage, the *Osprey* ended up being impounded by the local government. Then sometime in 1944 she was packed with stolen artwork and sailed up the river Loire to Orleans where, presumably, the artwork was loaded on a train headed for Berlin and the *Osprey* left abandoned.

She was subsequently discovered by some British army officers who got her ready for sea and sailed her back to the UK, where she was pressed into service with the Royal Navy and finally handed over to the Sea Scouts in 1982, who then sold her to me.

Several questions now arose. One, what had happened to the looted artwork? Second, was the Torres part of it? Third, could there still be stolen artwork, or even gold bullion, secreted away somewhere on board the *Osprey*? Fourth, why had the California PI been shot and killed in my workshop? And most importantly, fifth, what had happened to Nancy and my Torres?

I called DS Street.

'How can we help, Mr Nevis?'

I recounted what I'd heard about the history of the *Osprey*.

'Mr Nevis, I understand your concern for your friend. I'm sure there's a perfectly good reason for what she did. Give her time, I'm sure she'll turn up with an explanation for her actions. If it helps, I'll take the report on the missing guitar.'

'But don't you see, Sergeant? The *Osprey* was used to ship stolen artwork – who knows to what value? She ends up back in the UK after the war, is used by the navy, sold to the Sea Scouts then finally on to me.'

'Mr Nevis, I'm sure a man like you knows that boats are bought and sold all the time, many of them with a colourful history.'

'Ah, but how many of them will have the history of the *Osprey*? How many of them will have had the sales agent almost killed in a hit-and-run accident, the brokerage burglarised and the sales records stolen?'

'You do have a point there; I'll grant you that.'

'Then, to top it all off, I wake to find a dead body in my workshop!'

'Mr Nevis, I do realise you are under a lot of stress, but please, leave the policing to us.'

'But what about the fact I've recently discovered a rare valuable guitar, then – Nancy shows up under the pretence of having me repairing her grandfather's guitar and does a runner with it. Don't you think that it's all a bit odd?'

'Mr Nevis, you worry too much. You're letting your imagination run away with you.'

'But my guitar? And I'm sure something has happened to Nancy.'

'As I said, we'll report your guitar missing, and Mr Nevis, don't worry, I'm sure your friend will turn up with a perfectly reasonable explanation of what has happened.'

I could have sworn at her but realised I might need her help in the future. By now the sun had set and I was getting hungry. I poured myself a Jack Daniels and had a look in the fridge. I managed to find a steak that was still in date and went outside to the stern. As I stood up from lighting the barbecue and my eyes adjusted to the dark, I saw her standing on the end of the dock.

'Nancy?'

'Jack.'

'Where the hell have you been? And what have you done with my guitar?'

'Can I come on board – please? I can explain everything and I've brought your guitar back.'

I counted slowly to ten, then breathed out quietly between my teeth. 'Yes – yes, of course. Here, let me give you a hand.'

I walked back along the side deck and reached out to help her up onto the boat. Her hand was cold to the touch but gripped mine with a fierceness that sent a shiver down my spine. I opened the door for her and followed her in.

'Your guitar,' she said, passing me the case. 'Sorry, it's been damaged,' she sniffed, tears welling up. I wondered what or who was responsible for her left eye turning a nasty shade of blue.

'What happened to you – the bruise on your face?'

'Oh Jack, it's been awful.'

'Look, come and sit down. Want something to drink?'

'White wine, if you have any?'

I poured her a large Pinot Grigio, and waited for the trembling to cease. While I waited, I poured myself another three fingers of Jack Daniels.

She sniffed a couple of times, then downed the remainder of the wine and handed me the empty glass.

'More wine?'

She nodded, took in a deep breath and exhaled slowly.

I refilled her glass and sat down opposite her and waited.

'Jack, it was so awful.'

'Wait a minute, let's start at the beginning. First, why did you pretend to want to learn how to make guitars?'

'No, that was true, I do.'

'And the cock and bull story about your grandfather's guitar – you do know it isn't really a Fleta, don't you?'

'Yes and no. According to my mother, my grandfather was a trained cabinet maker who used to specialise in antique furniture restoration. His skills were in big demand and he travelled all over Europe. One summer he'd just finished a restoration job in one of the big houses near Barcelona. He wasn't sure what to do next so he went for a wander round the back streets and walked past the Fleta workshop. He got curious and asked if he could help there. In exchange for his work they let him make his own guitar.'

'And you want to follow in his footsteps?'

She nodded. Her face lit up and I saw the smile I'd become enamoured with return. 'He even pinched one of their labels and stuck it in his guitar. He just wanted people to like the guitar.'

'He didn't need to do that; the guitar is brilliant.

'I know; he was just like that.'

'So – my guitar, what's the story?'

'It was my husband's idea.'

'Your husband – I thought you said he was in Saudi Arabia working in the oil fields, or was it Germany?'

'That was what I thought, but the rat's back again, much the pity. He said if I didn't do what he wanted he'd harm my children.'

'Did he really threaten to harm your children?'

She nodded again and sniffed; tears welling up and running down her cheeks. I was in a quandary; on one hand I wanted to find out more about what was going on, and on the other I wanted to reach out and give her a hug, but that would mean getting up from my chair, walking over and sitting down beside her. I went over, sat down beside her, put my arms around her and held her close.

She buried her head in my chest and sobbed. 'He's not the children's father,' she said, between sobs. He died in Afghanistan, stepped on an IED. A few months later I was invited out there, along with other widows, to a special commemoration service. While there I met one of the Afghan translators, he'd been working with my husband's platoon when the explosion occurred. I suppose I was lonely and we just sort of got on well together. We were married within the year. At first, he was the perfect husband, treated me and the children well, then – you remember where you were on the sixth of January 2011?'

I nodded. 'I was in hospital. That was the morning after my family died in a car crash on the M1.'

'Oh, I'm so sorry.'

'That's all right, you weren't to know.'

'He changed, he became sultry, bad-tempered and moody, moaned continually about the weather. I think it was the first time in his life he'd had to deal with ice and snow. He shouted at the children when they asked him to take them out to play in the snow. We went out to dinner that evening, but I may as well have been on my own, when we got home he started shouting at me, calling me names. He slapped me in the face and called me a slut. Next morning, he was gone.'

'What did you do?'

'After a couple of days I reported him missing. And that was that, I thought.'

'What do you mean?'

'Two days later I was visited by two members of the foreign office; they asked me all kinds of personal questions about our relationship.'

'And after?'

'Nothing till a couple of days ago. He just showed up at the door as though he'd just been out to the shops.'

'So why did you take the Torres?'

'He said he was working for someone who would pay a lot of money for the guitar and I was to leave my grandfather's guitar in exchange. I didn't want to do it, but he was so angry, I really believe he would have harmed the children.'

'I thought you said they are with your sister?'

'They are. He doesn't know where she lives, and I was afraid to take the risk of going to them in case he followed me.'

'And he actually said he'd harm your children if you didn't do what he wanted?'

She sniffed and nodded.

'So – why did he want the Torres?' I asked, letting go of her. 'And also, how did he know about it?'

'I have brought it back.'

'So I see, but that doesn't answer the question how he knew it was here.'

'It was the photograph in the newspaper, someone recognised the guitar, someone that Achmed knows.'

I walked over to the table where I'd left the Torres, opened the case and looked inside at the disaster.

'He did that, my husband.'

The "that" was the almost complete destruction of the Torres. How he'd managed to rip the soundboard from the body and keep it in one piece was beyond me, but then I remembered the fretboard was loose when I'd found the guitar, though not completely off of the neck, a lucky break for the guitar. The bindings had popped loose when the soundboard had been ripped off. I looked closer at the edges of the soundboard and realised that with the guitar being closed up in the confines of the rear of the cupboard for all those years the glue had failed. In retrospect he'd done me a favour, all I had to do now was repair a couple of splits, clean the edges and re-attach the soundboard.

'Is it beyond repair? Oh, Jack, I'm so sorry,' she said, starting to sniffle again.

I passed her a kitchen towel. 'Are you really serious about making a guitar?'

She nodded. 'Why?'

'You can help me put the Torres back together.' The smile returned and at that moment I realised I was at the point of no return. I could no longer live in the present looking at the past; the present looking to the future was where I belonged.

'You hungry?' I asked.

'Want me to cook us something?'

'I was about to barbecue a steak, there's a second in the fridge?'

She smiled. 'You do the steaks; I'll see if you have enough vegetables to make a side salad.'

'There should be a couple of baking potatoes in the basket in the bottom cupboard.'

I could hear her singing as I turned our steaks; I smiled, sniffed and reached for my handkerchief.

> My broken heart can never mend
> So loving memories to you I send
> Remember me when you wander near
> As I stand in the rain and hide my tears
>
> When the gentle breath of spring, warms the winter air
> I'd hold you in my arms, and dream without a care.

◆

We ate dinner in silence in the wheelhouse, each avoiding the other's furtive glances.

Nancy spoke first. 'Can we start on your guitar after dinner?'

I nodded. looking at the clock. 'If you want, though it's getting late. Won't your sister and children wonder where you are?'

She was silent for a moment. 'Since my husband has returned and threatened the children, I've told my sister I will be staying away till he leaves. He doesn't know where she lives and I don't want to lead him there by going home.'

51

'Where will you stay, then?'

She smiled again and cocked her head.

'You want to stay here?'

'If you don't mind? I can sleep on the settee; it's not fair to take your bed.'

I shook my head. 'No, it's all right. You can have my cabin, just till your husband goes. Okay?'

'I left my stuff on the dock, be back in a minute.'

I headed for the galley to wash the dishes; she was back before I'd finished drying the plates. She hadn't brought much, just what she was wearing and a small backpack stuffed full of who knows what, I wasn't sure if I was relieved.

As I put on the kettle for coffee, she said, 'Right, ready to go to work on your guitar?'

I looked at the clock and regretted saying I'd work on it tonight, it was almost nine. 'Ok if you're that serious I don't see why not.'

She followed me down to the workshop. Carefully I removed the guitar from the case and laid it on the bench.

'Where will we start?' she asked.

'The fretboard is almost off already so might as well start there.'

I'd removed many fretboards over the years and this one was the easiest of all of them. I slid the heated spatula into the gap at the head and the fretboard just popped off. I looked at the glue and realised something was not as it should be. Usually on old instruments, when a glued joint fails, there is a tell-tale sign of crystallised glue. This joint had no glue, other than a spot just large enough to hold the board in place; it was almost as though someone had meant it to be easily removed – but why? It wasn't long before the answer became clear. Secreted in a hollowed-out section of the neck was a folded piece of paper.

'Is that usual?' Nancy asked, looking over my shoulder. Her scent making me momentarily woozy.

I shook my head. 'It's a new one on me.'

I carefully pried out the paper and saw it was a letter, folded several times to enable it to fit within the hollowed-out section. I unfolded it and tried to make sense of the handwriting. I turned it over and saw someone had obviously been bored – they'd doodled all over the back.

'What is it?'

'I've no idea, looks like a purchase order. See? There's a list of stuff, looks like it's written in German?

'Can I have a look?'

I passed her the letter.

'Definitely German – look at the date, *Februar* 1944'

She stared at it and twitched her nose. 'Hmm, not sure, but I think it's talking about some paintings See here on the list,' she pointed, 'Matisse, Picasso, not sure about Liebermann, but Vermeer, they're all painters. And look at these names,' she said, pointing at the first paragraph, and down there, look, Göering.'

'You're right. I wonder if this is a list of some of the paintings stolen by the Nazis during the war?

'Can I use your computer?'

'Yes, of course, why?'

'I'll transcribe the letter in German, then google the translation. Won't be perfect but at least it will give us an idea as to its contents.'

'Is there no end to your talents?'

'Maybe someday I'll answer that question for you.' She blushed and skipped off up the stairs then stopped half way 'Where is your computer?'

'Where you left it, in the wheelhouse. More wine?'

'Yes please.'

I followed a couple of minutes later with the bottle. She was a fast typist and within minutes had transcribed the letter and googled the translation. I rattled the ice in my empty glass as she read.

'It's only a rough translation; we should get someone who really speaks German to translate it for us.'

'It'll have to do for now. What does it say?'

Jeu de Paume
Paris
Feb 13 1944

Dear Hans

Burn this letter when reading. Our fat friend has dustup another with Herr Himmler was and is now on the warpath, and I do not want this letter traced to me. I have just returned from the Gare Montparnasse, and my examination of the latest shipment of recovered art of Orleans. As you know, it's all intended to Berlin and finally Führermuseum in Linz. Everything would be fine if it were not for the missing items on the manifest, which I later.

1. Both Matisse – Femme Assise
2. The great Picasso – Woman on the Beach
3. The two Liebermanns –Two Riders on the Beach, and The Basket Weaver
4. The Vermeer – The Art of Painting
5. The small Egyptian statue of the black falcon the Göering said that he would present to Fuhrer the personally, Göering says that we are not so small to be *Wicht, Wiesel* Himmler we know the small falcons have character.

I must assume that they are resisted by the French with the help of one of the guards on the train were spirited. I am not willing to let the SS because they ask too many questions.

Unfortunately, someone opened the cage and have left the nest gold flew the eagles. As necessary resolution to our little problem, could be a new manifesto that they. On the train, which create on Wednesday, which was one that sabotaged by the resistance fighters and robbed and send me load a modified version of the original left.

As always, your friend
Gerhard

'Well, what do you think?' she asked.

'I feel as if we have a few pieces of a jigsaw, and no picture.'

'I've got an idea. Pour me that glass of wine, please.'

I filled her glass and added a double shot of bourbon to my melting ice. When I returned to the wheelhouse she had just finished looking at the computer.

'Find anything?' I asked, handing her the refilled glass of wine.

'Since the war, those paintings listed in the letter have been recovered, though some are still in contention as to who actually owns them.'

'And?'

'So that just leaves the matter of the little black falcon statue and the eagles. Maybe the falcon statue was made of gold, painted black, and belonged to Cleopatra, or some other Egyptian royalty?'

'Maybe. Anything about the eagles?'

'No, though I was wondering if it might have been something to do with the German flag, it has an eagle on it.'

I nodded and took another sip of bourbon.

'Maybe it was a special flag and it simply got caught in the wind and was blown away?'

'That's possible, but I wonder – suppose the eagle referred to something to do with the US?'

'Secret plans for an invasion, and the underground managed to rescue them?'

I shook my head and our eyes met; I smiled, she grinned. She got busy again on the computer while I went out on the wheelhouse side deck and stared at a cloudless sky and full moon over Beachy Head.

'Ah-ha, found something!'

I went back in and closed the door. 'Yes?'

'The only serious reference I can find of a falcon statue is a brief note about the Knights Templar giving one to Charles V of Spain for the use of the island of Malta.'

'As I said, I think we're out of our depth. We need professional advice, but I've no idea where to get it.'

'What about the British Museum? They must have people there who know about Egyptian falcon statues. Though they may not be as helpful about World War 2 stolen paintings.'

'I am thinking the paintings are not part of our mystery.'

'Explain?'

'If the *Osprey* had been used to transport the paintings and they were somehow still on board, then all that has happened would make sense. But as we know from your search on the internet, all the paintings have been accounted for. So that leaves the black falcon statue and these mysterious eagles, which for all we know could still be secreted here on board somewhere. After all, the Torres was hidden since 1944, so why not the falcon statue and the eagles – whatever they are?'

She yawned and stretched her arms. I looked at the clock: it was twenty past one.

'But if they are, how could they be so valuable as to have caused all this trouble? Someone has died looking for them, remember.'

Only too well did I remember. 'Who knows? Let's get some sleep and have another go in the morning.'

Another night on the settee. I was beginning to feel like a husband who'd been put out to sleep with the dog.

5

The Cult of Horus

I didn't sleep well, this time Katie and Nancy were fighting over who would repair the Torres; I left them to it and woke up with a raging headache and to the sweet smell of coffee and bacon.

'Good morning, sleepyhead, breakfast's ready.'

'What time is it?'

'Half past seven, time to get up. Come on, we've got work to do.'

'Hang on, let me get dressed first.'

I looked up into her eyes and for a moment I imagined I was standing at the North Pole looking up at the Aurora Borealis, full of wonder, tinged with excitement and an element of danger. Then just as quickly as they appeared, they went out like a blown light bulb; the northern lights were replaced by the cold green of an Atlantic storm.

'All right, I take my coffee black and I like my eggs over easy.'

'Your wish is my command,' she said.

I went into the toilet to shave and get dressed.

Earworms are what they're called; tunes that go round and round in your head. This tune with the words were lethal to my solitary lifestyle:

> Now all I have are memories
> And your picture by my bed
> I stare at it as I fall asleep
> and dream of you, and what we had.
>
> When the gentle breath of spring, warms the winter air
> I'll hold you in my arms, and dream without a care.

♦

'Eggs okay?' she asked, as I mopped up the last of the yolks with my toast.

'Couldn't have cooked them better myself – you're hired!' Then I realised just what I'd said. Suppose she took it as a proposal?

'You're too late, I already have a job.'

She must have seen the embarrassment in my face for, before I could hide it, she said, 'I'm an apprentice luthier. That's what you guitar people call it, isn't that right?'

Either she'd misunderstood my comment or she was playing with me. I didn't mind either way.

'I've been busy,' she said.

'So I notice, dishes done and the place looks tidier than I can ever get it.'

'That's not what I meant. The British museum opens at ten – that gives you a couple of hours in which to start teaching me about guitars.'

We returned to the workshop. I grabbed my copy of *Step by Step Guitar Making* and, page by page, went through the steps of guitar construction with her.

'He makes it look so easy,' she said, looking at the photos of completed instruments in the back. 'Look at that bass guitar – can't you just see Paul McCartney playing it?'

'I believe his guitar was a left-handed solid body Hofner. If you look closely you'll see that the one in the book has a hollow body, and is right-handed.'

She continued to gaze at the pictures. 'Teach me to make one like that,' she said, pointing to the 00 sized rosewood guitar.

She had pointed to the guitar with the most intricate inlay work of all of the guitars in the book, and probably would take her months to complete.

'That guitar would take an expert about three hundred hours of construction – look at all that abalone and mother-of-pearl inlay. Each piece has to be hand cut then inlaid. You think you've got that much time and patience?'

She looked at me, eyes sparkling. 'I do, do you?'

I turned away from her gaze and saw that it was ten past ten. 'It's time to call the museum.'

We returned to the salon and I picked up the phone, 'Where's the number?'

'Here,' she said, passing me her notebook. Beautiful handwriting, I observed.

I dialled the number and waited for an answer. I got passed around a few times before getting the information I wanted. I said thanks and hung up.

'Well, what did they say? she asked, with the excitement of a teenager waiting for their exam results.

'They suggested we contact a Professor Stanton Lozinski.'

'Did they give you his number?'

'No, they said to try the Herstmonceux Observatory, he sometimes gives lectures there'

'That's a start.'

'Apparently he used to work at the museum but retired a few years ago to write a paper on his life's research.'

'Which is?'

'The study of monotheism through the ages.'

'What's that got to do with paintings and falcons?'

'Who knows? But since it's our only lead, I'll give the observatory a call. And I think lady luck is on our side today, it's a local number.'

I dialled the number and after sitting on hold for a few minutes was pleasantly surprised when Professor Lozinski picked up the phone. I explained about what had happened on the boat and the letter. Something I said must have intrigued him for he said to come right over, though why he wanted the guitar as well I could not figure out.

'Right, do you have a coat?' I asked Nancy.

'Yes, why? Are we going somewhere?'

'We're off to see the wizard, the wonderful wizard of Herstmonceux!' I tried to sing, but she just laughed at my attempt. 'Well, we will as soon as I can book a taxi – my car's being serviced.'

The taxi dropped us in front of a large two-storey whitewashed cottage. The professor's house was down a lane just past the pub in Wartling, within healthy walking distance of the old Herstmonceux observatory and castle. A climbing rose, still in bloom, struggled to hold on to its trellis over the front door. I rang the doorbell and waited. I wasn't sure what to expect, but was surprised to see a very fit man, probably in his early seventies, with a presence I could only describe as that of the eminent actor Sir Ian McKellen. He had liquid, clear eyes, and a look of eager expectation.

'Come in, dear boy, come in! And this, I assume, is your dear lady wife?'

Nancy blushed and shook her head. 'No, we're just working together, I'm Jack's assistant.'

'Welcome, come in.'

He ushered us through to his study and indicated an overstuffed settee facing his enormous oak desk. I wasn't sure why I thought his study would be tidy. In fact, the left side of his desk was piled with open books, and on the right was all the usual accoutrements of a busy communicator. There were jars of pens and pencils, several vintage fountain pens, a house phone, a mobile sitting in a charging stand, plus a calculator and stapler, while in the middle was an enormous computer screen. I looked round the room and saw all the bookshelves were full of neatly-arranged books and the three filing cabinets stood, drawers closed, like soldiers on parade.

'My wife will be with us in a minute, please sit. I expect you'd like some coffee? I'm not allowed any unless we have visitors, and unfortunately we don't get enough of them.' He grinned and shrugged. Seeing the look of puzzlement on my face, he added, 'I'd drink gallons of it, and I end up staying awake all night, with the subsequent lack of sleep making me grouchy.'

The door opened and Mrs Lozinski entered. Tall and regal, with long flowing grey hair, she spoke with an educated eastern European accent I put down to possibly Polish.

'Nadia, our guests are here – coffee?'

She smiled at him, pursed her lips and shook her head slowly and turned to Nancy. 'Would you like coffee?'

'Yes, please.'

'Coffee, Mr Nevis?'

I said yes and saw the smile grow on the professor's face.

Mrs Lozinski exited the room to brew up our coffees.

The professor began, 'You mentioned a letter and a newspaper?'

I handed him them both.

'Before I read these,' he said, 'tell me, where does your involvement with this matter begin?'

I started from the moment I'd heard what I'd assumed was the sound of the string on Dizzy's guitar breaking.

'So, you wake in the night to a Californian private investigator being shot in your workshop. I think first, we must ask why he was there?'

'Beats me, I've been wracking my brain over that these last few days,' I replied.

'Hasn't it crossed your mind that he must have had a prior reason to have travelled all the way from California to be on your boat that fateful evening? And how did his protagonist manage to coincide his rendezvous with the investigator? Think, Mr Nevis, think back at least two weeks, what did you do to attract attention to yourself and your boat?'

I worked backwards a couple of weeks and tried to remember anything that I'd done that would have drawn attention to me. Then I remembered, I'd taken a stand in the Winter Gardens at the exhibition for local businesses put on by the Eastbourne Chamber of Commerce. I remember being photographed with the local MP while holding the Torres. Of course I'd no idea at the time of its provenance, it had just been a surprise discovery of an old guitar in the back of a cupboard. That photo and subsequent paragraph about its discovery in the *Eastbourne Herald* must have been read by someone who understood its significance.

'So, you discovered the guitar, had it and yourself photographed for the paper – and I suppose you mentioned where your workshop was located?'

I nodded. 'Thought it was a good opportunity to publicise the business.'

'Looks like it did more than that.'

We were interrupted by the arrival of our coffees.

'Milk, sugar, Mrs Nevis?'

Nancy blushed again 'It's Mrs Rafsanjani. I'm Mr Nevis's pupil, he's teaching me to make guitars. Just a little sugar and a splash of milk, please.'

I'd never heard her surname before, and I suppose it shouldn't have surprised me, she did say she was married to an Afghan.

'Mr Nevis, milk, sugar?'

'Just black, please.'

'Mr Nevis,' said the professor, 'while you drink your coffee, I'll read the letter and have a look at the newspaper. Mind if I borrow the guitar? It will help me to think if I have the actual object in front of me. It will perhaps also aid in me imagining what was in the mind of the person who secreted the letter there.'

He laid the paper on his desk, turned on the reading light, and proceeded to ignore us. We sat in silence as though any interruption from us would break his concentration. Finally, he grunted, put down the letter, read through the newspaper one more time, then turned back to us.

'You will stay to lunch? I have much research to do before I can provide you with definitive answers with this matter. Then, looking at his wife, he said, 'Nadia, there will be four for lunch, a late one probably. Would you take Mr Nevis and Mrs Rafsanjani into the lounge and make them comfortable, please? You may have to provide them with a sandwich to tide them over.'

It was like a scene from a TV adaptation of a Miss Marples story. As we entered the lounge I saw there was a massive oak dining table and chairs at one end and, at the other, a huge settee faced an open fire. Overstuffed armchairs sat either side the hearth, completing the image of the Lozinskis spending many nights relaxing with family and friends. I half expected the local vicar to walk in at any moment. I was about to sit in the armchair beside the companion set when I saw a look of consternation grow on Mrs Lozinski's face.

'The professor's seat?' I asked.

She nodded, then relaxed, as I moved over to the settee and sat at the other end to Nancy.

We had to wait a further three hours before the professor joined us. He entered the room, walked over to the window and drew the curtains.

'Wine, dear, I think we'll try some of the merlot we had delivered yesterday.'

'It's breathing on the sideboard.'

'Thank you, my dear, as always anticipating my every move.'

'That's what happens when you've been married for forty-five years, Mrs Rafsanjani,' she said, laughing. 'Relationships change from that of lovers to that of a comfortable friendship.'

'Well, Mr Nevis,' the professor said, pouring substantial amounts of wine in the glasses, 'it appears you two are involved in a very serious matter, and I'm not just referring to the death of that poor Californian private investigator.

He put the glasses on a tray and handed them round before moving over to the fire and standing spread-eagled in front of it.

'Initially when you told me about your break-in and the death of the investigator, I wasn't really interested. But when you mentioned the letter, the art theft by the Einsatzstab Reichsleiter Rosenberg or ERR as it's sometimes referred to, and the fact the letter mentioned the little Egyptian falcon, alarm bells sounded in my head, though the bit about the eagles still puzzles me.'

'Let's have dinner before it gets cold, Stanton. Our guests have only had a sandwich since they arrived.'

'But of course, you'll need all your energy before this little adventure has run its course.'

I could see he was desperate to tell us about his findings, so as soon as the dessert had been served I said, 'Professor, I detect you have much to say. Is now the time?'

He looked up at his wife, who smiled and nodded.

'Mr Nevis, up until today I've been despairing about life, it's been plain, and simply boring. That is till you brought me the letters.'

'Letters plural, Professor? There are two letters?'

'Ah, yes, so there are, I was coming to that. If you'd looked further, Mr Nevis, you'd have discovered on the reverse of the letter what I'm talking about.'

'You mean that scribbling is a letter? I just thought it was just someone's doodles.'

'That's what you were meant to think.'

'Well, Professor, what does it say?' asked an excited Nancy.

'As you correctly pointed out the one letter is about the missing art treasures that were supposed to be shipped to Berlin, but mislaid on the way –'

'And the other letter, Professor?' interrupted Nancy.

'It's from a crew member of the tug – from what I can decipher he was staying in one of the big houses in the St Nazaire region.'

I wondered about that and asked, 'The name of the house in the letter, the one that was raided by the SS, is it the same as the house in the newspaper article?'

He picked up the newspaper and mumbled quietly as he read. 'Looks like that's the case – this is very interesting.'

'What is?' asked Nancy.

'Let me read you this letter, then I think you'll understand.'

'Okay but first I need to leave the room for a moment.'

'It's down the hall, the second door on the right, dear,' said Mrs Lozinski.

'Another drink while we wait? Mr Nevis?'

'Why not, since I'm not driving this evening?'

By now we were on brandy and I was wondering just where all this was going. Nancy was back in ten minutes, and none too steady on her feet.

'You all right?' I asked.

'Yes, bit warm in here, the fresh air in the corridor hit me, that's all.'

'Well, if we're all comfortable,' Lozinski began. 'Roughly translated, as I said it appears to be from one of the tug's crew. He is writing to a Lieutenant Hudson, informing him of the impending movement of the stolen art and the gold.'

'Gold!' exclaimed Nancy. 'How much?'

'Doesn't say exactly, just mentions a few boxes of gold coins.'

'So why did he hide the letter in the neck of the guitar?' Nancy asked.

'One must presume it was to keep it from falling in to the hands of the Gestapo. Remember they were taking the art and gold back to Germany, and whoever wrote the letter probably meant it to be read by this Lieutenant Hudson.'

'Wonder who Lieutenant Hudson was,' said Nancy, 'and what happened to him, Professor? Looks like he never got the guitar.'

'Obviously not, but I haven't been kicking my heels. This afternoon, I did a search for all Lieutenant Hudsons who'd served in the navy on the eastern Atlantic. I found four; three are deceased and the fourth is currently residing in a Royal British Legion care home called Nelson's Lodge. The website gives an address in Bexhill, not for from here.'

Funny, I thought, all this going on and not more than a few miles from where it all started. I looked at the professor and figured he'd come to the same conclusion.

'I'll go visit him tomorrow,' I said. 'Hopefully it will be the same man. What about the family living in the house?'

'I did look for the family, there are a few scattered round the south east. I'll get on to it tomorrow, too late today.'

'So the guitar was meant as a means of transporting a message to the British secret service,' said Nancy, 'how exciting.'

'MI5, even as far back as the second World War it was known as MI5, and yes, it looks that way.

'So one of the tug's crew found out about the imminent shipment of the paintings and the other valuables and decided to do what they could to prevent it, Professor. But why was he in still in France? I would have thought he'd be long gone by the time the Germans arrived.'

Lozinski shrugged. 'If he was here, Nancy, we could have asked him, but since he isn't we may never know.'

'Some things we do know,' I said. 'He was British, worked on the tug, was still around while the Germans were occupying the town and had links to MI5.'

'And don't forget he worked on guitars,' said Nancy.

'Ah, the guitar connection,' said the professor. 'We are assuming he worked on guitars – and if so, he must have had access to proper woodworking tools. Look how neatly the recess is carved – all done by hand and the bottom as flat as a billiard table.'

'So he might have been a cabinet maker,' said Nancy. 'My grandfather was one, and he made his own guitar.'

'It's possible this individual worked in the shipyard as a cabinet maker and volunteered to go with the tug to recover the private yacht from Monte Carlo,' added the professor. 'Finding out that he was destined for the Mediterranean, MI5 got in touch with him, possibly to act as ears and eyes for them, especially since war was imminent.'

'But it was more than imminent when he wrote his cryptic letter to Lieutenant Hudson,' I said. 'The Germans were wholesale stripping their conquered countries of the national treasures,'.

'I've seen the movie,' said Nancy, 'it was called *The Monuments Men*. The allied soldiers went round Europe after the war looking for stolen artwork and gold.'

'It was based on real facts, and sadly even now in 2016 – seventy years after the war – there are still groups of people trying to reunite World War 2 stolen artwork with the rightful owners.'

The professor was correct. I'd seen newspaper articles as well, and wondered how many guitars had suffered from the ERR. I watched, amused, as he sipped on the dregs of his coffee, looked forlornly at his empty cup, then at his wife.

'All right Stanton, just one more cup.' Turning to us she asked, 'Would either of you like more coffee?'

We both declined.

The professor grinned and leant forward with his empty cup in his outstretched arm, obviously eagerly anticipating his next caffeine fix. We waited for him to go through his ritual of sniffing the aroma, then taking a sip.

'Wonder what the gold would be worth in today's market?' said Nancy.

The professor picked up a pen and scribbled on a notepad. 'Gold in 1942 was valued at about twenty dollars an ounce, today that same ounce would cost you roughly,' he picked up a copy of the *Telegraph* and shuffled through to the financial pages, 'the princely sum of eight hundred pounds. That's an increase of roughly forty times.'

No one spoke. The fire crackled into life as Mrs Lozinski put on another log.

'Yes, quite a substantial amount,' said the professor, 'but unlikely to still be undiscovered. Most of these Nazi gold stories are just that. Stories made up to sell books and fill newspaper columns.'

'Pity, would be nice to have a share of however much it was,' said Nancy, smiling in my direction.

I thought of the *Osprey* and the upcoming dry-docking and engine service that I'd put off for lack of funds.

'Any ideas what might have happened to the gold?' said Nancy, her eyes wide open like a child who's just seen the presents under the Christmas tree.

'A valid question. Many people have sought the Nazi gold of World War 2. In fact, just a few weeks ago there was an article in the *Guardian* about a missing gold train hidden somewhere in one of Hitler's tunnels that the Nazis were digging in Poland. Supposed to be booby-trapped with explosives, but that's what I meant by gold stories.'

'So, do you think that is what this is all about?' I asked. 'The missing gold?'

I watched the professor's face; he was carefully considering his reply. He cleared his throat.

'Jack, Nancy, you must have heard of the stories of how Jason and his band of Argonauts searched for the Golden Fleece, or how King Arthur sought the Holy Grail, or Bilbo Baggins had to return the *One Ring to rule them all* to Mount Mordor for its destruction?'

'Of course I have, but those are just fiction, stories turned into movies by Hollywood.'

'Let me tell you a story,' began the professor.'

'Good, I like stories,' said Nancy as she moved beside me, hooking her arm through mine, and leaning her head on my shoulder.

The professor smiled. 'This story – and it is just a story – begins at the death of the Egyptian warlord and Nile god, Horus. What I believe we are dealing with, Jack and Nancy, is a resurgence of *The Cult of Horus.'*

'What's that when it's at home, Professor?'

'The worship of an Egyptian god, Nancy. Historical records tell us that Horus was the son of Isis and Osiris; some say he was a real man, though I've been unable to substantiate this. As a deity he was worshipped from the late pre-dynastic period and well into the Greco-Roman era. He was revered as a deity, the sun god, protector of the pharaoh, and most importantly to our present concerns, a god of war.'

'Who did he fight?'

'According to legend, Horus had a brother, Set. You may have seen the recent movie where Set is ruling the world and Horus has to take back control of the world?'

'Yes, I did, thought that the computer graphics was the best part of the film.'

'Well, it might interest you to know that the film was based on a real story, most likely a myth, but believed by many people all the same.'

'How close was the movie to the historical version?' I asked.

The professor's smile said it all. 'The main story goes like this – there are variations and embellishments. Set was the brother of Horus, and the son of Isis and Osiris; he killed his father. To regain the throne, Horus had many battles with Set. The final one was a boat race in boats made of stone. Horus used his cunning by making a boat out of wood and painting it to look like stone; Set's boat, being made of stone, sank. Horus was victorious and regained his position as god. These are a few lines of a hymn that would have been sung to him during worship.:

> Well do you watch, O Horus, who sails over the sky,
> thou child who proceeds from the divine father,
> thou child of fire, who shines like crystal, you who
> destroys the darkness and the night.

'So he really was seen as a god, someone to worship?'

'Absolutely, Nancy. The story of his passage into mythology is somewhat shrouded in mystery. But the story I have been able to unravel says that upon the moment the soul of Horus departed his body, the temple priests, using incantations now lost to the sands of time, managed to ensnare his soul in a hand-carved, black marble statue of a falcon figurine. Apparently after a period of time Horus came to be a symbol of the unification of his country. It is also recorded that the pharaoh was considered to be an incarnation of Horus.'

'What happened to the statue? Were you able to find out anything?'

'Not much about the early years, Nancy. Though it did eventually become the focal point of worship in the temple of Horus.'

'Probably just another myth to titillate the tourists.'

'You've got it wrong there, Jack. In 237BC a new temple to honour Horus was begun at Edfu, and still stands today.'

'Really, professor. Is it like most of the other ancient monuments in Egypt?'

'Not quite. Anyone can visit the temple of Horus, it's one of the main tourist attractions on the Nile riverboat cruises. One other very important temple on the Nile is at Philae, just past the lower Aswan dam. That's the temple of Isis, the mother of Horus.'

'And you say there is documentary evidence for this, Professor?'

'You could read it for yourself, Nancy. That is if you visited the British Museum and can read Egyptian hieroglyphs.'

'Thanks, I'll leave that to you and the other experts.'

'Since we are mentioning it,' the professor continued, 'I've found a very interesting story about the temple of Isis at Philae, and a man called Athanasius, he was the Bishop of Alexandria. After hearing reports of how local Christians were being mistreated by the local pagan community, he sent one of the junior bishops to the island of Philae to investigate; Bishop Macedonia, an orthodox Christian who was acting as the local governor. Upon arriving at the island he made a pretence of wanting to make a sacrifice to Isis. He was permitted to enter, and on doing so discovered a falcon in a cage being worshipped. In indignation he took the bird out of its cage, ripped its head off, and threw the remains in the sacrificial fire. Not long after, the whole community turned away from worshiping pagan gods to that of Christianity.

'A very potent image you paint, Professor.'

'Thought all those ancient monuments were just crumbling ruins.'

'Might have been, if it were not for the desert sands, Jack. Horus's temple at Edfu for instance, fell into disuse in about 390AD. With the passing of time, the winds of the desert covered it with over ten metres of sand and river silt. Excavations of the site started in 1860. Today you can park in the new car park, take a tour of the inside of the temple, see the statues of Horus and many very legible hieroglyphs on the walls.'

'The temple at Philae as well?'

'Uh-huh. Though it's not in its original position. When the upper Aswan dam was completed, the lower dam water level was raised and almost completely inundated the temple of Isis.'

'What happened to it?'

'It was moved, all forty thousand blocks, to an adjacent island and completely reassembled.'

'So do you think the statue was in the temple till – when did you say it was excavated?'

'1860, Jack. And no, I don't think it was there till then.'

'Why is that?'

'In about 572 BC, Nebuchadnezzar, King of Babylon, after a fruitless siege of Tyre, invaded Egypt as far south as the southern border at Sudan. On departing from Egypt, his troops took captive many of the people and looted the country of all of its treasures, especially the contents of the temples.'

'So our statue of Horus went to live in Babylon?' I asked.

'Just temporarily. Flushed with the spoils of war and full of self-importance. Nebuchadnezzar made a bigger than life statue of himself out of gold, then decreed that everyone must bow down to it.'

'Is that from the fiery furnace story in the Bible?'

'The very same, Nancy. You attend church?'

'No, just stories I remember from childhood.'

'As I was saying, Nebuchadnezzar is remembered as the king who made an effigy of himself out of pure gold. His kingdom lasted through to his grandson, Belshazzar.'

'The writing on the wall story?' asked Nancy.

'You do have a good memory for stories.'

'Thanks.'

'A few years later, in about 539 BC, Cyrus II invaded Babylon and –'

'Cyrus II, who was he?' asked Nancy.

'He was the king of Persia, modern day Iran. History refers to him as the King of the World, which included, after invading, Babylon, modern day Syria. In 539 BC, he invaded south and after a great battle at Opis where the inhabitants were massacred, the city of Sippar surrendered without a fight and Cyrus led his triumphant army, unhindered, through the gates of Babylon.'

'So the statue ended up somewhere in Iran, Professor?'

'Let me read you a short sentence from the Cylinder of Cyrus, currently residing in the British Museum:

> I returned to these sanctuaries on the other side of the Tigris, sanctuaries founded in ancient times, the images that had been in them there and I made their dwellings permanent. I also gathered all their people and returned to them their habitations.

The images mentioned here are, I believe, the temple implements and idols.'

'Including our friend Horus?' I asked.

'The very same.'

'So sometime towards the end of the fifth century BC, our friend Horus ends up back in Egypt in one of the temples?'

'Which temple is not clear, Jack. But presumably Horas was still in Egypt when Alexander invaded in 331 BC. Although he was only in Egypt for a few months, Alexander immersed himself in Egyptian life, especially their religious centres. He was so revered as a deliverer from the oppressive rule of the Persians, he was crowned pharaoh. Here, I've come across a translation of a temple inscription,

> Horus, the strong ruler, he who seizes the lands of the
> foreigners, beloved of Amun and the chosen one of Ra –
> beloved by Amun – Alexander, son of Zeus.

So you can see the power that goes with the name.'

'Destructive power, you mean,' said Nancy.

'Precisely. Everywhere Horus is involved, war, petulance and famine follow.'

'I thought that was the four horsemen, Professor?'

'Quite right, Jack, I shouldn't mix my metaphors. But you do see how dangerous this cult worship of Horus is – don't you both?'

Nancy nodded, and I asked, 'What came next?'

'Next came the Romans. You've no doubt heard about Anthony and Cleopatra?'

We both nodded.

'I am of course referring to the real man and woman, not the movie. Rome begun growing in about 753 BC, even earlier than the time of Nebuchadnezzar –'

'Something to do with twins being reared by a wolf?'

'Precisely, Nancy. The story of Romulus and Remus, but we're not going to focus on those events. When the Greek empire collapsed there was of course Hannibal, followed closely by the

Romans. When I worked in the museum I remember there was a gold ring from the Roman period. This ring showed figures of three gods: Serapis, Isis and Harpokrates. These three deities had been adopted from ancient Egyptian gods, Osiris, Isis and Horus.'

'Quite a family, they do get around!' said Nancy. 'Who's next?'

'Next is a bunch of jolly travellers.'

'The Templars?'

'Exactly, Jack. Remember I said Charles V of Spain had given them the island of Malta as an advance base to hold back Suleiman's advance?'

'And they must have found the statue and, according to what you've already discovered, they gave the statue to Charles V of Spain.'

'A most unfortunate gift to give. Shortly after Charles received his gift of the falcon statue –'

'Shit, the Holy Roman Empire, the Spanish inquisition. Thousands of Jews and Muslims died because they wouldn't convert to Catholicism. You're so right, Professor, we must find this bird and make sure it can't do any more damage. But where did it and its evil spirit go after that?'

'It is my belief, based on its past history, that it sailed with Cortez to the Americas, and we know what happened to the indigenous peoples when infectious diseases spread: whole populations were wiped out in a matter of weeks.'

'So where do you think it ended up?'

'I believe it ended up somewhere in Mexico, Nancy, and that's where it was until the outbreak of World War 2.'

'Mexico? World War 2? Doesn't make sense to me. Why do you think that?'

'During World War 1, Mexico was neutral; they had their own on-going revolution. Germany tried to get a commitment to not back the US but to go with the central powers. Fortunately, Mexico refused. When World War 2 started they waited till 1942 to join in the fight – that was after two of their oil tankers were torpedoed by German U-boats.'

'So there might have been some reluctance on their part to get involved?'

'Possibly. Though Mexico was important enough to Germany for it to have its own spy ring. It was headed up by a man called George Nicolaus under the watchful eye Osmar Alberto Hellmuth, who in turn reported directly to Heinrich Himmler.'

'Full circle.'

'Exactly, Jack. Himmler was a Satanist, just like his boss, and probably had his henchmen constantly on the lookout for interesting objects so he could ingratiate himself with the Fuhrer.'

'And you think this George fellow, found the Horus statue and sent it back to Germany via a U-boat?'

'It's the most likely scenario.'

'People just never learn, do they?'

'What do you mean, Jack?'

'We've just been listening to the history of the middle east, all the way back to the beginning of recorded history, and what you've been telling us could have come straight from today's headlines.'

'Indeed, the sad bit is, if society doesn't remember and understand the past, however are they going to prevent the past being repeated.'

'Come on, this is 2016, that's nothing more than a fairy-tale, professor,' said Nancy.

'If it's nothing more than a fairy-tale, why did Nebuchadnezzar loot it from the Egyptians? Or Cyrus, why did he repatriate it to Egypt after they invaded Babylon? Or Alexander, he seized it during his time in Egypt. The Roman Empire under Caesar treasured it in the temple of the gods. The Knights Templar gave it to Charles of Spain for the use of the Island of Malta, before it once more took flight in its never ending desire for bloodshed. Your letter confirms that there was an unspoken competition between Göering and Himmler to find the falcon. They sent their henchmen worldwide looking for it, and when found, they intended to present it to Adolf Hitler. I don't know if you go to the movies Jack, but back in the 1930s a movie was made about this bird, and to show you how sought after the real item is, in November 2013, someone paid four million dollars for the stage prop.'

'Maybe they thought it might be the real thing.'

'Maybe, maybe not, Nancy. But history tells us many have possessed it without knowing it; others have died looking for it, wars have been fought for it, and now it's my belief Horus is stretching his wings once again for the last time, ready for the final battle of good versus evil.'

'But it's just a bloody statue, probably just a carved piece of stone.'

'Possibly, but nonetheless, those who have possessed it, or sought it, believed it to have power far beyond anything the human brain could imagine. Power to control events, power to control nations, power to even control the weather. These people will stop at nothing to gain possession of it, they want it to rally those of like minds to their evil cause. Jack and Nancy, you are now in a race to find the elusive bird before it falls into the wrong hands, and like Bilbo, you must destroy it before it falls into those wrong hands.'

'What about the newspaper?' I asked. 'Nancy's had a read of it, but she says her French is not great.'

'Well, thank you!'

I laughed. 'You said it yourself, and Professor Lozinski is an expert. I just thought he might be able to read things you missed, that's all.'

Our first tiff, what was I thinking, she's just a customer, and a married woman to boot, keep your head Jack.

'Did you get the bit about the accidents in the dockyard?' the professor asked.

Nancy shrugged.

'Or the article about the U-boat?'

'No, my French is not as good as that.'

'Well, you did a great job of the German letter, very resourceful. Says here,' he turned the paper into the light to see better,

> On Thursday evening, a team of engineers working on a small tug were asphyxiated by a leaking exhaust and died while doing a test run on the engine that had just been repaired. Someone had accidentally shut the main hatch and locked it. By the time the rescue services had opened the hatch, all inside had died. The dock superintendent could not understand why it had happened; the engineers were the most experienced in the whole dockyard.

'Do you think that was the *Osprey*, Jack?' asked Nancy.

'Quite possible, who knows? Er – what about the submarine, Professor?'

'Ah, now that takes a bit of reading between the lines to understand.'

'Not following you.'

'I'll translate and interpret for you.' He was quiet for a moment, then grunted as though agreeing with himself about his understanding.

'Right, here's how I see the facts. The article describes how a U-boat that had been on an extended mission in the Pacific Ocean had got into trouble when trying out a new snorkel device fitted after her return. When submerging, sea water had entered and got into the main batteries. The subsequent chlorine gas had killed everyone on board.'

'Another accident, Professor?'

'What do you think, Jack?'

'I'm at a loss to see any significance – wait a minute, are you saying that this U-boat is the same one that had just returned from the Pacific with the gold and the falcon?'

'The very same.'

'Terrible accident, all those sailors gasping for air and stuck at the bottom of the sea.'

'More likely they were killed deliberately, Nancy.'

'Why, Professor? Who'd do something like that?'

'The Gestapo, they worked for Himmler, and he probably didn't want anyone to know about the gold, or the statue.'

'But that was murder.'

'I know, Nancy, but that was the way they were.'

I looked at the clock and thought of all the guitars sitting in my workshop waiting to be repaired. 'Professor, it's getting quite late, we must be going. Nancy needs to get home and I've got several guitars that I've promised to be ready for customers to collect tomorrow.'

◆

We sat in silence in the back of the taxi as it drove back to the marina. I paid the driver enough to get Nancy to her sister's and back again if needed, and I made sure the driver knew I'd recognise him in the daylight.

I was tired, my head was spinning, too much to think about. I fed Garboard and went to bed. I stripped off and climbed in thinking I would be able to sleep like a log, but as soon as my head hit the pillow she was with me, at least her scent was. I'd not changed the bedding and she'd been the last one to sleep in it. I breathed in deep, pulled the blankets tightly around my face and imagined the impossible.

It was no good, I couldn't sleep. I now realised why the professor was limited in his coffee consumption, the caffeine in his coffee would power a football team. I shook my head. Who was I trying to kid? It was the memory of Nancy that kept me awake.

I got out of my bed and grabbed my Galaxy tablet. I googled San Francisco and saw it was on the Pacific seaboard. Next I googled the U-boat's number and found she'd been launched in 1939, had never seen active service but spent her time at sea as an escort vessel while German warships were being refuelled, and she'd been into the Pacific. From what I read on Wikipedia she arrived in St Nazaire in September. Two weeks later, while doing submersion tests in the mouth of the Loire, a leak in some newly-installed plumbing developed and sea water leaked on to the main batteries creating a cloud of chlorine gas, which subsequently killed all the crew.

6

Hudson and Munroe

I woke once again with a raging headache: that was two days in a row, not good. I dressed and wandered over to the Harvester and breakfast. While drinking my third cup of coffee I wrote out a to-do list. First was to contact Greyspear and have him check with his man in Greenock and see if anything was known about the chap who worked on the *Osprey* during the war. Next was to see if the Hudson living in Nelson's Lodge was the same as the one in the letter.

♦

I would have driven, but my car was still in the garage. Instead it was a taxi ride to Pevensey and Westham station, a train ride to Bexhill and finally, after a further taxi ride, I was sitting in the day room with Lieutenant J Hudson, RNR.

'It's very good of you to see me, Mr Hudson.'

'Not at all my lad, don't get many visitors these days. In fact, other than the reporter who was here earlier, you're the only ones since my last birthday back in January.'

'You have no family?'

'Killed in the Blitz. My family now are the other residents here in the home.'

'As I mentioned in my phone call, I was wondering if you were the Lieutenant J Hudson who was in St Nazaire just as the Germans invaded France?'

He nodded, smiled, and stared off into the distance. I wondered what memories he must have locked away in the back of his mind. I waited patiently for him to return from wherever his memories had taken him.

'Nobody here wants to talk about the war any more. I suppose it's for the best. But yes, I'm the same Lieutenant J Hudson who was serving in the Navy.'

'Can you tell me anything about what went on just after the Germans arrived in St Nazaire?'

'I don't see why not; I've already told that young reporter, and the war was long ago.'

Alarm bells rang in my head. 'What reporter?'

'She was here, not just half an hour before you, said she'd a deadline to make.'

'This reporter – was she about my height, blonde hair cut short in a bob?'

'Yes, that's her. Do you know her?'

I nodded. 'We've talked.'

What the hell was Nancy up to? We could have come together if she wanted to meet the lieutenant. Her husband, the bastard, bet he was pulling her strings. It was all my fault; I shouldn't have sent her home in the taxi.

'Those eyes,' Hudson continued, 'never seen such beautiful green eyes. Reminded me of a time we were anchored in Honolulu and the water was so green.'

'1942, St Nazaire – you were telling me about your time there?'

'Ah, yes, so I was. I was in the navy, but not on a ship. When Germany invaded France our admiralty recognised the potential harm that could come from the Germans using the St Nazaire docks to service their warships. Up till that point the U-boats had been causing havoc with the transatlantic convoys. But with the advent of the Bismarck battlecruisers *Bismarck* and *Tirpitz*, along with other pocket battleships coming into service, the government had to take action.'

'I've seen some of those stories about sea battles on the television. Mostly grainy black and white.'

He nodded. 'The *Bismarck* was sunk during a sea battle with the Royal Navy in the straits of Denmark, leaving the *Tirpitz, Lützow* and *Admiral Scheer* anchored in Norwegian waters. Efforts to engage these ships produced no results, and the great worry for admiralty was that if these ships were able to get out into open waters and in to the North Atlantic shipping lanes they could cause untold damage, even might be the pivotal point of the war. The *Tirpitz* was the main focus, over 500,000 tons with heavy armour plating, complete with 15-inch guns. Nothing in the Royal Navy or US Navy could afford to go one on one with her. Sir Winston Churchill said at the time about the importance of putting the *Tirpitz* out of action for the duration: *the whole strategy of the war turns at this period on this ship.*'

'I've seen the movie about sinking the *Tirpitz*. Very brave men to have sailed in those mini submarines.'

'Yes, they certainly were. It was soon recognised that if those ships did manage to break free they would need a port to come in to for repairs, etc. The port of St Nazaire was the only suitable one on the west coast and it was already servicing a large U-boat fleet.'

'I've seen those pens, they're now a marina for pleasure boats.'

'Me too, made a pilgrimage there a few years ago to say goodbye to an old friend.'

'Your friend the guitar maker?' I asked. Or was that now a closed door?

He shook his head. 'No, just someone I knew from the war. We used to play dominoes in the café.'

So the guitar maker may still be around, I surmised.

'I was,' he continued, 'as I mentioned, not stationed on board a ship, but worked in a separate department in Whitehall –'

'MI5?'

He nodded. 'It was nothing like James Bond, mostly reading newspapers, listening to radio broadcasts, that sort of thing. Being fluent in German and French helped. When the decision was made to put the port of St Nazaire out of action, I was sent over to reconnoitre the base and observe what happened during and after the raid, which no doubt you've already read about.'

'Operation Chariot? Yes, I've had a look on Wikipedia.'

'Then you know all about the raid and how it put the docks out of service for the duration of the war?'

I nodded.

'I'd been chosen mostly because I'd lived in the area for several years prior to the war and had family living there. My cousin ran a bakery and that was my cover.'

We were interrupted by one of the staff wanting to know if we wanted more tea. I waited patiently while it was poured and biscuits nibbled on.

'Was there anything else you wanted to ask?' he said.

'Did you own a guitar?'

He smiled at a memory. 'Yes and no. My cousin owned a guitar and I borrowed it from time to time. He didn't play that well, his hands were the size of dinner plates, fingers like sausages. I used to play in the café down by the docks in the evening. Lots of German sailors came there; I used to eavesdrop on their conversations and report them back to London.'

'Do you remember who the maker of the guitar was, and what happened to it?'

He looked vacant for a moment, then said, 'I think it was made by a Spanish maker, don't remember who. I just played it, beautiful sound and so easy to play. It got damaged when some German sailors started a fight over one of the girls in the café. I took the guitar to a repair shop and never managed to get back to collect it. Why?'

'I believe I now have it in my workshop, and it still needs repairing., and there was a letter secreted in the neck that was supposed to be given to you.'

He looked puzzled. I explained about finding the guitar sealed in a secret compartment in the *Osprey,* about finding the dead Californian detective in my workshop, the subsequent stealing of the guitar and its eventual return and the discovery of the letter in the neck.

'Ah, of course, I was supposed to collect the guitar from the shop and pass it on to one of the resistance who was working on the tug. But when I got down to the docks the tug had already sailed and the soldiers were doing a house to house search on the street where the guitar shop was, so I never got to collect it.'

'Two questions.'

'Just two?'

I smiled. 'Yes, just two. First, who do you think put the guitar on the tug, and second, why was it necessary to secret it away? I would have thought that something so innocuous as a guitar wouldn't attract any unwanted attention?'

'I'm sorry, Mr Nevis, I have no idea.'

'Oh well, it was a question worth asking. I brought you a copy of the letter, sort of a memento,' I said, handing him a photocopy.

'So, the war goes on,' he said, reading the script on the back. 'I'm glad about the guitar, not that it's still broken, but rather that it still exists.'

I made a promise to him, bad habit of mine. 'As soon as it's restored,' I said, 'I'll bring it by for you to see, and play.'

He shook his head and held up his hands, 'Arthritis is a bitch.'

♦

Just what was Nancy up to, I wondered, while riding the train back to Pevensey and Westham. Why had she gone to see Hudson, was she out to feather her own nest by being one step ahead of me. Or actually, what was her husband up to, and more to the point, other than the threat of harming her children, what was he doing to make her do his will? I shook my head and swallowed the remainder of my coffee and stuffed the empty cup in the wastepaper bin as the train pulled into Pevensey and Westham station.

♦

I called Greyspear, a woman answered. 'I'm sorry, he can't come to the phone at the moment. Can he call you back?'

I said yes, hung up the phone and went down to the workshop. I wasn't in the mood to work on the Torres so grabbed one of the other classical guitars and got to work. I was working on the third guitar, re-fretting the top end of the fretboard, when Greyspear called.

'I have good news for you, Jack. I talked again with my yard manager and he said you need to talk to a Hamish Munroe. He worked on the *Osprey* during the war and got stuck behind enemy lines for the duration. He's living with his daughter in Port Glasgow.'

I wrote down the address and phone number of the daughter, said thanks to Greyspear and hung up. Next I called the daughter and asked if I could come up and talk with her father.

'No problem, Mr Nevis, he loves getting visitors. When were you thinking about visiting?'

I thought for a moment and had a gnawing feeling in the pit of my stomach that all was not well. 'How about tomorrow?'

'Lovely, I'll tell Father you're coming. He'll be so thrilled.'

I turned on the laptop and checked for flights to Glasgow from Gatwick: no seats available. I'd left it too late in the day and I didn't fancy trying any of the other airports. Next alternative was the overnight sleeper from Euston station. I went online to the booking website and decided that I would treat myself to a first class berth, I wasn't in the mood to share a cabin.

I caught the nine thirty-seven train from Polegate to Victoria, then the Victoria line to Euston arriving in plenty of time for my comfy bunk on the Caledonian Sleeper to Glasgow.

I tried to read, but the gentle motion of the high-speed train lulled me into a blissful slumber. I slept well and woke in Glasgow Central and saw that we had arrived five minutes early. The attendant's morning tea and sandwich had done nothing to satisfy my hunger so I grabbed my bag and made a beeline for a full breakfast at the Central Hotel.

I caught the nine fifty-five train to Port Glasgow, then a short taxi ride up to Hamish Munroe's daughter's house on Ivybank. It was a two-storey, semi-detached, solid sandstone building; typical of the houses seen all over the Clydeside.

I rang the bell and waited. The hall light came on and the door opened.

'Mr Nevis?'

I nodded, 'yes, and you are?'

'Agnes Kerr. Please come in.' She closed the door behind me and beckoned me to follow her down the hall to the back of the house. 'Father was so excited when I said you were coming to see him. He's already up, had his breakfast and is eager to chat. He's in the conservatory. It's light and airy when the sun's out.'

He stood as I came into the room, letting his lap blanket fall on the floor at his feet. At ninety-two he still had a firm handshake and his eyes were as bright as those of a man many years his junior.

'Mr Munroe! Sorry to be a bother and disturbing you.'

'Oh, it's no bother for him,' said Agnes, tucking in her father's blanket round his knees. 'He loves getting visitors, don't you, Father?'

'Don't fuss, lass, I'm not an invalid.'

'Mr Nevis, have you had your breakfast?' she asked.

I said I'd had something to eat at Central Station.

'Oh, then you'll still be hungry. You'll stay for lunch? we eat at twelve. I'm making a steak and kidney pie.'

I'd booked a seat on the thirteen-forty to Euston, so had just enough time for a quick early lunch. 'That would be lovely, thanks.'

'Good, then I'll leave the two of you to chat. Before I go, would you like a coffee?'

I looked at Hamish's face, then back to Agnes.

'Father, it's too early for a dram, have your coffee and after lunch we'll see.'

He shrugged in resignation as she closed the door behind her.

'Well – Mr Nevis, is it?'

I nodded. 'Jack Nevis. I've brought you a letter, something you might remember.' I handed him a copy.

He took it and stared at it, then nodded slowly and grinned. 'I'd completely forgotten about this. How did you get a copy?'

'You sent it to me, back in 1944.'

He repeated the puzzled look.

'I believe you hid it in the neck of a guitar? I now own the guitar and found the letter in a hollowed-out section of the neck. That's the reason I'm here, hoped you'd be able to help me make sense of what's been going on.'

'Hmm, it was a long time ago. I suppose I should start at the beginning. In 1939 I left school at fifteen and went to work for Fergusons in Port Glasgow. I later left the yard for a job crewing on the tug boat *Kestrel*.'

'It's now called the *Osprey*; the Sea Scouts changed its name.'

'That's bad luck. You should never rename a ship.'

'That makes sense, especially considering all that's happened. Don't worry, I'm fine, the *Osprey* is fine, it's just what happened to the poor unfortunate burglar I had last weekend.'

'What happened to him?'

'He got a bullet between the eyes in the middle of the night when he tried to rob me.'

'You shot him?'

'No, not me, someone else. The police are investigating.'

'Fortunate for you that you didn't interrupt him.'

'I hadn't thought of that before now. I suppose I have Jack to thank for that.'

'Jack?'

'Jack Daniels – I'd over-celebrated the evening before and slept deeply.'

'I've been there. Anyway, as I was saying, I'd only been with the company a short time when the company owner, Sir Archibald, sent us to the Mediterranean to bring back his private launch from Monte Carlo. We towed it to St Nazaire docks without incident. When we arrived to re-coal, it was the 9th of June. The docks were in chaos, people panicking. It didn't take us long to find out why. They'd just found out the German army was only fifty miles from Paris. We were in a bit of a state. We'd tried to keep up with the news and if it hadn't been for the need to fill the coal bunker we would have sailed right on.'

His narrative was interrupted by the arrival of Agnes with our coffees.

'Milk, sugar, Mr Nevis?'

'Just black, and no sugar, please.'

Hamish started coughing and picked up the glass of water from the side table.

'Here's your coffee, Father,' she said, taking the empty water glass from him. 'If that'll be all, I'll leave you two in peace.'

Before he continued, he reached over to the bottom of the grandfather clock, opened the door and retrieved a half drunk bottle of Talisker whiskey.

'It's a game we play,' he said, winking, 'I pretend she doesn't know it's there, and she pretends I don't know she knows it's there. Makes for a happy relationship. Here, hold out your cup.'

I sipped on my fortified coffee as he continued with his story.

'We tried to buy coal, but all the coal stocks had been impounded and we were stuck. The night before we were to leave I became very ill – I'd eaten oysters, and had to go to hospital. I was too ill to travel, so while the German tanks rumbled past the Arc de Triomphe, down the Champs Elysees to the Place de la Concorde, the rest of the crew boarded one of the last steamers headed for England. I was stretchered to Le Chateau de Chevalier, the home of the Count de Brissac. He has family in England and, to my advantage, he couldn't stand the Nazis.'

'So you were trapped. Did the Germans catch you?'

He shook his head. 'Even though I'd left school at fifteen, I could speak French well enough to be understood. That was one of the reasons I'd been selected to crew on the *Kestrel* to collect Sir Archibald's yacht.

'I gave up French at school, which is a pity, especially with all that's been going on.'

'I was fortunate to have a good teacher. To keep me out of the way of prying eyes I went to work in town with the Count's brother as an apprentice luthier. As I said, I spoke passable French. I enjoyed the life, but there was a war on so I resigned myself to wait it out and do what I could to confound the German war effort.'

'Sort of in a prison without walls?'

He nodded, 'You could say that. One day, I think it was late summer of 1944, while I was up in the attic, I heard the doorbell ring and the sound of heavy banging on the front door. I looked down out of the skylight and saw a big black Mercedes car and two large lorries parked at the side of the house by the stairs to the basement. Someone answered the door, I heard raised voices but couldn't make out what was said, then the visitor walked round to the basement door. I was very curious so I crept down to the basement and hid behind some boxes. I had just managed to get into hiding when the Count lumbered down the stairs. He opened the side door and the visitor came in. He was tall and stocky, I'd say just under six feet and looked like he'd eaten too many pies. I found out later he was Hermann Göering.'

'I've heard of him. Got scared of what was in store for him and committed suicide at the Nuremberg trials.'

'Yes, that was him, though if you'd seen him during the war you'd have seen a completely different man. There was an argument between the count and Göering, unfortunately I don't speak any German so didn't know what was said. Göering hit the count hard across the face causing him to fall against one of the

89

crates. As he got up, the front of one of the crates fell off and revealed a painting.'

'Was the count hurt badly?'

'No, it would have taken a lot more than a simple slap to hurt him, he was tough. Göering swore at him and smashed open some of the other crates; they were all full of paintings. When I asked the count later what it was about, he said Göering was going to take the paintings and send them to Berlin for the Reisch Museum. The count thought that Göering really wanted them for himself.'

'Sounds about right, Göering was well known to have amassed a huge quantity of stolen art work, well over three hundred pieces by the end of the war.'

'The count was very angry because the Germans had been looting many of the local chateaux and museums. He'd been busy trying to collect the art works before the Germans could get their hands on them.'

'Did he want them for himself?'

'No, his plans were to collect and hide them till after the war, then return them to their rightful owners.'

'Was he successful?'

'No, the SS came a couple of days later and removed them.'

'Well, at least they did eventually find their way back to the rightful owners.'

'What's that you say?'

'The paintings listed in the front of the letter were eventually returned. A friend of mine had a look at the list and all of them have been accounted for.'

'Ah, the letter, pity it never got to the Lieutenant.'

'But it did, I delivered a copy to him yesterday.'

'He's still alive?'

'Lives in a retirement home in Bexhill.'

'It would be grand to meet up with him again, especially after all these years.'

I did it again, and promised that when things had settled I'd arrange for the two of them to meet.

'Yes, the letter, I had fun with that,' he said, looking at the back of the letter.

'How did it come into your hands?'

'In a minute, it'll all become clear.'

I looked at the clock on the mantelpiece, still plenty of time.

'I thought that the incident with the paintings was all, but Göering said something to his men and they went out to the lorries and returned carrying small wooden boxes. I waited till they had left and crept over to them. I was surprised to see, stencilled on the side, *Property of the US Mint*. One of them had been opened and the lid not fastened back down properly, so I opened it and found it full of gold coins separated by sheets of, I think, some sort of cloth. I estimated there were about fifty coins per layer and ten layers per box.'

'How many boxes were there?'

'I counted the boxes, forty of them, each with about five hundred gold coins.'

Now that was a lot of money, I thought. Was this the reason the Californian detective was murdered? While Hamish sipped on his coffee I worked out how many coins were involved. Five hundred to a box, times forty boxes, made a total of twenty thousand coins, all presumably solid gold.

He put down his cup and continued. 'There were some smaller boxes that contained jewellery and figurines, one of which was an evil-looking bird carved from what I seem to remember was black marble. It looked like it belonged in the British Museum, sort of a bird of prey with a crown on top – like a falcon, that sort of thing.'

'What happened next?'

He shrugged. 'All I know is that Göering returned with his men a few days later and collected all the paintings, jewellery and gold. I heard later that the French resistance had intercepted the shipment before it got to Orleans – some of the paintings, jewellery and all but one box of gold coins were recovered. I laughed and thought it a bit ironic when I heard the Germans had used the *Kestrel* to take the paintings up the river Loire to Orleans.'

'And you know nothing about what happened to the shipment after the resistance intercepted the *Kestrel*, or the items that were not recovered?'

He shook his head and was silent for a moment as he tried to remember. 'A few days after Göering had removed the paintings and gold, there was another visitor. Scrawny individual, pudding-bowl haircut shaved high, Coke bottle glasses and wore a long black leather coat; he had his own chauffeur. I asked the count who he was. He said it was Himmler.'

'The master of evil.'

'Quite. He shouted and screamed at the count then left. I'd just returned from work as the German's tirade was ending and later asked the count what was going on. He said that Himmler was looking for the falcon statue. Almost had a catatonic fit when he found out that Göering had sent the statue and the art to Berlin. He said he'd promised the statue of the falcon to the Führer.'

'The letter – you were going to tell me how you got hold of the letter.'

'One of my resistance contacts came into the shop with it a few days later and explained that the shipment must never get to Berlin. If it did, the war could go on for many more years.'

'Did they say how they got the letter?'

'No, just that it had to get to British Intelligence as soon as possible; I suppose it was to show that what they were asking was genuine.'

'What did they want you to do?'

'They said I had to pass it on to British intelligence. In case it was intercepted, I wrote the details of what I'd seen on the back in code. That was one of the things Lieutenant Hudson had taught me. I hid it in a hollowed out section of the neck of a guitar I'd been working on, then I packed the guitar in the case, along with the newspaper.'

'I make and repair guitars.'

'Make a living at it?'

'Just.'

'Nothing's changed then. People who own guitars just don't really appreciate how much work goes into the making of them.'

'Sorry, I interrupted you.'

He shook his head, 'That's all right. The guitar was owned by Lieutenant Hudson; he was supposed to get the information back to MI5 in London, though I always thought he was MI5 himself.'

'How did you two meet?'

'He found me. Came into the shop one day and bought some strings for his guitar. His French wasn't as good as mine and it didn't take long for us to acknowledge the fact we were both English. From then on we'd meet once or twice a week for coffee and swap stories.'

'Were you friends for long?'

'From the day the Germans arrived in town. I regularly gave him bits of news, not sure how he got the information back to England. It was a bit of luck he'd left his guitar for repair, I hid the letter in the neck and made arrangements for it to be smuggled out of the country. The guitar was supposed to go along with some British consular staff who had been in hiding since the beginning of the war.'

'And Lieutenant Hudson didn't come for the guitar?'

'No, as soon as the destroyer blew up in the lock gates, the whole German garrison went into panic mode. People were being rounded up and questioned, didn't matter who you were. I never saw him again; thought at the time he might have been arrested by the Gestapo.'

'So, if the guitar was supposed to be smuggled out of the country, how did it end up on the *Osprey*, sorry, suppose I should be calling her the *Kestrel* when talking to you?'

'*Kestrel, Osprey,* I know what you mean. Maybe one of the resistance came and collected it, intending it would be passed on later when they stopped the *Kestrel*?'

'How did they know the letter was concealed in the neck of the guitar?'

'Not sure, I – I must have mentioned it to one of them. The guitar shop was used by them as a secret post office.'

'Like a message drop?'

'Yes.'

'And you think it's possible they hid it on the *Osprey*?'

'Who knows? One moment it was in the workshop, the next it was gone.'

'I know the paintings have been recovered, but what do you think happened to the gold?'

He shook his head. 'No idea on that either, maybe it was recovered by the resistance when they stopped the *Kestrel* on the river. I was never told the outcome. I did hide one of the coins in the guitar case with a note for the lieutenant.'

Now that was news to me. I'd had a good look at the guitar, but not the case, I resolved to do so when I got home.

'And you've no idea why the guitar was hidden in a cupboard in the *Kestrel*?'

'A complete mystery to me. Maybe the resistance chap who collected it hid it, thinking that Lieutenant Hudson would collect it later.'

'And you never met again?'

'No, sadly not. I assumed he'd either been arrested or escaped back to England.'

'Would you like to?'

'Oh, yes, certainly, but how?'

'Leave it to me, I'll see what can be arranged.'

We had lunch, I gave him one of my business cards and said to call me if he thought of anything else.

Agnes walked me to the front door, 'thanks for visiting Mr Nevis. Other than the doctor my dad doesn't get many visitors.'

I had an idea, 'does he have any wartime mementoes?'

She thought for a moment, shook her head, 'no, sorry. All he has is in an old case up in the loft, been there for years.'

'Any statues in it by any chance?'

'I doubt it, from what I remember, all that's in the case are his medals, some letters and his old uniform.'

I thanked her for her help and returned to Glasgow and my train ride home.

I now had a better understanding of the events of 1944, but not why the guitar had been hidden in the cupboard in what was now my bedroom. Or what had happened to the gold, the falcon, or the other jewellery and artefacts. Maybe another visit to Lieutenant Hudson was in order.

My taxi dropped me at the marina car park and I walked down to the *Osprey*. I climbed on board and found the door was unlocked and sounds coming from my workshop. My heart lifted: Nancy had returned. I opened the door, entered the saloon and stepped down into my workshop.

There was a well-dressed, heavy-set man sitting on my bench stool. He was brandishing a very business-like black pistol with a silencer, its infrared targeting laser pointing directly at my forehead.

7

Dr Kaufmann

'Good evening, Mr Nevis. I'm Dr Kaufmann, nice of you to join us.'

I stepped off the companionway steps and stopped three feet from him, wondering who the *us* were. I soon found out as the sound of familiar footsteps came down the steps after me. I glanced in their direction and saw Nancy, followed by a man I didn't recognise.

She'd been crying. I didn't know whether to walk over and give her a hug, or swear at her. All I could muster was a wry grin.

'Oh, I see you know each other,' said the doctor. 'Good, I like happy families. As I said, my name is Dr Kaufmann, and this gentleman is one of my associates, Hanse. Let's hope you never get to be friends with him.'

'Do you need to use my forehead for target practice?'

'With this?' he said, turning the gun away from me and looking at the barrel. 'No, of course not. Why would you think that?' he said passing the pistol to Hanse. 'Though sometimes in our line of work, killing is a necessity, a mere blip in the rhythm of one's day.

'It wouldn't be the first time that someone's forehead's been used for target practice on this boat.'

'Oh, I read something about that in the newspaper, Mr Nevis. Some speculation about you finding a World War 2 service revolver and a customer not paying their bill? Newspaper speculated you shot him and threw the gun over the side.'

What could I say to such rubbish? I just shook my head and glanced in Nancy's direction. She was saying no with her tear-filled eyes.

'Mr Nevis, let me introduce myself properly. As I said, my name is Dr Kaufmann. I'm what you might call a finder of lost property, who, when the item in question is found, returns it to the rightful owners. For a fee, of course.'

'Of course. What else could they do, but be grateful?'

'Exactly, Mr Nevis. Now, down to business. It has come to my attention that you have recently come into possession of an item of archaeological significance. I would like to pay you, handsomely of course, for your troubles and then having taken possession of the item, return it to its rightful owner. Now, what do you say to that fine offer?'

'I'd say you were living in cloud cuckoo land.'

How did he know, or actually, what did he know? Had I been followed to Port Glasgow? Had they talked with Hamish Munroe?

He chuckled. 'Mr Nevis, I think you'll do nicely. But that's all right, I like a man who knows how and when to bargain. We'll take this matter to a further level.'

'There's nothing to discuss, Doctor. I don't have this – this archaeological item you're going on about. Probably wouldn't know it if I ran into or tripped over it.'

I wasn't going to let him know how much I knew, but then Nancy knew almost as much as I did. Why didn't they just ask her? I glanced her way and gave her an inquisitive look; she shook her head very slowly. So they were only guessing. I wasn't sure if that was helpful or not.

'Hmm, let me explain,' Kaufmann went on, 'but first, we're guests in your home, why don't you ask us if we would like a drink and something to eat? Archaeological investigating creates a healthy appetite,' he said, looking at his watch. 'After all it is now gone nine in the evening. We'll stay down here and continue with our search, while you go and get us something to eat.'

Once again, the workshop was in a chaotic state but at least the guitars appeared to be intact. I was glad I'd returned the Torres to its hiding place, no room for safes on the *Osprey*.

'Nancy, would you help me with the food, please?'

As I started up the companionway steps, Kaufman said, 'Mr Nevis, I see you have a lot of very fine guitars down here. It would be a pity if any of them got damaged as we continued with our search. I suggest you think about that.'

When I was sure we were out of earshot I whispered, 'Nancy, what's going on? Just who are these people?'

She shrugged, then whispered, 'Associates of my husband. They must have been waiting outside my house when the taxi dropped me off.'

'What's this thing they're looking for?' I asked, wondering if they were aware of the gold.

'The black statue, the one mentioned in the letter, I think.'

So, it wasn't the gold, and I hadn't been followed. We didn't get any further with preparing the meal.

'Mr Nevis,' said Kaufmann, halfway up the companionway steps, 'I've seen all I need to for the moment. We'll leave you in peace to think things over. I believe I'm being a little too presumptuous to think you are ready to do a deal just now. Perhaps you have put it somewhere safe and are not quite ready to discuss a deal. Or – could it be there are others who have an interest in this matter? I think I'll give you a little time to reflect on things with your associates and then we'll talk some more. Come, Hanse, let us make our exit and leave these two lovely people to discuss what they should do next.'

As soon as they'd got to the end of the dock, I went down to the workshop, Nancy followed. What a mess! Every cupboard and drawer had been emptied and the contents strewn all over the floor. It was the same in my cabin, bedclothes in a heap on the floor.

'They've been all through the boat?'

Nancy nodded, tears trickling down her cheeks. 'I'm so sorry, Jack.'

'Why are you sorry? It wasn't your fault – they're the ones who made the mess.'

'No, it *is* my fault, I brought them here.'

'You brought them here? I don't understand.'

'I think Kaufmann believes Achmed and I are trying to find the same item he is after.'

'And are you?'

'No, of course not. I'd never heard of the falcon till I read about it in the letter.'

'And you say they've been following Achmed.'

'Who knows? For all we know Achmed is in competition with Kaufmann.'

'And since you two are married – that probably makes sense to someone like Kaufmann. So he's been following you, trying to get to Achmed?'

'And I've been following you,' she said, shrugging and turning bright red.

Interesting colour combination I thought: blonde hair, green eyes and a red face.

'I'm not sure what you mean by that.'

Her normal colour returned with her smile 'It's just I seem to be in the same place as you a lot.'

'Including a visit to Nelson's Lodge?'

'Oh, you found out.'

'Wasn't difficult, you and I were the only visitors he's had since his birthday back in January.'

'How sad. Doesn't he have any family?'

'Don't think so.'

'So, Mr Detective, what did you find out?'

'How about you? You talked to him first. What do you think about all this?

'I suppose it's like the professor said, everyone's looking for the statue of the falcon. Are you sure it's not hiding somewhere on the *Osprey*? Are you sure you've looked everywhere for it?'

99

I laughed at her assumption.

'Why are you laughing? What did I say that's so funny?'

I shook my head. 'Come on, I suppose you need to get home and I've got this mess to sort out.'

'You're not going to tell me, are you?' she said, a fierceness in her face that I'd never seen before. 'And while I'm asking, where were you yesterday? I came down to the boat for some lessons and you weren't here.'

I was about to answer her question when I saw the irony of it all. We were just acquaintances and she was wanting to know where I'd been! Maybe it was time to establish boundaries in our fledgling relationship.

'Listen, what I get up to –'

'I'm sorry, it's none of my business what you do or where you go. I – I should mind my own business. I'll go now, can you call me a taxi?'

The cold green of the Atlantic had returned, she'd embarrassed herself.

'If you're sure, I could drive you home,' I said, then remembered my car was still in the garage being serviced.

She shook her head. 'No, I think I should go. I've caused you enough trouble as it is today.'

'Look, we need to talk. There's too much going on for us to just keep beating around the bush.'

Her face relaxed, the smile returned. 'What do you propose?'

I looked at the clock. 'How about something to eat?'

She looked at the galley. 'It'll take me ages to get something made, especially with all this mess.'

'I didn't mean here on the boat; I know somewhere really close.'

'I can't, I'm not dressed to go out to dinner.'

'That's all right, where I'm thinking of is not formal, you'll be fine.'

'You sure?'

'Yes, of course I am. Let's get going, I'm hungry.'

'Okay, let me get my coat.'

We walked down the dock in silence, hands in pockets, each reluctant to start a conversation.

'This where you're taking me?' she asked as I pushed the door open for her. 'It's a gift shop.'

'Seasons is not just a gift shop. If you'll observe, this side may be a gift shop but if Madame would care to follow me through, you'll find it is in fact also a fine restaurant, deli, bistro and wine bar.'

'You get a commission for bringing people here?'

'No,' I chuckled, 'I just like the casual atmosphere, and of course the food and wine is great and they have free live music on Friday evenings.'

I chose a table by a window where I could keep an eye on the *Osprey*. I didn't trust the doctor to not pay another visit now we were no longer on board.

The waitress brought us the evening menu. 'Something to drink?' she asked.

'A glass of Pinot Grigio, please,' said Nancy.

I was about to order my usual Jack Daniels but decided to give the white wine a try instead. 'Can we have a bottle of the Calusari Pinot Grigio, please?'

She smiled, 'be right back with your wine.'

I looked at Nancy's face as the waitress poured her wine, lovely. Nancy took a sip of her wine, then asked, 'Well, Mr Guitar Maker, what do you have to say? What's so important that you take a girl out to dinner?'

'I – I just thought we should clear the air, for instance –'

My question was interrupted by the waitress returning and asking if we'd decided on what we wanted to eat.

'Yes, could I have the mixed stuffed olives,' said Nancy.

'Will that be for two?'

I shook my head. Nancy continued, 'Then as a starter could I have the rare breed pork and pancetta pâté.'

'And for your main course?'

She looked at me, smiled and said, 'Do you have the lobster?'

The waitress shook her head. 'I'm sorry, we're sold out.'

'Then I'll have the crab thermidor instead.'

'And for you, sir?'

'I'll start with the beetroot and goat cheese and follow with Moroccan chicken stew, please.'

'Thank you.'

I waited for the waitress to be out of earshot then asked, 'Tell me about your husband, what sort of hold does he have over you, other than your children? You've said he doesn't know where they are, so they can't be in any immediate danger.'

She picked up her glass and took a long, slow, sip of her wine. I watched her eyes, they were searching for something, looking for the end of the thread in the tangled ball of yarn that was her life.

'I loved my husband, we'd been married for four years when he got posted to Afghanistan. Jack – oh, that's your name as well – how odd.'

'It's the name my parents gave me; I didn't choose it.'

She shook her head, 'It just never registered before, how odd. Anyway, as I was saying, Jack was posted to Afghanistan – then one morning while out on patrol he stepped on an IED and was killed. They flew what was left of him home for a funeral – I was advised not to ask to see his body.'

'I remember watching the repatriation events on television, all those people lining the road, and the flowers being thrown over the cortege. I must admit to shedding a few tears.'

'The funeral was held in his home town of Colchester, that's where his parents live. A couple of months later I was invited, along with some of the other widows, to a special commemoration service at his barracks. That's where I met Achmed.'

'Your present husband.'

'You could call him that, I suppose. At first we got on well, he was charming and always attentive. For instance, if I needed space, he knew to leave me alone. At first I thought he was being kind, but now I realise he was just avoiding me.'

'You said he disappeared off to Saudi Arabia?'

She nodded. 'That was just after the London Olympics. He said we couldn't live on my income and since he couldn't find work in the UK he'd have to look elsewhere. He came home a few days later and announced he'd been offered a job in the Saudi oil fields as a translator. That was the last I saw of him, till he turned up last week.'

'And the doctor, how's he involved?'

'I've no idea, I assumed he was a business associate of Achmed's.'

'So you've never seen the doctor before this evening?'

She shook her head. 'You know, you should report Kaufman's visit to the police, especially the bit about the gun.'

'Kaufmann gave me the impression it was a toy.'

'And you believed him?'

'Good question, I don't know what to think. The last time I talked to the police they gave me the impression I was a bit of a nuisance to them.'

'Suppose it was the doctor who shot that detective on your boat?'

'I'll give the police a call, but not now, I'm hungry. I believe I see the waitress with our food.'

Between mouthfuls she told me about her childhood, of how she'd been born in a small village called Hanningfield, and grew up roaming the local Essex countryside. She did well at school and was all set to go to university to study horticulture, but changed her mind when she met and married Jack.

The waitress returned to remove the dinner plates. 'Would you like to see the dessert menu?'

I looked at Nancy; she nodded.

'I'll have the Bakewell tart,' said Nancy looking up from the menu

'Sir?'

'Make that two, and could we have coffee at the same time, please?'

'So, Master Jack, how about you? You now know all about me – what's your story?'

'I left school at eighteen and got a job labouring on a building site. Eventually I got tired of digging ditches, carrying bricks and getting soaked to the skin. I was fortunate to be hired by a local building firm as an apprentice carpenter, I'd always enjoyed working with wood. When the opportunity to learn about guitar making on an evening course at our local tech was advertised, I jumped at the chance. I kept my job as a carpenter and in my spare time started making and repairing guitars, nothing very glamourous. Eventually, after being made redundant too many times I went full time with guitar making.'

'What about your wife? Does it hurt to talk about her?'

'Katie, she was called Katie. No, it'– it's just. I suppose I've put the memories in a special place and only think about her and the kids when something happens to trigger a memory.'

'I know what you mean, happens to me as well.'

'That's something we have in common,' I said, smiling at the thought.

'Are you still willing to teach me how to make guitars?'

'Of course I am, why wouldn't I?'

'It just seems you are preoccupied with finding that stupid black bird.'

'No, I'm not, though it is intriguing, especially when you consider someone has died looking for it.'

'So, when do I start?'

'How about tomorrow morning?'

'Fine. When are you going to clean up the mess Kaufmann left behind?'

I'd managed to forget about that till she mentioned it. 'Good point, how about tomorrow afternoon, say about two?'

'No, how about we go back and clean up the mess now?'

I looked at the time on my phone, ten forty-seven. 'It's a bit late for that. I was hoping for an early night.'

'Really? I thought you boaty types stayed up all night partying?'

'Not thus one.'

'Look, it's not too late. I'll give you a hand and we'll be done in no time.'

I didn't fancy going to bed with the boat in such a mess, and even worse would be getting up to it in the morning.

'Okay, but when I say we're done, we're done. Okay?'

'Aye, aye, skipper.'

I paid the bill and we walked back to the *Osprey*. I made Nancy wait on the end of the dock while I climbed on board. There was no sign of Kaufmann having made a return visit. I signalled for her to follow me.

I stood in the main saloon and wondered where to start.

'You know your workshop better than I do,' said Nancy. 'Why don't you start there and I'll have a go up here?'

That made sense, so I went below.

It had been a good idea, and by eleven-thirty my workshop was back in shape ready for me to go to work in the morning. Nancy had the saloon and galley looking like I could never get it looking. There were only two areas left to put back in order, the wheelhouse and my cabin.

'What next?' asked Nancy.

'I need to have a look at the wheelhouse; would you mind having a go at my cabin?'

'Wheelhouse shouldn't take you a moment. I've had a look in your cabin: it's a right mess. Join me when you're done.'

We met in the main saloon.

'Don't you like to be close to me?' Nancy asked, when she realised I'd been avoiding helping her in my cabin. I must have turned red, because she said, 'Are you embarrassed being with me?'

'It's just – you're a married woman and I feel a bit awkward making a bed with you.'

'Would it make a difference if I wasn't married?'

'I'm sorry, I'm – it's just I'm a bit old-fashioned when it comes to relationships. I don't think it's right for a man to date another man's wife.'

'Suppose I wasn't married – would that make a difference? And who said we're dating?'

I thought for a moment, then said, 'It's late, and we have work in the morning. We're making a start on your guitar remember, that's why you're here. Also, have you told your sister where you are?'

'That's okay, I called her earlier and said I'd be staying at my house for a couple of days.'

'Oh, okay. I'll call you a taxi.'

I watched the taxi leave and felt empty. I'd hurt her feelings by being old-fashioned, but what' was wrong with that?

♦

I climbed on board, opened a fresh bottle of bourbon, dropped a few ice-cubes in the glass and made my way up into the wheelhouse. I needed to think, life was running away from me and I couldn't keep up with it.

♦

I managed to get a couple of blissful hours of unconsciousness, and woke to the sound of Nancy banging on the door. I looked at the bedside clock, seven-fifteen. I pulled on my clothes and headed for the noise.

She was beaming from ear to ear, eyes sparkling like emeralds.

'Come on, let's get going! It's a new day and I'm ready, even – if – you're not. Did you just get out of bed?' she said, looking me up and down like an impatient sergeant major.

I shook my head. 'Didn't sleep well.'

'Well I did. You go finish getting dressed and I'll fix us something to eat.'

She made cheesy scrambled eggs with sliced tomatoes and wholegrain toast, putting it on the table with orange juice and steaming cups of fresh coffee.

'Where are we starting this morning?' she asked.

I wanted to say where we left off last night, but said instead, 'The neck. I found a nice piece of mahogany that should do.'

'About last night,' she said. 'I'm sorry if I embarrassed you. I was just having fun and it obviously went a bit wrong.'

'Thanks, I suppose I was a bit tired.'

'You do like me – don't you?'

I breathed out hard. 'Yes, I do like you – very much.'

'It's just that I'm married?'

I nodded and thought, yes, you're a married woman and this conversation is going in a direction I don't feel comfortable with, so I said, 'It's a good piece of mahogany, straight grain with no blemishes. Should make a very stable neck.'

She smiled and reached out, taking my hand and giving it a squeeze.

'What was that about?'

She smiled again and said, 'Nothing. Just wanted to say thanks.'

'Oh, okay.' I smiled back.

'Is it difficult to make the neck? How do you bend the top?'

'Wait a minute, and I'll explain.'

I stepped down into the workshop for my copy of *Step by Step Guitar Making* and returned to the saloon. She'd cleared the table and was in the process of washing the dishes. I was in two minds whether to call the whole guitar-making thing off and just end it before someone got hurt.

'Kettle's on. Do you want more coffee or would you rather have tea?'

'Er – coffee please.' So much for ending something that hadn't really started – or had it? I grabbed the tea towel, dried the dishes and put them in the cupboard, then sat down at the table and waited for her to finish making the coffee.

'Right, Mr Luthier, teach me how to make a guitar.'

I opened the book to the making the neck section.

'Why start with the neck and not, say, the body of the guitar?'

'The neck is the best place because all the surfaces are flat and at right angles. Sort of gets you used to using the basic tools.'

'Such as?'

'Hand plane, ruler, square and hand saw.'

'Oh, okay, that makes sense, I think.'

I was explaining about how to make the scarf joint between the head and the neck when the police showed up at the door.

I let them in. There were three of them this time. I recognised the sergeant and the constable, the third one looked like he was the boss.

'Mr Nevis,' began the sergeant, 'This is DCI Buchanan, he's assisting us with the investigation into the death on your boat.'

'I've already told the sergeant all I know, Inspector.'

'Mr Nevis, can you tell me where you were between one-fifteen and six-forty this morning?'

'I was here on the *Osprey*. Why?'

'I ask the questions, Mr Nevis. Where were you?'

'Here, on the *Osprey*.'

'All night?'

'Yes, I've just told you that.'

'Can anyone corroborate your statement?'

'I can,' said Nancy. 'We spent the night together.'

'And you are?'

'Nancy Rafsanjani, Mrs.'

I was stunned. Why would she lie?

'Would you mind if the sergeant and constable have a look round your boat, Mr Nevis?'

'Sure, I mean, go right ahead. You wouldn't be the first people to make a search.'

'What do you mean, sir?'

'Two evenings ago I returned to the *Osprey* and found she'd been broken into, again.'

'Again, Mr Nevis? How often does your boat get broken into?'

'Last week was the first, you know when the Californian detective was found dead in my workshop.'

'And the next was?'

'Night before last. I'd just returned from a trip to Scotland and found two men and Nancy on my boat. One of the men called himself Dr Kaufmann.'

'Jerome K Jerome,' said the sergeant.

'Street!' said the inspector.

'Sorry, just me being funny.'

I shook my head, not understanding the sergeant's remark.

'Tell me about your visitors, Mr Nevis.'

'Not much to tell, Inspector. I climbed on board, heard sounds coming from the workshop and headed down there.'

'Weren't you concerned for your safety, going straight down to your workshop? The killer could have returned.'

I smiled at my thoughts at the time. 'No, I thought Nancy had come back to surprise me.'

'And was she down in the workshop?'

'No, not at that moment, she was in the wheelhouse with the other man. Kaufmann called him Hanse.'

'Just Hanse?'

'Yes, just Hanse.'

'And who was in the workshop?'

'He called himself Dr Kaufmann, no first name. He told me he makes a living looking for lost property, then returning it for a fee.'

'What were they looking for, here on the *Osprey*?'

'A statue of a black bird, possibly a falcon and some nonsenses about eagles.'

'And do you have it on board?'

'It was last seen in 1944. Inspector, since I bought the *Osprey*, at one time or another I've been all through the boat. If there was a statue of a bird on board, I'd have found it by now.'

We were disturbed by the return of the sergeant from my cabin. She was holding an evidence bag containing a black pistol, fitted with a silencer and an infrared sight.

'Your pistol, Mr Nevis?' asked the inspector.

I was flummoxed. 'Where did you find that?'

'It was under the mattress on your bunk, Mr Nevis, where you obviously forgot you'd left it.'

I was stunned. I knew I hadn't put it there and so that left only two options: either Kaufmann or Hanse had shoved it there before they left, or – and this thought chilled me to the bone – Nancy, had she put it there, but if so, when and why?

It couldn't have been last night when she was tidying my cabin – or could it? I'd drunk almost a fifth of bourbon and could have slept on a bed of nails and not noticed. For all I knew, Kaufmann had more than one pistol and he'd told Hanse to give it to Nancy to hide somewhere in my cabin. Then I realised the full horror of what the inspector was getting at. He was assuming I'd shot the detective and hidden the murder weapon. But they couldn't prove anything, my fingerprints wouldn't be on the gun – but that didn't mean anything, I could have wiped them off. But of course, it might not be the murder weapon. I wondered if they still did paraffin tests for gunpowder blast.

'You can't use that as evidence,' said Nancy. 'You don't have a search warrant.'

'We didn't need one, Mrs Rafsanjani. Mr Nevis gave his permission for us to look.'

'Oh, that's not fair! You tricked him.'

'He could have said no.'

I looked at Nancy's face, she had a scared rabbit look about her.

'Mr Nevis, I'll ask you one more time: were you on your boat all night?'

'Yes, of course I was.'

'And Mrs Rafsanjani, you say you were here with Mr Nevis all that time?'

'Of course we were, Inspector. Mr Nevis is teaching me how to make a guitar. We worked late, it was too late to get a taxi, so I stayed overnight.'

'Together?'

'What do you think, Inspector.'

Why was she lying? I hadn't done anything wrong.

'Can anyone else back up your story, Mr Nevis?'

'We had dinner at Seasons, ask them. We left about ten-forty then returned to the *Osprey*. Check the CCTV, there's a camera directly opposite the gate to my dock. That'll show you when we returned to the *Osprey*, and also it might show who shot the detective.'

'We will, Mr Nevis, we will.'

I looked at Nancy, why was she scared? It was me the police suspected.

'Constable' said the inspector, 'take their fingerprints and get them and the gun off to the lab right away.'

'Will do.'

'Mrs Rafsanjani, I understand you are married to an Achmed Rafsanjani?'

'Yes, why.'

'You've been apart for several years?'

'Yes, several years ago he abandoned me and the children. I was told he'd gone off to Saudi Arabia to work in the oil fields. For all I knew he was dead and out of my life.'

'Who told you that?'

'What?'

'That he'd gone off to Saudi Arabia?'

'He said something about it before he left. Then I had a visit from someone in the foreign office, apparently they were looking for him as well.'

'When was the last time you saw your husband?'

'A few days ago. Why?'

'Not last night?'

'I told you, I was here all night.'

Why was she lying? What was she trying to hide?'

'Mrs Rafsanjani, I'm afraid I have some bad news for you.'

I glanced at Nancy's face; the colour had drained from it.

'What?'

'It's about your husband. I'm sorry to say he was found dead in an alleyway off Langney Road this morning.'

'How – how did he die?'

'His body was discovered by the bin-men early this morning; it was dumped in one of wheelie bins.'

'What? How?'

'That's what we are investigating, Mrs Rafsanjani. We'll know more when the autopsy results are available.'

'How did he die?' Nancy repeated.

'Mrs Rafsanjani, we would ask you to please accompany us to the morgue for a positive identification. Then both of you will be taken to the police station to make statements.'

'Are we under arrest, Inspector?'

'No, Mr Nevis. You are helping us with our enquiries, voluntarily.'

Now my mind was really in a spin. Had Nancy shot her husband because of our conversation about her being married, and then subsequently wanted me to be her alibi? Or – and this thought really bothered me – was I supposed to find the gun, pick it up, and leave a nice fresh incriminating set of fingerprints on the gun stock?

8

Achmed

We bundled into the back of the sergeant's car, and drove off to the morgue. I'd never ridden in a police car before, front or back, and was pleased they let us travel together.

I sat in the car while Nancy, escorted by the sergeant, went to pay her last respects to her dearly departed. While I waited, I tried to make sense of what was going on. I'd seen Nancy to her taxi at about twelve-thirty. Surely the police would soon figure that out? But she'd been adamant that we'd spent the night together on the *Osprey*. Why?

When the police checked the CCTV coverage, they'd see us walking down the dock to her taxi, then me returning to the boat. But there was a problem with that. I'd gone for a wander round the marina after seeing her off in the taxi. It was almost three-thirty when I climbed back on board, and then I'd stayed up drinking in the wheelhouse till almost five. So I didn't have an alibi from one o'clock till after three-thirty, plenty of time to drive into Eastbourne, do in the husband and get back to the *Osprey*. In my favour was the fact I still didn't have my car back from the garage and there were no buses at that late hour. So unless the police could find a taxi driver who was prepared to lie and say he picked me up and drove me into town, they wouldn't be able to say I had a hand in the death of Achmed Rafsanjani. Of course I did have time to walk briskly into town and back.

But what about Nancy? Had she gone straight to her sister's when the taxi dropped her off, and where exactly did her sister live? I had a gnawing feeling that things were not good, and Nancy was in deep trouble.

She was back twenty minutes later, the scared rabbit now replaced by a vacant look.

'Are you all right?' I asked.

'I'm fine,' she replied, staring out the window, 'just fine.'

We sat in silence in the back of the police car as it drove from the hospital to Hammond's Drive, each not wanting to start a conversation. I suppose in case we said something to incriminate the other. We were escorted into the station and shown into separate interview rooms.

This was my first time in a police station; I'd only seen them on TV and this one wasn't much different. A bare room, mirror on the wall, table fixed to the floor with three chairs, and a recording machine on a shelf by the door.

The inspector and the sergeant entered and sat in front of me.

'Are you comfortable, Mr Nevis? Would you like a coffee?' asked the inspector.

'Black, no sugar, please.'

The inspector consulted his notes while the sergeant left the room for my coffee. I supposed they'd had theirs earlier. I was wrong, she returned with three cups.

'Mr Nevis, before we start, you're not under arrest. You are here voluntarily to give us a statement.'

That was news to me. 'I didn't think I had an option.'

'You could have refused.'

'And you'd have arrested me?'

He smiled and shrugged. 'We would like you to go over your earlier statement about the dead man found in your workshop.'

I repeated what I'd said earlier and watched his head nod as he read my earlier statement in time with my narration.

'What about the gun we found under your mattress?'

'I've no idea how it got there.'

'Are you sure, Mr Nevis? Something that bulky would have made sleeping difficult.'

I thought about that, thought about the bourbon, and shook my head.

'Remembering something, Mr Nevis?'

'Inspector, I was too drunk to remember much of what happened.'

'Do you remember returning from the restaurant?'

I nodded.

'That's a yes, Mr Nevis?'

'Yes, that's a yes.'

'What time?'

'About ten-forty.'

'Mrs Rafsanjani says she was with you all night?'

What was I to say? I thought for a moment, then realised trying to find an answer that would protect Nancy was not going to work.

'Not all night, I put her in a taxi about half one.'

'And you returned directly to your boat?'

The game was up; they'd obviously looked at the CCTV tapes. I'd hoped they would have only looked at the time Nancy left, but obviously they'd gone past that.

'No, I went for a walk.'

'Where?'

'Just round the harbour. I went out to the end of the breakwater and watched the moon.'

'Anyone see you?'

'There were a couple of fishermen, not sure if they saw me. I wanted to be alone and, before you ask, I didn't get back to the *Osprey* till gone three.'

'Go straight to bed?'

'No, I wasn't tired. I opened a bottle and sat in the wheelhouse thinking.'

'What about, Mr Nevis?'

'Ever been in love, Inspector?'

'I take it you were thinking about Mrs Rafsanjani, Mr Nevis?'
I nodded.

'Can't make up your mind if you're being played for a sucker?'

There was no way of avoiding that question. She could have put the gun under my mattress when she made up the bed, and drunk as I was I wouldn't have felt it. Had she killed her husband? But then why would she want to incriminate me? She wasn't to know I would have gone for a walk then returned and drunk half a bottle of Jack Daniels. But she'd have time that morning while I was shaving – she could have quickly slipped it under the mattress. Then the obvious struck me. It was as I first feared, I was supposed to find the gun, pick it up from under the mattress and leave a clear set of fingerprints on it, and just before the police showed up.

'Inspector, will you answer me one question?'

'Try me.'

'Did you get an anonymous phone call this morning, say half an hour before you showed up at the *Osprey*?'

His face said yes. 'That information is confidential, Mr Nevis.'

I smiled. 'I bet if you re-listen to the recording – it was recorded, wasn't it? If you listen again, you'll find someone with a German accent left the message that got you out here.'

'Are there any other questions, Mr Nevis?'

'Yes, the gun you found under my mattress. Was it the same gun that killed the Californian detective, and was it the same gun that killed Mr Rafsanjani?'

That stumped him for the moment.

'I'll take that as a yes, Inspector.'

'We're still waiting for the autopsy and ballistic reports.'

I smiled.

'I'll arrange for one of our officers to drive you back to your boat, Mr Nevis.'

'Mrs Rafsanjani, where is she?'

'She left half an hour ago, she was driven to her to her sister's, that's where her children are.'

'And where is that, Inspector?'

'Pevensey Road, Mr Nevis.'

I felt as though I'd been punched in the gut. Pevensey Road ran parallel to Langney Road.

He'd been watching my face, and had got the reaction he'd expected.

'Is she under suspicion for killing her husband, Inspector?'

'It's early days Mr Nevis, our investigations are on-going.'

'So, you're not going to say?'

'Not at the moment. Now, if you'll excuse me, I've got work to do.'

So that was it. Nancy was under suspicion of killing her husband – and it was my fault. I'd led her on to think that if she wasn't married, I'd be willing to start a relationship. Now what was I to do? More importantly, was she working with Kaufmann and not her late husband, and if so, was that where she got the gun?

I still didn't know where her sister lived, although I knew the road, but I couldn't go knocking on every door asking if there was a Nancy staying there. I chuckled at the thought, a single man wandering round Eastbourne looking for a Nancy.

The constable dropped me off in the car park outside Asda. I purchased some cat food, a sandwich, pint of milk, and a bunch of grapes that were on sale, then wandered over to the boat ramp. While I watched a forty-foot runabout being hauled out, I reflected on my visit to the police station. The gun found under my mattress was most likely the one that killed the detective, but was it the one that killed Nancy's husband, and if so, how did it get back to the *Osprey?* It was placed there to incriminate me, there was no doubt about that. Could Nancy have met her husband, shot him, disposed of his body, returned to the *Osprey,* hidden the gun, then returned home to her sister's? Not likely, she didn't have a car – or did she? I'd never asked. Why?

I'd read detective stories where desperate women did desperate things to be rid of unwanted husbands, like the *Double Indemnity* story. Could Nancy be playing me for a fool? No, she'd no way of knowing if I'd be on board sleeping. Even if she could get on board, she was taking a huge risk trying to hide the gun, it just didn't make sense. Then the only other possibility was Kaufmann. He'd been watching the *Osprey*, and saw me go off wandering round the marina and took advantage of my absence. But did that put Nancy in the clear? She could have been working with them from the start, and still could have shot her husband and had Kaufmann get rid of the gun for her. But at what price?

I finished my sandwich and walked slowly down the dock towards the *Osprey*. Nancy was sitting on the side deck waiting for me.

'Hello, Nancy.'

'Jack.'

I nodded to her, opened the door and beckoned her to follow me inside.

She shut the door and I turned to look at her. She reached out and pulled herself to me, burying her head in my chest.

'Oh, Jack,' she sobbed, 'did you kill Achmed?'

'Who put that silly idea in your head?' I said, pushing her back so I could see her face. 'I've never met your husband, and don't even know what he looks like.'

'The police, they say you went into town after I left. Oh Jack, I need to know the truth. I don't care if you did – he deserved it.'

'Now just wait a minute. After I put you in the taxi I went for a walk, but I didn't go anywhere near Eastbourne.'

'You didn't?'

'No, I didn't.'

'Then where did you go?'

'I wandered round the harbour to the end of the breakwater and watched the moon crawl across the night sky. I needed time to think.'

'About us?'

I nodded. 'I needed to sort out something.'

'You were going to say goodbye?'

I nodded again. 'You know how I feel about dating another man's wife – you were married.'

She shook her head. 'I wasn't really.'

'What do you mean, you weren't really? You either were or weren't!'

'Achmed already had two wives in Afghanistan; he was a bigamist. He only married me to get a British passport.'

'So why do you still use his name?'

She shrugged, 'I just did that with you.'

'But why?'

'I'd been hurt twice in my life by men who said they loved me, I wasn't going to let it happen again. I wanted to wait and see just how serious you were about me, so I let you think I was still married to Achmed.'

I pulled her close and hugged her tight; but there was still the nagging doubt – was she working for Kaufmann?

'So what do I call you?'

'What's wrong with just Nancy?'

'Come on, no more secrets.'

'It's Nancy Harrison.'

We stood like that for I don't know how long, just hugging each other tight; it felt so good. But also the little voice was still nagging, 'Be careful, Jack.' I tried not to imagine what the future might bring, then the sound of someone walking down the dock disturbed us.

'I could do with something to drink,' said Nancy.

'Cup of tea would be nice.'

The footsteps came to an abrupt end as someone climbed on board and knocked at the door. I opened it. I didn't recognise the woman standing there, though she did look familiar.

'Can I help?'

'Is Nancy here?'

'You're Sarah?'

'Yes.'

'Is she here?'

'Making a cup of tea, come on in.'

'Sarah! Where are the children?'

'Next door with Shadi, they're fine.'

'So why are you here then?'

'I heard you'd been arrested for killing Achmed.'

'Where did you here that? It's nonsense!'

'It was on the radio. They said the body of a middle-eastern man had been found dead in the alleyway down the road from the house. I just wondered if it might be your Achmed. So I took the children next door to Shadi and went to look. I managed to glance at the body as they were wrapping it in a body bag – it did look like him. Then when I got back to the house I heard someone had been arrested and taken to the station for questioning, I figured it might have been you. Why don't you answer your phone? I've been going crazy with worry!'

'I wasn't arrested, but I did have to go and identify the body, then went to the police station to make a statement, that's all.'

While they were having their chat the kettle came to the boil, I interrupted, 'Either of you want a drink?'

'I'll make them,' said Nancy. 'Tea, Sarah?'

She nodded.

I watched the two of them working together at the kitchen counter. Possible sister-in-law? I mused.

'So Jack,' said Sarah, 'did you do in Achmed?'

'Not you as well! And to answer your question, no, I did not kill Achmed. I've never even met him.'

'Sarah!' exclaimed Nancy. 'Enough of that.'

'That's all right,' I said, 'she's just joking.' But was she?

'Joking or not,' said Nancy, 'there's the Kaufmann character to worry about. I'll bet he killed Achmed.'

I glanced in her direction; the cold Atlantic was back, nothing to learn there. But I did ask, 'Why do you think Kaufmann would want Achmed dead?'

'I think they were working together and Achmed tried to double-cross him.'

'What did he know that would have caused him to try that?' I asked.

'I think it was something to do with your guitar, the one you found on the boat.'

That was when I remembered what Hamish Munroe had said about hiding the gold coin in the case. I decided to wait until Sarah had left – the fewer people who knew about it the better.

I was eager to retrieve the Torres and its case, but felt it would have been bad manners to abandon our guest. I smiled to myself and thought about what I'd just said: *our guest*!

I did my best to hide my impatience, but eventually, after another round of teas and coffees, Sarah said goodbye and left us. I was now in a quandary: should I tell Nancy everything, or continue to keep my cards close to my chest? It was Nancy who decided.

'Come on, tell me all.'

'Tell you what?'

'I've been watching you – you couldn't wait for Sarah to leave. What have you found out? Do you know who killed Achmed?'

I was back in the quandary. Could I trust her, or was she just a conduit to Kaufmann? *In for a penny, in for a pound*, was the adage my grandfather would use.

I told her all about my visit to see Hamish Munroe, including the bit about the gold coins.

'Do you think they're still on the *Osprey*?'

'I think one of them might be. Wait in the workshop for me, I'll be right there.'

I removed the Torres from its hiding place and headed for the workshop. Placing the case on the bench I removed the guitar and hung it on one of the spare guitar hangers. It took me ten minutes of gently feeling the lining before I came across the coin. It had been slipped under the lining in the back of the accessory compartment. Teasing it out I carefully slid it from its velvet bag, surprised at its weight and condition. What I had in my hand was a bright, shining, uncirculated US twenty-dollar gold coin. I looked at the year: 1933.

'Is that one of the coins Hamish Munroe was talking about?' asked Nancy.

'The one and the same.'

'What are you going to do with it?'

'Not sure at the moment, though a further chat with the professor might be a good idea.'

'Why do you think that?'

'Just a hunch. Hang on a minute, I'll give him a call.'

I had to wait while Mrs Lozinski went out to the garden and retrieved the professor. I explained what I'd found and asked what did he think. I listened to his reply, then hung up the phone and turned to look at Nancy.

Her face was alive with excitement. 'Well, what did he say?'

'He asked if I was sure it was a 1933 twenty-dollar gold coin.'

'And?'

'I said yes, and he said come right over.'

♦

He was standing at the door, waiting for us.

'Come in! You did bring it with you, didn't you?'

'Of course.'

'Great, follow me.'

122

We followed, as before, down the corridor and into his study. The professor went behind his desk, Nancy and I sat facing him. Mrs Lozinski shut the door and stood by it as if on guard while the professor took out a pair of white cotton gloves from his desk drawer.

'You haven't touched it? It is still in its little bag?' he asked.

I nodded, removed the bag containing the coin from my pocket and passed it to him.

He undid the drawstrings on the tiny velvet bag and gently slid the coin out on to his hand. After staring at it for a moment, he opened one of the desk drawers and took out what looked like a tiny version of a baking scale. He turned on his desk reading lamp with magnifier and carefully looked at the coin, then put it on the scale and weighed it. We waited while he stared at one side then the other, then he looked at the display on his computer screen. Finally, he turned and said, 'Suppose I told you this coin could be worth anywhere up to five million pounds, or even more?'

'I'd say you're sounding like you were trying to sell ice to the Inuit.'

'Jack, I'm perfectly serious. If this coin were allowed to appear at auction, it would realise at least five-million pounds. In fact, in 2002 one just like it was sold, at auction, in excess of seven million dollars.'

I was dumbfounded.

'Professor, Hamish Munroe told me he'd seen forty boxes, each containing five hundred of these coins.' At five million per coin, it was a sum too big for my tired brain to work out.

Jack,' interrupted the professor, 'I can almost hear the cogs whirring round in your brain. What I have to tell you, I believe is probably beyond your imagination? Why don't we sit down and I'll explain? First, though, I think something stronger that coffee is in order.'

'Stanton,' interrupted Mrs Lozinski, 'your knowledge is impeccable, your timing is not. If you'll observe the clock, you'll see it's dinner time.'

Once more we sat through an excellent meal while the professor wittered on about anything that came to his mind except the gold coins. At last we went through to the living room and a blazing fire. Mrs Lozinski sat in her chair, I sat on the end of the settee, Nancy followed and curled up beside me, her head on my shoulder and her perfume doing crazy things with my emotions. We sat and waited, while the professor stood, with his back to the fire brandishing a large overfull brandy glass.

He began, 'Nancy, Jack, as I said the last time you were here, I believe you are involved in a task most dangerous. So dangerous that if you fail it could alter the whole course of history.'

9

The Professor Speaks

We were committed. Everything the professor was about to tell us could, by this time tomorrow, be in the hands of Kaufmann. I toyed with the idea of making an excuse as to why we had to leave immediately, but realised that would be a fruitless gesture. What he had to say needed to be said, Kaufmann or not.

'Jack and Nancy,' he began. I suppose he saw himself as part of the team searching for the – which was it – the gold or the falcon? Or was it both? I thought of the *Indiana Jones* movie *Raiders of the Lost Ark* and could see the professor playing the part of Marcus Brodie. Then I realised if that was the case I'd be Indiana Jones with Nancy playing the part of Marion, and of course there were Nazis in that story as there were in ours.

'Jack, if we could have your undivided attention, I'll continue.'

'Sorry, Professor, my mind drifted a bit.'

He shook his head, 'An ounce of desire for a companion heart is more precious than a pound of gold. Do you understand?'

I nodded. I understood only too well.

He continued, 'This coin may seem to be just another gold coin, but let me tell you something of its history. As you'll see, looking at the date, this is a mint, 1933 20-dollar gold coin. In numismatic circles, it is commonly referred to as a double eagle. There were 445,500 minted in early 1933, hence the date on the coin. Yet, according to the documents I've been reading, all were melted down after being struck – they were never put into circulation.'

'So how does this one exist? Is it a forgery?' asked Nancy.

'A sensible question. Let me continue and I believe all will become clear. In 1933, in an attempt to bolster the US banking industry –'

'Was that the depression?' interrupted Nancy.

'Not quite, that was in 1928, though in 1933 the banks were still trying to do their bit and stabilise the economy. Anyway, back to what I was saying. To shore up the banking system President Roosevelt signed into law on the 5th of April, executive order number 6102, decreeing that all gold coins, bullion and gold certificates be surrendered by the 28th of April. After that date, a fine of ten thousand dollars per day would be levied, plus a jail sentence given.'

'A bit draconian, Professor?' I said. 'Did gold owners rebel – especially considering their losses must have been considerable?

'The government didn't think so. At the time of surrender, the value of gold was almost equal to the face value of the coins. And remember the country was struggling with the aftermath of the Great Depression and the government were desperately trying to put the economy back on a level keel. But there were exemptions for collector coins.'

'Still doesn't explain how this coin exists?' said Nancy.

I wondered why the professor was pursuing this line. What did a 20-dollar gold coin and the US overdraft have in common? He must have seen the question in my face.

'You're wondering where's the connection. Am I right?'

I nodded.

'Let me continue. As I said earlier, there were over 450 thousand of these coins minted, all of which were ordered destroyed. According to the story I read, one of the employees in the mint substituted about twenty of the 1933 20-dollar double eagle gold coins with 20-dollar gold coins of an earlier vintage, thus keeping the surrender value of gold intact.'

'Oh, I see,' said Nancy. 'So when the coins were counted there wouldn't be any missing? Though I don't suppose anyone actually read the date on all 450 thousand.'

'That's what the culprit was banking on.'

'An apt comment, Professor.'

'Very apt, Jack. The culprit probably figured the subterfuge would never be detected, but unfortunately for him it was, and the Treasury department and FBI have been chasing after these coins ever since.'

'So will they be after the forty boxes as well?' asked Nancy.

'Unlikely. This coin is probably all that remains of those forty boxes. During World War 2 the Germans, like the allies, counterfeited each other's currencies, trying to destabilise each other's economies. If you look on eBay, for instance, you'll find many of these coins for sale.'

'I thought you said there weren't any, Professor?'

'It's very likely, if we had those coins advertised on eBay assayed, we'd find they were probably mostly an amalgam of various base metals, with a thin layer of gold plating, and their only value is as war mementoes.'

'But this coin, Professor – are you saying it is a fake?' I asked.

'This coin, with it weighing two ounces and with its provenance, I'm convinced it is the genuine article. Ultimately to prove to the satisfaction of the worldwide numismatic society, it would require a full assay test done on it.'

'Professor, if this was the case, why did the Germans place so much importance on them, and if they were really gold, why not have them melted down in the foundry in the dockyard? Why send them back to Berlin?'

'Unfortunately we will probably never know the answer to that. Is there any chance they could still be hidden somewhere on your boat?'

'Unlikely, trying to hide a stack that big would be like trying to hide a small refrigerator. If the gold was still on board, I'd have found it by now.'

'So what's Kaufmann after then – the gold or the falcon?' asked Nancy.

'Wait a minute, we don't even know he's aware of the gold, do we?' asked the professor.

I had been wondering about that myself and decided that I should call Munroe's daughter and find out if they'd had any unwelcome visitors. With the possible existence of the gold, Hamish Munroe was now in the firing line if Kaufmann had found out about him. I looked at the time on my mobile, nine-fifty, not too late.

'Professor,' I interrupted, 'I must make a phone call, it's very urgent.'

'Certainly.'

I went out into the hall and called Munroe's daughter. I willed the phone to be answered but it wasn't. I hung up and redialled; this time it was answered in three rings.

'Munroe residence.'

'Agnes, It's Jack Nevis.'

'Oh, hullo Mr Nevis! How are you?'

'I'm fine, thanks.'

'Do you want to talk to Father?'

'Ah, not at the moment.'

'That's all right then, because he's not here at the moment.'

'Oh, where is he?'

'My son's driven him up to Inverness to see his sister, she's quite poorly.'

'When do you expect him back?'

'Not sure, he said if he wasn't back by Friday evening he would stay over till Sunday evening, wanted to go to the kirk. Can I give him a message?'

'No, not really. It was you I really wanted to talk to. I was calling to ask if anyone had visited him in the last few days, before he went off to see his sister?'

'Aye, there's been the minister and his wife, they came for tea, and auld Dan with his dog.'

'No one else?'

'No, should there be?

'No. How about phone calls, anyone with a German accent for instance?'

'Oh yes, there was a message on the answerphone yesterday.'

'Would you mind telling me what the message said?'

'Said he was a writer doing research about dad's wartime experiences in France.'

'Did he call back?'

'Yes. He wanted to come and interview father, said it was always better to do these things in person.'

'What did you tell him?' I asked, feeling the hair on the back of my neck bristling.

'I told them him he was wasting his time, my father was away and I didn't know when he would be back. I don't mind telling you, Mr Nevis, I didn't like the sound of his voice one bit, gave me the creeps.'

'Do you think he'll call again?'

'Oh, aye, he did. Not long after we hung up, the phone rang again. It was someone else though, said he was the secretary. Said his boss had other people to interview in Glasgow and would stop by when he'd talked with them.'

'Did he give any indication when that might be?'

'Aye, said they'd be by Monday morning.'

'Agnes, do you have somewhere safe you could go stay for a few days?'

'Yes – why? What's going on, Mr Nevis? Is it that German fellow?'

I pondered for a moment, wondering if I should draw her into this mess. 'Agnes, these people are bad. They have some sort of grudge about something that happened during the war when your father was working in France. Until the police catch them it would be better for you and your father if you were not there when they call.'

'Did my father do something bad, and these people want revenge?'

'No, it's nothing like that. They think your father knows where something is that they want, that's all.'

'What is it? Did Father steal it from them?'

'No, Agnes, your father didn't steal anything,' Then I thought of the double eagle ensconced in its velvet bag and tucked in with my notebook in my jacket pocket. Better not to say.

'No, it's some sort of memento they are looking for; they seem to think your father might know where it is.'

'Oh, if that's all then, I'm sure Father will put them straight on the matter when he gets home.'

'Agnes, these men are really dangerous – you need to be away when they call.'

'Mr Nevis, how do I know that it's not *you* that's after this memento? Maybe you are trying to get us both out of the house so you can break-in and steal it?'

That stumped me. How could I convince her I wasn't interested in breaking in and stealing anything?'

'Mr Nevis, I'm sure you mean no harm, but if it's all the same to you, I'll stay put till Father comes home. He'll know what to do. Goodnight.'

The phone went dead, call over. Today was Friday, I had till Monday morning to get to Port Glasgow and convince them both to get out of the house and to safety till Kaufmann and Hanse were under lock and key. But how did Kaufmann know about Munroe? Had Nancy told them? Either way I didn't have much time. But what should I do with Nancy, if she was working for

Kaufmann? If I left her behind, as soon as I was gone she'd get in touch with him and warn him that I was on the way to Port Glasgow. The only option was to take her with me. But would she go?

And what was I going to do with her till we flew to Glasgow? I had a look at the Skyscanner app on my phone and saw I could get a flight Sunday evening at 19:35 to Glasgow, arriving at 21:05. The price was horrible, but I was stuck. Of course there was the sleeper on the Saturday night train, but that meant sharing a cabin. I booked the flight, two returns to Glasgow. Now what about the weekend? I stuffed the phone back in my pocket and returned to the dining room.

'All well, Jack?' asked the professor.

'I'm not sure. I just talked to Hamish Munroe's daughter, she said Kaufmann had called.'

'What did he want?'

'He said he wanted to talk with her father, made up a cock and bull story about writing an article about Munroe's life in St Nazaire during World War 2.'

'What did you say to her?'

'I asked her if she had somewhere safe where she and her father could go till Kaufmann was out of the way.'

'Excellent plan.'

'Would be if she took my advice.'

'She's staying?'

'Till her father returns. Problem is, that will be on Sunday evening. Kaufmann said he'll visit on Monday morning.'

'Doesn't give them much time.'

'No, it doesn't.'

He saw the look of indecision on my face. 'What are you planning, Jack?'

I looked at Nancy, then back to the professor. 'I've booked a flight to Glasgow on Sunday evening.'

'Going to read them the riot act, sort of thing? Good idea.'

131

'Not quite Professor, just going to help them to see reason, and hopefully have them out of the way while Kaufmann is on the prowl.'

'Can't we just call the police and have Kaufmann arrested?' asked Nancy.

'That would be the best thing, but he's not yet been found guilty of any crime, my dear,' interrupted the professor. 'What are your plans for when you get to Port Glasgow, Jack?'

'I'll hire a car, head to the house and hopefully be able to convince them to leave.'

'Where will they go?' asked Nancy. 'You can't just show up and expect then to pack their bags and leave for – where?'

'I'll pay for a couple of rooms in a hotel for them, it'll only need to be for a couple of nights. When Kaufmann can't find them, he'll get bored and leave.'

'It's a plan,' said Nancy, 'but Munroe's daughter doesn't sound like she's the type of woman to allow any man to tell her what to do. How are you going to convince her?'

I had a moment of inspiration. 'I'm not. *you* are.'

'Me? Are you saying you want me to come with you to Glasgow?'

'Port Glasgow actually, and yes, I do. That is, if you want to?'

'What about my children?'

I shook my head. 'They'll have to stay with your sister. I'll have the taxi drop you off on the way back tonight and I'll pick you up on Sunday afternoon on the way to the airport.'

'I told Sarah I was staying with you.'

Who was watching who, I wondered? 'So is that a yes?'

She smiled and nodded.

'Excuse me,' said Mrs Lozinski, 'would anyone like a nightcap?'

I looked at the clock and saw it was almost midnight.

'My dear, you are right, it is getting late,' said the professor, 'but, I have a wonderful idea.' He turned to us. 'Why don't you

132

two stay here this evening? Bit late to be calling a taxi. We have plenty of rooms, don't we dear?'

'Yes dear, we do have plenty of rooms.'

'Good, that's settled.'

He got up from his chair, placed a couple of logs on the fire and satisfied the fire would burn for the next few hours turned and said. 'Well, if that's all settled I think it's time for some brandy, Nancy, a glass of brandy?'

'Stanton, a word, please,' said Mrs Lozinski as she stood and walked over to the door.

'Oh dear,' said Nancy grinning, 'I think the professor's in trouble.'

'I doubt if it's the first time.'

'Or the last. I think he's actually a lonely man.'

'Think they both are lonely. Have you seen any pictures of children?'

'There's one on the mantelpiece,' I said, getting up and going over to the fire.

Nancy got up, walked over and leaned on me, a bit too close for comfort. I could feel the warmth of her body and she was wearing that perfume again. She picked up the small, framed, yellowed photo.

'What do you think, Jack? His parents? The young man bears a resemblance to the professor.'

'My son and his wife,' said the professor. who'd just come back into the room.

'They were killed in an aeroplane crash while working in the Amazon,' added Mrs Lozinski, who'd followed her husband into the room.

I looked at Nancy: a new face, this one was pure empathy. That was when I realised just how much she must have loved her first husband, Jack, and how great the loss must have been when she got the news of his death. I put my arm around her and held her tight.

'Jack, Nancy, my husband was being presumptuous in assuming you would want to stay here at such short notice.'

'We'd love to stay, as long as it's not too much trouble for you, Mrs Lozinski?' said Nancy.

She smiled. 'It would be lovely to have guests again, especially a young couple like you two.'

Oops, an awkward moment I thought, so I explained, 'We're not quite a couple, Mrs Lozinski, we're just good friends.'

Chicken, I said to myself, you know you love her, and she's *not* married.

'I understand. As Stanton said, we have plenty of rooms.'

I looked at Nancy. She was grinning from ear-to-ear at my discomfort.

'Stanton, you offered brandy to our guests,' said Mrs Lozinski.

'Oh, yes. Nancy, a brandy?'

'You must excuse my husband, Nancy. He thinks he rules the roost, I know better.'

Nancy smiled and walked over to the professor who'd just poured her a large brandy.

'Jack, a brandy?'

'Do you have any Jack Daniels?'

'Ah, smooth Tennessee whiskey. *We do things a little differently around here – and that's what gives Jack Daniels its distinctive character.* Isn't that what they say, Jack?'

'I've no idea Professor, I just drink the stuff.'

He dropped some ice in the glass, poured me a large measure, then passed the drink to me before resuming his seat beside the fire.

'Are you all right, dear?' Mrs Lozinski asked Nancy.

She nodded. 'Some memories just don't go away. How do you live with your loss?'

'It was many years ago and we cried so many tears. I didn't think I could cry any more. Then, just when you think it's all over, something happens and you live it all over again.'

134

Nancy nodded. 'I know exactly what you mean. I lost my husband in Afghanistan: a stupid bomb, buried at the side of the road. Doctors said he never knew what happened, all over in an instant.'

I looked at them, two women with an ache of emptiness that nothing would ever fill adequately.

'So, what are we going to do with the rascal Kaufmann?' said the professor, attempting to divert the conversation.

'Trying to get him arrested isn't going to work at the moment,' I said. 'The next best thing would be to thwart his attempts to find Munroe.'

'And you think going to Port Glasgow and persuading him and his daughter to hide out will do that?'

'Best idea I have at the moment.'

'Yes, you're right, it's just like preventing fires.'

'There you go again, Stanton, talking in riddles,' said Mrs Lozinski.

'No, my dear, the analogy is quite correct. For fire to happen you require three things: fuel, air and source of ignition. Without any one of these – no fire.'

'And what is Mr Munroe? Fuel, fire or ignition?'

'I'd say fuel, my dear.'

'But what does he know that could help Kaufmann?' asked Nancy.

I'd been wracking my brains over that. Anything he knew was over seventy years old. Of course if Munroe told him about the double eagle I'd found, that would be like a red rag to a bull. No matter what Munroe told him, Kaufmann would assume where there was one coin, the others wouldn't be far away. And if the coins were to be had, why not the falcon?

The professor had also come to the same conclusion. 'Yes, Jack, you must get Mr Munroe away from Dr Kaufmann at all costs. If the doctor is as determined as you make out, I don't hold out much hope for Mr Munroe to see the dawning of a new day.'

'But why, Professor?' asked Nancy. 'What drives Kaufmann? Surely even he must realise it's unlikely the gold exists? And the statue is nothing more than a stone carving, be it old – but not worth the trouble he is taking to acquire it.'

'It's just possible, Nancy, there is more to the story regarding the gold than we are privy to.'

'What do you mean?'

'Well, we have Mr Munroe and Lieutenant Hudson's sides of the story – but suppose there's a third element, one that only Dr Kaufmann is party to?'

'I hadn't thought of that,' said Nancy.

I had, and I didn't like the where my imaginings were taking me. Lieutenant Hudson should be fine, he only had a small part to play in this unfolding drama. It was Hamish Munroe who was in the firing line, he actually saw the gold. Suppose Kaufmann thought Munroe had spirited it away and hidden it somewhere in St Nazaire? But if that was the case, why leave it there? Then a thought struck me. Munroe had said he'd been over to St Nazaire to say farewell to a friend. Suppose that old friend had been the gold, and he had decided to dump it? Now that could be awkward if Kaufman didn't believe him. All the more reason to get Munroe out of harm's way till Kaufmann had been dealt with.

Of course there was another issue altogether: suppose Kaufmann, being German, had contacts with former SS officers who were involved? Suppose there was a German version of Munroe who'd told Kaufmann all about the gold that was in the chateau that night? I glanced at my watch, just gone midnight, past time for bed. But there was still the matter of how to keep Nancy close till we reached Port Glasgow. It was Mrs Lozinski who offered the solution.

'Have you ever been to the Observatory, Jack?'

'No, why?'

'Tomorrow after breakfast Stanton and I are going to pay a visit. Stanton is giving a talk on how the Egyptians regarded the stars. While he's giving his talk I thought the three of us could go for a wander round the grounds and gardens and if it's open to visitors, take in a tour of the castle. When he's finished, Stanton can then join us for afternoon tea. What do you think?'

Nancy decided for both of us. 'Sounds like fun, we'd love to.'

I dreamed Nancy and Katie were washing each other's hair and Kaufmann kept draining the water from the sink.

10

The Visitor

I woke to hear birds chirping outside an unfamiliar window, then realised where I was. Picking up my phone, I saw it was almost ten so dressed and went downstairs. Following the sound of voices, I ended up in the kitchen, to find Nancy sitting at the table with Mrs Lozinski, coffee cups in their hands.

'Good morning, Jack,' she said, eyes sparkling and dimples showing in her cheeks. 'Sleep well?'

I nodded, remembering too late not to move my head too vigorously. 'Is there any coffee left?'

'Plenty, just made a new pot,' interrupted Mrs Lozinski. 'Why don't you sit down and I'll make your breakfast? What would you like?'

'What is there?'

'I made scrambled eggs for the professor, how does that sound?'

'Fine. Is he around?'

'No, you've just missed him. He likes to be early for his lectures, we'll catch up with him later.'

Although I'd lived in the area for several years, I'd never taken the time to explore the surrounding countryside, and Herstmonceux was part of that unvisited countryside. After breakfast, we piled into Mrs Lozinski's well-used Volvo estate and drove the short distance to the Observatory. I paid the entrance fee to the grounds and with the instructions to purchase the castle tour tickets from the office we parked directly across from the castle.

'If you ladies wait by the tea room I'll go get our tickets for the castle.'

I exited the castle reception with three tickets for the tour, and walked across the bridge. Nancy was standing on her own.

'Where's Mrs Lozinski?'

'The professor called her, something about an assistant was going to be late. She's gone to help with him get started with his lecture, she said not to worry, she'll be back in time for the tour of the castle.'

'So it's just you and me?'

'Looks like that,' she said with a huge grin, her eyes sparkling.

'So where shall we start?'

Nancy opened the guide, twitched her nose and said, 'Let's start with the rose garden, then walk through to the others, I'd especially like to see the herb garden.'

'You wish is my command.'

We set off past the Zimbabwean sculpture exhibition and through the gate into the rose garden, I almost grabbed her hand, but resisted the urge.

We spent the morning wandering through the grounds, out to the folly and back to the castle tea room where Nancy said we'd meet Mrs Lozinski for the castle tour at one o'clock.

I found the guided tour very informative, though my mind was elsewhere wondering how I was going to convince the Munroes of their need to be out of the way for a while. I'd noticed that Nancy and Mrs Lozinski were deep in conversation most of the time, and I didn't want to intrude.

'Are you with us, Jack?' asked Nancy as I lagged behind them.

'Oh, yes, just admiring the view.' And still trying to figure out what to do if Munroe didn't play ball I mused. She just smiled back at me.

We exited the castle and saw the professor sitting under one of the huge chestnut trees.

'Ah, there you are, Stanton, how did your talk go?'

'Excellent, my dear. A very appreciative audience, thanks for your help early on.'

'Let's have tea,' said Mrs Lozinski.

It was as bizarre as I could imagine. Here I was sharing an afternoon tea with three people who would have been complete strangers a week ago, but now were more family than I had had in years. Wasn't life just wonderful?

I drove back with the professor while Nancy went with Mrs Lozinski.

I was beginning to feel awkward; we'd originally come over Friday afternoon to see the professor about the coin, and now we were weekend house guests. At some point I needed to get back to the *Osprey* and collect a change of clothes for the both of us before we flew up to Glasgow.

'Jack, I don't know about you, but I could do with a change of clothing before we fly tomorrow.'

'Just what I was thinking.'

'Take my car,' said Mrs Lozinski.

♦

I parked the car, walked down to the *Osprey* and climbed on board. I didn't bother with turning on the main saloon light as the harbour lights provided enough light for me to see. I climbed down the stairs to my cabin for my clothes and Nancy's backpack. I turned on the cabin light and saw the backpack sitting on the bunk. I grabbed my small roll-around suitcase, shoved a shirt, socks and some underwear in it, along with my travel kit – remembering to check to see if it still had my deodorant stick and the small tube of toothpaste.

I climbed back up into the main saloon and heard something swish past my ear, then all went black.

I came to sitting in a chair in my saloon, my arms tied behind me and a wiry-looking individual staring at me.

'Who the hell are you, and what are you doing on my boat? And more importantly why all the violence?'

'Mr Nevis,' he said in an accent I couldn't quite place, 'I'm looking for a small item of historic importance that I believe you have in your possession, or at least you know of its whereabouts.'

I shook my head – a big mistake, it felt like it was about to fall off. 'I have no idea what you are talking about, now untie me.'

'When you've answered my question. Where is the statue, Mr Nevis?'

So that was what this was about. I was glad the double eagle was still with the professor. 'I have no statue. If you want money, all I have is in the change jar over there on the counter.'

'So it seems. Not a very profitable way to earn a living, repairing guitars, Mr Nevis?'

'I get by.'

'Did you shoot the detective?'

'What? Shoot who? Oh, I get you. You think I shot that detective in my workshop?'

He nodded very slowly and walked over to where I was sitting. I hadn't seen it before but now he was close I could see the barrel of a very business-like automatic pistol.

'Mr Nevis, I've had a look round your boat and not found what I am looking for. I am going to untie you and I advise you not to make any sudden movements, do you understand?'

'Yes, I understand. But answer me a question, if you can?'

'If I can.'

'What's all this nonsense about a statue?'

He was about to speak, then stopped to think. Instead he went behind me and untied my arms. It felt good to have the ropes off till the blood started to flow again: my arms burned. He returned to the settee and made it obvious that he had the upper hand, the muzzle of his pistol was pointing directly at my crotch.

'Mr Nevis, I'm going to tell you a bit of history. Sometime in late 1941, a German submarine, operating in the Pacific, boarded and searched a US merchant vessel, the La Paloma, bound for San Francisco. We don't know if the Germans had specific information about what was on board, but during the search a small statuette of a falcon was removed, along with jewels and a shipment of forty boxes of gold coins being returned to the US mint. Thirty-nine of the boxes of coins were subsequently recovered later in the war. Which leaves one still unaccounted for. The bird was of no consequence to most people, but a thing of great importance to the jihad.'

'Jihad – your struggle? Someone else once used that phrase. His name was Adolf Hitler, except he called his struggle *Mein Kampf.* Ever heard of it?' I asked, while trying to get the circulation back into my arms.

'A great man, pity he failed in his task, but then he didn't know the truth.'

He was losing me in his rhetoric.

'You have strange friends.'

'In Jihad, the end justifies the means.'

'So you think this thing, this statue, is some sort of talisman?'

He nodded again.

'Then if you'll leave me your phone number, I'll call you when I find it.'

He stood, walked over to the door and stopped. 'Mr Nevis, if I find out you are lying to me … ' he made a gesture of drawing a knife across his throat, and with that gesture vivid in my mind, he opened the door and was gone.

That was just great. Not only was I trying to keep an eye on Nancy in case she was tied in with Kaufmann. I also had him looking over my shoulder and now some sort of jihadist was threatening to decapitate me. I grabbed my roll-around and Nancy's backpack and was back in the professor's house in forty minutes. I didn't tell Nancy that someone had been on the boat again.

'What took you so long?' she asked.

'I was about to cross the bridge and got attacked by Balrog.'

'Balrog?'

142

I shook my head. 'It's a creature in *The Lord of the Rings*. I'm here now, that's all that matters.'

Nancy gave me one of those looks that said, *I'll talk to you later.*

I went upstairs and left my roll-around at the foot of the bed, went next door to Nancy's room and left her backpack on her bed, then went back downstairs.

'Jack, Mrs Lozinski has a suggestion.'

'Oh, what's that, Mrs Lozinski?'

'It's, Nadia, Jack. Mrs Lozinski sounds so formal.'

'Okay, Nadia.'

'Why don't you two go out for dinner? Stanton has preparation to do for a radio interview tomorrow and I was going to call my sister in California.'

I looked at Nancy. 'How about it? Fancy a gourmet meal? I'm buying.'

She smiled again and did that thing with her nose as she nodded.

'I'll call a taxi,' I said, 'I don't fancy going out for a nice meal and driving.'

Nancy was ready in fifteen minutes and stood at the front door like a puppy excited about going for a walk.

'You know The Swan in Westham?' I asked the taxi driver when we got in.

'The fish and chip shop?'

'That's the one, by the roundabout. The best fish and chips in all of Sussex.'

'Okay'

I saw Nancy's reflection in the driver's rear view mirror, and smiled. This will teach her for teasing me. The taxi stopped halfway on the pavement and let us out. I paid the driver and saw him wink; a fellow conspirator. I gave him an extra big tip.

'Well,' said Nancy, 'you certainly know how to treat a girl, don't you? Cod and chips twice, is it?'

'With mushy peas, don't forget the mushy peas.'

'Of course, and salt and vinegar to taste, I suppose?'

'Come here, you silly billy,' I said, and pulled her close. 'We're not going for fish and chips; we're going next door to Simply Seafood. I called earlier and made a reservation.'

It was becoming too easy for me to hug her; I should be more careful. I looked her in the face; it shone like the sun coming out from behind a cloud, the smile was back.

We were shown through to the conservatory and, to my surprise, directly under a huge grape vine. I watched her as she tried to make up her mind what to eat.

'Oysters, they have oysters!' she squealed with excitement.

I didn't see that coming and reluctantly agreed to share the six she ordered, not quite my cup of tea. She followed the oysters with tomato and basil bruschetta, then the lobster. As usual I started with the soup, a really tasty smoked haddock chowder, then stuffed myself with the surf and turf. We didn't bother with desserts, but settled for the cheese tray and brandy.

It was gone midnight when the taxi dropped us at the professor's. The moon was full and cast a surreal glow over the garden. Neither of us wanted to go in and draw the evening to a close. Had there been somewhere to sit and talk, we would. I reluctantly said goodnight at her bedroom door and went to my bed. I woke at four and tried to figure out just why we were going to see Munroe. If he went into hiding, fine. If he refused, what could the four of us do against the power of Kaufmann? I managed to drift off to sleep again, only to be confronted with that night's viewing of Nancy and Katie fighting over how to iron my shirts.

♦

Nancy sat in front of the fire in the living room reading, I couldn't concentrate, my mind was full of questions about what to do when we reached Glasgow. At last it was time to drive to the airport. Nadia drove the old Volvo, with the professor providing unwanted and un-needed directions. I was quite pleased about the ride, at least I didn't have the expense of the taxi.

♦

The flight was uneventful and within an hour of us landing I'd collected the hire car, shoved our small overnight case in the back and we were on the M8 heading towards Port Glasgow.

I parked in front of Munroe's house and pressed the doorbell, willing that no one would answer. I was out of luck.

'Oh, it's Mr Nevis! What brings you back?'

'Agnes, has your father returned yet?'

'Oh aye, he's just having his tea. Come on in. Aren't you going to introduce your friend?'

'Oops, sorry. Agnes, this is my friend, Nancy. We're working together.'

'Pleased to meet you, Nancy. This way; Father will be surprised.'

Not half as much as he would if Kaufmann showed up, I thought.

Agnes opened the door to the living room. 'Father, it's Mr Nevis and his friend.'

'Mr Nevis! What brings you back so soon?'

'You remember the story you told me about the crates of gold you saw in the chateau?'

'Oh aye, but that was years ago. They'll no be there now, the Germans came and took it all away. Ah told you all that already.'

'I remember what you said, but there's a problem. I met a German last week who's certain you know where the gold is, and he'll stop at nothing till he gets his hands on it.'

'But the Germans took it! There *is* no gold.'

'Mr Munroe, I have it on good authority that thirty-nine of the boxes were recovered just before the war ended. But there is still one box unaccounted for and, if found, it could be worth many millions of pounds.'

'So what does that have to do with me?'

'Mr Munroe, this German is looking for the gold, amongst other items, and I believe he has killed two people in the last two weeks while trying to find it. He believes you know where the gold is. Now do you understand why you have to go somewhere safe till he is arrested by the police?'

'But where can I go? I'm not a young man, and there's Agnes.'

'Don't worry, Father, we'll go to Jimmy's. We'll be safe there.'

'Jimmy's?' I asked, 'Where's Jimmy's?'

'It's my son's flat,' said Agnes, 'it's not far from here.'

'Where's not far?'

'Top of John Wood Street, just across from the station.'

'You have a car?'

'No, we always call a taxi if Father has to go somewhere, I have my bicycle.'

'I'll drive you both, my car's outside.'

'What about the house?' asked Agnes.

'We'll stay here and make sure no harm comes to it, it's your father they're after, not us.' I said, with a conviction I didn't feel.

For a man in his nineties he managed the stairs up to his grandson's flat quite well; all but being a bit out of breath, he was fine.

'Stay here tonight, and I'll come get you tomorrow. It might be quite late; we don't know when Kaufmann will show up.'

'Thanks, Mr Nevis. We'll be fine here with Jimmy till you come back,' said Agnes.

I drove us back to the Munroe's house, but instead of parking outside I parked the car down the hill in front of a row of cottages.

'Why are we leaving the car here?' asked Nancy.

'I want the house to look as empty as I can. If I park the car out front, Kaufmann will be certain there is someone in.'

'That makes sense.'

We walked up the rest of the hill and let ourselves in. I locked and bolted the outside door, locked the inner front door, and went room to room making sure all the windows were shut and locked.

146

I also went room to room making sure all the lights were off, and as a precaution I placed a chair in the middle of each room, just where someone would bump into it in the dark should they have come in through a window.

'What now?' asked Nancy.

'We wait, but not here in the lounge, let's use the small box room under the stairs – should give us the option of making a dash to the front door if needed.'

'You certainly know how to treat a girl; you fly them off to exotic places then treat them to a night in a cupboard.'

'It's all part the service.'

'Tell me again, why are we here?'

I was beginning to wonder that myself, then whispered, 'If we hadn't come up here, Munroe would never have left, and he wouldn't have lasted ten minutes at the hands of Kaufmann. Besides I don't believe Kaufmann when he says they will be here Monday, more likely for him to show up in the middle of the night.'

'Of course, that makes sense.'

I was correct in my reasoning about Kaufmann. At about twelve-thirty I heard a thud and a muffled curse coming from the downstairs toilet.

'Is that them?' Nancy whispered.

'No, probably just one of them, most likely Hanse. He's probably the only one fit enough to climb through a small window.' Then I realised if he could break in to this house, why not the *Osprey*? Did that mean he shot the detective? I traced his path by the sound of his footsteps down the corridor, heard the inner door open, then the outside front door.

'Are they asleep?' It was Kaufmann's voice.

'Don't know, whole house is quiet.'

'You go upstairs, wake the old man and get him down here, I'll search the downstairs.' It was Kaufmann's voice again.

We could hear Kaufmann going from room to room. Then the sound of Hanse returning. Without actually hearing what was said, Kaufmann's anger could be understood by his tone of voice. There was the noise of other doors being opened and closed then the inevitable happened: Hanse opened the door to our hideaway.

'Mr Nevis, I presume?' said Kaufmann. 'How opportune! Why don't you come out and join us? We can have that chat I mentioned earlier.'

I tried to push Nancy back into the dark of the cupboard, but to no avail.

'Ah, Mrs Rafsanjani – would you please join us as well? Hanse, please show our guests into the living room. You may shoot them if they cause trouble– but only in the legs – wouldn't want to come this far and not collect what we came for.'

We stood, like naughty schoolchildren who'd been sent to the headmaster's office.

'Hanse, have a look through their pockets and see what little treasures they bring to the party.'

He went through mine and threw my cash, wallet, car keys and mobile phone on the table. He had less success with Nancy, she only had her purse. He rummaged through it, made a rude remark about the contents and threw her phone on the table beside mine.

'I think we'll hold on to their phones, Hanse, they can have the rest back.'

'Oh look, said Hanse, as he scrolled through my phone, 'it's full of photos of guitars.'

'I suppose everyone has to have a perversion,' laughed Kaufmann.

I shook my head slowly and wondered how we were going to extricate ourselves from this inconvenience.

'Look, boss, 'said Hanse, opening the door at the bottom of Munroe's grandfather clock and extracting the bottle of Talisker, 'something to keep us warm on a cold night, and it's got a brother to keep it company. You want a drink, Doctor?'

'Why not? I'm sure Mr Nevis would like one, especially having spent time in that dusty cupboard.'

'No thanks.' The last thing I wanted to do was drink alcohol; I needed to keep my wits about me.

'Come, come, Mr Nevis. This is no way for us to have our little, tête-à-tête. I find a little libation helps one to think, brings one's thinking to a pleasurable conclusion. Just a short one – surely that won't dull your senses?'

'With ice, I only drink whiskey with ice.'

'Hanse, ice for Mr Nevis. I must tell you, Mr Nevis, I find it difficult to trust a man who declines to share a drink with me. Makes me wonder what ulterior motives he may have for refusing. Mrs Rafsanjani, would you care to join us in a little celebration?'

I glanced at Nancy, caught her eye and shook my head.

'No thanks, I'm particular who I drink with.'

Hanse returned from the kitchen with a tray of ice cubes and reached for the bottle to pour the whiskey. I grabbed the glass. 'Ice first.'

He slid the ice tray over and I extracted four large cubes, then poured a short measure over the ice and waited for the whiskey to cool.

'Interesting. Now Mr Nevis, why don't you two sit and we'll have our little chat? Hanse, two chairs for our guests.'

'Doctor, like I said before, I don't know what it is you are looking for. Why don't you describe it to me, and maybe, just maybe, I can be of assistance?' I said as we sat.

'My, you are the canny one, no doubt about it. All right, let me tell you what we are looking for. Two items really, one might say they are both ornithological in nature; yes, indeed, you could almost describe them as that. The first is a figurine of a black bird, not just any bird, and certainly not a black enamelled, jewel-encrusted gold one. No indeed, what we are searching for, Mr Nevis, is a figurine of a falcon. It stands about eight inches high, is carved from black marble, and has a little crown on the top.'

The professor didn't say that. Wondered what else Kaufmann knew. 'Doctor, why would a marble figurine of a falcon have any value?'

'It's very old, Mr Nevis. A genuine historical artefact. Some say it's as old as history itself, a relic of ancient Egypt.'

'I don't understand.'

'Mr Nevis, suppose I told you there are certain people who would pay a king's ransom and more to boot for the bird?'

'More fool them.'

'Yes, indeed, but that would be their decision.'

'So, what's it worth to you if I were to get it for you?'

'So you do know where it is? My, you really are the canny one. One question Mr Nevis, would I be correct in assuming that there are no other bidders?'

I let my face go blank and waited.

'So there is another bidder! This is exciting, isn't it, Hanse?'

Hanse looked up from scraping dirt from under his fingernails with an evil looking knife and shrugged.

I raised my drink to my mouth and sucked in one of the ice cubes, then put the glass back down on the table. The whiskey level had dropped noticeably, the ice cube tasted of ten-year-old Talisker.

Kaufmann was thinking, working out just how much information to tell me, hoping I would play ball.

'Let me tell you something, Mr Nevis. Something that will help you decide selling the falcon to me makes the most sense financially. As to the falcon figurine, I'm willing to advance you, say, twenty thousand pounds – in cash – for your troubles so far, and a further thirty thousand on delivery. Now, what do you say to that fine offer?'

'And the other bird, what does it look like? Just in case I overlooked it while cleaning out my budgie cage?'

'Very funny, Mr Nevis, but I must tell you, a bird indeed it is. A magnificent specimen of its ilk. The other bird I am looking for could be described as an eagle.'

He was getting too close to the truth.

'So, you want to find this Egyptian falcon figurine and an eagle figurine? Don't tell me you're going to re-establish the Holy Roman Empire, are you?'

That stopped him in his tracks; obviously he'd not considered it as an option.

'Mr Nevis, you amaze me! Not even I had thought of that. But, excellent an idea as it might be, the eagle I am looking for is not related to the falcon figurine. The eagle is in fact imprinted on some US gold coins that went missing back in 1941.'

'So you're nothing more than a treasure hunter?' said Nancy. 'Got your map, doctor? Does X mark the spot?'

'Thank you, Mrs Rafsanjani. The gold coins I'm referring to are part of a collection of gold coins imprinted with eagles. Their rightful owner is eager to get them back. Is that descriptive enough for you, Mr Nevis?

I nodded.

'Well, Mr Nevis, where are they?'

'Flown south for the winter?'

'Now, now, Mr Nevis, we're friends – no need to be sarcastic. I'm offering you a simple business proposition. I'll pay for the coins at the current gold value and take the bird off your hands for, as I said, fifty thousand, in cash. What do you say we shake on the deal?'

I needed time to think. He was fishing; he didn't know what I knew.

'I'm sorry, Doctor. I'd love to oblige, but I just don't have these coins or the bird.'

'Then tell me, Mr Nevis, why are you here – in this house? What has brought you all the way from Eastbourne this very evening? Was it to warn Mr Munroe that I would be paying him a visit?'

I sighed a sigh of relief; he knew nothing about what I knew. I smiled and stretched. 'Doctor, the *Osprey*, the boat where I work and live is a museum piece. I've been tracing its history, and while doing so, I found out that Mr Munroe used to work on her while she worked on the river Clyde, that's all.' Bull's-eye, knocked the conceited pig for six.

'And Lieutenant Hudson, did he work on the boat as well?'

He'd bowled a bouncer. Think fast, Jack! I shrugged and said, 'His name came up while going through the paperwork, something about him being in the navy. I suppose he worked on her after the war. Why?'

'Is that what he told you?'

I shook my head. 'Never talked to him, don't even know if he's still alive.'

'Mrs Rafsanjani, what did Lieutenant Hudson tell you when you went to visit him?'

That'd torn it – how did he know about Nancy's visit?

'Come now, Mrs Rafsanjani. Do you think someone as beautiful as you can wander the streets of Eastbourne and not be noticed? Hanse has been your constant companion for the last couple of weeks.'

So that was it. She hadn't been passing information to Kaufmann at all. He'd simply had Hanse follow her everywhere. Then another thought struck me, had Hanse shot Nancy's husband as well as the detective?

While everyone's attention was directed at her I leapt up, grabbed the whiskey bottle from the table and hit Hanse hard in the face. Being almost empty, and in such a confined space, the bottle didn't have the weight to do any real harm. But it did feel good. Hanse fell back over a coffee table and the momentum of lashing out with the bottle took me after him. In falling, I managed to land with my forearm across his throat. I wasn't able to do any more damage to Hanse as, within seconds, Kaufmann grabbed me from behind and hauled me to my feet.

'Mr Nevis, this will never do, Mrs Rafsanjani might have got hurt in the brawl. You need to be more careful. Do you understand?'

I nodded.

Hanse was tougher than I thought. He got to his feet and came close enough for me to get a whiff his vomit-smelling breath.

'You'll wish you never did that, Nevis,' he said, as he backhanded me across the face with his pistol.

'Hanse, take them to the car. We'll continue our conversation in more comfortable surroundings,' said Kaufman. 'There doesn't appear to be anything of interest here for us after all.'

That at least was good news. Munroe and his daughter could now go about their business in peace without the fear of Kaufmann returning.

It was good to get outside into the fresh night air. I was squashed between Kaufmann and his suitcase in the back, while Nancy sat beside Hanse, who drove. We didn't go very far and ended up driving into a cul-de-sac to what appeared to be a row of abandoned terraced houses, hidden behind scaffolding.

I was bundled out of the car first and pushed up the stairs to the front door of one of the houses. Hanse banged on the door and waited. A few minutes later it creaked open by someone who I took initially to be a watchman, then realised it was my visitor with the cosh. So he was working with Kaufmann. I wondered if Kaufmann realised that his friend was playing solo as well as on the team. We were escorted into the hall, where we waited for Kaufmann to finish his conversation with my night visitor.

'Hanse, take our friends and follow Snyder, he'll show you where you can put them till I'm ready to continue with our little talk.'

We were pushed down a dusty corridor to one of the rooms on the left at the back of the house. It had been a formal room at one time. Now void of any furniture it appeared to be the decorators' store. At least there were a couple of plastic milk crates to sit on. We sat side by side, backs to the wall.

'Mr Nevis, I'm sorry you had to cross swords with Hanse, he's usually a very mild-mannered person. Has the bleeding stopped?'

'I'm a fast healer, Doctor.'

'Good, that's what I like to hear. No need to call a doctor then!' he said, laughing at his own joke.

'You're a brute,' Nancy said to Hanse, as she mopped at the dried blood on my face.

'I'm going to lose this tooth, all because of you,' he said, kicking me in the leg as he continued to spit blood on the floor.

'Is it deep?' Nancy asked me, while dabbing at the cut on my face.

I shook my head and gently pushed her hand away. 'It's fine, no need to fuss.'

'Mr Nevis, we'll leave you two alone to think things over. When you're ready to talk, just shout.'

Hanse gave me a look that said he wasn't finished with me, and shut the door. We could clearly hear the lock click as the key turned.

'What are we going to do, Jack?'

I managed to get to my feet and walk over to the door. I could hear the sound of muffled voices and a radio, coming from a room somewhere further down the corridor. I fumbled in the dark for the light switch and flicked it on. The bulb struggled to push the light out through the months of builders' dust, but it did provide enough light for me to see the chances of making an easy escape were slim. The previous owners had obviously been concerned about burglars; the only window had stout metal bars set into the stone windowsill on the outside. I rummaged round the room for a weapon, something that might help redress the balance of power, but the only thing I found that could pass as a weapon was a broken broom pole.

'Jack, I'm worried, he means what he says,' said Nancy. 'They've already killed twice, what's to stop them killing again? And I don't like the way that Hanse looks at me.'

'It won't come to that,' I said, struggling to believe my own words. But would it? I'd no training in martial arts, and I'd only boxed a bit at school. The only weapon I had to hand was the short length of broken broom pole. To these people, killing was a way of life. What was it the doctor said, *killing is a mere blip in the rhythm of one's day.* I needed to be an interruption to his rhythm, but how? I had Nancy to consider. Then a thought struck me: Nancy, she could be the answer, or at least part of the answer.

I sat down beside her and explained my feeble plan.

'It might work – if he's a typical man. I'll give it a try.'

'But not yet, give them time to finish the whiskey, their brains should be more befuddled by then.'

In the meantime, I pulled off my jacket, shoes and trousers.

'What on earth are you planning to do?' Nancy asked.

'You'll see,' I said, stuffing some of decorators' rags and scrunched-up newspapers into the trouser legs.

'Ah, now I understand,' she said. 'Here, let me help.'

It took us twenty minutes to make a dummy that resembled my body shape. We dragged it over to the far corner of the room and threw one of the small dust sheets I'd found over it. I suppose even I would assume it was me sleeping on the floor in the corner of the room. When we were satisfied the scene was set to our best advantage, I wrapped one of the other dust sheets round my shoulders, sat down beside Nancy and waited for the whiskey to run out.

I waited till I heard a time check on the radio, two o'clock, and figured it was time. I took my place behind the door, broken broom pole at the ready and waited for Nancy to do her bit.

'I'm going to enjoy this,' she whispered to me.

I almost dropped the broom pole to cover my ears, as she yelled, 'Hey, you out there! I need the bathroom!'

155

No response. She stood in front of the door and hammered on it with an old metal paint pot, while yelling. It had the desired effect – Hanse was there in three minutes.

'What you want?'

'I need the bathroom.'

'Pee in the bucket, the doctor said no one gets out of that room till you are ready to talk.'

'But I need the bathroom.'

'So, I said, pee in the bucket.'

'You don't understand. I'm a woman, it's that time of the month.'

I could almost hear him thinking through the door, trying to work out what to do. I tensed as I heard the key turn in the lock.

'Stand well back from the door, I want to see both of you standing at the far end of the room when this door opens, and no tricks, I will shoot if necessary.'

I raised the broom handle above my head. The door swung in slowly as he pushed it with his outstretched leg. All he'd be able to see from the hall light was Nancy standing at the end of the room and the outline of a sleeping body lying on the floor.

'What's up with Romeo?'

'He's sleeping – that beating you gave him did him in.'

Satisfied he was in control of the situation, Hanse stepped into the room. I stepped out from behind the door and hit him over the head as hard as I could.

I was now holding a much shorter section of broken broom handle. Hanse was kneeling on the floor, rocking back and forth in pain, cursing me while holding his scalp and trying to stop the blood from running down his face.

'Face down, hands behind your back,' I said, shoving him face down on the floor with my foot, while trying to sound menacing, but not so loud I'd have Kaufmann and Snyder in here wondering what was going on.

Nancy handed me the strips of torn dust sheet she'd ripped up earlier and I tied Hanse's hands and ankles. Then with great joy I stuffed a piece of rag in his mouth. Next I tied a strip around his face to stop him from pushing the rag out with his tongue and shouting to alert the others. Satisfied that Hanse would not be able to free himself in the near future I put my trousers and shoes back on and picked up my jacket from the floor.

'What now?' asked Nancy.

'We leave, quickly and quietly.'

I grabbed the protesting Hanse by the ankles and started to drag him across the floor, away from the door. As I did, I heard the sound of something falling from his pocket. I unceremoniously let go of his ankles and leaned down to see what had made the noise. It was his pistol, the nasty black one he'd hit me in the face with. I went to pick it up then stopped.

'Nancy, any of those rags you cut up left?'

'Here, this do?' she said, passing me a handkerchief-sized piece of cloth.

I reached down, wrapped Hanse's gun in the rag and placed it in my jacket pocket. I then resumed dragging his protesting body over to the far corner of the room where I threw a dust sheet over him.

'Now do we leave?' asked Nancy.

'Now we leave.'

Hoping that no one had heard the scuffle with Hanse, I peeked out into the hall. No sight of any thugs waiting to pounce on us. I closed and locked the door behind us, pocketing the key. We turned right and headed for the front door. I put my hand on the handle to open the door and saw the door was bolted as well as deadlocked, that cost us precious seconds. A noise distracted me and I turned and saw the shadow of someone coming out of the room at the far end of the corridor; it was Snyder. I heard Snyder's voice. 'How should I know what's happened to him? Am I his mother's keeper?'

157

'*Brother*, you dummkopf! It's brother, not mother!' shouted Kaufmann, as he barged through the door and into the unlit hallway.

I motioned Nancy to keep quiet and head for the stairs. I gestured up the stairs and loped after her. We stopped to catch our breath on the landing as Kaufmann and Snyder hammered on the door to the room we'd just vacated. All was quiet for a minute, then they discovered Hanse was locked in the room. It must have been the bulk of Kaufmann that got the door open; Snyder just didn't have the same mass. I couldn't make out what was said, but figured Kaufmann was really mad at us getting away. We listened to their footsteps as they searched room by room and realised any minute now the search would extend up the stairs. I pressed the light button on my car key-fob and saw by its dim light that we were in what once must have been a large reception room, now being converted into two separate bedrooms. I groped for a light switch and saw bare wires sticking out of the wall.

I shone the dim light of the fob into the room and saw, extending all the way across, a new stud wall partially covered with plasterboard. I motioned Nancy to follow me through the doorway in the new wall. We got behind the plasterboarded section just in time to see the beam of a flashlight scan across the floor.

I bent down and quietly picked up a piece of four by two timber and waited. Once again it was Hanse who got poleaxed. We were getting good at dragging unconscious bodies across floors. We dropped him behind a workbench and listened for any other footsteps. Next was Snyder; he was panting like a twenty a day smoker. Once again I took up my position behind the door and waited. He must have been a really heavy smoker as he stopped to catch his breath just the other side of the opening. Come on my beauty, I thought, just another couple of steps and its bye-bye birdie.

'Snyder,' yelled Kaufmann, 'where's Hanse?'

'Isn't he with you?'

'No, I sent him upstairs. There's no sign of our lovebirds down here, they must be upstairs somewhere. Hanse, where the hell are you?'

The sound of Kaufmann's voice must have penetrated the unconscious mind of Hanse for at that moment, half-conscious, he tried to stand. In doing so he pushed over a pile of wood offcuts.

'Hanse, is that you?' yelled Kaufmann again. 'Where are you?'

'Upstairs. They're up here somewhere, the shits hit me over the head again.'

We stood deathly still in the darkness as Hanse, illuminated by Snyder's torch, staggered past us and out of the room.

'Hanse,' said Snyder, 'wait here by the door. I'm going to check out the other rooms.'

Now we were really in trouble. To get out of the room we would have to get past Hanse, who was leaning on the doorframe holding his head and quietly cursing. Snyder was only a couple of rooms away, but at least we had the darkness on our side.

I pressed the key-fob's on button and carefully scanned the room. The only substantial item in the room was the workbench, and directly above I saw what looked like a hatch into the loft. I got down on my hands and knees, motioned to Nancy to follow me, and crawled across the floor to the workbench. I climbed onto it and reached up to the hatch; no good, I was at least a foot short of reaching it with my hands.

'We need something to climb on,' I whispered. 'See what's over by the far wall.'

I waited patiently realising that if any of them shone a torch into the room I would make a perfect target.

'Here, will this do?' asked Nancy.

It was another plastic milk crate. Why would builders want plastic milk crates? I wondered briefly. I could hear footsteps approaching the room. I placed the milk crate on the workbench and gave Nancy my hand to help her up, then had to hold her round the waist, lifting her up till she could grab the hatch opening.

'You okay up there?' I asked, in a hushed voice.

'Yes, I'm fine. Hurry, they could be here any moment.'

I stepped up onto the crate and reached for the hatch opening. Thankfully I was quite fit and with a bit of a struggle managed to pull myself up into the loft. I glanced back down wishing there was some way of taking the crate with us. But without a piece of rope it wasn't going to happen. Shining the fob-light round the loft it was obvious that it had been used as a room at one time and the rafters were boarded over. Although we were out of immediate danger, we were now more trapped than when we first made our escape.

In the centre of the loft we were able to stand upright. With the use of the dim light of the key-fob, I took stock of our options. We had none – we were trapped.

'What now, Jack?' asked Nancy.

'We wait, and hope they assume we've somehow escaped and go looking for us elsewhere.' I sat down to consider our situation.

Nancy stood. 'Can I borrow the key-fob?'

'Yeah, why?'

'Just thought I'd have a look around.'

I handed it to her. 'Don't go wandering off too far.'

'I'm not going anywhere, just want to see what's at the other end of the loft.'

'Okay.'

I watched the light gradually diminish as she made her way to the end of the loft, then it disappeared. I heard a crash and anxiously waited for the light to reappear. Then I got worried. 'Nancy, where are you? I can't see you, are you hurt?'

No answer.

'Nancy – where are you?' I whispered, as loudly as I dared.

Still no answer. I carefully groped my way across the floor to where I'd last seen the light, but there was no sign of her. Then I realised I wasn't in complete darkness; above me was a skylight. But where was Nancy? I continued towards the end of the loft; it took a turn to the right and I tripped over the same pile of suitcases that she must have, falling flat on my face.

'Quiet, you'll give us away,' said Nancy, from somewhere in the darkness.

'Where are you?'

'Here, behind you.'

I turned and looked for the tell-tale illumination of the key-fob.

'I can't see you. Where are you?'

'Up here.'

I made my way back, over the suitcases, to where her voice emanated. 'Flash the key-fob, I can't see you.'

'You won't, I'm up here.'

I looked up and saw her silhouette framed in an open skylight.

'What are you doing out there? It's dangerous!'

'Not as dangerous as staying inside. Come on, we can escape this way.'

As I reached up for the edge of the opening, I saw with horror a torch shine directly up through the ceiling hatch, Worse still, someone's hands were gripping the edge. I walked quickly over and, with malice, stamped down hard on the fingers. I heard a muffled curse then the sound of someone falling on top of someone else. I chanced a peek over the edge of the hatch and saw that it had been Hanse's fingers I'd stood on. He'd let go and fallen back on top of Snyder, who'd fallen on top of Kaufmann. I would have liked to stay and watch their discomfort, but Nancy and freedom were waiting. I crept back to the skylight and reached to pull myself up. It was then I realised what Nancy meant by our escaping this way. The roof was in the process of being retiled and where we were seated the tiles had not been replaced and the new

161

battens provided us with a safe way to clamber down onto the scaffolding.

'You are a smart cookie,' I said.

'I've been right to the end and it looks like there is a ladder all the way to the ground.'

I took one last look inside the loft and saw the beam of a flashlight shining up through the hatch again.

'Let's go,' I said, 'it won't take them long to figure out where we've gone.'

Fortunately, or unfortunately, it was a moonlit night. We were able to work our way along the scaffolding planks to the end where Nancy had seen the ladder. All went well till we reached the last stage of scaffold. We were about eight feet off the ground and found the roofers had tied a scaffold board to the last section of ladder. It was tricky to slide down and hold on to the sides of the ladder, but we managed.

'What now, Jack?'

'The car – can't be too far away, it only took Hanse a few minutes to drive us here.'

Nancy came over, put her arms around my waist, reached up and kissed me. 'I love you, Jack Nevis. Let's get out of here – now!'

My pulse was racing as we worked our way past piles of building debris until I saw what I was looking for. It was a passageway that ran between the houses and out into the street at the front. Caution made me stop before we exited. I put my hands to my lips and motioned Nancy to stay back in the shadows. When I looked out into the street there was no sign of any of them; they could be still working their way through the house, or maybe they were already on the roof looking for us.

I beckoned Nancy to follow, and within ten minutes we were well away from the immediate danger. Now all we had to do was blend in with the crowds as we made our way back to the car. Problem was, at three o'clock in the morning, the only crowd was a solitary milkman doing his rounds.

It was further and took us longer than I'd figured to reach the car. When we did, I realised it was going to be more difficult getting away than I first supposed. Standing beside the car, talking on his radio, was a policeman. We waited in the shadows to see what he would do. We didn't have to wait long. He stuck what looked like a parking ticket on the windscreen, then got back in his car and left. I waited till I was sure he wasn't going to return, and sauntered over to see what he'd stuck on. It wasn't a parking ticket as I'd first assumed, it was instead a *Police Aware, Do Not Move* notice.

I took out the car keys and unlocked the door. I waved to Nancy that all was safe, and to join me.

My earlier plan was to get to the car, drive to Munroe's grandson's, and tell them it was now safe to go back home. Though now I wasn't so sure about flying back to London. As soon as Kaufmann realised we'd escaped, he'd head first to the airport, probably hoping to persuade us, by force probably, to go with him. But to do that he'd need bait. I shook my head. Munroe and daughter were still a target.

'Where are we headed?' Nancy asked.

'Straight to the airport, but first we need to fill the tank with petrol. I'm not going to pay for the car hire company to fill it up.'

'What about Mr Munroe and Agnes? Shouldn't we tell them what's happened?'

I was about to say I'd phone them, but realised I didn't have the grandson's phone number, or my phone with the number in the memory.

'All right, we'll go there first.'

I parked the car round the corner from John Wood Street and walked up the stairs to the grandson's flat.

It took several rings on the bell before a very suspicious voice asked through the closed and locked front door, 'Who's there? What do you want?'

'Mr Munroe, it's Jack Nevis. We need to talk to your grandfather.'

'It's four o'clock! Come back later, he's sleeping.'

'No good, we must warn him of the danger.'

'Oh, all right, just a minute.'

We stood on the landing while the front door was unbolted.

'Come in. Agnes has gone to wake him.'

We sat and waited while Agnes woke her father.

'Sorry to wake you at this hour, Mr Munroe. But I'm afraid the doctor is on the war path.'

While Agnes made us tea, and much needed bacon butties, I explained what had happened during the previous four hours and that he and his daughter were still in danger.

'I'll drive us all back to see Jenny,' said the grandson.'

'Jenny?' I queried.

'Father's sister, she lives in Inverness.'

'Brilliant idea, but you need to be gone as soon as possible.'

Nancy and I helped them down the stairs with their cases and into the car. I relaxed when I watched them turn right at the bottom of John Wood Street and head for the motorway and safety.

11

Colintraive

We got back in the car and drove up the M8 towards the airport. We left the motorway at the airport sign and drove into the nearest petrol station. As I walked into the shop to pay, I glanced at one of the redtop newspapers on the stand by the door. There I was, not in full colour, but certainly recognisable. It was a copy of the picture in the *Herald* of several weeks earlier. The headline said I was wanted for questioning with regards to the deaths of an American and an Afghan in Eastbourne. The broadsheets were more reticent in accusing me, just mentioned the two deaths in Eastbourne and the fact the police had not been able to locate me for further questioning. I wondered if I should turn myself in.

'What time is our flight?' Nancy asked, as I did up my seatbelt.

'It's not.'

'Cancelled?'

I explained about the newspaper and the fact the police were now looking for me.

'Shouldn't you turn yourself in?'

'Not just yet. I need time to think and do something to stop Kaufmann.'

But just what could I do to stop him? I didn't even know where he was at that moment.

'Any plans in that head of yours?'

'We need somewhere to hide out till I can see the wood from the trees.'

'What do you propose?'

'A quiet hotel, somewhere off the beaten track, somewhere the police or Kaufmann would never think to look for us.'

'And where would that be?'

'First, we should return the car. Be best if you did that.'

'Why?'

'Because, my dear, it's not you they are looking for.'

'But the car's in your name.'

'Not an issue. This is Scotland – there must be thousands of men with the name Nevis. I'll drive us into the car park, you take the keys in. If they say anything, just point to me and say I'm not well, and need fresh air. Joke about celebrating too much last night. I'll mope around outside the office and try to look the part.'

'Okay, I'll give it a go.'

All went well with the drop off. Then, feigning a desperate hurry to catch a flight, we cadged a lift to the terminal from a passing shuttle bus.

'Follow me, my dear.'

'Where to?'

'The entrance I want,' I said as we walked down the row of entrance doorways, 'is this one on the end.'

'Why?'

'Starbucks is directly inside on the left.'

'I see, I think.'

Trying to not look up and into the CCTV cameras, we walked over to the Starbucks coffee counter.

'What would you like?' I asked.

'I'll have whatever you're having.'

I ordered two americanos and a couple of cinnamon rolls. The coffee came in paper cups, just what I needed. I didn't intend to hang about.

'Aren't we taking a risk?' Nancy asked, as I pointed to a seat at the back of the café.

'What do you mean?'

'Sitting here drinking coffee?'

'We're here for a reason.'

'What's that?'

'I don't know about you but I'm skint, and before this adventure is over we're going to need some cash for food and accommodation. Also, I want to give the impression that we've just arrived by plane.'

'That makes sense – I think,' she said, with a quizzical expression.

'So, my fine friend, the closest place I can think of to find a cash point is here in the airport.'

'Is that what I am?'

'Sorry, you lost me on that?'

'Me. I'm just your fine friend? I thought I was more than that.'

'Of course you are, it's just – huh – look, can we discuss this later? We're in a hurry.'

'Sorry, shouldn't put you on the spot like that. How can I help?'

'It's okay. If I give you a couple of my cards, would you take out the maximum and I'll meet you back here?' I said, pointing to the door we'd just came in. 'And bring your coffee cup with you.'

'But why don't you take out the money yourself?'

'I would normally, but in case it's slipped your attention, airport terminals are full of CCTV cameras and this one is no different. Remember, it's me they are looking for, you'll be less conspicuous.' But that wasn't necessarily so, I mused – she'd stand out in any crowd.

I handed her three of my debit cards. 'The pins are all the same: one-three-two-three.'

She looked at me and smiled. 'Are you sure you can trust me not to run off with the family fortune?'

'Of course I trust you, I'd trust you with my life. Now hurry before someone recognises me.'

'Is that likely? You haven't slept properly or shaved for two days.'

'Going off me?'

'No, of course not. It's just you don't look much like the picture in the newspaper that man is reading.'

I looked in the direction she indicated at the newspaper, then at my reflection in the window. She was right, I didn't look like myself. I relaxed one notch on the worry throttle.

I looked back at my reflection and smiled. I really did mean it: I could trust her with my life. I sidled over to the exit and waited for her to return.

'I took out nine hundred,' she said, passing me the cash and my cards.

'Thanks, this should keep us incommunicado for a couple of days.'

'It would keep me and the children going for a couple of months. Are you really that rich?'

'What gave you that idea?'

'I have one bank account where my money goes; by the end of the month it's all spent.'

'For your information, my lass, one of those cards is my personal account, the other two are for my business and, like you, at the end of each month they are almost empty.'

'Oh, something else we have in common. I like that.'

I estimated where the middle of the bunch of notes was and handed Nancy half.

'Paying me off?'

'No – you silly goose – this is just in case we are separated.'

'Or get pick-pocketed?'

'There is that. Now, let's get going.'

Cups in hand, Nancy pulling my small overnight case, we headed out the door to the taxi rank.

'What's the plan?'

'Many years ago my parents took us to Scotland on holiday. We stayed at a small B&B in a village called Colintraive, I thought it would be a good place to stay till we can figure out how to extricate ourselves from the mess we're currently in.'

'So how are we going to get there?'

'There's a taxi rank just outside the arrivals area.'

'Won't that cost a lot?'

'It's just to get us to the station.'

'You think of everything.'

I hoped I was thinking enough to keep us out of the police and Kaufmann's clutches.

'Thanks. I plan to get us to Wemyss Bay by train, then ferry to Rothesay. When we get there, I'll call the B&B. If they're not able to help, I'm sure we can find a suitable hotel in Rothesay.'

'Why, Mr Nevis, are you asking me to run away with you?'

'I suppose I am. Do you mind?'

'I don't know – do I have a choice?'

I thought about our present situation and said, 'I'm sorry, Nancy, I shouldn't have got you involved.'

'That's all right, I was involved the day I married Achmed.'

I smiled. 'Thanks for being so understanding.'

I opened the door of one of the waiting taxis. 'Can you take us to Paisley Central, please?'

It felt strange buying two singles to Wemyss Bay. Firstly, a single ticket meant a one-way journey, and with Kaufmann looking for us it could be just that if he caught up with us. Secondly, I was running away with a married woman – well, technically she was now a widow. I supposed I could accept that. She'd been married twice, once legitimately and her second one illegitimately, with a bigamist husband now presumably lying in the Eastbourne morgue. But that wasn't really the cause of my uneasiness, there was still the memory of Katie floating just under the surface of my consciousness.

We'd done something similar once. I'd found a cheap holiday in France and we'd dashed off on the train to London, then caught the Eurostar to Paris. It was our first time away alone, not even our parents knew where we were – caused quite a ruckus when we returned.

'Penny for your thoughts?' said Nancy, as the train approached Port Glasgow.

I jerked to attention, hoping that none of Kaufmann's thugs would be waiting on the platform. 'Keep an eye out for Kaufmann's people, they may be watching the station.'

'But that would be to see if we get on, not for us to be already on the train.'

'All the same, let's be careful.'

We didn't see anyone looking for us on the platform when the train pulled in. It stopped to let off some passengers, then, as the train left the station, standing at the foot of the footbridge was Hanse. He was deep in conversation with Snyder.

'Do you think they saw us?'

'I don't know, I don't think so,' I said, without conviction.

I half expected them to come running after us, then realised it would not make any difference – all the doors were electronically locked. They couldn't get on the train even if they wanted to.

Outside Port Glasgow the train switched onto the branch line for Wemyss Bay. We had only got minutes to spare between the train arriving and the ferry departing for Rothesay. We followed the crowds to the ticket office. Then once again following the crowd, we went on board and climbed up onto the upper deck to watch as the ferry left.

What was it about sea air? I pondered. Its unique smell was tied inexorably to childhood memories of our family seaside holidays. Sandcastles on the beach made from upturned gaily-coloured pails, looking for sea creatures in tide pools. Ice-cream cones with chocolate flakes sticking up like truncated telephone poles. Fish and chips with lashings of salt and vinegar, and sleeping in an overly hot and stuffy caravan.

'Hungry?' I asked.

Nancy nodded. 'Could do with another cup of coffee and breakfast if it's available.'

We went into the lounge and stood in line at the counter. 'What do you want to eat?' I asked.

'Not sure. What are those round pies?'

'I think they're called Scots pies.'

'Sounds fine, I'll have one with my coffee.'

We found a table in front of the window and, while we ate, watched as the ferry made its way across the Firth of Clyde.

'This is just like a mini-cruise,' said Nancy.

'Sailing down the Clyde on the steam-powered paddle-steamers used to be the highlight for many Scots families on weekends and summer holidays.'

'I saw a news item a few months ago about the *Waverley*, something about it being the only remaining steam-powered working paddle-steamer in the UK.'

'I think it used to sail round the UK coast, stopping off at seaside towns that still had piers big enough for it to tie up against safely.'

'Does it still do that?'

'No idea. The commentator in the film I watched said the people were off on their holidays, "*going doon the watter*". Apparently in the days when pubs in Scotland were not allowed to open on Sundays, the only way to legally get an alcoholic drink was to be a traveller. So the enterprising Scots figured out that if they went for a Sunday afternoon sail down the Clyde, they could drink to their hearts' content. Which many of them did, thus creating the phrase "steaming drunk".'

'Now you can get drunk any day of the week you want. So sad.'

'With so many of the passengers drinking on the trip, by the time they reached Rothesay they all needed to relieve themselves, thus making famous the recently restored Victorian toilets on Rothesay pier.'

'Where did you hear that bit about the toilets?'

'Over there on the wall – there's a notice about it by the tourist board. It now costs more than a penny to spend a penny! They've become an actual working museum.'

The journey was short and forty minutes later we were standing on the pier at Rothesay, queuing up, like so many before us, to use the toilets.

'What do you think?' I asked Nancy, when she came out.

'You were right when you described them as a working museum. I've never seen, or used, a public toilet that looked and smelled so fresh. Your side the same?'

'Have a look, last person has just left.'

'It looks brand new – difficult to realise it's as old as it is.'

I nodded.

'What now, my illustrious tour guide?'

'Would madam like to see the pyramids, or flaunt with the natives in the Kasbah?'

'How about a hotel, a bath, a sumptuous meal, and a good night's sleep?'

Since Kaufmann had liberated my phone, it was then I realised just how accustomed to using it I had become. In normal times I would have just googled the information about the B&B and then called them.

'For that we will require the tourist information office, then a taxi.'

It turned out that my childhood memories of a dainty, whitewashed B&B were actually of a small hotel with just four bedrooms. The tourist information lady said it was a short taxi ride and an even shorter ferry one across the loch, back on to the mainland. She called the hotel and was able to ascertain they had a room available. I asked for it to be held for us.

First, I thought breakfast was in order before going to the hotel.

'Fancy something to eat?'

'Not at the moment. In case it's slipped your mind, we need some clean clothes, especially since the ones we are wearing have been over the roofs of a building site! I don't know about you, but

I could do with some fresh underwear, and I should let Sarah know where I am.'

'You're right.' I said running my hand through my hair and trying to shake out the dust.

Suitable clothes purchased, we took the taxi and ferry rides and were soon standing in the lobby of the hotel from my memories.

'Mr Nevis, is it?'

'Yes.'

'And for how many nights would you be wanting the room?'

I looked at Nancy; she shrugged.

'Could we say three nights?'

'That will take you to Thursday night. That will be fine, we're fully booked this weekend,' she replied, handing me the key. 'Your room is at the top of the stairs on the right. Just ask at the bar if you need anything, my name's Moira, I'm the manager.'

Top of the stairs meant no lift and the spiral stairs creaked under my weary legs. I opened the door to our room and froze. Facing me was a double bed.

'What is it? What's the matter?' asked Nancy.

I grinned and nodded to the bed.

'Great,' she said, walking into the room and sitting on the edge of the bed. She bounced up and down a couple of times. 'Very comfortable, we should be able to get a good night's sleep.'

She lay back on the pillow, yawned twice and within minutes was fast asleep. I pulled the case into the room, then shut and locked the door. It wasn't till I heard her slow, steady, breathing that I realised how long it had been since I'd slept properly. I went round to the other side of the bed and pulled the duvet over her. Grabbing a spare blanket from the wardrobe, I sat in the chair in front of the window, trying to figure out what to do next. I kept looking out at the ferry as it plied its way back and forth across the narrow channel. I half expected at any moment to see Kaufmann and gang emerge, though I had no idea what sort of vehicle they would be driving.

◆

I tried to wake but my brain was in a muddle. How did the duvet get on top of me? I could hear the sound of the shower running in the bathroom. Was it Katie? Then I remembered where I was, and who I was with. I reached over to pick up my phone to see what time it was then remembered I no longer had a phone.

Nancy stepped out of the bathroom wearing only a towel, her hair wrapped like a turban with another towel. She stood rubbing it into her hair and looked at me.

'You awake?'

I nodded.

'How did you sleep?'

'Confused dot me.'

'Shower's good and hot, dinner's in half an hour.'

'What time is it?'

'Five-thirty. You snore.'

'I was tired! Do you?'

'You'll have to find that out for yourself!' She went back into the bathroom singing that song. I listened intently as she sang and realised she was singing about us, or more specifically about me.

> What if he's the one, can this love last
> Will his love fill this cold and empty heart
> For if his love is true, the past can fly
> And I'll dream again the dreams gone by.
>
> When the gentle breath of spring, warms the winter air
> I'll hold you in my arms, and dream without a care.

More earworms for me listen to.

I threw off the duvet and saw she'd removed my shoes. I sat up and stared out the window. The ferry was loading, getting ready to make its way back to the island. I watched it make two crossings before Nancy emerged from the bathroom, fully dressed. She was wearing the new jeans and top she'd purchased earlier that day. I liked what I saw. I noticed she'd moved her wedding band back

174

to the ring finger of her left hand. Now why had she done that? Ever since she heard that Achmed was dead she'd been wearing it on her right hand, now it was back on the left. Was she embarrassed to be with me, or proud?

'Bathroom's available, come on sleepy head, I'm hungry,' she said, throwing a dry towel at me.

I grabbed a change of clothes and headed for the shower. It felt good to stand under the hot water but, no matter how I scrubbed, I couldn't wash away the feeling I was cheating on Katie. I tried reasoning with myself that she'd been dead for several years. I was single, and so was Nancy. Why shouldn't I have a new relationship? But Nancy's children – what would they think about someone new in their lives? I hadn't even met them; all I knew were their names. Then a thought struck me – did they know what was happening to their mother? I got out of the shower, dried and dressed.

Nancy was sitting in front of the mirror brushing her hair. '

'Shouldn't we try to get in touch with your sister? Your children need to know what's going on.'

'I already did.'

'When? And how?'

'Earlier today in Rothesay, while you were in the changing room trying out your new trousers.'

'And the how bit?'

'My phone.'

'I thought they took it from you?'

'They did, but when you were fighting with Hanse I saw it sitting on the table, so when Kaufmann was busy dragging you off, I picked it up and stuffed it in my pocket.'

That wasn't all that we'd managed to take with us. I still had the pistol, though for the life of me I didn't know quite what to do with it. Should I just chuck it in the loch, or hand it to the police? If I dropped it in the loch it would be gone for ever, but it still had Hanse's fingerprints and DNA on the handle. Should the police do a ballistics check on it, would they find it was the same pistol that killed Achmed? No, I'd have to hold on to it, it was the best way of clearing Nancy from having killed her husband.

'Why didn't you tell me you had your phone? It would have been easier to call the hotel.'

'You never asked. I just assumed you knew what you were doing.'

'How are they?'

'Who – my children?'

I nodded.

'Missing their mum.'

'What did you tell them?'

'I said I was away on a business trip and should be home by the weekend.'

'Good thinking, let's hope we *can* be home for the weekend.'

'You ready for dinner? I'm starving – two cups of coffee and a Scots pie is not enough to keep me going.'

We were shown to a table by the window. It was just like we had been invited for a home-cooked meal. Being spoiled and made to feel like we were honoured guests was just what our tired bodies and minds needed.

I watched with pleasure as Nancy scanned the menu. She was licking her lips and making little, squealing, happy noises. Like a child being shown the ice-cream menu at a Baskins Robbins for the first time.

'Have you decided, Mrs Nevis?' asked the waitress.

There it was again: Mrs Nevis. Why didn't Nancy correct her?

'Could I have the langoustines, please?'

'And to follow?'

'It's got to be the rib-eye steak.'

'How would you like it cooked?'

'Medium rare, please.'

'And Mr Nevis?'

'Are the king scallops really fished locally?'

176

'Oh, yes, hand-dived by local divers.'

'Then I'll start with the king scallops, and could I have the steak and Guinness pie?'

'Certainly. Have you decided on the wine?'

I was too tired to go through the list, so said, 'We'll take whatever the chef recommends.'

'Oh, he'll just love that. He's always saying he wished people would ask him, especially since he's doing all the cooking. Anything else? Would you like water with your meal?'

'Yes, please,' said Nancy.

'I'll be back in a minute with your drinks.'

'This is fun,' said Nancy. 'I've never had an adventure like this before.'

An adventure I suppose it was, complete with the damsel in distress and gangsters out to do us an injury in the attempt to get what they wanted.

'You like adventures? I asked.

'Don't really know. I suppose being married to Jack was an adventure in wondering if I'd ever see him again.'

'Can't imagine what that was like. When I was married to Katie, we went everywhere together.'

'When Jack asked me to marry him I was over the moon, a starry-eyed teenager of nineteen. I had no idea what army life was about. My friends said not to do it because too many soldiers get wounded, lose limbs, or even killed.'

'Not all soldiers get injured.'

The conversation was interrupted by the waitress bringing our drinks. 'I'll be right out with your starters.'

'Thanks.'

'I knew about the possibility of him getting wounded, but thought he'd be one of the lucky ones,' continued Nancy. 'Probably what all soldiers' wives think.'

'I suppose that's a sort of self-preservation motive.'

'Makes sense. As the wife of an active soldier I was so naïve. I had never even been to an army base. My only experience of army life was watching a BBC television show, I think it was called *New Recruits*. It looked just like any other job to me. The dying bit never crossed my mind.'

'Shall I pour your wine?' asked the waitress.

'Yes, please.'

'I remember a friend who'd been in the navy saying something about it being just like any other job, except you got paid to travel.'

'The day I found out about Jack, I'd just come back from the shops. I'd been looking for wallpaper for the twins' room. Jack said we'd redecorate it when he was next home on leave. As I walked up from the station, a hearse drove past and I froze. I suddenly just knew something terrible had happened to Jack.'

'Was the hearse part of a military funeral?'

'Don't know,' she said, shaking her head slowly. 'It was just a hearse, but I had one of those feelings that something had happened.'

'Sort of a second sense?'

She nodded. 'I remember opening the front door and the phone ringing. I tried to pick up the receiver, but my hands were shaking so badly I dropped it three times. Finally, when I got it to my ear, it was Sarah. She'd just heard that there had been a massive explosion outside the base where Jack was stationed and the news report went on to say there were many civilian casualties.'

'What did you do?'

'I said thank you for calling and put the receiver back down.'

'You were in shock.'

'Maybe. Later that day there was a knock at the door but I didn't answer it. I thought if I didn't go and open the door, it would all be fine. Jack would be all right and it would have been a mistake, a mix-up of identities. Why put myself through the anguish? I asked myself.'

'And you went through all of that on your own? You had no one to help?'

'The police called Sarah and she let them in. She found me on the bedroom floor, holding one of Jack's sweaters and bawling my eyes out.'

'Did you have anyone else – other than your sister, to help?'

'The army was wonderful during all the repatriation, and of course Sarah was a true friend. She watched the children while I fell apart, and then helped put me back together again.'

I think the waitress had heard part of the conversation and didn't want to disturb us, so she quietly, without a fuss, placed our starters in front of us then made a discrete retreat to the kitchen.

'I went to the airfield and watched them bring Jack home. I so wanted to run up to the coffin and tell him I was here, that all would be fine. I wanted to tell him about the twins' room and what colour paint I'd chosen. But deep down inside I realised this was welcome home and – goodbye.'

'I know the feeling. I kept expecting Katie to barge in the front door, arms full of shopping and jabbering on about what the children had been up to that day.'

'For the first few months I kept catching myself thinking he was still on tour, and would be home soon. We used to catch up with the occasional phone call, but after – after– there were no more phone calls.'

'For the first few days I kept picking up the phone to check that it was still working. I'd catch myself looking at the clock, thinking Katie will be home soon'

'I thought the trip to Afghanistan to the commemoration ceremony would put things to rest, but it just brought back too many memories. I suppose I was vulnerable, and Achmed recognised this and took advantage of the situation.'

'Did it take long for you to get over the initial pain?'

She nodded. 'It was hard at first, but gradually life went on, one day at a time. But it didn't stop me from watching the news headlines each hour, for months after.'

'For me it was all over in a flash.'

'What do you mean?'

'What I mean is, I saw a flash of headlights as the truck rode over the centre divider and hit us head on. The next thing I remember was three days' later when I woke in hospital and the doctor, in her best bedside manner, told me I was the only survivor.'

'We have a lot in common, haven't we?'

'How was your steak, Mrs Nevis?' asked the waitress, as she cleared the plates.

I expected Nancy to blush, but realised she was getting used to the idea of us being a couple.

'Absolutely lovely, thanks, just the way I like it.'

I don't think I'd ever had such excellent service in a restaurant before. The food arrived and the empty plates departed, wine glasses were filled when required, all without any interruption to our conversation.

'Would you like to see the dessert menu?'

I looked at Nancy and knew the answer to that one right away.

'Yes, please, and could we have coffee?'

'Certainly. Desserts this evening are: chocolate fudge cake, sticky toffee or hot croissant puddings.'

Nancy chose the sticky toffee, while I had just got room for a couple of scoops of ice cream.

We finished our meal and walked through into the bar.

'Yes, sir? Can I get you something to drink?'

'Nancy, what would you like?'

'Could I have a – do you have Baileys?'

'And sir?'

'Jack Daniels, with ice, please.'

We took our drinks and went and sat by the fire.

'It's been quite a day! Can't remember ever having so much fun,' Nancy said.

'You call that fun? Wouldn't want to share a bad day with you – no that's not really true, I think I could share any day with you, no matter how bad it was.'

'Thanks. I think I could share all my days with you.'

'Does that mean we're dating?'

'Could be. I'll keep you posted.'

'Cheeky! Have you thought about what's next? I don't suppose we can just fly home as though nothing has happened.'

'No, I suppose we can't.'

'So, what are we going to do?'

'If I had my phone I could call the detective in charge and explain what's happened to us.'

'Why don't you? We have my phone.'

'But not Sergeant Street's number, and I can't imagine calling 999 or 101 and trying to get them to forward a message.'

'There must be someone you could call? Someone who you can trust?'

'How about your sister, Sarah? She'll know the detective in charge, maybe she's got her number.'

'It's a bit late, but I'll give her a try.'

I watched the fire consume another log as Nancy called and chatted with Sarah.

'Any luck?' I asked, as she hung up.

'No, she remembered there was a woman police officer, but has no idea how to get in touch with her. Can you think of anyone else? Someone who knows the sergeant?'

I had a moment of inspiration. 'I just might know someone.'

'Who?'

'Remember me saying I was trying to trace the history of the *Osprey*?'

'Yes, of course I do. I was with you.'

'Well, the day the investigator was found dead on board I mentioned to the sergeant I was trying to find out about the boat's history and she said she knew someone who might be able to help.'

'Who was it?'

'A guy called Nathan Greyspear. I think he's got something to do with boating, maybe someone in the family owns the company. It was him who put me on to Munroe.'

'Great, do you have his number?'

I shook my head.

'If he's got something to do with the boat building company, maybe someone at the head office will know how to get in touch with him?'

'That might work if we have the office number.'

'Google it. Here, use my phone, the battery's still got a charge.'

I googled Greyspear boats and found to my surprise that not only did Nathan Greyspear have something to do with the company – he owned it.

'What now?' asked Nancy.

'Bit late to call this evening, I'll call first thing in the morning.'

'Wonder where the doctor is? Be good to know he's not going to come barging in the door at any moment.'

'We can! Why didn't I think of that before.'

'Think of what?'

'*Where's my phone?* – that's a Samsung app. All I need to do is log into my account and ask the app to tell me where my phone is. Kaufmann has my phone, so wherever my phone is, he is. Can I borrow your phone for a minute?'

'Yes, here.'

I logged into my account and pressed the *Where's my phone?* button.'

'Well, what does it say?'

'He's still in Port Glasgow, probably wondering where we and Munroe have got to. At least Munroe's safe as long as he stays away, and we should be safe as long as we keep our heads down.'

'Could I have another drink?' Nancy asked, holding up her empty glass.

I returned from the bar to see her staring into the fire.

'Here's your drink. Are you all right? You look far away.'

'So much has happened these last few days. Seems that it was ages ago that Achmed showed up and made me bring you my grandfather's guitar. Yet it was only last week.'

'It was Sunday morning for me when this adventure started.'

'When you found the dead man in your workshop?'

I nodded. 'So much in such a little time.' I smiled, and wondered what sort of song Dizzy would concoct if he knew what had happened.

'What's funny?'

I told Nancy about Dizzy and his weird ideas for songs.

'I'd like to meet him someday.'

'Stick around and you probably will.'

Nancy drained her glass and yawned.

'Tired?'

'Yes, that nap we had this afternoon wasn't enough. I need a full night's sleep to recharge.'

I crunched on my remaining ice cube as I followed her up the stairs. I unlocked the door and followed her into the room.

'Be right out,' she said, as she entered the bathroom.

I waited patiently for her to come out, feeling like a groom on his first night with his new bride.

She came out wearing my new shirt. The image of her of her with the sleeves and cuffs flapping around her hands and arms reminded me of a scene in a movie I'd long forgotten. Barbara Streisand in *Funny Girl*. Nancy walked over to the bed, threw the blankets back, and climbed in. She pulled the covers up over her, snuggled down and yawned. This was my cue to get ready, but I felt a bit awkward – I didn't wear pyjamas.

I was fumbling around in the case wondering what to do. I turned round to say something and saw she was already asleep. I sighed and was annoyed at myself for feeling relieved. I had a long, hot shower, changed into some fresh clothes and once more picked up the spare blanket and took my place in the chair by the window.

I was used to sitting in the wheelhouse of the *Osprey* at night and watching the marina scene as the sun set and night lights took over, illuminating the harbour. This was different; apart from the occasional car headlights, and a couple of navigation buoys on the loch, all was total darkness.

I don't know how long I sat there, wondering just what I'd got us into, and how I was going to extricate us from the mess. At least the doctor was nowhere near. But where was he? Surely not on the way back to the *Osprey* again.

◆

'You sat up all night?'

I opened my eyes. She was standing in front of me, staring into my face.

'I – I thought it best. I wanted to be ready should the doctor show up unexpectedly.'

'You're blushing. You really are old-fashioned, aren't you?'

'I'm sorry, it was –'

'Talking about Katie last night? Too many memories?'

I nodded.

'That's all right, I understand. It just makes me love you all the more.'

'Hungry?' I asked, trying to change the subject.

'I'll get dressed and meet you downstairs.'

◆

I made my way down the stairs and into the dining room.

'Good morning Mr Nevis, will Mrs Nevis be joining you for breakfast?' asked the waitress.

Funny how the brain accepts things unquestionably, yet the heart holds out, waiting to be absolutely sure.

'Yes, she'll be down shortly.'

I felt, rather than saw, her arrive; she bent down and kissed me on the cheek. 'Good morning, ordered yet?'

'Er, no. Been waiting for you.'

'I've brought my phone, if you want to call Mr Greyspear?'

'It's Nathan, he's called Nathan.'

'Okay.'

'I'll call after breakfast.'

We ate in silence; I suppose she was wondering if she'd overstepped our fledgling relationship.

I dialled the number on the website and ended up at the Greyspear London office. I was told that Sir Nathan didn't take direct calls and was redirected to his office in Eastbourne.

'*Sir* Nathan – you do move in rarefied circles.'

'It's news to me – I just thought he was another boater being helpful.'

'Did they give you his phone number?'

'Not quite, I have the number for his office in Eastbourne.'

'Are you going to call him?'

'Not quite sure what to ask.'

'Ask for his help – tell him that we're stuck here in Scotland with Kaufmann looking for us and the police want you to come in for questioning.'

'Not sure if that would work, especially since he's a Sir – probably won't want to get his good name in the papers.'

'From what you've told me about him so far, I doubt he'd go running to the police – more likely to send out the heavies to catch Kaufmann.'

'Where did you hear that sort of language – the heavies?'

'Oh, you know what I mean.'

She was right, getting in touch with Greyspear was the right thing to do, plus he already knew the detective-sergeant. But not here in the dining room. I figured the less people who could overhear the conversation the better.

'Let's go back to the room, be a bit more private there.'

I put the phone on speaker and dialled the number.

'Greyspear Yachts. How can I help?'

'Could I speak to Sir Nathan, please? It's Jack Nevis, he was helping me trace the history of my tugboat. We're neighbours.'

'Jack Nevis?'

'Yes.'

'I'll see if he's available, please wait.'

We listened to a few bars of *Sailing By*, before the phone was picked up again.

'Mr Nevis, Sir Nathan is not available just now, but he asks if you could call back after four this afternoon? He will be available to talk then.'

'Will do, thanks.'

I hung up, looked at Nancy and shrugged.

'Well, at least he's agreed to talk to us, that's progress.'

'Yes, indeed.'

'Suppose, just suppose, they kept us on hold long enough to trace the call?'

'I doubt it. If we'd called the police, possibly, but I doubt if that was the case with our call to Greyspear.'

'That's good to know, now I can relax. So, tell me Jack – what should we do with the rest of the day while we wait to call Sir Nathan?'

Then a thought struck me. Suppose Kaufmann was trying to track us by using my phone to trace Nancy's?

'Hang on a minute, – do you have GPS turned on, on your phone?'

'Probably, why?'

'How about mobile broadband?'

'Yes, I have unlimited roaming in my package. Why – why would you want to know that?'

'Remember how I used your phone to find where my phone was, and subsequently to find Kaufmann?'

'You think he'll do the same to find us?'

'Possibly. Can I see your phone?'

I looked at the settings and found that GPS was on. I turned both it and the phone off.

'I think we should leave it off, except when we are making calls. Just in case.' Then I remembered someone once saying that it was possible to track a phone, even when it was switched off.

I handed her the phone back. 'What was it you asked before I interrupted?'

'Nothing,' she said shaking her head, 'doesn't matter. What shall we do while we wait?'

'How about a walk along the loch-side and a picnic?'

'Not quite what I meant, but sounds a lovely idea. What about food?'

'I'll ask in the kitchen, I'm sure they could fix us up with something suitable. I'll meet you at the front door.'

I left Nancy to finish getting ready and went downstairs to the kitchen. I found Moira in the bar getting ready for the lunchtime visitors.

'Moira, do you think we could have some sandwiches made for our lunch, please? We are thinking of going for a walk along the loch and stopping for a picnic.'

'No problem, I'll get James to make you up a picnic lunch.'

I sat on a bar stool and waited for Nancy, and our picnic.

'Here you are, Mr Nevis. There's cheese and pickle, and salmon and cucumber sandwiches. There's some fruit for you to eat as you walk, and a couple of slices of Victoria sponge cake and a thermos of tea.'

'Moira, you've outdone yourself! That's fantastic. Thanks.'

'Do you have a bag to carry your picnic?'

'Er, no.'

'Not to worry, we've got a couple of backpacks you can borrow. They were left by a guest last year and they didn't want them sent on.'

'We'll take good care of them.'

'I've also packed you an old blanket to sit on, the ground can be quite damp at this time of the year.'

'Thanks.'

♦

Nancy and I walked slowly along the road, looking at the loch-side cottages, and wondering what it would be like living in such a quiet environment.

'Look, Jack, look at the clouds lying on the hills; they look like a huge, soft, fluffy blanket resting on a giant's shoulders.'

I watched the spectacle, and yes, I could almost imagine some giant pulling a blanket over his shoulders.

Halfway up the hill the path turned to the left and sloped down away from the road. We walked down and found that the path we were now on was what was left of the original road. The new road wound its way round the shoulders of the hills and out of sight.

We walked aimlessly along the old road, passed splendid houses and humble cottages, each with a unique view of the loch. Some stretches of the road resembled more of a track than a road with trees right down to the loch edge and their gnarled branches covered with lichen.

We turned back at the end of the old road, looking for a suitable spot for our picnic. We walked for about forty minutes till we came to an open area where we had a lovely view of the loch.

'This should do,' said Nancy.

'Fine with me.'

I passed the blanket to Nancy and watched as she spread it out on the grass. 'Can I have the backpack?'

I handed it to her and watched. It felt so good to be here, watching her lay out our lunch on the blanket. For a moment, I saw Katie and the children and thought of that last summer.

Nancy turned and looked at me. 'Lunch is served. What's the matter – are you crying?'

I nodded and sniffed. 'Just an old memory, something that happened a long time ago. Can we eat? I'm starved.'

'Yes. You want milk and sugar in your tea?'

'Please Did you bring your phone?'

'Right here, in my pocket, why?' She pulled it out and showed me. 'Do you need to call someone?'

'No, just wondering what time it was.'

She pressed the on button and waited. 'Ten past two. That's funny.'

'What is?'

'I have a watch, so do you, yet the first thing we look at is our phone.'

'They're always on time, and besides you can't check emails or texts on wrist watches.'

I could see the face of the phone and her screen saver: it was of her children. How odd. We'd known each other for several days now, and yet never really talked about our children. As I framed that thought, I realised she still had hers, while mine were just memories. How thoughtful of Nancy not to broach the subject.

'Your children are lovely,' I said. nodding at the screen.

She swiped the screen and tapped one of the photo apps.

'This is Stephen.'

'And these two cute ones?'

'Stephanie and Sandra, they're twins.

'Must be nice to have children.'

'Was that why you were tearful a moment ago?'

'We'd been camping in the Lake District. Katie had taken a week off work, the children were on their summer break from school. It was a hot dry summer, the kids had spent the afternoons swimming in the lake, or hiking up the hills with us. Each evening we'd walk down to the water's edge and have a picnic dinner. It was the perfect summer, and the last one we would ever have.'

'You all right?' she said, turning to me and looking intently into my face. 'You must have loved them very much, I'm sorry I've brought back the past for you.'

'I still do love them. I'm sorry, Nancy.'

'Sorry for what? Loving your family so much? Look at me, Mr Jack Nevis,' she said, putting her hands on my cheeks, gripping my face like a concerned mother. 'That is why I love you, you care.'

'You do?'

'Of course I do, you doughnut. Now let's have our lunch before the tea gets cold.'

We ate our sandwiches in silence, each thinking of the past and wondering what the future could now bring. I lay back on the grass and stared at the clouds passing overhead.

'I could lie here all day, it's so peaceful.'

When I got no response from Nancy I looked at her: she was fast asleep.

I lay back down and closed my eyes. The sun was out in full spring glory, the air had lost its winter chill and I felt at peace.

I was back in the Lake District. Katie was clearing up after our lunch and the children were down at the lakeside splashing in the shallow water. I closed my eyes and rested. Katie lay down beside me and snuggled up. I was in turmoil. How could I tell her things had to change, we couldn't go on this way? I told her I would always cherish what we'd had, but the time had come for me to move on. I said I had a new love in my life and it was now time to say goodbye.

'Goodbye, Jack. I'll always love you too.'

'Goodbye, Katie.'

'What was that?'

I woke and found Nancy lying beside me. It wasn't Katie who had snuggled up to me.

'Who were you talking to?'

'No one, I was just dreaming.'

'Okay.' And she put her head back on my chest.

'Nancy, tell me about your kids. I want to hear all about them: school, grandparents, the lot.'

♦

'How was your picnic?' asked Moira, when we returned.

'Lovely, we had it on a lovely grassy spot by the loch.'

'Moira, do you have a mobile phone I could borrow? I'll pay for the call,' I offered, dropping a twenty pound note on the counter.

'Oh, you don't have to do that, we have a phone in reception you can use.'

'Thanks, but I need to trace my phone. Yesterday when we were travelling I think I might have left it in the taxi in Port Glasgow. I can find its location by using another mobile phone.'

'Oh, I know what you mean! My mother loses her phone all the time and uses mine to find it – it's usually down the back of the sofa. Here you are.'

I logged on to my account and after a moment found to my dismay that my phone was on the move, not southwards, but down the Clyde. Kaufmann must have locked on to Nancy's phone at some point, but where?

'Other than this afternoon, when was the last time you used your phone, Nancy?'

'When we were in Rothesay, yesterday, why?'

'Kaufmann's on his way across the Clyde to Rothesay.'

'That's torn it. Do you think he can find us here?'

I shook my head. 'Very unlikely. We got off the ferry and other than the brief bit of shopping, we came straight here.'

'What about the tourist information lady? If they ask her, she'll send them right here to the doorstep.'

I'd had a similar thought; it was the sort of thing I would do in similar circumstances.

'My cousin did the same thing,' interrupted Moira.

'What was that, Moira?' I asked.

'Her husband used to beat her up, especially when he was drunk, and that was even after they were divorced.'

'Did she go to the police?' asked Nancy.

'Yes, but they said she'd have to press charges against him, without that their hands were tied and they couldn't interfere.'

'So what did she do?'

'She and her boyfriend ran away from him. Is that what you're doing?'

'Sort of, Moira,' said Nancy, 'but it's not my ex-husband we're trying to avoid, it's some of his friends. We think they are angry over a business disagreement.'

'And now they're after you?'

'Unfortunately, yes.'

Thanks for the use of your phone, Moira, you sure I can't pay you something for using it?'

'No, that's all right. Do you want anything from the bar?'

I shook my head. 'No, thanks. Nancy?'

'Me neither, I'm going to go up and get ready for dinner. Jack, are you coming?'

It took me a moment to figure out what she meant, then I saw it was past four o'clock, time to call Greyspear.

'Ah, Moira, could I use your phone for one more call?'

'No problem, go right ahead.'

'The number is in our room, be right back down.'

'Take the phone with you, I don't mind.'

I followed Nancy up the stairs and into our room.

'Such a nice girl, make sure you leave her something for the phone call.'

'I will. Pass me the paper with Greyspear's phone number, will you?'

I dialled the number then pressed the speaker button so Nancy could hear what was said. The same voice answered the phone.

'Hi, it's Jack Nevis. Is Mr – er – I mean, Sir Nathan, available?'

'Please wait, Mr Nevis, and I'll get him for you.'

'Jack, it's Nathan Greyspear. How are you?'

'Fine – at the moment.'

'Police have been asking for you.'

'Thought they might be; the redtops are having a field day. That's why I called.'

'How can I help?'

'I need to get in touch with the sergeant in charge of the investigation. I have information that could sort this mess out.'

'You want me to contact her?'

'Not really, I thought if you could get me her mobile number, I could give her a call.'

'Why don't you hand yourself in to the nearest police station?'

'Not that easy; we're being chased by the same people I believe killed the private investigator and the Afghan chap last week.'

'Where are you just now?'

'A small hotel in Colintraive, it's across the loch and up the coast from Rothesay.'

'How long will you be there for?'

'Not sure, I think we're safe for this evening, at least we will be after the last ferry.'

'What are your plans?'

'None at the moment, that's why we called you.'

'We? You mean you and Mrs Rafsanjani?'

'Yes.'

'Ever read any John Buchan stories?'

'No, why?'

'Because you're living one. Give me your number and I'll see what I can do then call you back.'

'When do you think you will be able to call us back?'

'Had dinner yet?'

'No.'

'Then go have dinner, I'll call you after cheese and biscuits.'

I finished getting dressed, then opened the door to go downstairs with Nancy. I immediately grabbed her by the arm, put my finger to my lips, and drew her back into the room.

'What's the matter?'

'They're here.'

'Who's here?'

'Kaufmann, Hanse and Snyder. I got a look at Snyder, his hand was hovering over the till.'

'Typical. What will we do? We're trapped again!'

'Wait here, I'll go see.'

I opened the bedroom door and crept out onto the landing and listened,

Moira was talking. 'I'm sorry, Mr Kaufmann, but we're fully booked. There's a nice hotel in Clachan, you could try there. If not then you need to be quick, the last ferry of the day will be leaving in ten minutes.'

'Ah, I was hoping to catch up with my niece and her husband. They said they'd be staying here; she has blonde hair, and very pretty green eyes?'

'I'm sorry, Mr Kaufmann, there's no one of that description staying here. Maybe the hotel in Clachan can help? It's only about ten miles up the road. Shall I call them and see if they have rooms?'

'Never mind. Come Hanse, Snyder, our search goes on.'

I ducked back into the bedroom, went over to the window and hid behind the curtain to watch. Relieved at our narrow escape, I saw the three of them pile into their car and head off to catch the last ferry.

'Are we safe?' Nancy asked.

I nodded. 'For just now we are. But tomorrow, Greyspear or not, we need to be on our way again.'

Moira was tending the bar. I handed her phone back, with a twenty-pound note folded inside the cover.

'All sorted, Mr Nevis?'

'I think so, Moira.'

'Good. Do you want to go through for your dinner, or do you want to wait?'

I looked at Nancy. 'Hungry?'

'Yes. We haven't tried the rest of the menu yet – I fancy the smoked salmon tonight.'

I don't remember much of the conversation at the table. My mind was on the issue of how to get back to Eastbourne without our's and Kaufmann's paths crossing. That, and waiting for the phone to ring. I was picking at my ice cream when Moira came into the dining room and said I had a phone call in the bar.

'Hello?'

'Jack, it's Nathan. How are your sea legs?'

'Run that past me again?'

'I've arranged a ride for you and Mrs Rafsanjani –'

'It's Nancy Harrison.'

'Okay. Anyway, I've arranged a ride down to Eastbourne for you both.'

'Where will we meet?'

'You say you're in Colintraive still?'

'Yes.'

'Captain Bracewell will pick you up at the ferry terminal at five tomorrow morning.'

'First ferry isn't till five-thirty.'

'That's okay, he'll bring his own boat. He's doing a delivery tomorrow and I've asked him to pick you and Nancy up. Be ready at five at the ferry terminal.'

'Okay. Thanks.'

I hung up and returned to the table, and Nancy.

'Greyspear?'

I nodded.

'You look puzzled. Can he help?'

'Yes, he's sending one of his boats to pick us up at five, at least we'll be half an hour ahead of Kaufmann should he have managed to track us down. That will mean an early start.' I looked at the clock on the wall. 'It's eleven-thirty. I think we should be packed and ready to go by four-thirty – no taxis for us tomorrow morning.'

'No nightcap?'

'Just a quick one, we can't afford to sleep in.'

We walked back through to the bar.

'How was dinner, Mr Nevis?'

'Fine, thanks. Moira, we have to leave early in the morning so could we settle our bill before we go up to bed? We'll probably be gone before anyone is around tomorrow.'

'Certainly. Would you like a drink before you go up?'

The quick nightcap meant we went up to the room at one.

I tucked Nancy into bed and stood back.

'Aren't you coming to bed?'

I shook my head. 'As long as Kaufmann is out there, I can't sleep, I'll sit here and keep an eye on the road.'

12

At Sea

I sat in the chair fully dressed and looked out the window into the darkness. At about four I was sure I saw lights down by the ferry terminal and what looked like a small dinghy making its way across the short distance from the far shore. Surely not Kaufmann? Could he be this desperate to try to catch us sleeping? When I thought of the stakes, yes, he certainly could.

'Nancy, wake up. Hurry, we must get out of here.'

'What, who?' she said struggling to untangle herself from the blankets.

'I think it's Kaufmann. He's somehow got a hold of a dinghy and is coming across the channel.'

Nancy climbed out of bed and walked over to the window; she leaned on me and put her arm around my waist. I could feel the warmth of her body stirring something in me, a longing to take her in my arms and hold on to her for ever.

> When the gently breath of spring
> Warms the winter air
> I'll hold you in my arms
> And dream without a care

'What was that you were singing?'

'Our song. Come on, Kaufmann or not, we need to be out of here in twenty minutes.'

Nancy dressed in the darkness. I was glad we'd thought to pack the previous evening.

I thought we were first up, but when I we got to the bottom of the stairs, Moira was waiting for us.

'Got everything, Mr Nevis?'

'Yes, thanks,' said Nancy. 'When this is all over, we'll come back again. Thanks for making us feel so welcome.'

I almost felt we were escaping as we walked quietly down to the ferry terminal. I was on edge all the way, expecting to be accosted by Kaufmann, or one of his thugs. What I didn't expect was Greyspear to be waiting for us.

'Good morning Jack, Nancy!'

'How did you get here?'

'We flew up last night and took delivery of the boat when we arrived. We left Greenock a couple of hours ago to meet you here.'

'In a dinghy?'

'Ah, I should have explained. We have a customer in Kent whose yacht needed to be delivered. When you called, I thought why not fly up to Greenock with Captain Bracewell, collect the yacht and swing by for you two?'

I was a reasonable sailor, wasn't sure about Nancy. The thought of a long sail from the Firth of Clyde to Eastbourne didn't appeal, even to me. Though we would certainly be out of the way of Kaufmann for several days at least.

The ferry, tied up at its mooring with lights on and engine idling, was getting ready to start its day. We carefully walked down the ferry ramp to the waiting dinghy. I wondered how big this yacht was that could carry a dinghy big enough to hang a huge outboard from the stern.

'Jack, Nancy, this is Simon Bracewell – he's my senior captain.'

'Hi, Jack, Nancy, good to have you aboard. - Just call me Simon, we keep the captain bit for the customers.'

'Thanks, Simon. Er – where's the yacht?' Nancy asked.

'Moored in the channel, we couldn't get in to tie-up because of the ferry.'

'I'm not a very good sailor.'

'No problem, Nancy, the yacht's fitted with stabilisers.'

'How long will we be at sea?'

'Hope to be in the marina sometime late tomorrow night.'

'I am assuming the yacht is not a sailboat, Simon?' I said.

'Correct, the *Beatrice* is one of our fly-bridge motor yachts,' replied Greyspear.

'How big is it, or should I say she?' asked Nancy.

'Eighty-eight foot overall, twin caterpillar turbo-charged diesels, with a top speed of just under thirty knots.'

'I've never been on a yacht that size,' said Nancy.

I thought of the *Osprey*; she was ninety-two feet long, but certainly not in the same league as the *Beatrice*.

'Here – let me help you with your case,' said Greyspear.

'Thanks.'

Greyspear pushed us off from the ferry slipway and Bracewell motored the dinghy backwards out into deeper water.

'Where is the *Beatrice*?' asked Nancy.

'See the red light, over there?' said Greyspear, pointing to a solitary red light shining against the darkness of the hills.

'Yes.'

'That's her port navigation light. The owner ordered her with a blue hull, makes it difficult to see in the dark.'

Bracewell motored us towards the solitary red light. As we approached the stern the deck lights came on, showing for the first time the magnificence of the yacht. One of the two deckhands steadied the dinghy as we stepped out on to the *Beatrice's* swimming platform. We climbed the steps onto the lower deck and watched as the deckhands hoisted the dinghy from the water and slid it into her inside storage garage.

'Have you two had breakfast yet?' asked Greyspear.

'No, we were up and straight out the door. We didn't want to be late for you.'

'Right, follow me into the main saloon. Andy will have breakfast ready in a few minutes, traditional English. Okay for you both?'

I nodded and looked at Nancy; her face was pale. 'You okay?'

'I'm not a great sailor.'

'You should be fine on the *Beatrice*,' said Bracewell. 'The weather in the Irish Sea area is reported as fair, and with the stabilisers you won't even know we are at sea.'

I noted he didn't mention what the weather would be like as we went round Land's End. I decided not to mention it either.

We followed Greyspear into the main saloon. I was immediately taken by the sumptuousness of the interior. It made me think the interior of the *Osprey* looked more like the inside of an average family caravan.

'Do people live on boats like this?' asked Nancy.

'I doubt it,' replied Greyspear. 'Most people who can afford one of these have full-time crew who sail it to a desired destination, while the owners fly out for a holiday. Most of them, if they plan to stay for longer than a few weeks, will stay in a hotel and just use the boat for entertaining friends and family.'

A bell rang somewhere in the bowels of the boat, then the *Beatrice* shook as the engines were started.

'Breakfast is ready,' said the one Greyspear had earlier referred to as being called Andy. 'If you'll be seated, I'll serve breakfast.'

He beckoned us to follow him over to the table.

'This is just for us?' asked Nancy.

'The Queen was busy today, and sends her apologies,' said Greyspear, with a laugh. 'Come on, let's eat.'

I'd never seen a table set so extravagantly on a boat – we could have been at the Ritz. As I buttered my toast I realised the sun had risen and the darkness of the loch had been replaced by a warm glow to the east.

'Like to see your cabin?' asked Greyspear, as we finished breakfast.

'Cabin?' echoed Nancy.

'Of course, I don't expect you to sit up all night.'

'We actually get a cabin?' she said, shaking her head.

'Yes. I've chosen the owners' stateroom for you. If you'll follow me, I'll show you where it is.'

'After you,' I said to Nancy.

I followed Nancy and Greyspear out of the main saloon, towards the wheelhouse, and down a flight of stairs. These were carpeted, unlike the companionway steps on the *Osprey*.

'This way,' he said at the bottom, as he opened the door to our accommodation. 'Here you are. This will be your cabin till we get to Eastbourne.'

'But it's fantastic! Are you sure this is for us?'

Greyspear smiled. 'All for you.'

'Just for us?'

'Just for you.'

'No one else?'

Greyspear shook his head, and smiled again.

'It's wonderful! Those windows – they won't break, will they?'

Greyspear smiled. 'They're made from toughened glass, similar to those of an aeroplane cockpit.'

'Oh, well that's okay, I'd hate to think what would happen if one of them broke.'

'Where will *you* sleep?' I asked Greyspear.

'I'll be in one of the guest cabins. Sleep well.'

I pulled the suitcase into the room.

'I'll leave you to get settled,' said Greyspear, 'I'll be in the wheelhouse if you need me.'

He shut the door behind him and we were alone.

'Jack, this is fantastic, and all for us! I can't wait to tell the children.'

'Remember, it's just for the trip, Nancy. I'm sorry to say it will then be back to the *Osprey* for me, and your house and children for you.'

'That's all right, I'm going to enjoy this while I can. But what are we going to do about Kaufmann? We can't spend the rest of our lives trying to avoid him.'

'It's not Kaufmann who worries me,' I replied. 'It's Hanse – he's the cold-blooded killer amongst them. I'm sure it was him who killed Achmed.'

'What about the private investigator in your workshop?'

'Probably Hanse shot him as well. Kaufmann may have a foul temper, but I just can't imagine him pulling the trigger himself.'

'What about Snyder?'

'Unlikely. Did you take a good look at him? He's probably good at taking orders – when it suits him. I reckon he's out to feather his own nest, so not likely to be a hit man for Kaufmann.'

'You think so?'

'I do. Remember when I went back to the *Osprey* to get our clothes?'

'Yes.'

'Well, he was on the *Osprey*, searching it.'

'He was searching the boat? What did you do?'

'It was more a case of what he did.'

'And just what did he do?'

'He hit me over the head with a cosh, then tied me up.'

'Why on earth didn't you tell me?'

'I didn't want to worry you.'

'Worry me! Jack – this has to stop. No more heroics. How did you escape?'

'He untied me, told me what he was after, then left.'

'Just like that? So what was he after, or should I not bother guessing?'

'He said he was after the falcon statue, something crazy about his jihad.'

'Isn't that what those fighters in Syria are all about?'

I thought about Snyder's parting gesture. 'Nasty bunch, all of them.'

'So what are we going to do?'

'We need to neutralise Hanse somehow; getting him arrested would be the ideal solution. Once he's out of the picture,

Kaufmann and Snyder will be easy to deal with. But in the meantime, I'm going to get some sleep; remember I sat up all night.'

I stripped to my underwear, climbed into the bed as the *Beatrice* streaked south at almost thirty knots and drifted off into a troubled sleep.

I dreamed I went to look for Katie at our old house, but no-one answered the front door. I pushed at it and the door swung in on creaky hinges. I stepped into the hall and called her name: no answer. I climbed the stairs to our bedroom and saw the bedclothes thrown back on one side. There was no sign of her; the room, the house, were empty. I saw one of Katie's jumpers lying on the bed. I picked it up and pressed it into my face; it didn't smell of her perfume; it was a new smell.

I woke and found I was holding Nancy. She'd climbed in beside me and had snuggled up close, her soft fragrant hair rubbing against my cheek as she breathed. She was sleeping so soundly, occasionally making a sniffing sound. I lay beside her, holding her tight, listening to the deep rumble of the twin diesel engines propelling us ever southward through the Irish Sea.

I didn't want to move, I wanted this oasis of peace to go on for ever. To hell with Kaufmann, the gold and the blasted falcon. This was what I wanted – this moment to last forever. I glanced over my right shoulder and looked out the huge window at the darkening sky and realised we must go on. Kaufmann had to be stopped.

I untangled myself from Nancy's embrace and quietly slid out of bed, got dressed and went up to the wheelhouse.

'Sleep well?' asked Bracewell.

'Yes, thanks, could have stayed there for another week.'

'How's your lady doing?'

'My lady? Oh, Nancy, she's doing fine, out like a light in a power failure.'

'Being at sea does that.'

'Where's Nathan?'

'On the phone in the main saloon. He's making arrangements for refuelling.'

I'd wondered if that would be needed. 'Thanks, I'll go see how he's doing.'

I stood for a moment and looked at the dashboard in front of Bracewell. It wouldn't look out of place on a modern jet liner. Poor *Osprey*: it only had a steering wheel, throttle handle and a compass for the helmsman to play with.

I walked back into the main saloon and waited for Greyspear to finish his phone call. While I waited I glanced at the surroundings. When we'd boarded earlier, I wasn't really aware of anything except my need for sleep. I sat on the settee opposite Greyspear and could see through the window behind him we were near to land. The saloon was huge, especially compared to that of the *Osprey*. The furniture wouldn't be out of place in any modern apartment. I looked forward into the wheelhouse. To the right of Bracewell's shoulder, I could see the lights of what I took to be a ferry heading westwards into the setting sun.

Greyspear hung up from his call.

'All settled?'

'Yes, our first fuel stop will be in Holyhead.'

'I thought the range of a yacht this size would be greater.'

'Ever run out of fuel in your car?'

I nodded. 'Once when we were driving down to Devon. Took the AA over an hour to get to us, dreadful night, raining cats and dogs.'

'Just imagine doing the same while you are out at sea, at night, and in the dark with a storm brewing. Also the yacht performs slightly better at sea with full tanks.'

'How far could you go with full tanks?'

'We could get from the yard in Greenock to Lands End in one go, providing we had calm seas, but that would be at reduced power.'

'Makes sense.'

'We'll also have dinner while we are tied up. I've asked Andy to heat some soup and make a couple of rounds of sandwiches.'

'That sounds just right.'

'The run to Falmouth, round Lands End, will be a bit rough according to the weather report. If it's still bad when we get to our next fuelling point we'll wait out the storm – another reason to eat now.'

'Where are you planning to stop next?'

'Swansea.'

I didn't like the sound of bad weather. I'd been across the Irish Sea in bad weather, and that was in a large ferry – didn't fancy doing the same in such a small craft as the *Beatrice*. I got up and walked through to the wheelhouse. Bracewell was on the radio getting instructions as to where to tie up for refuelling. Once again I wondered how well the *Osprey* would do in tight quarters. Unlike the *Beatrice*, the *Osprey* didn't have twin screws and bow thrusters. The crew made the manoeuvre look so simple, and within a few minutes the fuel was gurgling into the *Beatrice's* tanks. I watched the dials on the fuel pumps and wondered how much the *Osprey* would take for her run to the repair yard for her overhaul. The dial stopped at 3800 litres for the *Beatrice*. Bracewell looked at me and saw the consternation on my face.

'If you were putting that lot in your car it would be in the region of £4,700. At least marine diesel is cheaper, no duty.'

'Thanks, I had wondered.'

Greyspear went ashore and paid for the fuel, while the crew prepared the *Beatrice* to move off the fuel dock. I was surprised how much she was like a modern car when Bracewell started the engines. He simply took a key out of his pocket, inserted it into a keyhole on the dashboard and turned it. Bells started ringing angrily.

'No oil pressure, that's the alarm,' said Bracewell. 'Until the oil pump has circulated enough oil and is up to running pressure, the engines won't fire.'

The bells continued for a couple of moments, then the engines fired and the bells stopped. They were replaced with the reassuring rumble of the twin Caterpillar V8's.

Bracewell signalled to the deck crew to untie the dock lines. By skilful use of the throttle and bow thrusters, Bracewell manoeuvred the *Beatrice* further down the dock, away from the fuel pumps. We tied up at a vacant space, and I went into the main saloon to ask how long we'd be there.

'Just long enough to have something to eat,' replied Bracewell. 'I want to get round Land's End before Katie arrives – what's wrong, Jack?'

At the mention of the name "Katie" I'd almost fainted. 'You said Katie?'

'Yes, it's the name the Met Office have given the next Atlantic storm, that's all.'

'My late wife was called Katie. She and the children died in a car crash.'

'Oh, I'm sorry, I didn't know.'

'That's all right, it's just one of those things I'm learning to live with.'

'What storm?' asked Nancy, who'd just entered the saloon.

'Nothing to worry about, if it gets really bad we'll head in to the nearest port till the worst has passed.'

'Good to hear that.'

'Don't worry, we should be well ahead of it,' replied Bracewell.

'Where are we?' asked Nancy.

'Holyhead, we've just stopped for fuel. We'll be heading off again as soon as we've had a bite to eat,' said Greyspear.

'Okay, but I'm not very hungry.'

'It's not a fancy meal, just sandwiches and hot soup.'

'I think I can manage that, thanks.'

'Sleep well?' Nancy asked me when Greyspear left for the galley.

'Uh-huh, how about you?'

'Fine till you left me alone in that big bed,' she smiled, gently punching me on the arm.

'I thought you were sleeping.'

'I was – just teasing.'

Andy brought us two mugs of soup with a plate of cheese and pickle sandwiches.

'You can watch from the wheelhouse,' said Greyspear. 'There's a bench seat on the port side.'

'Won't we be in the way?' asked Nancy.

'No, there's plenty of room,' replied Bracewell. 'If it was warmer, you could have sat outside on the sun deck, but I wouldn't recommend it tonight, not with the approaching storm.'

I followed Nancy and Bracewell into the wheelhouse. While we ate our soup and sandwiches we watched the crew get the *Beatrice* ready to go to sea again.

We motored out of the harbour at a sedate pace till we were clear of the harbour wall then Bracewell opened the throttle. The *Beatrice* leapt ahead and we were on our way south again.

'How fast are we going?' asked Nancy.

'Abut twenty-five knots,' replied Greyspear.

'Seems so fast, yet if you closed your eyes you could almost imagine you are standing still.'

'You are,' I said. 'It's the boat that's moving!'

'Very funny.'

Two hours further south and waves were starting to break over the bow. Bracewell reduced speed – we were now down to a sedate fifteen knots.

'Looks like Katie is early,' said Bracewell, as another wave broke over the bow and washed its way almost up to the wheelhouse.

'Is this the storm you were expecting, Simon?' Nancy asked.

'Looks like it's a bit early, I'd hoped to be a lot further south before we ran into it.'

'Will we be all right? Will we have to head for a port?' asked Nancy.

Bracewell shook his head. 'No, these yachts are designed to handle this type of weather. We may have to reduce speed a bit more. The weather report says the storm should have passed north-east within the next two hours, this is probably the worst it's going to get.'

I looked at Nancy; her colour was fading. 'You all right?'

'I think I'll go lie down.'

I followed her below and tucked her in.

'Sorry, Jack, guess I'm not a great sailor.'

'Nonsense, you've been through a lot these last few days, you're just exhausted. Get some sleep and we'll talk later.'

'I love you, Jack.'

'I know you do, and I love you, too. Sleep well.'

I bent down and kissed her.

'Where are you going?'

'I'm going to sit with Simon in the wheelhouse for a bit, I'll be down later. If you need anything, there's a phone beside the bed, press 0 for the wheelhouse.'

'Okay.' She yawned, closed her eyes, snuggled down into the blankets and before I'd reached the door I could hear the tell-tale sounds of gentle snoring.

I climbed back up the stairs to the wheelhouse.

Greyspear was at the helm. 'Your lady not a good sailor?'

'Nancy? Not sure, she's been under a lot of stress lately. I suppose it's having a missing husband suddenly reappear, your children's lives threatened, then your husband found dead in an alleyway, and finally ending up being kidnapped. I suppose that could cause a bit of stress.'

'I'm sure it would.'

'Where's Simon?'

'Turned in, he's back on at four am.'

'Want company?'

'Sure. It gets lonely at night sitting in the wheelhouse on your own, staring out into the darkness.'

'I know what you mean.'

'Didn't realise you were a sailor.'

I laughed. 'I'm not. What I mean is I quite often sit up late into the night on the *Osprey*.'

'On your own?'

'Unfortunately yes, the sad life of a widower.'

'Your wife died?'

'Wife and children: all died in a car accident.'

'I'm sorry to hear that.'

I looked at his face, he was wearing my sadness. I could see it in his eyes, the emptiness of a lost love. 'You too?'

'Twice.'

'I struggled with losing one, don't know how I'd cope with losing two.'

'Memories do that, stick their foot out when you're not looking.'

'Just thinking about the children, and what could have been.'

'How many did you have?'

'Three. Two boys and a girl.'

'I never had any. My first wife died of cancer.'

'How long had you been married?'

'Five years, five glorious years. Then one day my world turned from summer to winter. Angela felt a lump and went to see the doctor. Tests were done and the results were devastating. The cancer had already spread. Two weeks later, on our fifth anniversary, I held her in my arms one last time and said goodbye.'

I was at a loss with what to say to that, so asked, 'Want something to drink?'

'Simon made a pot of coffee, there should be plenty left in the thermos. I take mine black, no sugar.'

209

I could have done with something a little stronger, something with a kick, and poured from a bottle over ice in a glass. I settled for a cup of black coffee with no sugar too and re-joined Greyspear in the wheelhouse.

'Thanks for the coffee. Even though the auto pilot is doing its job, I still prefer to remain at the helm.'

'Hope you don't mind me asking, but what is your connection with the Greyspear Yacht Company?'

'Not at all. I own it.'

'I had wondered. How did you get started?'

'It's a long story.'

'Fine by me, I'm not going anywhere.'

'I joined the army after leaving university. It was at an inter-services rugby game that I met my first wife.'

'Were you playing, or watching?'

'I was playing. That's when I met Angela.'

'Love at first sight?'

'You could say that. It was a bit more physical than romantic in the beginning, but after a while we grew to love each other very deeply. I hated it whenever I got posted and was unable to take her with me.'

'Did that happen often?'

'Not too often, thankfully.'

'What did you do in the army?'

'Special ops. Took me away from home for a couple of weeks at a time, usually.'

'Where did you go? That's if you are allowed to talk about it?'

'There's no restriction on me discussing it now as it was quite a few years ago. I was in Iraq with an intelligence unit, mostly eavesdropping on local radio chatter.'

'And your wife went with you?'

'No, not to Iraq, she went with me when I travelled in Europe. It was just a couple of times, that was all, but nice to have a friendly face with me.'

'You were telling me how you got into boatbuilding?'

'We met at an inter-services game between the navy and the army. I was playing for the army. Angela came along with the army team as a supporter. She was the team's unofficial mascot. We met in the bar after the game.'

'Did you win?'

Greyspear thought for a moment. 'Lost the game, but won Angela's heart.'

'Sounds quite romantic.'

'I suppose it was. Shortly after we met, Angela's father had to retire from the army to run the family business. We didn't know it at the time, but he was quite ill – kept it to himself.'

'What did the business do?'

'It made plastic toys for children. A real irony, there he was, in charge of a toy factory, and no grandchildren to make them for. Research and development and prototyping was done in the UK, manufacturing in China.'

'Not uncommon these days. Most of the guitars I get to work on are made in China, quite good some of them.'

'Then one day, at a toy exhibition, he keeled over and died. Heart attack. Since there wasn't anyone suitable to run it, I resigned my commission and took over running the family business.'

'And no one knew about his heart condition?'

'No, not a sign. We used to play on the same polo team, he regularly played squash to competition level. Angela was devastated when it happened.'

'What about Angela's mother? How did she take it?'

'She'd died the previous year.'

'Broken heart?'

'Sorry?'

'Do you think he could have died of a broken heart? Quite often when one partner in a marriage passes, if they were really close the other follows soon after.'

Greyspear nodded. 'I've heard that statistic as well. Could quite well be the case with them, Angela said they were very close.'

'What did you do next?'

'Turned out I had a flair for business and over the next three years the company trebled in turnover.'

'My ex in-laws are still alive, get a Christmas card every year from them. Doesn't bring Katie and the children back though.'

'What were their names?'

'David was the eldest, next was Harry. The youngest was Tina, it was her birthday party we were returning from when we had the accident. Katie's parents were devastated; her mother had arranged the party at their house. I think she still blames herself somewhat.'

'Because she had arranged the party?'

'Who knows? Graham, that's her husband, says she only breaks down occasionally now, says the doctor is pleased with her progress.'

'I've no children. You'd think someone as fit as a rugby-playing army major could have children by the dozen, but the irony is I can only shoot blanks.'

I looked at him, illuminated by the digital displays on the console. His eyes were looking for something just over the horizon of history.

'I know what you felt.'

'You do?'

'One minute I was a happy family man, then – then blackness, despair and a long empty, lonely, road to walk down with nowhere in particular to head for.'

'You know, Jack, we're like ships travelling on parallel courses, but at least there is daylight ahead for me.'

'What's that?'

'I'm engaged to a wonderful woman.'

'I'm glad to hear that. How did you meet?'

'We met in my office, just over a year ago. You've talked to her; her name is Susan.'

'I have?'

'When you call my Eastbourne office.'

'Your secretary?'

'Not at first, she was working in our marketing department when we first met. I promoted her to be my PA.'

'Lucky lady.'

'Lucky me. Anyway once I'd climbed out of the fog I got stuck into running the company. Expanded the line and yet again turnover and profits soared.'

'Were you still playing rugby?'

Greyspear shook his head and backed off the engines a few revolutions. 'I got out of shape; all those long hours running the business. Nope – I took up horse riding. Horses were new to me. Fell in love with them, regardless of size, shape, or temperament.'

'You said you'd been married twice?'

'I met Althea at the stables where I stabled my first horse. It was she who helped me learn to ride. I would come over to the stables on Saturday at lunchtime, have a lesson, then go out for a ride. At first that's all there was to it. Occasionally, after the lesson she'd come out for a ride with me. Then one Saturday I asked her out to dinner. She said yes. We were married three months later.'

'Katie and I were married within six months of us meeting. Little David was on the way.'

'Most men's dream, a son to carry on the family name.'

'If you don't mind me asking, what happened to Althea?'

'Jack, if Eugene O'Neil was still around writing stage plays, my life would make perfect material. I was coming to the realisation that being a happily married man was not going to be my lot in life. As I said earlier, my first wife died from cancer, my second died in a car crash,'

'We do have something in common. Our car was hit by a truck, came right through the central barrier late on a wet and windy night. The police said the truck driver had fallen asleep at the wheel. When they checked his tachograph it showed he'd been driving for seventeen hours without a proper break.'

'Foreign driver?'

'Don't know. These days with so many Europeans living in the UK it's hard to tell who's who just by a name. I hate driving at night when it's wet, especially when an oncoming car comes too close.'

'I can understand that, especially if you're tired and it's late.'

'You were telling me how you and Althea met.'

'We met at her stables, and they were her stables. She'd inherited them from a spinster aunt. We'd gone to the Horse of the Year Show, stopped for a meal afterwards. We should have stayed overnight, but one of the mares was foaling and Althea insisted we drive across London that evening to be there in case there were any complications. We were hit head-on by a drunk driver, crossed the road on a corner. Althea was dead on arrival at the hospital, I got off with hardly a scrape.'

'How long ago was this?'

'Last Friday evening would have been our eleventh anniversary and the sixth anniversary of her death.'

'I'm so sorry, I shouldn't have asked.'

Greyspear shook his head. 'It's all right, it helps to talk about it, better out than in. That's what the doctor said.'

'Do you still have the stables your wife inherited?'

Greyspear swallowed the last of his coffee. 'No, those stables were in London. There were too many memories for me there. It was then I found out just how valuable land in London was. I put the stables up for sale, rejected all offers for it as a going concern and found a property developer looking for a suitable brownfield site to build expensive houses on. I bought an old run-down manor near Eastbourne and turned it into a country club with the proceeds. Then built stables and converted the grounds into a golf course. The perimeter fields I reserved for cross-country riding.'

'What about the boatbuilding? How did you get into that?'

'Ah yes, I was coming to that. I'd gone down to Devon for a holiday, trying to make sense out of life, and basically feeling sorry for myself. I have no other family. I was staying in a small hotel in Dartmouth.'

'I've never been to Dartmouth.'

'You should, make a wonderful place to go on honeymoon.'

'Are you suggesting I should marry Nancy?'

'No, I'd never do that to anyone, but you two do make a lovely couple.'

'Thanks! You were saying?'

'One evening in the bar I was told about a local boatbuilding company about to shut down – on the verge of going bankrupt. The directors had had enough and were only too eager to get out. They did have some very excellent designs, but unfortunately the factory was not fit for purpose and most of the skilled personnel had already left.'

'Bit of a risk, you not knowing anything about boats?'

'Maybe, but I did know about business and marketing. I shifted the construction to Greenock, and built a whole new factory complex to build our boats. Then I put an ad in the local job centre for fitters and laminators.'

'Get much of a response?'

'Mostly young men wanting me to sign their cards; so they could continue to draw their dole. Though there was an amusing story about one of the chaps who came to work for us, I think his name was Bill Kelley.'

'What did he do that was so memorable?'

'Apparently he was a bus driver in Port Glasgow. The story was he'd been driving for several years and was fed-up with driving in the city. One day saw one of our posters advertising for boat fitters.'

'What did he do?'

'He parked the bus at the bus stop, turned off the engine and headed straight to our office to apply for the job.'

'Did he get it?'

'Yes, but that wasn't the amusing part of the story.'

'Oh?'

'When he parked the bus, it was still full of passengers.'

'Desperate man! From what I see of your boats you must have managed to turn things around.'

'It was difficult at first, but when those who stuck out the training started to spend their pay packet down the pub on Friday night, we had more staff than we could find tools for. Today the factory wins industry awards for excellence.'

'And you've never remarried?'

'What do they say about twice shy?'

'Till I met Nancy, I'd despaired of ever meeting someone to share my life and dreams with.'

'That's why I'm taking the plunge again.'

'I'm happy for you. When's the big day?'

He smiled. 'Wedding's set for June. Never imagined it could happen to me again.

'You said she was your PA?'

'Not at the start. I realised early on that to be a successful business it didn't matter how good your product was if your potential customers couldn't either find you or what you make. One of those who applied for a position was Susan. She'd worked for several local companies in sales and said, according to her job application, *I'm looking for a new challenge with responsibilities.*'

'Did that include being married to you?'

'Ha, ha! I suppose it does now. When I first met her in a sales meeting I was very impressed with her professionalism. The head of sales had just left on maternity leave and Susan stepped in to chair the meeting. I kept an eye on her –'

'You kept an eye on her?'

'I was referring to her business acumen, although I must admit just seeing her made my heart jump with joy. It was her sales results that helped me decide to promote her to head of marketing.'

'Quite a lady.'

'She is. But marketing wasn't her only business skill. My PA left the company, so I asked Susan to help out, just till I found a replacement. She was already meeting with customers and suppliers, so was a natural person to step in. She was magnificent, so I asked her to do the job permanently, with a suitable raise in pay to compensate.'

'She must have been very happy.'

'Not quite, her business life was fine, it was her home life that was a shambles. Her marriage had broken down long before I met her. She came to us looking for work, initially to get out of the house and put some money aside for the day she did finally leave.' Greyspear took a deep breath and continued, 'Within weeks she knew more about our yachts than anyone else on the sales team – our clients would ask for her by name. She was becoming such an asset I couldn't afford to lose her, that's why I asked her to be my PA. And that, as they say, was that.'

'Sounds like both of our lives have taken a turn for the better.'

'You and Nancy engaged?'

'Not quite, we only met – gosh, we only met two weeks ago! Seems like we've been together for years.'

'You're in love – it does that to one's brain. Bit of a whirlwind romance, eh?'

'A bit of a whirlwind, yes. Romance – I'm not quite sure. I am sure I love her, and she says she loves me, it's just there's so much baggage between us.'

'Memories of previous relationships getting in the way?'

I nodded.

'We – that is Susan and I – went and saw someone who helped us with that.'

'Not sure what they could do with anyone like me and Nancy. Her husband, who wasn't really her husband, threatened to harm her children if she didn't do what he wanted.'

'When Angela, and then Althea, died I couldn't imagine starting a new relationship. In fact it was the furthest thing from my mind. I'm a typical man: give me a problem to solve and I excel; relationships, I'm a mess.'

'Something else we share in common.'

'So how did you and Nancy meet?'

'That's part of the problem. The first I knew of her was a phone message on my answering machine – she wanted me to teach her how to make guitars.'

'As a way of meeting, that was quite original.'

'Can be quite frustrating; lots of people want to learn, but have very poor manual dexterity or aptitude for the intricate work involved.'

'Found the same thing when I set up the factory in Greenock. It was a big learning curve for some, others took to it like the proverbial ducks to water.'

'The problem I run into in guitar making, is interpretation of the customer's request.'

'Why would that be difficult?'

'I suppose in boatbuilding, customers specify, size, colour, engines etc?'

'Yes, we have a specialist team who get that information.'

'In guitar making, the customer usually has some sort of nebulous idea of a sound they once heard and want me to reproduce it.'

'Is that difficult?'

'Can be. I just tell them I produce guitars that have a similar sound, usually have a few on display for them to try. I sometimes use an analogy of wine.'

'I see: all the grapes come from the same vineyard each year, just each vintage will have slight variations in taste and flavour?'

'Exactly so. I also have the problem that no two pieces of wood will be the same, even from the same tree. Also with the introduction of the CITES convention on endangered species, woods we would have used, such as *Dalbergia Nigra* –'

He shook his head. 'Latin was never my favourite subject.'

'Sorry, *Dalbergia Nigra* is commonly called Brazilian rosewood. It is reputed to make the best-sounding guitars. There are many substitutes still available, though not quite as good. The variations in sound quality depend on the types of wood used. I like to use European spruce for the soundboards, Sitka is getting difficult to obtain.'

'We have the same issue with teak for decking, quality is nowhere as good as it was thirty or forty years ago.'

'I cover all that with new students. It still amazes me how many people don't know anything about wood or basic woodworking tools.'

'So – is Nancy a good student?'

'No idea – so far we've only got as far as discussing the basics. We had a slow start due to the dead detective in my workshop.'

'So you haven't actually started making a guitar yet?'

'No, we kicked off our relationship with her bringing me her grandfather's guitar for repair. Very nice one it was, just needed cleaning up, some frets re-seated and a new set of strings. She said he made it in the Fleta workshop and had tried to pass it off as one of the old master's guitars.'

'Like people do with Stradivarius violins?'

'Yeah, but with the case of the guitar it was actually made in the Fleta workshop, with their materials and probably under their supervision.'

'So does that make it a real Fleta?'

'More like a student guitar, but still quite valuable.'

'You think Nancy used that as a way of getting to know you?'

'I don't think so, it was her husband who put her up to it – threatened to harm her children if she didn't comply, though Nancy did a good job of keeping them safe.'

'How did she do that?'

'They've been staying with her sister, and she's been staying with me.'

'So what was his plan?'

'The plan had been to bring me her grandfather's guitar, and swap it with the guitar I'd found while doing some work on the *Osprey*.'

'Why would he want your guitar?'

'The guitar I'd found was a lost Torres – he was an 18th century guitar maker who revolutionised guitar making.'

'I'm afraid you're losing me on all of this.'

I spent the next twenty minutes going over all that had transpired during the previous weeks.

'And you still have the double-eagle coin?'

'Yes, well hidden from prying eyes.'

'Weird, to think that little coin is more valuable than this yacht we are currently on.'

'It would be if it could be legitimately sold. Unfortunately, if I were to let it be known I had this coin, the US treasury officers would be knocking at my door demanding it back.'

'And this Dr Kaufmann thinks you know where the other 499 coins are?'

'Yes, and that's just part of the problem.'

'There's more?'

I explained about the falcon and Kaufmann's desperation to find it. 'I think he's hedging his bets. If he gets the gold he'd be one of the richest men in the world, with power to boot. If he finds the falcon, he'll be the most powerful man in the world, with money to boot. Either way he wins.'

'And if he gets both?'

'It could be the end of the world as we know it.'

'You really think so?'

'I do. If it wasn't for Nancy, I'd just close shop and disappear for a few months till Kaufmann got tired of looking for me.'

'But you can't, or won't, is that it?'

'Till I met Nancy, I'd despaired of ever meeting someone to share my life with – but now –'

'Change of allegiance?'

'Sorry?'

'When you met and married Katie, you thought it was for life? Poured your heart and soul into the relationship?'

I nodded.

'And now you've met Nancy and you're struggling to let go of your feelings for Katie?'

I nodded again and asked, 'How did you deal with it? You've been through it twice.'

'I don't have a simple answer. I suppose it was because I buried my grief way down inside myself and got really involved in expanding and developing my business so I didn't notice what was happening. One minute I was alone, then –'

'Much like me and Nancy, I suppose. I do understand how it is to feel attracted to another person, it's – it's –'

'The closeness, sharing everything, allowing yourself to become vulnerable to the other person – being accountable?'

'Yes, I suppose it is.'

'When Susan's husband died, we realised we were free to live together, get married even.'

'What happened to him?'

'He was in an accident: drowned while swimming in the marina. It was all over the local news when it happened.'

'Oh, sorry to hear that. Bet Susan was distraught?'

'In a way it was a blessing. She was a battered wife. He was a drunk; when he was on one of his binges he'd shout at her. And the bruises – they made me mad with anger, especially when she would plead with me not to go after him.'

'Why didn't she just leave him?'

'Long story, but simply put, if she divorced him she would have been penniless.'

'But you'd have taken care of her, wouldn't you?'

'I was working on it. I'd bought the engagement ring and was going to propose the night she disappeared.'

'And I thought I was living through an adventure.'

'I'd taken her out to dinner, and tried to get her to make the break. We argued, she ran away and I ended up going home alone with the engagement ring still in my pocket. The police found her a few days later. By that time, her husband was on the run as a suspected embezzler and murderer. The police eventually caught up with him. I'm surprised you didn't read about it in the papers.'

'I don't get much time for newspapers. So you were dating a married woman?'

He turned back to the control panel, increased the engine's revolutions. 'In life, Jack, you play with the hand you're dealt with. At first it was strictly business, but with her being my PA and us travelling together so much, we simply grew into a couple.'

'Just like Nancy and me.'

'Will you get married?'

'I suppose it's inevitable now her husband is dead.'

'You don't sound very enthusiastic about the prospect.'

'I'm just a bit tired and confused at the moment.'

'That's not what I'm talking about. Do you love her enough to want to spend the rest of your days together – no matter what?'

'Now you're sounding like a vicar conducting a wedding ceremony.'

'Sorry, didn't mean to.'

'I think – no, I'm sure I do. But the one thing I'm not sure of is, what am I to do about her children?'

'Adopt them. Be the dad to them that you would have been to your own children.'

'I've never met them, only seen a photo on Nancy's phone. I have no idea if they would even like me.'

'You're doing yourself an injustice; they'll just love you. Just think, Jack. How many kids have a dad who builds guitars, lives on an old tugboat, and charged all around the country with their mother in a life-threatening adventure? You'll be a hero to them.'

'Suppose so. They never knew their real father. Nancy's next husband did a runner as soon as he got his UK passport. The poor kids have never really known parents – except for Nancy and her sister. I just don't know if they'd accept me.'

'Their mother obviously does. I'm sure she's thought the whole thing through and realises that if she and you get together her children become part of the equation. I'd say you're the only candidate for the position of being their dad.'

'I'd never thought about it that way. I suppose you are right. Mothers do tend to be very protective of their children, wanting the best for them. But how can we have any chance of a family relationship with Kaufmann breathing down our necks?'

'Do you want help?'

'You?'

'Why not?' he said, as he adjusted the throttles to increase *Beatrice's* speed.

'But it's not your fight, and, in case it's slipped your mind, you're getting married in a few months.'

'Oh, I don't mean blowing the bugle and charging in with the cavalry. There are other ways I can help. You remember I said I was in the army and had spent time intercepting radio chatter?'

'Are you saying you worked for the secret service?'

'No, army intelligence is a different department. What I'm getting at is I still know a few people who might be able to spike Kaufmann's gun.'

'Interesting metaphor, especially since he never carries a gun.'

'That's good to know.'

'What about the police? They think I killed Nancy's husband.'

223

'Ah, that might be a bit more difficult to sort out – not quite what I had in mind.'

'Then there's little hope.'

'I didn't say I can't help; I've just got to be careful how I go about it.'

'Good morning, Nathan,' said Simon.

Our conversation was over – for now.

'Simon, good morning. You're early?'

'Thought I'd see how the coffee situation is before relieving you at the helm. Morning Jack, been up all night?'

'Hi Simon, just talking. I suppose I should hit the sack.'

'Where are we, Nathan?'

'Still in the Irish sea, weather's moderated a bit, I've pushed the speed back up to twenty-five knots, should be at the fuel dock in a couple of hours.'

'Staying up, Jack?'

It took me a moment to realise Bracewell was talking to me. 'For a minute, not really tired.'

'Well, I'm going to turn in,' said Greyspear, ''Night Simon, Jack.'

I was in a quandary. Part of me wanted to return to the cabin, climb into bed with Nancy and just give in to the inevitable. Yet on the other hand, now that Greyspear had volunteered to get involved, the dynamics of the situation had changed. I decided to sit up for a while and think.

'Simon, is there anything to drink on board, other than coffee?'

'You could try the bar in the galley – there was a launch party yesterday afternoon and I don't think the owners had the bar cleared afterwards.'

I walked back into the main saloon and through to the galley. I was in luck. I discovered an open bottle of JD. I grabbed a glass, found some ice in the fridge and retired, with the bottle, to the saloon. I poured a stiff shot into the glass and swallowed it in one,

224

being careful not to swallow the ice cubes. I poured another shot and leaned back in the settee to think.

♦

I woke in darkness; my head was resting on a pillow and a travel blanket keeping me warm. I squinted at the bottle and realised I'd managed to drink it dry, not a good omen for a fledgling relationship. I lay there wondering what to do next when I realised I could hear voices coming from the wheelhouse. It was Nancy – she was in conversation with whoever was on duty.

I threw back the blanket, and being very careful to not let my head fall off my shoulders, I made my way through to the wheelhouse.

'So this is what you look like in the morning after a party?' asked Nancy. 'Whatever possessed you to drink a bottle of bourbon?'

'It wasn't full when I started.'

'It certainly was empty when you finished.'

'Please, my head's falling off. Is there any coffee?'

'I should let you get your own, but I see you are punishing yourself just nicely as it is – sit down and I'll get you a cup. Nathan, coffee?'

'Yes please, Nancy.'

'Where are we?' I asked.

'Those lights on our left, they're the night lights of Bournemouth. We should be home in Eastbourne in the early hours.'

'What time is it now?'

'Just past eight. You must have been really tired?'

'He hasn't slept for three nights,' said Nancy, returning from the galley. 'Here's your coffee, I made it extra strong.'

I took a sip and realised it could support the proverbial spoon.

'I've also brought you some painkillers, should help you uncross your eyes.'

'Thanks.'

'You drank the whole bottle on your own?' she asked, while shaking her head like a disapproving mother at a naughty child.

I was about to shake my head but managed to resist the urge. 'No, it was only a third full when I started.'

'Well, it's empty now.'

'Thanks – I needed to know that.'

'You're sounding like a Merle Haggard song.'

'Sorry?'

'Oh, never mind.'

'I think I'll go have a shower and change,' I said, trying to lighten the mood, 'I've been in these clothes for two days now.'

'Probably smell better as well.'

'Thanks – sorry, been under a bit of stress these past few days.'

'While you're showering, I'll make you something to eat. What would you like?'

'What is there?'

'Not sure, I'll have a look in the galley.'

'There should be plenty of eggs and bacon,' interrupted Greyspear.

Cup in hand I headed down the stairs to our cabin. I stripped and climbed into the shower, standing there letting the hot water melt away the tension in my neck. Finally, feeling a little bit like normal, I dried, shaved, dressed and returned to the wheelhouse.

'I recognise that face, feel better?' Nancy asked.

'Yes, thanks.'

'I've made you a bacon and egg sandwich. Like a coffee to go with it?'

'Could I have a cup of tea?'

'Coming right up. Why don't you sit down and I'll bring it out to you?'

I sat down on the settee, my back straight, and found I'd clasped my hands in front of me like a schoolboy in the headmaster's office.

'A formidable lady, your Nancy,' said Greyspear, with a huge grin. 'She really loves you.'

I leaned back and almost laughed. 'She's not bad. I think I'll let her keep me.'

'What was that, Jack?' said Nancy, from the galley.

'Oh, nothing, just something Nathan said.'

'Here's your food, eat it while it's hot.'

I smiled and wondered what I'd done in life to deserve such a gift, then thought maybe it's not what I'd done, but what I would do to deserve it. I suddenly felt very humble.

'How do you feel – better?' she asked, as I washed down the last of the sandwich with my tea.

'Yes, thanks to you.'

'We've been talking.'

'We?'

'Nathan and I.'

'Oh really, what about?'

'Things, just things.'

'And about your good Doctor Kaufmann,' interrupted Greyspear.

'I can assure you, Nathan, he's definitely not my good doctor, or anything else.'

'Just a figure of speech, Jack, that's all.'

'So what have you two been cooking up?'

'While you were sleeping, this afternoon –'

'I really slept fifteen hours?'

'You haven't slept properly since this whole adventure started. I didn't want to wake you.'

'Thanks. Can't wait to get home and back into my own bed.'

'As I was saying,' continued Greyspear, 'I made a few enquiries this afternoon and it might surprise you to hear what a bad piece of news the doctor is.'

'Like what?' I asked.

'For a start, he's not a medical doctor. His doctorate is in philosophy. Instead of working in his field, he uses it as a front to conceal his nefarious affairs.'

'Such as?'

'The one that stands out the most, happened a couple of years ago. Apparently, he'd chartered a yacht in an misguided attempt to import a substantial amount of cocaine into France from South America.'

'What went wrong with his plans? Do you know?' asked Nancy.

'Some enterprising Venezuelan treasure hunter managed to substitute the shipment with bags of harmless chalk.'

Serves him right, I thought. 'What happened when he tried to sell it?'

'It was tested and found to be just chalk dust.'

'How embarrassing it must have been for him,' said Nancy. 'Bet his backers wanted their money back?'

'According to my sources, he was self-financed through a grant from UNESCO.'

'And they didn't want their money back?'

'He was supposed to be surveying the effects of low rainfall on the Amazon river. He made up a story about how he had lost two of his team to incidents in the jungle, blamed it on illegal loggers. Said his team had been attacked and he had to abandon the project.'

'So, is that why he's still at large?' I asked.

'Jack, Nancy, you need to be very careful with this man, he is dangerous.'

'You're telling me – I've been on the receiving end of his anger,' I said, still feeling the ebbing pain from Hanse's backhander across the face and Snyder's cosh.

'What I'm saying is,' continued Greyspear, 'two people died on that expedition, supposedly by the hands of the illegal loggers, but my source says that was a cover for what really happened.'

'Death stalks him, like vultures after a dying man,' said Nancy.

'A poet in our midst,' said Greyspear.

'Not really, I just write songs, or at least I try to.'

'You were telling us about the doctor, Nathan?'

'Not much more to tell except my contact says the powers that be like to keep tabs on him. Not for his doings as such, but more to do with his connections. Apparently he leaves a very visible trail behind him.'

'Did they say anything about his current obsession?'

'They were surprised when I mentioned it. They thought he was harmlessly stumbling around in the dark trying to locate some ancient Egyptian artefacts, not the sort of items my contacts are interested in.'

'So they've lost interest in him?'

'In a word, yes, but I had them ask about the American coins.'

'And what did they say?' asked Nancy.

'It took a bit of cajoling, but in the end they said Kaufmann was looking for some World War 2 gold coins'.

'The double eagles!' exclaimed Nancy.

'When pressed, the US treasury official denied the existence of any coins, said that all have been accounted for. And, as such, are not interested in what Kaufmann is up to. Their man said it was just another one of those conspiracy stories put about by ignorant people.'

'So Kaufmann's free to do what he wants, without fear of anyone checking up on him?' I asked.

'Looks like that.'

'Then what was that Snyder doing on the *Osprey* last week?' asked Nancy.

'A bit of freelancing. My contact said he turned rogue when he was working for the US treasury department, something about a bank robbery that went bad. Snyder was supposed to be on a stake-out for a robbery at a concert when the local bank was robbed instead; suspicion pointed to him as the person who tipped off the gang.'

'So the US treasury says it's just another conspiracy story?' said Nancy.

'Typical government way of going about it. First they make fun of the story, then secondly, when it starts to have a following, they ridicule it.' I said.

'And thirdly? There's always a thirdly,' said Nancy.

'Thirdly, they say they knew about it all along, but said they were keeping the story quiet to protect the innocent, or some such suitable verbiage.'

'And we vote for them?' said Nancy. 'I suppose the US treasury really believes that the gold does exist then?'

'Looks that way.'

'And, more importantly, so does Kaufmann,' I added. 'Were they asked about the falcon statue?'

'Yes, but they said they didn't believe it had any significance, thought it was just a story written in the 30's about a jewel-encrusted gold statue, just another one of the doctor's wild ideas of getting rich quick.'

'If it still exists,' Nancy added.

'Kaufmann seems to think it does, and I suppose those who he intends to sell it to do as well,' I replied. 'But I'm confused about the coins. Surely, if they exist, and the US treasury recovers them, they will only have the gold value. Five hundred of them released on the market will kill their intrinsic value.'

'True.'

'But then they wouldn't do that, would they? They'd probably only release five to ten a year at auction, then they'd get the price they wanted.'

'That makes sense, Jack,' said Nancy. 'Nathan, what do you think we should do?'

'A famous general once said: *never let the enemy pitch the battle site.* I believe you should do just that.'

'Set a trap?'

'As the good general also said: *in case of doubt, attack and may the good Lord show them mercy, because I won't.*'

'Do you have a suggestion,' I asked, 'without resorting to blood and gore?'

'Your boat, the *Osprey*, seems to be the focal point of his obsession. I suggest you start there.'

'Ah, I have a problem with that.'

'Why?'

'She's got a bad leak, some of the rivets down near the keel have rusted pretty badly. I'm worried they might just fall out and sink the *Osprey* at the dock.'

'When were you planning to have the work done?'

'The yard where I was planning to take the *Osprey* says they have a slip free for the next few weeks, but I can't take advantage of it just now.'

'Why is that?'

'Getting her to the yard. I don't have a licence to operate a boat the size of the *Osprey*, and also, the engine hasn't been run in years.'

'No problem,' said Greyspear 'I'll lend you Simon and the boys. Do them good to handle a boat as old as the *Osprey*. When can you be ready to move?'

'Probably sometime next week. I've a few guitars to repair first.'

'I could help,' said Nancy.

I looked at her; the smile said it all. I was going to enjoy my future.

13

A new Family

We arrived back in Eastbourne marina at three in the morning. As we had catnapped most of the remainder of the journey, neither of us was tired. I knew in myself, and by looking into Nancy's eyes, that neither of us wanted the moment to end. Bracewell and Greyspear had left us alone for most of the trip, just like we were honoured guests, which I suppose we were. So we decided to spend the remainder of the night on the *Beatrice* talking about what had happened during the last few days and what awaited us on our return to Eastbourne.

I realised Nancy was waiting for me to make a move, to take our relationship to the obvious conclusion. Stupid really: I wanted to propose and I knew she wanted me to propose, I just couldn't find the words. I suppose it was the feeling of not wanting to be rejected that made me reticent. I did realise that sooner or later I would ask her, and I was just as sure she would accept, but I was not sure when. It didn't feel right to ask her – and the children of course – to join me in a permanent relationship when there was so much danger happening in my life.

'Where are you going?' I asked Nancy, as the *Beatrice* approached the lock-gates.

'I could do with some fresh air. Also I'd like to watch what happens when we go through the locks and into the marina.'

Bracewell steered the *Beatrice* towards the open left-hand gate and tied up to the pontoons. The gates closed behind us and water started to fill the lock. Bracewell climbed down onto the pontoon and talked with the lock-keeper while the water level raised to that of the inner harbour. The gates opened and the *Beatrice* moved forward. Nancy put her arms round me. I pulled my jacket round us both and held her tight as we moved silently between the moored boats. I put my free hand up to push the hair back from my face and felt the moisture from the damp air had settled on it; I wiped my face with my hand, so refreshing.

Other than the quiet gurgle of the exhaust there was not a sound in the marina. We continued on past the bascule bridge and ended the voyage by tying up in front of Greyspear's house.

Bracewell and the crew turned in. Greyspear left to go home saying, 'I'll get in touch in a couple of days to finalise arrangements for the *Osprey's* refit. In the meantime, the *Beatrice* is yours to enjoy.'

'Fine, and thanks for getting us home.'

'No trouble.'

'Yes, thanks. Nathan. Thanks for everything,' said Nancy.

'It was my pleasure, and remember our conversation. Don't forget.'

I stood in the main saloon and watched him walk down the dock and up the path to his house. As he approached the door it was opened by a tall blonde woman; they hugged and went in, closing the door behind them. Would Nancy be waiting for me when I came home from a busy day? Of course she would, and I was looking forward to that.

'How many guitars do we have to repair?'

'What are you not to forget?'

'Oh, nothing.'

'Nothing? You're keeping secrets from me already?'

'Of course not, just holding on to something. I'll let you know one day.'

I almost felt threatened, the woman in my life keeping a secret from me. But I suppose since Greyspear was involved, maybe I shouldn't pursue it. I decided it was best not to press the matter.

'Okay, if that's the way you want to play it.'

She laughed and threw a pillow at me. 'How many guitars do we have to repair?'

I did a mental inventory and replied, 'As long as Dizzy stays away, I'd say about eight. Mostly straightforward servicing: new strings, fretboard cleaning, setting the action, that sort of thing.'

'It may be straightforward to you, to me it's all double-dutch.'

'Don't worry, I'll hold your hand through it all.'

'Won't that be a bit awkward?'

Why do women always have to find double meaning in everything? 'Relax, it's just a figure of speech. Don't worry, I'll explain everything to you before you start.'

'Good, I'll hold you to that.'

More innuendo; life certainly had taken a turn for the best. What could go wrong now?

♦

What went wrong was the *Osprey*. I went to push the key into the lock and saw there was no lock. Where it should have been there was now a seventy-millimetre hole. Sawdust and brass shavings lay on the deck directly below and, in the middle of them, sat the lock.

'What is it?' asked Nancy.

'Kaufmann's been here, or at least one of his henchmen,' I said, pointing to the hole in the door.

I gently pushed the door open and went inside. To say that a hurricane had blown through would have been an understatement. Not one cupboard door was shut, or drawer in place, all their contents were strewn across the floor. With trepidation, I descended into my cabin: shredded pillows, ripped blankets and clothes thrown everywhere met my gaze.

'Your workshop – what will that look like?' asked Nancy.

I expected chaos to reign there as well and I wasn't wrong. My big fear was that whoever had invaded my boat had decided to trash everything. At least I was only partially correct. For some unknown reason none of the guitars had been touched, just the contents of the drawers and cupboards had been hit again.

'Kaufmann?' asked Nancy.

I nodded. 'Looks that way. One parting shot, a final desperate search for something that probably doesn't exist.'

'Well, at least he didn't damage the guitars.'

'It might have been better if he had.'

'Why do you say that?'

'The fact he didn't damage the guitars means this was not a vengeful, or spiteful attack, he's still looking for his gold coins and falcon.'

'But surely it means he's done with us and any involvement we might have?'

I wished I could believe that. 'Let's hope so. In the meantime, we've got work to do.'

By the time we had thrown out all the ripped clothes and bedding, put everything that was to be retained back where it belonged, and cleaned the spilt food from the galley floor, it was dinner time.

'I've just realised something,' I said.

'What?'

'Your children. Shouldn't you go see them?'

'I talked to Sarah and the children this morning, before they went to school.'

'Oh.' Not sure why I felt disappointed. After all I'd never met them, or even talked to them.

'I'll call Sarah. If what you say about Kaufmann is true, I certainly don't want to lead him back to them.'

'Mother blackbird, that's what you are.'

'What do you mean?'

'When a mother blackbird thinks her nest is in danger, she pretends to be lame and tries to lead any predators away from it.'

'But I'm not leading anyone.'

'Still the same – you're protecting your brood.'

I watched her climb the steps into the main saloon. She turned at the top to look at me and said, 'You too. Come on, it's time you got to talk to the children.'

'Er – I'm not quite ready for that. Do you mind if we put it off till after this mess is sorted?'

'Chicken,' she said, gently shaking her head. 'Of course I don't mind, time enough later.'

I picked up my notebook with the list of guitars to be repaired and read down it. I picked out a couple for Nancy to start on and waited for her to make the phone call. I didn't realise she would bring the phone down into the workshop.

'Phone's on speaker, so don't say anything you don't want heard,' she said. 'Don't worry, Sarah's gone to get the children, all you have to do is listen.'

I did just that. Part of me wanted to say hello, while part of me felt I was intruding in someone's private life. Get over it, I said to myself, this is your new family. I listened to Nancy chatter with the children and when she said goodbye, I joined in.

'Who's that?' asked Stephen.'

Oops – should have kept quiet.

'That's Jack, he's teaching me to make guitars.'

'Hello, Jack. Do you live on a boat?' asked Stephen.

It all came back to me, the innocence of childish chatter, the off-hand questions. It felt so good I wanted it to go on and not stop.

'Have you made a guitar for anyone famous?' he asked.

I thought of Dizzy and his lifelong desire for prominence in the musical world.

'Have you heard of Dizzy?'

'No.'

'That's all right, I'll introduce you to him one day.'

There followed a ten-minute conversation of how, when Stephen grew up, he wanted to be a sea captain, or maybe a pilot and fly big jet aeroplanes. I'd done it, I'd stepped into their lives, there was no going back now.

'Thought you weren't going to say anything?' Nancy said, poking me gently in the ribs after she hung up.

'Couldn't help it, just wanted to – just wanted to be part of what was going on, that's all.'

'I see.'

I was sure she did, but I didn't mind. I'd finally broken the ice; the next step would be to meet them.

'Dinner? Or do we go straight to work?'

'Dinner – an army marches on its stomach, that's what I've been told.'

'Bit odd, that?'

'It's a figure of speech, not to be taken literally.'

I ordered a take-away from the Thai Marina restaurant and, while we waited for it to be ready, I went over what I wanted her to do on her first guitar.

We worked well as a team and, by eleven o'clock, four of the eight guitars were ready to go home to their owners. At this rate all the guitars would be ready to go back by the end of the week, just in time for me to start getting the *Osprey* ready for her refit. We went to bed exhausted, kissed goodnight and fell immediately asleep.

14

The Children

'Good morning, sleepyhead. Breakfast is ready.'

'What time is it?'

'Watch your –'

'*Ouch*.'

'I was going to say "head". One of the disadvantages of living on a boat like this is where the bunk goes under the side deck.'

'I think I still prefer the *Osprey* to the *Beatrice*.'

'Why?'

'Because this is where you live.'

'It could be us.'

'Why Jack Nevis! Are you proposing?'

'I – I suppose I am.'

'In that case, I accept. Not quite the getting down on the knees proposal, but I'll take it all the same.'

I smiled and felt a bit weepy.

'Are you crying?'

I sniffed. 'No, just happy, never imagined this could happen. Thanks.'

'Breakfast, you said?'

'Yes.'

'What are we having?' she asked, reaching out with her hand, the familiar smile dimpling her cheeks, her green eyes alive with excitement.

'There's one thing we will have to do first.'

'And what is that?'

'We must rename the *Osprey*.'

'Why?'

'I'm not starting my married life living on an unhappy boat, especially since someone was murdered on it.'

'You mean we should call her the *Kestrel*? As she was on the day she was launched?'

'Absolutely. I agree with what Mr Munroe said, remember, *It's bad luck to rename a ship*?'

'Then *Kestrel* it will be. When the yard repaints the hull we'll have the name repainted, how's that?'

'Fine.'

♦

I was in the workshop re-fretting one of the remaining guitars when Nancy called down the stairs.

'Coffee?'

'Thanks, I'll bring up my cup.'

'How's it going? Almost done?'

'Yep. I'll let you dress and polish the frets while I get on to the last guitar.'

'Dolls I've dressed, frets never.'

'Don't worry, I'll get you started.'

'I'd like to tell Sarah about us.'

'Of course. What about the children?'

'Would you mind if we wait? I'd like to break the news to them personally.'

'I understand. It'll be a big shock to them.'

'Maybe, maybe not.'

'What do you mean? What have you told them?'

'I didn't need to tell them anything, other than you are a good friend. They're smart, Jack, they suspected something was going on.'

'Just like their mother.'

While Nancy called Sarah, I thought about my phone and wondered if I would ever see it again. Reluctantly I resolved to call Vodaphone and report it stolen.

'Sarah, guess what? Yes, this morning – before breakfast! He's here with me on the boat – hold on.'

Nancy pressed the speaker button.

'Hello, Jack. Congratulations.'

'Thanks, Sarah.'

'Glad you finally got round to it! We've been waiting for you to ask.'

'We?'

'Nancy, me, and the kids.'

'The kids know?'

'Not officially, they're waiting for their mum to tell them.'

I'd made the right decision. What was more important – I was wanted. I was a family man again.

'Nan, what does Kaufmann look like? I think I saw him this morning?'

'Where?'

'When I dropped the kids off at school. I saw someone who looks like him sitting in a car.'

'Was he a large man, black greasy hair?' I asked.

'I think so.'

'Was he alone?'

'No, there were two others in the car with him. Why?'

Not the news I wanted to hear. Not only was Kaufmann still around, he was still with Hanse and Snyder.

'Sarah, do you think he recognised you, or the children?'

'Doubt it, Jack. Nancy and I don't look that alike.'

Not quite what I thought, having seen them together.

'What time do you go to collect them?'

'Don't worry. I reported the car to the school – they called the police.'

'What did the police do?' I asked, in the vain hope Kaufmann et al had been arrested.

'I waited to see what would happen. As soon as the police car showed up, your friends tried to move on.'

'And then?'

'The police stopped them, got them out of their car, then made them stand against the school fence.'

'What then?'

'One of those big police vans showed up and your friends were put inside and driven away.'

'Sarah – they are not our friends. They killed Nancy's husband.'

'Interesting way of looking at it.'

'Jack,' said Nancy, 'if Kaufmann and friends are in jail, Sarah could bring the kids over. I'm sure they'd love to see the *Osprey*.

'How do we know they're still in jail – if they ever were in the first place?'

'You could call your police sergeant and ask her?'

'Bit risky. We don't even know if they still suspect us.'

'She doesn't need to know where we are, does she?'

'I'll call her,' piped up Sarah, 'after all I was the one who reported them in the first place. I'll pretend I'm a concerned mother, worried that her children are going to be kidnapped.'

'Excellent idea, Sarah. Let me get you the sergeant's phone number.'

I retrieved the business card from the desk that constituted an office in my workshop and read it out to Sarah.

'I'll call you back as soon as I've any news. 'Bye for now,'

'What now?' asked Nancy.

'To work, we've still got three guitars to repair.'

We didn't hear back from Sarah till gone four o'clock.

'What did you find out?' I asked.

'They're being held pending further enquiries.'

'What enquiries? Did they tell you?' I asked.

'No, just that they were being held, and for me not to worry – the police enquiries had nothing to do with children.'

I wasn't sure if I liked that news, what there was of it. I'd hoped they'd been charged, but then there would be very little evidence to support this, especially since I still had Hanse's gun.

'It's getting late. Do you still want me to bring the children over?' asked Sarah.

241

I looked at Nancy. 'What do you think?'

'Sarah, tomorrow's Saturday – how about you bring them over after breakfast?'

'Fine by me. We'd planned to have popcorn and watch a movie this evening anyway.'

'Sarah,' I interrupted, 'the weather is supposed to be fine tomorrow. How about we have a barbecue? You could bring your kids along as well.'

'On the boat?'

'Why not?'

'Great, I'll tell them in the morning – I'll never get them to sleep otherwise.'

'How will you get them here?'

'In the bus.'

'You have a bus?'

'No, it's a VW seven seater; the kids call it the bus.'

I left them to get on with the arrangements for the visit and returned to the workshop and the remaining guitars. I'd just finished the last one when Nancy joined me in the workshop.

'How do you do it?' I asked.

'Do what?'

'Not being able to be with your children.'

'It's only since I met you that they've spent so much time with Sarah.'

'So much in two weeks.'

'What do you fancy for dinner?'

'Want to go out somewhere?'

'I'd rather stay in, get used to my kitchen – oops, sorry – galley.'

'There's not much to eat on board.'

'Why don't I pop over to Asda? I'm sure I can find something there that will take your fancy.'

She cooked us grilled lamb chops with baked potatoes and veg.

'Jack, where are the children going to live?'

'The *Osprey* will need to be modified inside. The forward compartment would be best. We could strip out all the old shelving and lockers and turn it into two cabins, one with double bunks and the other as a single.'

'Didn't realise there was a forward compartment – how do we get to it?'

'Through the workshop, there's a door in the bulkhead at the far end.'

'I don't remember a door.'

'It's not very visible. it's where I hang my guitars while they are being worked on. There's a curtain behind the guitars to stop them bumping against the bulkhead. I'll show you it in the morning.'

'Why not now?'

I was hoping for an early night, but I didn't want to blunt her enthusiasm.

'At least with you finishing all the repairs, there's no guitars to move,' she said, as I unhooked the curtain from the bulkhead exposing the door.

'Is it locked?'

'Not necessary. It's where I store all my timber and finishing supplies. There used to be metal cots for the crew; I threw out the old rotten mattresses and used the frames as shelves. Haven't been in there in months.'

Nancy tried the door. 'It's locked. Where's the key?'

I shook my head. 'Don't think it's locked. Possibly one of the curtain rail screws have gone into the door as well as the bulkhead. Let me get my screwdriver.'

It only took a few minutes to unscrew the offending screw. 'Now try it.'

Nancy once again tried the door: this time it reluctantly opened on its rusty hinges.

'Hope you've been charging these spiders rent?'

I was amazed just how many spider webs there were, and how much fine sawdust had filtered through the cracks in the bulkhead.

243

'It's going to take hours of work to just get it clean,' she said.

'I never said it would be easy.'

She looked into the compartment full of shelves loaded to the ceiling with chunks of spruce, rosewood, maple, and mahogany. I realised I needed to get in there more often.

'How do you manage to know what and where everything is? And do you really need all this wood?'

'Probably not, but when Dave calls and says he's just got a new delivery of triple A grade timber, I just can't pass up the opportunity. I suppose I could sell most of it and never go short.'

'Aren't you worried about fire, especially with all this timber and – are those tins of lacquer?'

'Not all of them are lacquer, some of them are paint for the boat, but since I don't smoke and there aren't any electrical appliances in here to cause a spark. I don't see there is much of a fire risk.'

'What about the light bulb? I've heard that they can break and cause a fire.'

'You know what?'

'No, enlighten me.'

'I think you worry too much.'

'Typical man.

'Thanks for caring.'

'I have a thought.'

'What's that?'

'Your workshop. It would be better if it were situated in here, and where you have your workshop now, would be better suited as the children's cabins. Look, your present workshop is wider than the forward area and would make bigger cabins for the children.'

It had taken me a year to get my workshop configured to how it worked best. I thought about her suggestion for a minute and reluctantly came to the same conclusion. I could just get my workshop in there, and, if I did, the children's cabins would be part of the living area of the boat, making it more like a home.

'You're right, I could relocate my workshop into the forward area. It will need to be gutted first, then all my benches and tools moved in here before I can start on the children's cabins.'

'I'll help,' she said, putting her arm around me and holding me tight. 'A home for our children.'

15

The Refit

I heard, rather than saw, them arrive. I was down in my workshop with measuring tape working out how best to create two cabins with a walkway between them through to my soon-to-be relocated workshop. At the sound of six pairs of children's feet charging round the deck, I went up to welcome my new family. I felt like I wanted to not be there. Strange that, part of me was desperate to see them, while, on the other hand, I was unsure. I think it was not wanting to be rejected, wanting to be accepted.

It was easy to see which kids belonged to which mother. Sarah's kids all had dark curly hair, while Nancy's had straight fair hair.

'Hi, Jack,' said Stephen, looking down from the wheelhouse railing. 'Neat boat! How fast is it?'

'Er – not very.'

'Stephen, where are your manners?' interjected Nancy.

'That's all right,' I replied. 'Glad you like it, Stephen.'

The wheelhouse door slid back and the twins came out, followed by Sarah's three. 'Stephen, guess what?' said one of the twins.

'What?'

'It's got a steering wheel!'

Stephen followed the girls back inside to investigate, leaving me to wonder about safety on board.

'Nancy, do they know how to swim?'

'Don't worry so much, Jack. They're all good swimmers.'

'Hi, Sarah, how are you?'

'I'm fine, Jack, thanks for inviting us.'

'No problem. How about your kids? Do they swim?'

'Like fish, no need to worry.'

I did worry, the kids were a virtual whirlwind of excitement. I was glad the mast on the *Osprey* was short, just high enough for the navigation lights to be seen over the wheelhouse. By the time I had the barbecue ready, the children had been everywhere except the engine room – that inspection was reserved for going home time.

The barbecue was a success – at least the sausages were edible – and the visit to the engine room met with mixed responses. Sarah's kids weren't very interested, while, much to my joy, Nancy's wanted to explore every nook and cranny.

'Can we start the engine?' asked Stephen.

I shook my head. 'Not today, it's not in running condition.'

Eventually the time came for them to leave and I wasn't sure if I wanted the empty quietness to return. I'd enjoyed the chatter, questions and happy noise. I don't know why I said it, but I just came out with, 'Would you kids like to sleep over? Just for one night?'

Nancy's children jumped with joy, while Sarah's looked bored.

Nancy and Sarah turned to me and gave me an, *are you mad,* look.

Nancy asked, 'Where would they sleep, Jack?'

'Mine can't,' interrupted Sarah. 'Their dad will be home from work soon and he hasn't seen them all week.'

'I bagsy the wheelhouse,' said Sandra.

'Me too,' said Stephanie.

'Stephen, where would you like to sleep?' asked Nancy.

He shrugged. 'How about here in this room, on the upper bunk?'

The upper bunk he referred to was where I kept things I had nowhere else to store.

'Do you have enough blankets, Jack?' Nancy asked.

'Not sure.'

'Look,' said Sarah, 'if the children are going to live on board why don't I go collect their clothes and some blankets and bring them back with me?'

'Sarah!' said Nancy.

'Oops, sorry sis! But you all look like such a happy family.'

'We're going to be living here with Jack?' asked Stephen.

'Yes, here on the boat,' replied Nancy.

'All of us?' asked Sandra.

'Yes, all of us.'

'Even Aunty Sarah?' asked Stephanie.

'No, definitely not,' answered Sarah, with a laugh.

'You'll have your own cabins,' said Nancy. 'Jack is going to build you two of your own.'

The children were quiet for a moment, then Sandra asked the one question I didn't know if I'd ever hear. 'Does that mean you are going to be our new daddy?'

I looked at Nancy for an answer.

'Jack has asked me to marry him.'

'Good,' said Stephen. 'I didn't like that other one.'

'Neither did we,' said Stephanie.

Out of the mouths of babes and children come such simple truths. I was to be their new dad, simple fact, no argument; I liked it.

'I'll be back in twenty minutes, Nan,' said Sarah, as she escorted her brood out the door and on to the dock.

'Well, Jack, hope you're serious about all this. I wasn't going to mention us getting married to the children for a while.'

I shrugged. 'It just sort of came out, and besides, it was Sarah who let the cat out of the bag.'

Not for the first time that day our conversation was cut short.

'Jack, where are our cabins going to be?' asked Stephanie.

'Follow me,' I said, heading below to my workshop. 'There will be a cabin on each side,' I explained, drawing an outline on the floor with a piece of yellow chalk. 'Stephen's on one side and you girls on the other. There will be a corridor down the middle so I can get to my workshop.' I saw a look of consternation on their faces. 'Don't worry, all my tools and benches will be moved into their new workshop.'

'Where will that be?' asked Sandra.

'Behind that curtain there's a door that leads into another room,' I said, pointing to where I hung my guitars. 'Not quite as big as this one, but big enough for my workshop.'

'Can we have a look?' asked Stephen.

'Not just now, it's dusty and needs a good clean,' said Nancy, who'd followed us down from the main saloon. 'Maybe tomorrow.'

'*Aw*, we wanted to see everything! After all, this is our home now,' said Stephanie.

'Tomorrow, I promise,' said Nancy. 'Now it's time to get ready for bed. Aunty Sarah will be back in a few minutes with your clothes and blankets.'

It took an hour to get them ready for bed. While Nancy was bathing them I made up bunk beds in the wheelhouse for Stephanie and Sandra and relocated my stuff from the upper bunk in the main saloon for Stephen. By ten-thirty we were all tucked up in our beds, one big happy family.

I lay awake late into the night thinking about just how lucky I was. Two weeks ago, I was a single man, minding my own business, repairing musical instruments. Now, two weeks later, I had a woman who loved me enough to marry me, three children who wanted me to be their dad, new friends, and oddly, to top it all, I possessed a twenty-dollar gold coin worth about seven and a half million dollars if it could ever be sold. I had a priceless new family and an old coin that was basically worthless. What a wonderful life!

But what of tomorrow and the ensuing days? What of them? Unless the police could charge Kaufmann with the murders of the California P.I. and Nancy's husband, and get a conviction, my new family and I were still in danger. I did, of course, still have Hanse's gun tucked away under the mattress at the foot of the bed; that needed to get to the police. But unless they had the gun and Hanse in their possession at the same time it would be difficult to get a conviction. What was needed was for Hanse to be arrested, tried and convicted of the two murders. Then Kaufmann to be convinced I did not now, or ever, have in my possession the falcon or double eagles.

'You awake?' asked Nancy.

'Sorry, did I wake you?'

'No.'

'What time is it?'

I looked at the bedside clock. 'Four-thirty.'

'I've been lying here thinking just how lucky I am.'

'Don't worry, you'll get over it.'

'Cheeky so and so!'

'Just joking. We're both very lucky.'

'Those children, I was worrying myself silly how to tell them about us.'

'I'm glad they seem to like me.'

'You have a boat, that helps. And of course the fact you're here where they can talk to you, and you're willing to listen to them, makes a big difference.'

'Was Achmed really that bad as a father?'

'Worse – he ignored them at best and if they made any noise he would shout at them. I was glad when he disappeared.'

'How long was he around?'

'About six or seven weeks.'

'That all?'

'He waited till his passport came through, then did a runner.'

'What a –'

'Jack, I'm worried about the children. What are we going to do about Kaufmann?'

'The police have him. Don't worry, we're safe for now.'

'But will they be able to keep him? Do they have enough evidence to charge him?'

'I don't know. I suppose I could call the police and ask them.'

'They must be confident if they've arrested him.'

'Not necessarily. They may only be holding him pending enquiries.'

'How long will that take?'

'He and his gang can only be held for 24 hours without charge, unless they apply to a judge for an extension.'

'So, if they arrested them Friday morning, the police have till Saturday morning to either charge them or let them go?'

'Looks that way.'

'Jack, we have to do something. We can't just sit here and do nothing.'

'Sunday evening we'll to take the kids back to Sarah's – she will still look after them, won't she?'

'Of course she will, she's my sister. She knows I'd do the same for her.'

'Good. After we've done that we'll come back here and work out a plan of how to deal with Kaufmann.'

'Ok, but in the meantime, I think we should get some sleep, we've a busy day tomorrow.'

'You mean today?'

'You're so right, night, night.'

♦

We woke to the sound of the children running on the deck.

'What time is it?' asked Nancy.

'Seven-thirty. Do your children always get up this early?'

'They're excited, Jack. It's not every day they get to wake up on a boat.'

I made a huge stack of pancakes for breakfast and watched three hungry children devour them. For entertainment I cleaned out the dinghy and motored us round the harbour to where the *Beatrice* was tied up.

'She looks so much bigger from down here,' remarked Nancy, as we drifted past.

'Is it bigger than the *Osprey*?' asked Stephen.

'No, Stephen. The *Osprey* is two feet longer.'

'Wow! Really?'

'I thought I heard voices.'

We looked up and saw the smiling face of Greyspear.

'Out for a sail?'

'Not quite,' I replied. 'Just showing the kids the boat we spent the last couple of days on.'

'Would they like to see around her?' asked Greyspear.

I didn't have to ask.

Greyspear was the perfect guide and we ended up being invited to join him, his fiancée, and friends in another barbecue.

I motored us back to the *Osprey* as the sun was setting.

'Do we have to go to bed now?' asked Stephanie. 'We want to explore our new home.'

'Tell you what,' said Nancy, 'you can stay up another half an hour. Then it's bed.'

'Where will we start?' asked Stephen.

'I know,' said Sandra, 'we haven't been into the forward compartment, the one Jack's going to make into his new workshop. Bet there's plenty to see in there.'

'Jack?' said Nancy.

I raised my hands. 'No problem, there's nothing in there they can break that's not going to be ripped out when the new workshop is built.'

As they headed down the companionway to my workshop and through to the forward compartment I poured Nancy a coffee.

'Are you sure they're all right exploring in there?' asked Nancy.

'Sure they are, it's perfectly safe. Nothing can harm them.'

What is it that's said about famous last words? I'd no sooner spoken when we heard the sound of something crashing to the floor.

'Jack, you said they'd be safe!'

'You kids all right?' I yelled.

'Yes, just an old box fell on the floor.'

An old box? I didn't remember any old boxes being in that part of the boat. It was just piles of guitar-making lumber.

'See, I told you they'd be fine.' I replied, feeling uneasy about the box that had just materialised.

'Well, what do you think of your new family?'

'Can I think about it – for at least the next hundred years?'

'Very funny. Seriously, I'd hate to see them hurt again. They never really knew their father, and Achmed, well, he was just a name on the occasional letter from the Home Office.'

'Will you please relax, I love them. Just hope they'll grow to love me in turn.'

'They will – I did.'

There it was again: a quickening of the heartbeat, the warm fuzzy feeling inside, a sensation of complete peace.

'I think they're too quiet,' said Nancy.

I looked at the clock and realised half an hour had passed.

Nancy followed me down the stairs, two at a time, and into the forward compartment. Three pairs of eyes looked at us, then back to the floor. What they were looking at was a large, grey, wooden box, with the words *US Treasury* stencilled on the side. The top had partially opened and some of its contents had spilled onto the floor.

'We're sorry, Jack, we didn't mean to break it,' said Stephanie.

'They just fell out on the floor,' said Stephen, holding a fistful of coins.

'What happened?' Nancy asked, as I bent down to look at the box.

'Sandra was trying to climb into that cupboard,' explained Stephanie, 'and she grabbed something to pull herself up and the box fell out.'

'Is it pirate treasure?' asked Stephen.

I stood up and looked at the children. 'It's quite all right, nothing is broken. It's just an old dusty box in an old dusty cupboard. And Stephen, yes, if you want, you can call it pirate treasure, but it's not the kind you can spend.'

'Pity, we thought if we found treasure we could give it to you and Mum, then you could make the *Osprey* nice like the *Beatrice*.'

'Thanks, kids. That's very thoughtful of you.'

'Right, that's enough excitement for one day,' said Nancy. 'It's bed for all of you.'

'Can we keep the treasure?' asked Stephanie.

'Let me see what else is in the box and I'll tell you in the morning.'

'Just one, please, Jack?' said Sandra. 'If it's just pretend pirate treasure we could put it under our pillows and maybe if we wish hard enough it will turn it into real treasure.'

I looked at Nancy for an answer.

She smiled and shrugged. 'Okay, just one each, and we'll see what happens. But don't get your hopes up.'

We waited till the children were asleep, then I suggested to Nancy that we swap the coins for crisp twenty-pound notes.

'I think that's a lovely idea, and the kids will love that.'

Nancy held the door, as I lugged the heavy box through to my workshop.

'It's locked and I certainly don't have the key,' I said, reaching for a pry bar.

Three hefty whacks on the pry bar with a hammer had the lid of the box free.

'You open it,' I said to Nancy.

'Chicken,' she replied, taking hold of the broken hasp. Even though it hadn't been opened for almost seventy years the lid swung back effortlessly, revealing a piece of velvet cloth.

'It's just got to be them,' said Nancy as she lifted the cloth.

It *was* them – all 499 US 1933 double-eagle gold coins, minus the three that were at that moment lying under pillows fuelling dreams of futures not yet lived. Those, plus the one in the guitar case with the Torres guitar.

'How much did you say they're worth?'

'You are looking at three and a half billion dollars of antique gold coins.'

'Can we sell them?'

I shook my head. 'As soon as the US treasury hears about them they will do their damnedest to confiscate them.'

'What will they do with them?'

'Probably melt them down. Don't forget these coins don't exist, they were never issued as currency.'

'How much would they be worth if melted down?'

'Not sure, but I imagine somewhere close to a million pounds.'

'Still enough for the Americans or Kaufmann to try and get their hands on.'

'So what are we going to do with all those coins?'

'Let's put them back in the box for now.'

'But we can't just leave it sitting on your workbench.'

'Follow me, I have a plan.'

Nancy opened the door to the forward compartment, and between us we managed to bury the box of coins deep inside a pile of rough-sawn maple neck and body blanks.

♦

Sunday morning, we all slept in and, unlike Saturday, we couldn't get the children motivated. Stephen had gone up to the wheelhouse with bowls of cereal. I found the three of them sitting cross-legged on one of the settees chattering.

'Do we have to go to Aunty Sarah's?' asked Sandra. 'Can't we stay here?'

'You will, soon. Your mum and I need to make rooms for you first. You can't live here in the wheelhouse.'

'We wouldn't mind, honestly, Jack.'

'Can we watch TV?' asked Stephen.

'Er – sorry, I don't have a TV.'

'No TV?' chorused three incredulous voices.

'What I meant is, I watch TV on my Galaxy tablet.'

'Can we borrow your Galaxy, Jack?' asked Stephen.

'Be right back.'

'They usually watch TV on Sunday morning. My one day of the week to sleep in. Were they eating cereal?' asked Nancy, when I told her about the children.

I nodded. 'They told me they don't want to go to Sarah's, they said they want to stay here.'

'Can't blame them. How many children do you know get the opportunity to live on a boat?'

'Good point.'

'In that case, let's make a start today, after we've dropped the kids off at Sarah's.'

'We should do something for Sarah to say thanks for looking after the kids.'

'Some pirate treasure?'

'That, my dear, would be an albatross.'

'An albatross? Thought we were talking about eagles?'

'What I mean is, she could never spend it, and if it were known she had one, people like Kaufmann could make her life an absolute hell.'

'I was joking, she wouldn't take anything. We're family, and that includes you.'

'Thanks.'

'What are we going to do with the gold?'

'Stuff it back where it came from for now. It's been hidden well enough for the last seventy years, should be good for another few months till we decide what to do with it.'

'Couldn't we just turn it in? Get the newspapers involved and then Kaufmann would be off our back for good?'

'There's still the matter of the falcon statue. If he thinks the gold is gone he'll redouble his efforts to find it. Let's keep him guessing – no that won't work, you're right, we should turn in the gold. But not today, we need to get the *Osprey* ready for its refit and we need to work out how we're going to rearrange the boat for the children's cabins.'

'Pity, I was just getting used to the idea of being a billionaire.'

'I have an idea.'

'Yes?'

'When we get the *Osprey* into dry-dock, we'll make an announcement about finding the gold during the refit. That way we won't be interrupted before we get out of the harbour.'

'Okay, I'll go along with that.'

It was with a sense of loss Sunday evening when I said goodbye to the children at Sarah's.

♦

Nancy put the kettle on while I retrieved my drawing board, ruler and pencil from the workshop.

'Where do we start?' she asked.

'I did some basic measurements when I first set up the workshop and, 'I said, sketching out a three-dimensional drawing of what I thought the new cabins would look like, 'this is what I had in mind.'

'Can I choose the colours?'

'Of course. I'd probably paint all the vertical surfaces with magnolia and the ceilings white.'

'Thought so. What's the matter? You've gone all quiet.'

'Just wondering if Kaufmann's still in custody, and why the police haven't been round to check on us. After all, we were the prime suspects.'

'There must be some way of checking.'

'I know a way,' I said, heading up to the wheelhouse to retrieve my Galaxy.

'You going to google it?'

'Not quite. *The Herald* website is quite good for local news. It's usually up-to-date with what's going on.'

'What does it say? Anything about Kaufmann?'

'Hang on, I'll read it out.

> Three men taken in for questioning on Friday morning have been released on police bail pending further enquiries, DS Street said in a brief report issued this afternoon. When questioned further she said the police were still following up several lines of enquiries.'

'Are we one of those lines of enquiries, Jack?'

'Most likely, although I can't understand why they haven't been here to question us by now.'

As if on cue there came a knock on the deck.

'You were saying? Shall I pack us a bag?'

I stood and looked out the window. 'Relax, it's Simon.'

'Phew, I was worried for a moment.'

I opened the door. 'Hi, Simon.'

'You look like you were expecting someone else?'

'The police. Kaufmann and gang have been released on bail pending further enquiries.'

'I wouldn't worry about them.'

'And what should we be worrying about?' asked Nancy.

'The weather. I had a look at the long-range forecast this morning. If you want to get to the yard for your refit, I suggest we head out on Wednesday at the latest. There's some strong westerlies due at the end of the week.'

I looked at Nancy, her colour had already changed two shades lighter.

'What do you propose?'

'Nathan suggested I bring a couple of the lads over tomorrow morning and see if we can get the engine running.'

'And if you can't?' asked Nancy.

'Then you've got a problem. Though it's possible your yard has some sort of vessel capable of towing you.'

'Doesn't Nathan have a boat we could use?' asked Nancy.

'Not for towing a heavy displacement vessel like the *Osprey*.'

'Well, let's hope we can get her engine running. What time will you and your guys be here in the morning?'

'Considering how little we know about the *Osprey's* engine and running gear, I think an eight o'clock start would be advisable.'

'Want to have a quick look while you're here?' I asked.

'Why not?'

'You get to the engine room from my workshop,' I said, leading the way, 'the door is on the right at the bottom of the stairs.'

'What do you think, Simon? Can you get it started?' I asked, once he'd had a look, hoping he'd say something like *'No problem'*. What he did say filled me with foreboding.

'The engine starting batteries are flat and need charging – that is if they'll accept a charge.'

'Oh.'

'I'll get some tools and be right back. Er – you weren't planning anything, were you?'

'No, just working out some ideas about the relocation of my workshop so the kids will have their own cabins.'

He smiled. 'Nathan will be pleased to hear that.'

Simon was back in twenty minutes in a runabout with his tools and one of the *Beatrice's* crew.

'Back again. This is Russell – our resident engineer. If he can't suggest a fix,' he said, pursing his lips and shaking his head, 'it isn't fixable.'

'Hi Russell, welcome on board,' I said shaking his hand.

We followed Simon and Russell down into the engine room and crouched silently under the limited headroom.

'I see what you mean,' said Russell, as he took a sample of the battery acid.

'What are you doing?' asked Nancy.

'Testing the specific gravity of the battery acid. It's a best way to determine if the battery needs charging.'

'And do they?'

'Most certainly, they're as flat as the horizon in the doldrums on a windless day.'

'How are you going to charge them? They look like they'd need a crane to lift them out of here.'

'Not a problem, Nancy. The *Osprey* has its own built-in charger.'

That was news to me. Of course I'd never needed to start the engine and with the boat already wired for 240 volts I'd never given the batteries a second thought.

'How long to charge them, Simon? That is if they will accept a charge.'

'We'll have an idea in a minute,' said Russell. 'Just need to trace the cables and make sure the charging circuit is still in place.'

We waited patiently as Russell, in his blue engineer's overalls, climbed all over the engine. At last he stood up and smiled.

'Well, is it?' asked Nancy.

'Not only is it still there, the wiring looks quite new.'

'Of course,' I said, 'before I bought the *Osprey*, someone broke in and tried to strip it of its copper wire. Fortunately, they were discovered before they could get it all out. The Sea Scouts' insurance paid to have it replaced.'

'Hold on and I'll see if the old girl will behave,' said Russell.

We watched patiently as he checked each cell of the enormous batteries. 'Not quite ready, folks. Will need to add some water to a couple of the cells, they're too low to charge.'

'Do you have any water for them?' I asked.

'Not enough for these two.'

'How much water do you need?' asked Nancy.

'At least a couple of gallons to make sure.'

'Asda should be still open – it's only half past three,' I said.

'Make sure you get the distilled type; stuff you use in your iron.'

'Why is that?' asked Nancy. 'What's wrong with spring water?'

'Too many impurities, they can short out the cells.'

'In that case, I'll be right back,' I said.

260

'I'll help,' said Nancy.

We bought four jugs of distilled water and were back in the engine room in twenty minutes. However, Russell and Simon's faces said all was not well.

'What's the problem?' I asked.

'Two main things: the engine oil has water in it and the fuel tanks need flushing out. The tanks being almost empty have had water vapour condense in them and that, with the old diesel, might damage the engine if we tried to start it.'

'Then we can't take the *Osprey* for its refit?' asked Nancy.

'I did say if Russell couldn't fix it, it's not fixable,' said Simon.

'And is it fixable, Russell?'

'I'm sure the batteries are chargeable and the oil can be replaced here at the dock. It's just the issue of how to supply the engine with clean fuel. But while we work out a fix for that, let's get the batteries on charge. Pass me one of those bottles of water.'

Once again Nancy and I crouched in the confined space and watched Russell, helped by Simon, top up all the cells on both the batteries.

'Now,' said Russell, 'the moment has arrived – let's wake them up.' He reached over to a large switch on the electrical panel and flicked it up. The needle on a large meter swung over to the right.

'Good, the charger works; now let's see if the batteries will take the charge.'

He rotated a large black knob and another meter, beside the first, came to life.

'Gently does it, my lovely.'

'Russell talks to his machinery,' explained Simon. 'I'm sure he loves them more than any woman.'

Russell laughed. 'At least they don't argue with you, and they don't get headaches.' He climbed over to one of the batteries and shone his torch into the cell. 'Good, just what I like to see.'

'What do you see?'

'Engineer's champagne.'

'What?' said Nancy.

'Tiny bubbles in the cell. Tells me there's a current flowing. We'll leave it an hour and see how they do. In the meantime, while I'm here, may as well have a look at the steering.'

'What about the brakes, Russell?' asked Nancy, a mile-wide smile on her face.

'Very funny, but I suppose while we are here we could have a look at the ground tackle.'

'Now you're making fun of me.'

'No, not really. A vessel this size can do a lot of serious damage if it is unable to stop when operating in a confined space like a harbour.'

'Does it really have brakes?'

'Not like a car. It should have an anchor that can be dropped to stop it in an emergency.'

We spent the next two hours following Russell around the *Osprey* as he first checked the steering cables, then the anchors, both bow and stern. Finally, we returned to the engine room and the batteries.

'Perfect, just what I'd expected. We'll leave them on a gentle charge for the next couple of days. Should have enough in them by Wednesday – by then we should have got the engine oil changed. Possible a new filter's in order.'

'And the fuel tanks? How are we going to sort them?' I asked.

'Got an idea about that,' said Russell. 'I'll think it through tonight and, if it's a goer, I'll tell you in the morning. Where are you having the work done?'

'It's a small yard in Chichester. It was the only one I could find that had a railway big enough, could work on steel hulls, and had space to haul out the *Osprey*.'

'Sounds perfect. Oh, what time's breakfast?'

'Russell, if you can get the *Osprey* to sea for its refit, I'll start making breakfast now,' I said.

'How about six?'

'Six!' I exclaimed, looking at my phone. 'We'd better get to bed if we're to be up at six and be any good tomorrow.'

'Six it is. Good night!'

16

Kidnapped

I was lying under the shade of a palm tree on a beach somewhere in South America. I was cradling a glass of something cold, fruity and fizzy, when Nancy woke me. 'Jack, wake up. There's someone on the boat.'

I opened my eyes and stared into the gloom of five-thirty. 'How do you know?'

'I'm sure I heard noises coming from the workshop.'

I pushed back the covers.

'What are you going to do?'

'Go see. Don't worry, I'll be careful.' I picked up my dressing gown and slid my arms into the sleeves

'Hold on, I'm coming with you.'

'No, you're not. You are going to lock yourself in the toilet till I come back.'

'But what will you do? Suppose they have guns?'

I almost smiled. Nancy had escalated what she thought she'd heard, to a gang of gun-toting brigands.

'I'll be fine, don't worry. It was probably something to do with the batteries charging.'

One of my side-lines as a luthier, combined with living on board a boat, was the art of simple rope-work and sewing. Since the *Osprey* had now been broken into three times, and the law of the land denied me the right to defend my home with a firearm, I'd stitched up a small leather cosh and filled the end with lead shot as a means of defence.

I made sure Nancy was secure in the toilet then made my way through the passageway into the workshop. It took a few minutes for my eyes to focus on the shape that was Snyder. My turn to make the surprise entrance. I crept up on him in the dark and hit him hard on the back of the head. He grabbed for a box of odd ends of timber lying on the bench, then collapsed on the floor like the proverbial pole-axed ox.

The noise brought Nancy out of hiding.

'Jack,' she whispered, 'are you all right?'

I turned on the light. 'Yes, I'm fine.'

'Who – who is it?'

'That, my dear Nancy, is Snyder.'

'Is he dead?'

'No, just sleeping.'

'But how did he get here? I thought he was locked up with Kaufmann?'

'Habeas corpus.'

'What's that?'

'In Britain you are still innocent till proven guilty, that and the fact you can only be held by the police for a maximum of twenty-four hours without charge.'

'So that means the doctor is on the loose as well?'

'Looks that way.'

'Did you check the forward compartment? I'd hate to be surprised by him.'

I'd wondered about that myself, but had discounted the idea immediately. To make sure I opened the door and looked inside: all was as it should be.

'Empty, no sign of the doctor. Here, help me get Snyder up of the floor and into the seat.'

For a big man, he was also heavy and muscular. I was glad I'd got the drop on him this time. I hoped he'd have a headache like mine when he woke but, before he did, we tied his arms and legs to the chair and waited for him to come round. While we waited, Nancy went off to get dressed and I had a look through his pockets. Nothing of interest in the trouser or jacket pockets, but the wallet was interesting. Where I thought a US Treasury badge would have rested, now only showed an imprint.

I slapped him on the face a couple of times. 'Good morning, Mr Snyder! We meet again.'

I let him wake sufficiently before I asked my next question. 'What are you doing here, and how the hell did you get in? I changed the locks.'

'Good morning, Mrs Rafsanjani, I see you've found a new bed to sleep in.'

'And I see you still haven't learned any manners.'

I would have hit him again for that insolence, but decided there was no point in antagonising him further.

'Snyder, why are you here?'

'I thought I'd see if you have thought over my proposal.'

'At five in the morning?'

'I have a job to do.'

'I still don't know where your statue is.'

'How about you, Mrs – er – what do I call you?'

'You don't call me anything. Get lost.'

'Pity you've chosen to be unreasonable. I'd hoped since you've had time to think things over we could work together.'

'You're just out to line your own pockets,' said Nancy.

'Oh, you know so little about nothing.'

'Jack told me what you're after; and we don't have any of it.'

'Snyder,' I asked, 'tell me what it's like to be a treasury officer? Good salary – lots of free travel – a good pension plan? Does the good doctor know you are moonlighting on him?'

'Go to hell.'

'So what happened, Snyder? Got caught with your hand in the till?'

He lowered his head and stared at the floor. 'Three years ago. I was on a stake-out at an event in Chanhassen in Minnesota. We'd been following the trail of a gang of opportunist thieves who had been robbing high cash events.'

'And what was so special about this event?' Nancy asked.

'The reason we were there was because Prince was going to make a guest appearance, and since some tickets were selling for up to a thousand dollars a time we felt it was worth the effort. We'd got a tip-off about the gang targeting the event.'

'What happened? Did you catch them?'

He looked back up at us. 'No, we'd been made to look like fools. The concert robbery was just a diversion. While we were staked out at the concert, they robbed a bullion van in town and got away with almost a million dollars in untraceable cash.'

'So how come you lost your badge?'

He looked up at me with an intensity I'd only once seen in a rabid dog.

'In jihad, there are no national boundaries.'

I had a moment of inspiration. 'You were the inside man for the gang, weren't you? You'd tip them off anytime there was to be a stake-out. You were helping them raise funds for their cause, their jihad. Your bosses got suspicious and fired you – that right, Mr Snyder?'

His face changed from red of frustration, to grey of anger, and I was glad we'd tied him up tight.

'And Max, he was sent to stop you. Did you kill him?'

'I don't need a gun.'

'Thought you people hated anything to do with idols – that's what the statue is, isn't it?'

'Mr Nevis, what I want is the just the statue. We're willing to pay a lot of money for it.'

'So you can use it to rally the troops? Forget it, not interested.'

'We will win, Mr Nevis, no matter the pain we have to endure. In jihad, the end justifies the means.'

'The mantra of a mad man,' said Nancy. 'Why don't we just send him on his way?'

'You mean we should kill him?'

I caught the colour of Snyder's face turning white.

'You can't do that! This is England,' he whined.

'Nancy, I'm hungry, let's go have breakfast. Russell will be here in a few minutes; we'll talk it over with him, see if he agrees with you.'

I was wondering what to do with Snyder till Nancy made her suggestion. Now I knew.

I made sure he was tied tight and followed Nancy up into the main saloon.

'Jack,' she whispered, 'I didn't mean we should kill him.'

I smiled. 'I realised that, but Snyder doesn't. To him killing is just a part of his belief system. You start breakfast and I'll get dressed.

As good as his word, Russell showed up at six. In a hushed voice I explained to him about Snyder.

'Best to just let him go,' Russell suggested.

I nodded in agreement. 'That's what we thought. But first we need to help him escape. Be right back.'

I climbed back down into my workshop. 'It's two to one we nix you, Snyder. Russell hasn't made up his mind yet, but it looks like you're to be dumped overboard in the channel on Thursday when we go out.'

He shook his head. 'Others will follow, Nevis. My death will be avenged; your blood will flow.'

I made sure I looked decidedly worried.

'You're mad, you need locking up!'

I walked behind him and said, 'Wouldn't want there to be bruise marks on your arms when you're fished out of the channel,' as I slightly loosened the knots. 'I'll be back in a few minutes, when we've voted.'

I returned to the main saloon and motioned for Nancy and Russell to follow me outside. As I did so, I said, loud enough for Snyder to hear me, 'Russell, Nancy, we need to check the towing gear on the stern before we head out into the channel.'

We stood on the stern deck and waited for Snyder to untie himself and make good his escape.

◆

'Look at him run!' said Nancy, as we watched Snyder jump from the *Osprey* on to the dock and on up to the carpark.

'He'll probably be back,' said Russell.

'Maybe, but we'll be ready for him next time,' I replied.

'Breakfast's getting cold,' said Nancy.

'So, what was that all about, Jack?' asked Russell, as we sat down to breakfast.

'He seems to think we have a statue hidden somewhere on the boat.'

'Must be very valuable to threaten to kill you over. Is it a rare bronze something or other?'

'No, supposedly it's just an old Egyptian black marble stone carving of a falcon –'

'Supposed to have evil powers,' interrupted Nancy.

'As I was saying.'

'Sorry.'

'It is supposed to have some sort of occult powers so that whoever possesses it can get others of equal persuasion to rally to their cause.'

'A talisman. Read a story about that once, real creepy stuff.'

'Dennis Wheatley?'

Russell nodded. 'I have just had a brilliant idea.'

'What?'

'Why don't you let him have it, if he shows up again?'

'Don't follow you.'

'If it's as old as you say, then who knows what it looks like? Why not buy a statue that resembles the one he's after and tell him you've found it and want it and him gone from your lives?'

'Great idea, but where would we find something that looks several thousand years old and resembles a falcon? And would he believe us if we just said come and get it?'

'I know,' said Nancy, 'garden centres have all sorts of stone garden statues. I'm sure I could find one. In fact, I seem to remember there's a garden statue place on the A23 – it's near Handcross Hill, you drive past it on the way to London.'

'Or you could try eBay,' suggested Russell.

'I think I may have a better idea,' I said. 'Yes to getting a suitable statue, but instead of letting Snyder just have it, I think we could pretend to have found it during the refit, and somehow or other have it get lost during the work.'

'We could say it was accidently thrown out with the rubbish and went off to the tip,' added Nancy.

'Either way, we've got work to do. Russell, last night you said you thought you had a solution to the fuel tank issue?'

'Ah, yes, I think I do. My idea is to strap some plastic fuel tanks to the deck, then run a flexible fuel hose down to the day tank in the engine room. No need for a pump as gravity will do the job.'

'Won't that be risky?' asked Nancy.

'No, these are tanks that farmers use for fertiliser, made of thick plastic and contained in a steel cage. Perfectly safe.'

'How will we stop the fuel from overfilling the day tank?' I asked.

'We'll just have to keep an eye on it and turn the tap on and off at the fuel tank as and when needed.'

'That sounds workable, as long as we can get the engine started,' I said, thinking back to the last time it had run. It was on the day the *Osprey* had been moved to its present berth, almost three years ago. Would it start? Tomorrow would tell.

'Have you looked at the batteries?' asked Russell.

'Not yet, we've been busy,' I replied.

'Well, if you two are going to work on the engine, I've got dishes to do,' said Nancy.

I followed Russell into the engine room and watched as he checked the batteries.

'Perfect. The SG is up and they're still charging, should be fine for a test start tomorrow.'

'Good. What's next?'

'I've got to get Andy and some tools, probably will need to do an engine oil and filter change before we try starting the engine. It should have a factory service if it's been sitting idle for so long.'

'Could you do that?'

'No, needs a professional engineer, experienced in this engine, for that.'

'Does that mean you may not be able to get it started?'

'We'll see.'

Russell left to find his tools and collect Andy, while I went back to the wheelhouse to see what Nancy was up to.

She was on my laptop.

'What you looking for?' I asked.

'Not looking any longer – see what I've found.' She passed me my laptop.

I looked at the picture on the British Museum's shop page: it was a replica of a statue of a falcon.

'It's a replica statue of Horus, even has the double crowns.'

I read out the information posted on the website.

> A reduced-size replica of an ancient Egyptian statue, measures approximately 6 inches tall. The statue is of a falcon – the animal representation of the god Horus. It is likely that the statue was commissioned by a wealthy follower of one of the many cults that worshipped Horus as a votive offering, a gift to a god. This ornament is ideal as a history gift or as a cultural display for your home.

'Well done, Nancy.'

'Thanks, and it's not too expensive either,' Nancy remarked.

'Quality product, not like one of those cheap trashy tourist things you see at the shops and airports,' I added. 'I think we'll order one.' I typed in my card details and selected the next day delivery option. I waited for the confirmation of purchase email then switched off the laptop.

'What next, captain?'

'There's the last two guitars to hand over to their owners. I thought we could deliver them and then go have lunch and discuss what's needed for the children's cabins.'

'I like that. But what about Russell? Won't he need your help?'

'I doubt it. I think I'd only be in the way.'

'Okay, let's go.'

♦

We arrived back on board at four-thirty to find Russell and Andy standing on the fore deck strapping down a huge square fuel tank.

'Sorry to be so late, Russell. Traffic on Seaside Road was crap – can't figure out who all those people are that get to go home at four o'clock in the afternoon.'

'Teachers,' said Andy.

I wasn't so sure about that. Eastbourne is a popular seaside town with many venues to entertain and educate visitors. The busy roads were more likely holidaymakers making their way back to their accommodation for tea before the evening commute began.

'We've had to run the fuel line down through the deck vent in the forward compartment and your workshop,' said Andy, 'it was the best way of getting a straight run down to the day tank in the engine room.'

'No problem with running it through the workshop, I won't be using it till after the refit.'

'You use all that wood on the shelves?'

'Not really, I'll be selling most of it prior to moving my workshop into the forward compartment. Where my workshop is now, is where the children's cabins will be.'

'Then we're almost all done, Jack,' said Russell. 'We've changed the oil and filter, and managed to bar the engine over.'

'Bar?' I asked.

'Rather than exhaust the batteries, we put a crowbar in the front of the engine and rotated the crankshaft by hand. We were fortunate that it wasn't frozen.'

'Frozen?' remarked Nancy.

'Let me explain,' said Russell. 'When an old engine, like the one on the *Osprey*, sits for several years without turning over, there is the danger of the pistons being stuck in the bores. With a petrol engine it is a simple job of removing the spark plugs and spraying some WD40 or similar type of spray down the bores to free the pistons and provide some initial lubrication.'

'What about diesel engines?'

'We can remove the glow plugs if fitted, or injectors if not.'

'And that's enough to get it to start?' asked Nancy.

'No, there's still the issue of stale fuel and dirty injectors that could cause problems, but don't worry, we'll replace the fuel filter and purge the system before we try to start the engine. I wasn't able to find an air filter locally, so I've ordered one on an overnight delivery, should be here by nine o'clock.'

'Good, I think. How do we get fuel, Russell?' I asked, 'Can't see us carrying that tank all the way down to the fuel dock.'

'Sorted, Jack. Andy and I took some jerry-cans in the dinghy down to the fuel dock. We've put thirty gallons on board, more than enough to get the engine started and get us down to the fuel dock.'

'So we're all ready to go?'

'Not quite – Andy's going to go over the side and scrape the prop and rudder. In three years of sitting at the dockside, your boat's grown quite a beard of weeds.'

I was beginning to wonder just how much this was going to cost me. If it hadn't been for the rusting rivets causing the leaks I would have been quite happy to ignore the need for the *Osprey* to be serviced.

Russell must have seen the concern in my face. 'Don't worry about the cost; Nathan says you can pay for the materials, the labour is free.'

'But you've been working on this for two days now.'

He shook his head. 'We'd just be sitting around on the *Beatrice* anyway. When the yard sends out new boats there's virtually nothing to do on them, and she's not due for delivery till next week.'

I relaxed. The fuel and oil I knew I'd have had to buy anyway, I just hadn't figured how complex the preparations would be to get the *Osprey* ready to go to sea. I was glad to have friends like Nathan and hoped I'd be able to repay the friendship someday.

Andy, standing on the stern deck, suited-up in his diving gear, reminded me of a photo I'd once seen of Jacques Cousteau, though Andy was quite a few years younger.

'I'm going to start dinner,' announced Nancy.

I watched Andy slide off of the dock and under the stern of the *Osprey*. I followed the line of bubbles as he made his way along the underside of the hull to the rudder. Within a few minutes the water had turned green as he scraped at the rudder and propeller. Twenty minutes later Russell and I helped him out of the water.

'All sorted,' said Andy. 'Your boat does need a haul-out, there are weeds and barnacles everywhere. We'll be lucky if we can make more than four knots on Thursday.'

I didn't like that. Being at sea on the *Beatrice* with twin engines, auto-pilot and stabilisers at thirty knots was one thing, but the *Osprey* had none of those niceties and plodding along at four knots wasn't my idea of fun.

'Probably only at the start,' added Russell, when he saw my face. 'Don't worry, when we get going a lot of the weeds will wash off, and besides, I didn't think you were in a hurry.'

'When are you due to slip, Jack?' asked Andy.

'Saturday morning. The yard said they may be able to get the *Osprey* out of the water Friday afternoon if we're there before they close for the day and they're not too busy.'

'Where are you going to stay while the boat's out of the water?' asked Russell.

'Nancy's house,' I replied, realising that I'd never been to it.

'We can give you a lift back then – Nathan's arranged a ride for us.'

'As long as there'll be room,' I replied.

'Plenty, it's the company's mini bus.'

'You guys staying for dinner?' asked Nancy, who'd just walked down the side deck to the stern. 'I've made paella, at least my version of it. Went through the fridge and sort of put in what looked good.'

'Russell, Andy, fancy staying for dinner?' I asked. She's a great cook and we've some really nice wine.'

♦

'How did you two meet, Nancy?' asked Andy as we opened the fifth bottle of merlot.

'You know the scene from Romeo and Juliet?'

Andy looked puzzled.

'What she means is,' I said, 'I was standing on the wheelhouse side deck, Nancy was standing down on the dock waiting for me to answer the door. I looked down at her and thought, not bad, there's someone I'd like to get to know better.'

'I looked up when he spoke and thought what a nice body he had,' Nancy giggled. 'I went home that night and said to Sarah, my sister, I'd just met the man I was going to marry.'

'You were that sure?' asked Russell.

Nancy nodded.

At eleven-thirty we said goodnight to Russell and Andy. I had a look at the batteries – still charging – and headed for bed.

♦

We woke to the sound of a ringing phone: my land line. I let it go to the answer machine and turned over to try and get a few more minutes of sleep.

'Who was it?' asked Nancy.

'Don't know, let it go to the answering machine.'

'It might have been Sarah.'

'Okay, I'll go see.'

I climbed out of bed and walked through to the workshop. The display on the machine said I'd missed three calls so I pressed the

275

play button and listened. The first two were from yesterday, something about an accident I was supposed to have had and would I call this number to start my claim for compensation. Stuff you, I thought, and pressed the delete button.

The third call, the one that had woken me, was different. It was from someone called Sally at the local BBC station. She wanted to know if she could send a crew over to the *Osprey* to interview me about the restoration of my classic tug boat. That was news to me. I thought all I was doing was usual maintenance, not restoration.

'Well – who was it?' asked Nancy.

'The BBC, want to interview me about the restoration of the *Osprey*.'

'Will you?'

'Not sure. Never been on television before, not sure what I'd say.'

'Sounds fun to me, what harm can it do? Just think of the publicity for your guitar business.'

I thought about the last time I'd tried to promote my business and the subsequent problems we were still working through. 'I suppose there's something in that. Okay, I'll give her a call, I doubt that lightning will strike twice in the same place.'

I called and arranged for them to come over and do the interview late that afternoon. I didn't want them to get in the way of the work being done to get the engine started.

I was in the wheelhouse checking my emails when I saw Russell and Andy walking gingerly down the dock. I saved them the trouble of knocking on the door and opened it as they stepped onto the *Osprey's* side deck.

'Good morning,' I whispered, 'you two look like you need something to get you going. Want some breakfast?'

'Black coffee, if there's some on the go,' replied Andy.

I noticed Russell try to nod in agreement. 'A piece of toast is all I think I could manage,' he added.

'You sure? Nancy's making scrambled eggs.'

Russell shrugged. 'Ok, I'll give it a try.'

'Two more for breakfast, Nancy!' I called through the open door.

Forty minutes later, the four of us sat round the table while a newly animated Russell went over the plans for starting the *Osprey's* engine. It basically came down to fitting the air filter, turning the engine over with the starting motor and bleeding all the fuel lines to make sure only new fuel was in the lines to the injectors.

Our meeting was momentarily interrupted by the delivery of the statue. Nancy unwrapped it and put it on the shelf behind the settee in the main saloon.

'Is that what I think it is?' asked Russel.

'Not quite.' I replied. 'It's a decoy to hopefully distract Kaufmann and keep him off our backs for good.'

'Sounds like a plan. Shall we see if the engine will start?'

At first the engine turned slowly on the starter motor, but after a few revolutions it started to wheeze like it wanted to get going.

By the time the moment to start the engine arrived, we'd collected a large pile of diesel-soaked rags.

'What do you want me to do with these, Jack?' asked Nancy, while holding a couple of Tesco shopping bags stuffed full of the rags.

'Put them in the workshop for now, I'll get rid of them later.'

'Okay.'

'Right,' said Russell, 'time to give it a go. Andy, you take the engine room, watch for fuel leaks, shout on the radio if anything looks iffy.'

It was then that I saw they'd each got small walkie-talkies clipped to their belts. Nancy followed Russell to the wheelhouse, while I went with Andy down to the engine room.

'Ready, Andy?' came Russell's voice over the walkie-talkie.

'Ready,' he replied.

There followed the sound of the fuel pump drawing fuel from the day tank, then silence. I looked at Andy; he smiled. Next was an audible click of the solenoid engaging the starter motor and then the sound so many motorists have experienced at one time or other, an engine trying to start with a tired battery. I exhaled in submission; it was no good, the engine wasn't going to start.

But I'd given in too soon. Russell tried again, the starter motor engaged, the engine turned, and then I heard the sound I'd been waiting for: a thumping, wheezing sound, the engine was trying to start. Russell kept the starter engaged, and moment by moment the irregular thumping, wheezing sound increased till finally the engine burst into life.

I went out onto the deck to listen to the engine and was shocked to see the huge cloud of black smoke hanging over the *Osprey*.

'Is that normal Russell?' I asked.

'Yeah, especially when an old diesel hasn't been run for a long time. It'll clear in a few minutes when the engine warms up.'

And it did. Russell let the engine run for a couple of hours, then with the throttle on idle, put the gear lever forward. I was pleased to see the dock lines tighten. Nancy and I made our way back to the stern, a great stream of greenish-coloured water flowed away from it. I smiled inside, the *Osprey* was ready to go to sea.

Russell and Andy spent a further two hours in the engine room checking things over before leaving us to get the interior ready for going to sea on Thursday.

♦

The BBC crew arrived at three o'clock. There were four of them: a camera-lady, a sound man, the interviewer, and the producer.

We sat in the main saloon. The camera-lady set up two cameras, explaining the one on the tripod was for long shots and the other, which she slung over her shoulder, was for close-ups.

The questioning followed the story of how I'd first come across the *Osprey* and gone on to trace its history, and the fact I was now embarking on a full restoration of the boat.

I tried to explain that, during the refit, the outside would be cleaned up and repainted in its original colours, but the interior was to be made suitable for three children to live on-board. I deflected questions about the dead man in the workshop and steered the conversation back to the *Osprey's* part in the war. The question of how three children could live on a boat was asked, and I duly explained that all over the world children were growing up on boats. That they would still go to school every day, and have their own cabins.

'Will you travel, Mr Nevis?'

I shook my head and replied, 'No, I don't have a licence to operate a boat this size.'

'So, you'll just be living on board and working from home?'

'A very modern way of life.'

They finished by taking a couple of shots of Nancy and me walking round the deck and then through the interior.

'When will the interview be broadcast?' asked Nancy. 'I'd like the children to see it.'

'This evening's news. Not sure what time slot we'll get it into. I'll call you when I know.'

♦

Something was niggling at the back of my mind. It wasn't the actual interview, that had gone off well, it was – it was something I couldn't quite grasp, something I'd said maybe, but no matter how I tried nothing came to mind.

The children were over the moon with excitement, looking forward to seeing their mum and their new home on television.

As the day wore on, I made sure all my tools were secured, tripped over the temporary fuel lines a couple of times, and Nancy gave the galley another once-over and declared the boat was ready to go to sea. It was then we realised there was nothing on board to eat.

'Fancy a pizza?' I asked.

'Sounds fine. I'll order – where's the menu?'

♦

We sat my laptop on the binnacle and munched our way through the pizza as we watched the evening news. The interview was a lot shorter than I'd supposed it would be, but with Brighton winning three matches in a row, it bumped our interview down to three and a half minutes.

Within moments of the airing of the interview, Nancy's phone rang: it was Sarah. I left them to chat while I contemplated the new problem. I now realised what had been niggling at the back of my mind all afternoon. During the initial part of the interview the camera had been focused on me, but when Nancy spoke, the camera panned to her face and in doing so provided the viewer with a clear shot of the falcon statue sitting on the shelf behind us. I wondered who would have seen it, and noticed it? After all, it had only been in the shot for a couple of seconds. I now had the issue of wondering if Snyder or Kaufmann had seen the broadcast, and, if so, what would they do next?

♦

After dinner we drove over to Sarah's to say hello to the children and answer the inevitable questions about how soon their cabins would be ready, how big would they be and could they have a pet? I was not sure how to answer the pet question till Nancy interrupted and told them about Garboard. I wouldn't have mentioned him due to his habit of letting you pick him up before he decided to open your face with his claws, but since he'd decided to allow Nancy to be his friend, I hoped he would extend this courtesy to the children. I waited for the plethora of questioning to end, and for Nancy to finally say goodbye to the children, then drove us back to the *Osprey*.

'What is it, Jack? You look worried.'

'Did you notice anything in the interview? Anything odd, out of place even?'

'No, the only thing I thought didn't look quite right was my makeup – my face looked too pink. Why?'

'You didn't see the falcon sitting on the shelf behind us?'

'No, I was too busy watching us.'

'Let's hope Snyder and Kaufmann were too busy to be watching the local news.'

'Oh, I hadn't thought of that! What can we do?'

'Good question. Keep the doors locked for a start, I suppose.'

'What time are we leaving in the morning?'

'Russell and his crew will be here about five, just after sun-up.'

'That gives us,' said Nancy, looking at her watch, 'about eleven hours to go. Shall we stay up all night?'

'Might be wise, but first we should make the boat as secure as we can.'

I went outside and pushed the *Osprey* a little further away from the dock by inserting some larger fenders between the hull and the dock. These wouldn't prevent someone climbing on board, it would just make it a bit more difficult. Next, I went round and made sure all the dock lines were taut, then finally went back inside, dogged down all the portholes and finished off with locking the door from the inside.

'You realise we are trapped?' said Nancy.

I nodded. 'Can't think of doing anything else. Let's sit up in the wheelhouse. We should see, and hear, anyone if they walk down the dock.'

◆

We took our coffees and climbed up into the wheelhouse, turned off the lights and sat in the dark to wait – for nothing, I hoped. Garboard meowed at the door to get in for his dinner.

'Can you remember what you were doing this time last month?' Nancy asked.

'Let me see – ah, yes, I was just about to reset the neck on an old Gibson J40.'

'Sounds like something a chiropractor would do,' she said, stroking Garboard as he purred.

'Not quite, it involves pulling the neck out of the body, and, by shimming and paring the dovetail, bringing the neck angle back to where it was when the guitar was new. How about you? What were you doing?'

'At one-thirty on a Thursday morning, I'd be sound asleep.'

'That's not quite what I meant.'

'I know. I was wishing my life could be a bit more exciting. One of my friends had just gone off travelling. She and her boyfriend went to India for six months.'

'You've done a bit of travelling these past two weeks – and had a sea voyage on a luxury yacht.'

'And don't forget the bit about being kidnapped. No, I suppose you are right, things have been a bit exciting since I met you. Is this the way our life together is going to be?'

'Let's hope not. I've had enough excitement to last a lifetime. In fact, we only have a few more hours to go then it's off to the refit, where we can announce the finding of the gold coins and the falcon statue that was unfortunately lost in the rubbish when the *Osprey* was being stripped out.'

'Pity we can't keep the coins. Are you sure we can't just hold on to them? After all, we found them on your boat – isn't that like finding treasure in a field?'

'I think that when treasure hunters go out into fields looking for buried artefacts, they are supposed to get permission from the landowner. They in turn usually share fifty percent with the hunter. Though I seem to remember there is something about a treasure trove law, where the Crown seizes the find then splits the value with the landowner and the finder.'

'Well, why don't we make sure the Crown seizes the coins and shares its value with us? Half of – what did you say they were worth?'

'As individual coins, about five million pounds each.'

'Times four hundred if we count the one on your pocket. Divided by two, is a great deal of money.'

'But that would never happen. Remember what I said before? If you flood the market with hundreds of uncirculated gold coins, as rare as these are, you'd be lucky to get a hundredth of the price.'

'I wouldn't say no to that.'

'What was it the professor said their value as gold was? Do you remember?'

'I think he said up to three-quarters of a million pounds depending on the value of gold at the time.'

'We could retire on that.'

'You think so? Just wait till the kids want to go to university, then we'll both be working to support them.'

'Do you think we'll get a reward for turning in the coins?'

'Not if we just call the US Embassy and tell them we've found their long-lost gold.'

'What do you think will happen?'

'We'll get a knock on the door from genuine treasury officers demanding we return their lost property.'

'Would they say please?'

'You kidding? I read about a recent case where a family found nine of these coins in their family's safety deposit box. When they tried to share the good news with the government they were turned down flat.'

'So they lost their money?'

'No. They appealed to the US supreme court and the government was forced to return the coins – something about statute of limitations.'

'How long ago was this?'

'Just last year.'

'How do you know all this?'

'It's all to be found on the internet.'

'So what will we do?'

'Negotiate.'

'I thought you said the US government would refuse to do a deal?'

'What we'll do is to get a good lawyer –'

'Is there such an animal?'

'Be nice. We'll get a good lawyer to write to the US government saying he has been contacted by an anonymous source regarding the desire to repatriate the coins to the US treasury, and if the treasury is not willing to cooperate, then the coins will be disposed of.'

'You think that will work?'

'Should do. Client-lawyer privilege, he doesn't need to disclose who his client is.'

'You sure about that?'

'Who knows? At the moment it's all I can come up with – more coffee?'

'Yes, please. When are Russell and Andy going to be here?'

I looked at the clock on the wall: two-thirty. 'Only another three hours to go.'

'Good, seems like we are going to survive after all.'

It was half an hour later when I heard the tell-tale sound of the dock lines creaking. It could mean only one thing: one of Kaufmann's gang had decided to pay us a visit.

'What is it, Jack? What's wrong?'

'Someone is walking down the dock.'

'Russell?'

'Too early, he's not due for another two and a half hours. Shush, they're almost here.'

We sat in the dark waiting to see what would happen. I gripped my cosh tight. If someone came on board and tried to climb up into the wheelhouse, I'd have the upper hand.

Impatience got the better of me and I stood up and looked out the window to see who was out there.

'Who is it? Can you see?'

'Someone wearing a hat, and a long coat. It could be anyone.'

But instead of the sound of someone climbing on board, there was just a single knock on the door, then the sound of departing footsteps.

'Be careful, Jack,' said Nancy, as I crept down the stairs and walked over to the door.

'What is it?' she asked, as I closed the door and returned to the wheelhouse.

'Someone has returned my phone. I don't understand.'

'Could it be some kind of a message?'

'Don't know,' I replied, pressing the on button.

'Well, what is it?' she asked, as I stared at the screen.

'It *is* a message, look.' I passed her my phone, face first.

'The children! How did you get their picture? You lost your phone in Glasgow when Kaufmann took it. Oh no, he can't – he just can't have the children, can he?'

Nancy picked up her phone and called Sarah.

I waited, willing the phone to be answered, realising it was probably a futile action. The call went to voicemail.

'Sarah, when you get this, call me. It's urgent.' Nancy hung up and immediately redialled. While she waited, I looked again at the photo of the children and noticed it hadn't been taken in Sarah's house. It looked like it had been taken while the children were sitting in a bus shelter. Then I had a closer look and realised it wasn't a bus shelter, it was a railway platform. I enlarged the picture as much as I could without it blurring and could just make out the station name in the background: Pevensey and Westham. Now why would Kaufmann have done that? Then the obvious hit me. Stupid me! They wanted us off the *Osprey* so they could search it.

'Nancy, we have to go. I know where the children are.'

'You do?, Where?'

'They are waiting at Pevensey and Westham station.'

'How do you know that?'

'Look at the photo. See, in the background, there, the station name?'

'Are you sure?'

'Yes, I'm sure. Call 999 and tell them your children have been abducted from your sister's house and you think they are at Pevensey and Westham station.'

'What did they say?' I asked, when she hung up.

'They'll send a car to investigate. Did you bring your phone?'

'I left my phone on the boat. Pound to a penny they were tracking it and waiting to see if we had figured out where the children were. That would leave them a clear run at searching the boat.'

'Oh, Jack. I'm sorry! Shouldn't you stay in case they do come back?'

'Who cares about the stupid statue, or the gold? It's the children who are important.'

17

Arson Suspected

I could see the flashing blue lights as we crested the hill just before the crossing. I parked on the pavement and had to run to keep up with Nancy. There were five policemen with the children.

'Mum!' shouted the children, in unison, as we ran along the platform towards them.

Nancy crouched down to hug them, while one of the policemen pulled me to the side. 'Are you the children's father, sir?'

I shook my head. 'No, they belong to Nancy.'

'Why did you leave them alone?'

'Pardon?'

'I asked you why you went out and left the children alone?'

This was nuts. Then I realised just what was going on. 'Constable, if you call DS Street, she'll explain everything.'

'We will, sir, from the station.'

'Are you arresting me?'

'No sir, just asking you to accompany us to the police station so we can get statements from you all.'

'Nancy and the children, as well?'

'That's all right, sir. Social services will look after the children.'

'You're taking them away from their mother?'

'Come with me, sir, the car is just over there.'

Nancy was sitting beside me in the back of the police car; she was in tears as she watched the children being driven away by social services. This was not what I expected. I'd hoped we would be in time to collect the children, and also inform the police who we thought had abducted them.

'Sarah? What's happened to Sarah?' Nancy asked me, between sobs.

'Constable, Nancy's sister – she was babysitting when the children were abducted. We're worried about her, and her children. She won't answer her phone; we have to go see if she's all right.'

'Where does she live?'

'Pevensey Road, just behind the Hippodrome Theatre. I called her but got no answer,' said Nancy.

He radioed the address to the control centre and said he would go there first. With blue lights and almost empty roads we were outside Sarah's house in a few minutes.

'Do you have a key, ma'am?' the constable asked Nancy, as we stood on the pavement.

'Yes, er, somewhere. Just a minute.'

Nancy rummaged around in her handbag for Sarah's key. 'Here it is,' she said, handing it to him as DS Street arrived.

'Good morning, Mr Nevis.'

'Sergeant.'

'Mrs – er – what do I call you?'

'Nancy will do for now.'

'And later?'

'We'll see.'

'Your children are being looked after and will be returned to you shortly.'

'Thanks.'

'Sergeant, I can tell you who kidnapped the children.'

'You say they were kidnapped? We received a report about three children sitting in the shelter on the station platform.'

'Bet whoever phoned had a German accent,' said Nancy.

'Would you both wait here while we go and check if Nancy's sister is all right?' requested the sergeant.

We held on to each other as the sergeant, the constable and his partner let themselves into Sarah's flat.

The sergeant was back in three minutes. 'Your sister is all right; it appears she was given something to make her sleep.'

'Her kids?'

'Fast asleep in their beds.'

'Oh, thank God for that!' said Nancy. 'Can we go in and see her?'

'Please, you'll find her a bit woozy. We've called for an ambulance, just in case she needs to go to hospital.'

'I thought you said she was all right?' said Nancy.

'Just a precaution, we don't know what she was given. Could you look after her children if she has to go to hospital?'

'Of course I will. But what about my children, when can I have them back?'

'Social services will make sure they're all right, then return them to you, where you are staying?'

'I'm living with Mr Nevis; we're engaged to be married.'

'Thank you, your sister is waiting for you.'

I followed Nancy into the flat. Sarah was sitting on the settee, sipping a cup of tea. I stood back and let them cry together. I went into the kitchen and put the kettle on. It was about to boil when an excited DS Street joined me.

'Mr Nevis, I'm afraid I've got to leave you. We've just had a report that there's a boat on fire in the marina with possible fatalities.'

'What?'

'A message about a boat on fire.'

'Does it say what type?'

'You think it could be yours?'

'Just a horrible feeling I've got.'

'Hang on, I'll see if I can get more information.'

I followed her out to her car and waited while she talked with the control centre.

It was as I feared, the *Osprey* was on fire. Kaufmann had a lot to answer for. I told Nancy I'd be right back and went out to DS Street and a ride to the harbour.

'The latest from control is that the fire is mostly out and the damage appears to be confined to the front section,' she said.

I wasn't sure if that was good news or bad. I'd have to wait till I got there and saw the damage for myself.

There was a sizeable crowd watching the spectacle. I approached the gate to the dock and met Russell.

'What does it look like, Russell? How bad is it?'

'Fire department have just rolled up their hoses. I tried to get down there earlier, but they said it was too dangerous.'

'Any idea what caused it?' I asked, knowing full well who was behind it.

'Fire chief said it looked like someone had turned on the taps to the fuel tank on the foredeck and let it drain down into the inside of the boat.'

'But you used proper fuel lines – they would have to be deliberately cut!'

'That's what I thought. I suppose we'll never know; fire chief says the fire was so hot that some of the deck plating has buckled.'

'Will they let me on board?'

'You'll need to ask.'

I wandered off to find the fire chief. I found him talking to DS Street.

'Excuse me, chief, any chance I can get on board?'

'Who are you?'

'Sorry, Jack Nevis. It's my boat that was on fire.'

'You can with one of my men; they are not finished damping down inside.'

'How bad is the damage?'

'It appears to be confined to the forward section. On first investigation it looks like your deck-mounted fuel tank taps were left on and started to leak, draining down into the compartment underneath.'

I shook my head. 'Those tanks and fuel lines were installed by professional marine engineers. The fuel lines didn't spring a leak; all the fuel taps were shut off when I went ashore two hours ago. Yet I've been told they were found turned on when you came to fight the fire?'

'In that case, sergeant,' the chief said, turning to DS Street, 'it looks like you will be setting up a crime scene.'

Our discussion was interrupted by the arrival of one of the firemen.

'What is it, Murray?'

'We're all done, been through the whole boat, the fire's completely out.'

'Good.'

'Can I go on board?' I asked.

'Murray, would you go with Mr Nevis and show him the damage to his boat?'

♦

I followed Murray down the dock and on board. It was a shambles. Though the fire had been confined to the forward compartment, the main saloon smelled like charred wood and burnt mattresses.

'Be careful when you go forward, sir. You won't fall through the floor, but watch out – it's very slippery under the debris.'

I thanked him and his team for their work in saving the *Osprey* and said goodbye.

I stepped down into what should have been my workshop and saw that anything within a yard of the forward bulkhead had charred pretty badly. At least the *Osprey* was still afloat and we were going to strip out the workshop and forward compartment anyway, so other than the loss of some of my tools, which could all be replaced, I'd got off quite lightly.

I heard another set of footsteps and Nancy's voice. 'Jack, are you in there?'

'Down here, in what's left of the workshop.'

I waited till Nancy joined me.

'Oh, Jack, how could he do this? He's so spiteful.'

'We don't know it was Kaufmann; could be just an accident.'

'You can believe that, I'd rather believe in Santa Claus.'

'It's not as bad as it appears. I can replace the damaged tools, and the fire has saved us the work of stripping out the compartment.'

'Jack, the gold,' she mouthed.

We made our way gingerly across the workshop floor. Although the door was made from timber and had completely burnt out, the bulkhead was steel and gave us a view into the carnage of the forward compartment. Not one piece of the timber racking I'd kept my expensive timber on existed. The old steel bunk frames were twisted out of all recognition and hung from the side of the hull like piles of black spaghetti.

We carefully picked our way through the large pile of charred timber and ashes where I'd hidden the bullion box the previous day. There was no sign of it. Kaufmann had found it.

'The statue,' said Nancy. 'Is that still in the main saloon?'

'Who cares? Kaufmann's beaten us. He's got the gold and, knowing his luck, he'll probably sell the falcon for millions as well.'

'We've still got each other, that's worth more than all the gold in the world.'

'And the children. Two weeks ago, all the family I had was a feral cat. Now,' I turned and kissed her, 'now I have you and the children. Definitely worth more than the gold.'

'I suppose that means we're done with Kaufmann and his band of merry men? Pity the police didn't catch him.'

'I've still got Hanse's gun. Wonder if the police would like that?'

'Where?'

'It's under the mattress in our cabin. I put it there when we returned from Port Glasgow.'

'It'll be a waste of time; he'll just deny it's his. The police would have to catch him with it in his possession, and then he would only get a slap on the wrist. He'll probably make up a story about how in Germany it is still legal to own a gun.'

'You're missing the point, my love. A ballistic check will prove that gun is probably the one that killed Achmed and possibly the detective found in my workshop. It will have Hanse's fingerprints all over it.'

'Yours as well.'

I shook my head. 'Remember when I picked it up, I used a piece of rag?'

'Of course. Then all we have to do is to invite Hanse and the sergeant to tea, introduce each other, then it's bye-bye, Hanse.'

'If only it was that simple.'

'What about the first gun? You know, the one the police found in your cabin?'

'Who knows? Someone like Hanse most likely has more than one, it will probably be the second one that he used to kill your husband.'

'Achmed *wasn't* my husband – he was a bigamist, remember. My husband was an honourable man, he died fighting for his country in Afghanistan. Sorry – that wasn't called for.'

'That's okay, I should be more sensitive.'

'Does it bother you when I talk about him?'

'No, not really. Does it bother you when I'm thinking about Katie?'

'No, of course not.'

'They're like best friends we haven't seen for a long time, aren't they?'

'Friends who've gone off to live in a faraway country that we can't journey to.'

'Not in this life, anyway.'

293

'So how are we going to reunite Hanse with his gun and at the same time get him arrested by the police?'

'Don't know at the moment. Just now I can't think straight, I need some sleep.'

'We can't sleep here; the smell of the fire is too overpowering.'

'Your place?'

'Can we collect the children first? After last night, Sarah's got enough with her own kids.'

'And your car, do you think it will still be at the station?'

'Probably, though hopefully without a parking ticket.

'When this is all over we should do something really nice for Sarah,' I said, as we walked across the car park to the waiting taxi.

'Send her and the children on a holiday?'

'I know, why don't I – *we*– pay for all of us go to Disneyland in Florida? The kids will love that.'

'We have that much money?'

'The *Osprey* was well insured; if we do the repairs ourselves, there should be enough left to cover the cost of a holiday.'

'You're on, now let's collect your car and the children and get some sleep.'

18

Beached

Sleep, if you could call it that, consisted of a dream about Katie getting married to a soldier while children were dancing on the wing of an aeroplane and the wedding ceremony was being conducted by Mickey Mouse with Donald Duck playing a trumpet.

'Did you get any sleep?' I asked Nancy, as she passed me a cup of coffee.

'Catnapped on the settee, I'll catch up later. You were exhausted, snored like an elephant.'

'Sorry! Did I keep you awake?'

'That's ok, you needed your sleep.'

'What time is it?'

'One-thirty. Want some lunch?'

'Are the kids awake?'

'Watching TV.'

'How about you get some sleep, and I'll look after the children?'

'I was making them beans on toast; juice is in the fridge.'

I kissed her and watched her eyes flutter closed, by the time it took me to pull up my trousers she was fast asleep.

I sat through *Finding Nemo* and a movie about a monster in a Scottish loch before Nancy woke. I suggested we go out for dinner, and after a debate about the various benefits of pizza and hamburgers we settled on pizza.

Though we'd been up all the previous evening, and had only managed a few hours of sleep during the day, Nancy and I were still wide awake at eleven.

'Are you pleased with the way things have worked out?' Nancy asked.

'I never thought I'd get to do that again; it was so good to read a good-night story to my new family.'

'You're a big softy. That's why I love you,' she said, snuggling up close.

'We can't just let Kaufmann get away with what he's done.'

'Oh, why don't we just let the police deal with it? You could turn in Hanse's gun, make a statement, and leave them to clean up the mess. After all, that's what they're paid to do.'

'I suppose so, it just pisses me off to think he's got away with it, that's all.'

♦

For the first time in days I woke completely refreshed. I left Nancy to sleep and headed for the kitchen. I needed coffee. I stared out the window on the back garden and realised just how lucky I'd been. If it hadn't been for the fire department's quick response, the *Osprey* would probably have burnt out and be beyond repair. As it was, the fire had only hastened the relocation of my workshop and the building of the children's cabins. Of course Russell would have to repeat the work of providing temporary fuel tanks as the ones he fitted were now burnt out and unusable.

Rummaging through the kitchen drawers till I found a note pad and pencil, I started to sketch out my new workshop. I found the process very therapeutic and was well into the positioning of tool racks when Nancy came into the kitchen.

'Is that fresh coffee I smell?'

'Just made it,' I said, picking up a mug from the draining board.

'What shall we do today?' she asked between sips of her coffee.

'Go look at the damage in the daylight?'

'You sure you're up to it?'

'Of course I am, need to check dimensions. See, I've already started doing a layout of my new workshop,' I replied, showing her my sketch.

'What about the mess?'

296

'We'll deal with that when we're out of the water. Don't fancy trying to drag all that burnt lumber and ashes down the dock, besides we'd probably get in trouble for dumping the stuff in the harbour bins.'

'What about the kids?'

'How about we let them fish from the stern? You could keep an eye on them, while I check the dimensions. Then we could go to the park. Do they like trains?'

'Trains? What do you have in mind?'

'Out on Lottbridge Road, there's a golf course and driving range, and next door there's a miniature railway. They have a café where you can get food. We could make it our first family picnic.'

'I'll get them ready. You do your measuring, and when you come back we'll have our first family picnic.'

I parked the car and with tape measure and notepad headed for the *Osprey*. To my surprise, Russell and Andy were on the foredeck removing the remains of the fire-destroyed fuel tank.

'Hi, Russell, Andy.'

'Morning, Jack.'

'Didn't expect you two to be here.'

'We've a job to do if you're going to get to the yard by Monday.'

'You think we can get it running that quickly'

'The engine's fine, all that's needed is a new fuel tank and the fuel hose replaced. You should be ready to go tomorrow morning if you want. Oh the air filter's been delivered.'

'Where is it? Hope it wasn't on the *Osprey*.'

'No, I've got it on the *Beatrice*, thought I should hold on to it till needed.'

'Fine, we're not sure what we're doing yet. Could you hold on to it till I let you know?

'Sure thing, just call me when you're ready.'

'We're going to be a couple of days late, but I suppose under the circumstances that will be understood. I'll have to call the yard and let them know.'

'Already done. I called them this morning, explained you'd had a fire on board and said you'd be a couple of days late.'

'I don't know how I will ever be able to repay you guys.'

'Don't worry about it, Nathan is paying us for our time.'

I went below and with my tape measure took the critical dimensions of both the former workshop and forward compartment.

♦

After the excitement of the last couple of weeks, riding round on the miniature railway with the children was just the excitement I needed. We whooped and screamed our lungs out as the train went through the tunnel, then watched the fishermen catch carp in the lake and ate our picnic lunch on the benches in the family area.

'You all right?' asked Nancy, as we went to bed.

'Couldn't be better,' I sniffed.

19

The Eagle

We'd just gone to bed when the doorbell rang. I got up, put on my dressing gown and went to see who was there. Somehow I wasn't surprised to see Kaufmann.

'Ah, Mr Nevis, can we come in?' he asked, barging past me. He was followed by Snyder and Hanse who I saw, without surprise, had his left hand and forearm heavily bandaged.

'Dr Kaufmann, why aren't you on the run? I hear the police are after you.'

'With no thanks to you – my friend.'

'He's not your friend. What more do you want? asked Nancy, who'd joined us in the front room. 'Aren't you satisfied with abduction, assault, false imprisonment, and arson? I assume it was Hanse who almost destroyed our boat?'

'Ah, a small matter, is it not, Mrs, er, what do I call you?'

'Piss off, we don't want you around.'

'Mr Nevis, I'm sorry if I have offended your dear lady. I can assure you that has never been my intention.'

'Well, you've certainly managed to do so.'

He turned to Nancy. 'In the absence of a name, I think I will refer to you as Mrs Nevis. Yes, I think that will be perfect. I assume that is where your relationship is destined?'

'Don't sully the name by speaking it,' replied Nancy.

'I can assure you, Mr Nevis, all I want is to find the real falcon statue.'

'You already have it. You, or one of your friends, stole it from the *Osprey*.'

'Ah, such a fine specimen: £25 plus post and packing from the British Museum shop, I think. Am I correct, Mr Nevis? No, I'm afraid that little trinket will not do. No, sir, it certainly will not do at all.'

'That was the only one we had, Doctor. I'm afraid you'll have to take your search somewhere else.'

'And the small matter of the eagle? Do you happen to have an example of one of those hidden somewhere?'

I looked at Nancy and slowly shook my head. Why was he asking about the gold? Up till now I'd been assuming he had it all in his possession.

'Snyder, how are you? Been doing a bit of double-crossing?' I asked.

He looked puzzled. Good, now to go to work.

'Doctor, do your boys work exclusively for you?'

'Why would you ask that?'

'Just wondering if they can be trusted – implicitly?'

'Mr Nevis, I'm not sure what you are hoping to gain by this – this– verbal intercourse. I can assure you I trust both my friends here implicitly.'

'Oh, in that case, are you aware that your Mr Snyder used to work as a US treasury agent?'

I watched Kaufmann's expression; it was obvious he wasn't.

'And the fact he was drummed out of the service for supporting organisations that didn't see eye to eye with those who paid him? Have you thought to ask him about the eagles, Doctor?'

'Snyder, is this true?' asked Kaufmann.

'Sure it is, but that was a long time ago. It has no bearing on what we are looking for.'

'Why didn't you think it necessary to tell me, Snyder?'

'It just never seemed important.'

'You didn't think it was important? Dummkopf, of course it's important! Don't you see this puts you in a position of conflict? How can I continue to trust you?'

All this time I was watching Hanse. Even with the bandaged hand and arm, his eyes were emanating evil intent. Perfect.

'But Doctor,' said Snyder, 'don't you see what he's trying to do? He's just trying to put a wedge between us.'

'Of course I do, Snyder. Now here's what we are going to do. Mr Nevis, you, me, and Hanse are going to go to your boat, where you will show us where the real falcon is hidden. And just in case you are thinking of being some kind of hero, Snyder will remain with Mrs Nevis, just to keep her company, you understand?'

Yes, I did, and I didn't like it one bit. I'd tried to play them off against each other, but this was different. Time for plan B, Jack. But what was that? I decided to play for time.

'You can't expect me to go like this, can you?' I asked, pointing to my dressing gown.

'Mrs Nevis, you stay here. Hanse, go with him and make sure he doesn't try anything stupid. And take his phone from him, don't want him calling the police.'

I didn't like dressing in front of Hanse, especially the way he stared at me. I put my clothes on as quickly as I could and we were back in the living room in five minutes.

'No tricks, Hanse?' asked Kaufmann.

Hanse shook his head.

'Good, then we'll go and collect a falcon.'

I had now worked out a fledgling plan, not a great one, but a plan nonetheless.

'Doctor,' I said, putting my plan into action, 'it's possible that, due to the fire, my friend has moved the statue to a safe place.'

'Your friend? Now you are expecting me to believe you have another accomplice?'

'Why not? You have Snyder and Hanse.'

'Mr Nevis, you never fail to amaze me. Under different circumstances I believe I could grow to like you. Snyder, make sure she doesn't try anything that might endanger her children. You understand what I'm saying, Mrs Nevis?'

Kaufmann led the way down the stairs with Hanse following behind. I wondered if Hanse was dangerous without his gun, but it didn't matter, there was Snyder in the flat with Nancy and the children to worry about. We climbed into Kaufmann's rental car, me driving with Hanse beside me, and Kaufmann in the back.

'You will drive carefully, Mr Nevis,' said Kaufmann, 'and not attract attention to us by running any red lights, or anything like that.'

'No, Doctor, I'll drive like my granny is in the back seat.'

We arrived at the marina and instead of parking in the marina car park, I parked in front of the cinema.

'Why are you parking here?' asked Kaufmann.

'It's closer.'

'Oh, don't see why. It doesn't look any closer than the marina car park.'

I shrugged and started walking. What I didn't say was that the cinema car park was better lit and covered by CCTV cameras. Round one to me.

As we approached the boat, I fired my second salvo.

'Hope you brought a torch, Doctor?'

'Why is that, Mr Nevis?'

'There's no electricity on the boat, got turned off after the fire.'

'I've got my phone, there's a flashlight app on it,' said Hanse.

Damn, shot deflected. Or was it? I had no idea if the power was still on. I'd assumed the fire department would have had it turned off, and, if they had, would the batteries be able to keep the bilge pump running? Was the *Osprey* still afloat? Still, with Hanse only using the flashlight app on his phone, it would make it easier for my plan to work.

I could see by the harbour lights that the *Osprey* was still floating, though in total darkness. Good.

'You have your keys, Mr Nevis?' asked Kaufmann.

'Don't need them. Thanks to your friend Hanse and his fire-starting antics, the fire department broke the lock to gain entry.'

I gingerly stepped up onto the deck and pushed the door open. I could have found my way anywhere on the boat in the darkness and found it amusing to hear the muffled curses coming from Kaufmann and Hanse as they tripped over what was left of my workshop.

'It was up here in this cupboard,' I indicated, in the pale light of Hanse's phone.

'Where? I don't see anything,' said Kaufmann.

'Must have been moved. Maybe it's in the main saloon,' I said, climbing back up from the burnt-out workshop.

'That's where you hid the dummy,' said Kaufmann, now sounding a bit annoyed.

'Last place to check will be my cabin,' I said, diving down the stairs. Before Hanse could follow me, I had reached under my mattress and retrieved his gun, still wrapped in its cloth. I tucked it into my trouser waistband and pulled my sweater down over the butt to hide its outline.

'Well, Mr Nevis, where is it?'

I made a big pretence of shaking my head in exasperation. 'It was on the boat; my partner must have moved it. We'll need to call him.'

'Do it now,' said Kaufmann, passing me his phone.

'No can do.'

'Why?'

'Nancy has the phone number in the flat.'

'Mr Nevis, if you are trying to trick me, if you are playing for time, hoping someone will come to your rescue, all I can say is Snyder hates children.'

'Listen, Kaufmann, I don't give a shit about your statue. I just want you out of our lives. For good.'

'Then let's adjourn to your flat, you will call your friend, and he will bring the statue. And then, Mr Nevis, we'll be gone.'

I walked on their left. Hanse's gun was stuck in the left-hand side of my trousers and I didn't want them to see it just yet. Getting it back into Hanse's possession at the right time was crucial to my plan.

I drove as carefully as I could and we were back in the flat in twenty minutes. Nancy was sitting on the settee, reading a book and drinking a cup of tea.

'I'm waiting, Mr Nevis. Call your friend and have him bring the statue.'

Nancy gave me a shocked look; I stared back at her and shook my head imperceptibly.

'Nancy,' I said, 'remember that phone number I asked you to look after? I need to call it.'

This was the weakest part of my plan; if Nancy didn't twig which phone number I was after, I would have to resort to desperate measures.

'Yes, it's in my handbag in the kitchen. I'll get it for you.

Kaufmann nodded to Snyder to follow Nancy. Thankfully he didn't follow her into the kitchen, instead he leaned on the doorframe and picked at something under his fingernails with a knife. That I didn't like; knives can be very dangerous in a close fight.

Nancy came out of the kitchen clutching a piece of paper but before she could hand it to me, Kaufmann grabbed it from her and read the number out. He looked at it, shrugged, then handed it to me with his phone.

I shook my head and said, 'Won't work, unless my number comes up on their display, they won't answer.'

'All right, use your own phone.'

I looked at Hanse and put out my hand.

'Give him his phone, Hanse,' said Kaufmann.

I wanted to grab his hand and rip his arm off, but decided to wait; it wasn't his time – yet.

I made a pretence of dialling Russell's number while pressing the speed dial number for DS Street. I listened to the phone ring, hoping she would answer. Every eye in the room was looking at me, us all willing for the call to be answered. The voicemail kicked in and I hit the hang-up and immediately redialled her number.

'Don't worry, Kaufmann, it's a prearranged code we have for out of hours.'

Come on Street, answer your phone, I willed. She answered by the fifth ring. 'Russell, it's Jack – yes, Jack Nevis – who else is going to call you at two in the morning? No, I'm not on the boat, you need to bring the statue to Nancy's apartment. Yes, the doctor's waiting for it, says as soon as we give him the statue he'll be gone. Okay, we'll be waiting.' Before Kaufmann could grab the phone I hung up.

'Nancy, it's going to be a few minutes before Russell can get here – could you make us some coffee?'

'Okay, back in a minute.'

I needed her out of the way for the last part of my plan. I counted seconds in my head, wondering how long it would take DS Street to get a team together and reach Nancy's apartment. I positioned myself so as to be able to make a lunge at Hanse.

She was quicker than I thought and the first sounds of police sirens startled the silence of the room. Kaufmann looked at me and instantly realised he'd been tricked. I lunged at Hanse and in the ensuing fight, managed to get his gun back into his jacket pocket. He must have thought I was trying to use it for he brandished his newly-returned toy above his head before pointing it directly at my chest.

I had only moments to take in the full horror of what was about to happen. I remember Kaufmann turning the door-handle in a bid to escape, Snyder right behind him, and the evil grin on Hanse's face as he pulled the trigger. I flew back on the impact of the bullet hitting my chest, bumped into Nancy coming out of the kitchen, then passed out into total blackness.

20

Horus

I woke in hospital. Nancy was sitting in a chair at my side; I tried to turn and see her better and winced with pain from where the bullet had entered.

'You're back?'

'Didn't realise I'd gone anywhere.'

'The doctor says you were very lucky; the bullet went right through your shoulder.'

'It came out the back?'

'No, they had to cut it out. Doctor says you will be laid up for quite a while. I'll let them know you've come round.'

She was back in ten minutes with a tall blonde with a pony tail.

'Good morning, Mr Nevis. I'm Doctor Karlsson, I performed the surgery on your injury.'

'Thanks – I think.'

'It will get better. I had to go in through the front of your chest, the bullet was lodged behind your shoulder blade. If it hadn't been for your lucky mascot, the impact of the bullet would have shattered it.

Lucky mascot? What was she talking about? I looked at Nancy, who just smiled and held up the double eagle coin, which now had a finger-sized hole in it. Since the fire, I had returned it to my inside jacket pocket for safekeeping. How fortunate. I would have laughed, but the thought of ripping open the stitches made me just smile. I took it from her and stared at what was once five million pounds, now reduced to a hundredth of its original value.

◆

I stayed in hospital for a week, then went to recuperate at Nancy's.

Kaufmann, Snyder and Hanse had all been stopped before they'd reached the A259 on their way to the Newhaven ferry. Hanse had been stupid to believe he could outshoot the police marksmen and had taken two bullets in the leg before surrendering. At their trial, the evidence pointed to Hanse as the killer of both the detective and Achmed. Kaufmann and Snyder, with the help of expensive counsel, managed to avoid a jail sentence and immediately departed for pastures new, and presumably on with their never-ending pursuit of the falcon. Hanse was given a double life sentence, with the requirement of serving a minimum of thirty years.

After two weeks I was able to get up and move about, but instructed not to do anything too strenuous. Russell and Andy kept an eye on the *Osprey* for me till the doctor gave me the all clear and I was fit to drive again.

Three weeks later I decided it was time to get the *Osprey* over to the yard for its long overdue refit.

Nancy and I said a reluctant goodbye to the children at Sarah's, saying we would be back later that day to take them out for pizza. We then drove over to the marina where Russell and Simon, with two others were waiting for us on the dock.

'Jack, good to see you looking so well. How's the shoulder?' asked Russell

'Fine,' I replied, carefully swinging my arm in an arc over my head.

'You two set the date yet?' asked Simon.

'No, not yet,' answered Nancy.' But watch this space.'

'Just make sure we get an invitation,' replied Simon.

'Don't worry, you will.'

'We're all ready to go, Jack.'

'Thanks, Russell.'

'Made a bit of a mess running the new fuel line, had to climb over the remains of your wood store. Sorry, Nancy, we've tracked quite a few footprints across the floor.'

'That's okay, Russell, we're going to have to strip a lot of the interior due to the fire anyway. I imagine it will get a lot worse before it gets better.'

I felt like a spare groom at a wedding as I watched Simon take charge of the *Osprey* and head her out through the harbour locks, into the English Channel and westward to the repair yard.

Nancy and I spent the day trying to sort out the mess inside the main saloon. Although the fire hadn't travelled as far as the saloon, the smoke, ashes, and firemen's boots had. There was a fine covering of ash everywhere with several pairs of blackened fireman's boot prints going between the main door and the stairs down into the workshop. After an hour of fruitless cleaning, that and the need to constantly go out on deck for fresh air, we gave up and climbed into the wheelhouse with cups of tea and reminisced about the last time we were together in the *Beatrice* coming down the Irish Sea.

The journey along the coast was uneventful and as the sun approached the horizon we tied up at the pontoon beside the marine railway.

'That's going to hold the *Osprey*?' exclaimed Nancy.

'That's what I was told,' I replied, looking at the rusty steel cradle sitting on railway lines running down from the concrete covered yard and into the water. 'I expect once they have hauled the *Osprey* out of the water they will put her on blocks with props to hold her up while they work on fixing the leaks.

'The yard will take it from here, Jack,' said Russell. 'You still coming back with us in the mini-bus?'

'Yes, we told the kids we would take them out for pizza. We'll drive over tomorrow for the haul-out.'

We piled into the minibus for the drive back to Eastbourne.

'You planning to do all the interior work, Jack?' asked Andy, as we sped along the A27.

'Not all. As part of the insurance coverage, the yard is going to strip out all the burnt-out interior. All Nancy and I will be doing at that point is shovelling up the debris into piles for the yard to remove through the overhead hatch.'

'What about later, after the strip-out is done?'

'We've drawn up some plans for the cabins and my new workshop, all fairly straightforward.'

♦

Another tiring day. The trip to the pizza parlour was a huge success and it was two exhausted people who climbed into bed at ten-thirty.

I was almost asleep when Nancy sat bolt upright in bed.'

'You all right?'

'Yes, give me a minute.'

'What woke you up?'

'The gold, Jack? Where *is* the gold?'

'Kaufmann got it, just before Hanse set the boat on fire.'

'You sure? He didn't look like someone who'd just got their hands on two billion pounds of gold.'

'Three quarters of a million in gold you mean. As soon as he tried to sell any of those coins, the US treasury would be on to him in a flash, and take the lot.'

'So you think he'll just melt them down and sell the gold?'

'If he has any sense.'

'Unlikely, he's got as much sense as the proverbial lemming.'

'And is as devious as a barnyard rat.'

'Suppose he does melt the gold down – how will he dispose of it? Can't see him walking into a bank with half a dozen ingots and asking to deposit them in his current account.'

'He'd probably go through a commercial dealer, though he'd probably sell it through more than one to keep suspicion down.'

'It's just not fair, a man like that goes through life messing up other people's lives then gets away scot-free to enjoy himself.'

'Life will eventually catch up with him, wish I could be around to see it.'

♦

Next morning, we woke to a day of promise. I looked out of the bedroom window and saw blue skies from horizon to horizon.

'Come on, sleepyhead,' I said to Nancy, 'we've got work to do.'

'What time is it?'

I glanced at the bedside clock. 'Five forty-five.'

'Must we get up so early?'

'We've got a long drive to the yard and I want to be there when the *Osprey* is hauled out.'

'Coffee, I need coffee,' said Nancy.

I shuffled into the kitchen and put the kettle on to boil then returned to the bedroom to dress. Nancy was in the shower. 'Kettle's on.'

'Thanks. Are the kids awake?'

'Don't know, haven't checked,' I shouted back, over the noise of the running water.

An hour and a half later all five of us piled into my car, and after stopping for breakfast, we drove off along the A27 towards Portsmouth and the yard where the *Osprey* was waiting to be hauled out on to the marine railway.

I parked the car in the yard in front of the chandlery and looked through the fence at the *Osprey*. The yard workers had already moved her into the cradle and looked like they were preparing to pull her out of the water.

'Come on everyone, we're just in time for the haul-out.'

I held Stephen's hand, Nancy held Sandra and Stephanie's and we walked over to the crew and owners' waiting area to watch.

It wasn't till they had the *Osprey* completely out of the water that I fully appreciated the size of her. Like an iceberg, there was considerably more under the water than above.

'What are they going to do next, Jack?' asked Stephen.

'They'll take a hose and wash all the weeds and barnacles off the bottom.'

'Then are they going to fix the leaks?'

'Not right away. When they've finished cleaning the bottom I think they will move her up close to the boatshed where they can work on her.'

'In that big shed with the other boats?'

I shook my head. 'No, the *Osprey* won't go into the shed. They'll probably just haul her up to the doors and park her there.'

Even with the pressure sprayers it took almost an hour to rid the bottom of weeds and barnacles. Then, just as I suspected, they hauled the *Osprey* all the way up to the end of the railway in front of the workshop doors. I was surprised to see how easy it had been to haul her out of the water.

Having the boat parked at the top of the yard beside the boatshed worked out better than I'd first imagined. For a start it was beside the shed where the yard workers had their tools and machinery, it was close to the toilets and café, and was out of the way of boat movements. So the kids could play on the ground without being in the way. Come Monday all would change, of course, the shipwrights would be out with oxyacetylene torches, heavy duty drills, sledge hammers, a mobile forge to heat the rivets, and who knew what else. I was hoping they wouldn't need to replace any of the hull plating but just the offending rivets, as the money I'd put aside for the work would only go so far.

We gave the kids an area where they could play, with strict instructions not to stray away from it, while Nancy and I, dressed in our grubbiest work clothes, set to clearing the fire debris.

'I think the big stuff first,' I said, as we surveyed the fire detritus in the forward compartment.

'There's so much of it,' said Nancy, pushing back an errant strand of hair from her face, leaving a long slick of charcoal dust on her face. 'The fire appears to have reduced most of your wood supplies to charcoal.'

I thought of all those hours spent at Dave's going through the wood piles, selecting the best pieces of spruce for soundboards and bracing, the flamed maple and mahogany for the necks, and the exotic hardwoods for the backs and sides. They were now all reduced to charcoal. How would I ever get the money together to replace them? The insurance had only offered a paltry sum, not understanding the uniqueness of my collection.

311

I went through into my workshop to see what was salvageable. Because the worst of the leaks had been in the hull at the forward end of the boat, I'd realised the floor would have to come up for the hull repairs to be carried out, so clearing my workshop was a job that had to be done prior to the haul-out anyway. At least in preparation for the haul-out I'd managed to box up all of my edge tools in stout wooden boxes, and they had only suffered from charring on the outside and the contents would live to carve another day.

I'd just started to pass them up into the main saloon when Nancy popped her head through the doorway.

'Jack, you need to see this.'

'See what?'

'Just come in here and see what.'

In the few weeks that I'd grown to know her, I realised that she could be very tricky, in a nice sort of way. So I put down the box of Marples chisels and followed her through into the forward compartment.

'Do you see it?' she asked.

'See what? All I see is destruction and piles of charcoal.'

'All that glitters is…'

'Is – gold?'

'Don't you see it?'

'See what? I've no idea what you are talking about.'

'You're standing on it.'

I looked down at the floor and saw what she was referring to. Under the piles of charcoal and black dust, shone the glitter of gold.

'It must have melted in the fire and run out over the floor'.

'So Kaufmann never found it! No wonder he was so pissed off.'

It was a moment that could have played out in the movie *Treasure Island*, where the pirates dived into the sandpit looking for Flint's treasure. Though at this moment we didn't have Long John

Silver standing over us with cutlass in hand and a parrot squawking *pieces of eight, pieces of eight*. We were on our knees and, with our bare hands, swept and poked at the charcoal and dust trying to see just how large the sheet of melted gold was.

Thankfully the gold hadn't stuck to the floor and we were able to peel up the rivulets that had run out from where the box containing the double-eagle coins had been hidden. I estimated we had somewhere in the region of thirty pounds of the stuff, all in bits and pieces. But what to do with it? We couldn't just stuff it in our pockets.

'What are you thinking, Jack?'

'Just wondering what to do with all this gold. Especially since it's now no longer recognisable as coins.'

'We could just say we discovered it while stripping out the interior after the fire. It was found on our – oops, sorry – *your* boat.'

I smiled at her and said, 'No, you were right the first time. It's *our* boat, and *our* gold.'

'So, what do we do? If we take it back to the flat we could lose it all to some opportune thief, but equally we just can't leave it here on the boat.'

'I have an idea.'

'What?'

'I'm going to call the police and tell them what we've found. Lost property rules should apply.'

'And what are they?'

'The police will come and take the gold into custody. We'll be credited for finding it on our property and, when no one can prove it's theirs, ownership will revert to us and we can dispose of it through the proper channels.'

'You think that'll work?'

'Can't think of anything better. And at least when the word gets into the press, as it will, Kaufmann will realise what has happened and his chances of getting the gold will be lost forever.'

'And we'll be able to live without wondering if he's hiding round the next corner.'

♦

It didn't take long for the press and TV news to react to what had happened. One SMS to the BBC had reporters and camera crews flocking to the boatyard. The news about the fire was still fresh in the pipeline, so a continuing story like the finding of the gold also lit a trail from the newsrooms around the world to the *Osprey's* deck. When asked about how it got there, we just shook our heads and said we didn't have any idea, must have been there since WW2.

The local press had the children stand side by side holding chunks of the gold, just like they'd been at the beach and found strands of seaweed. We decided to let the local television channel on board to film the gold being stuffed into police evidence bags and being carted off in a security van. It was a bit of a blur for the kids, who'd not been party to any of the goings on, and with the professor being the only one who knew of the existence of the coins, I felt the story would play out in the news very quickly, to be replaced by some salacious story or other.

♦

'Sorry we don't have at least one of those coins as a memento,' I said to Nancy, as we sat with the children in the hotel bar sipping on our champagne.

'Would you have liked to have had one as a memento?'

'I suppose it would have been nice.'

'Really? After all we've been through? We could never let anyone see it.'

'I suppose you're right, at least we have each other and the children, that's all that matters.'

There was the one that had stopped Hanse's bullet, I thought; I still had that. The police weren't interested in its value, only that it was evidence in an attempted murder case. They'd returned it to me after the trial and I had wondered just what to do with it, especially since it now had a ring-sized hole in the middle, and that was when I had the brilliant idea.

◆

The *Osprey,* now officially renamed the *Kestrel,* made her return to the water and the marina. Complete with cabins for the kids and a nice new workshop for me.

The first morning back in the marina, I got up early and made Nancy breakfast in bed, complete with a special present.

'What is it?' she asked, picking up the small box from the breakfast tray.

'Open it and see.'

I watched as she undid the ribbon and pulled the box lid off.

'Jack! You – how did you do it?'

'I found a jeweller who specialised in custom jewellery. I told him I had a gold coin with a hole in the middle, and could he make it into a wedding band. It's a bit bigger than a standard one, but I thought it was the best use of the damaged coin.'

I watched as she took it out of the box and tried it on.

'Not many women have a five-million-pound wedding ring! How thoughtful of you. Pity it's too big to wear – I'll still treasure it, though.'

◆

Eventually the time ran out on anyone claiming the gold, so, with the aid of a broker, it was sold and a nice large cheque went into our bank account. I did get phone calls from people wanting to help us invest our newly-found wealth, but we just ignored them and found a trusty, local, financial advisor instead.

Nancy finished writing the song she'd been working on and promised she'd sing it to me one evening. I completed the restoration of the Torres and took it to Bonhams to be auctioned.

◆

We were sitting in the wheelhouse drinking coffee when Nancy said, 'You remember you told Mr Munroe you'd bring him down to meet up with Lieutenant Hudson?'

'Hmm, you're right, I did. I'll call his daughter and see if he would still like to make the journey.'

Nancy poured me another coffee as I dialled Munroe's number. Agnes answered by the third ring

'Agnes, this is Jack Nevis. How are you, and how is your dad?'

'Oh, I'm fine, Mr Nevis. Father's fine as well.'

'I was wondering if he would like to come down to Eastbourne and meet Lieutenant Hudson? We'd pay his fare.'

'Oh, I don't think he's up to travelling on his own.'

'Sorry, I meant the both of you. I'd arrange the flight and come pick you up at the airport.'

'I'll ask Father and call you back. He's napping just now and I don't want to wake him.'

Next on the list was to call the nursing home and talk with Lieutenant Hudson.

'Wonderful idea! Any day is fine, I'm not going anywhere.'

Agnes called back and we arranged for the following Wednesday for her and her dad to fly down to Gatwick airport.

Nancy and I drove up and took them to see Lieutenant Hudson.

Prior to the Munroes visit I'd found out that the nursing home provided overnight accommodation for a visiting family, so there was no need to get them back to the airport that day.

I arranged for us all to have dinner at the Grand Hotel, so it was an odd gathering of combatants round the table. The press got wind of the meeting of the two World War 2 veterans, and even the local BBC station did a sensitive interview with them.

It was a sad moment when we said goodbye to Agnes and her dad at Gatwick. I realised it would probably be the last time we'd get to talk and it was with a great sense of loss when we heard two weeks later that Munroe had passed away peacefully in his sleep.

But the biggest shock was what followed later in the week.

'Nancy, there's someone at the door. Can you get it? I've got glue all over my hands.'

'Okay.'

I heard her talk with whoever had rung the bell, the door close and Nancy's footsteps on the stairs.

'Who was it?' I asked.

'Parcelforce. Are you waiting for a delivery?' she asked, walking into the workshop.

'No, not that I remember. Bring it over here and we'll open it on the bench.'

It had a return address from Port Glasgow.

I cut through the packing tape and found a note inside.

'What does it say?' asked Nancy.

Dear Jack and Nancy, before he passed away, my father said to send you this, he'd completely forgotten he had it in his case. He'd meant to bring it with him when he came down, but was so excited about meeting Lieutenant Hudson, he completely forgot.

'Well, what is it?' asked Nancy.

I put down the letter and picked up the bubble-wrapped package. As my hand closed around it I knew immediately what it was, and realised our peace could be about to be shattered.

'Well, what is it? she repeated.'

'The thing that dreams and nightmares are made of.'

Only the sound of wavelets on the hull and bubble-wrap being peeled back could be heard as I unwrapped the statue of Horus. That bird – that bird who'd evaded the clutches of many hands down through the millennia.

'Is that the falcon? Is that Horus?' asked Nancy.

'I'm sure it is. But what to do with it? We can't – no, daren't – let the press know we have it. If Kaufmann even got a sniff that we have it, we'll just have to go through all the crap we've just gone through.'

'So what will we do with it?'

'Let me think for a moment.'

'I know, why don't we just throw it over the side and pretend we never saw it?'

I shook my head. 'I've thought of a solution.'

I took my phone and called the one person who I could trust to deal with the problem.

'Professor, it's Jack Nevis. Professor, we have a problem and need your advice.'

'What did he suggest?' asked Nancy.

'He said to bring it right over.'

We packed the kids in the back of the car, locked up the *Osprey* and headed for Wartling and the professor's house.

Mrs Lozinski showed us into the professor's study. He was plainly agitated with excitement. As we entered the room he drew the curtains. Mrs Lozinski took the children out to the kitchen to sample the chocolate chip cookies she'd just baked for them.

'You have brought it with you?' he asked, rubbing his hands together.

I took it out of the shopping bag and handed it to him.

We sat down and waited while he looked the statue over with his magnifying glass. Finally, he looked up and said, 'This is genuine, Jack. What are you going to do with it?'

'Carry it to Mordor and throw it in the river of fire?'

'Ah-ha, Tolkien. No, I have a better idea. If it's all right with you, I propose to take it in to the British Museum tomorrow. I'll find a nice quiet shelf and, with an appropriate obscure label stating this to be an unclassified, nondescript representation of the god Horus, and just park it there. It will live there in obscurity in perpetuity. Fully on display but no one will be any the wiser about its heritage.'

The End

I stand in the rain and hide my tears.

I watched you go, dressed for the fight
into the night sky, and out of sight
They swore you'd return, but not that way
Draped with a flag, you passed my way.

When the gentle breath of spring, warms the winter air
I'd hold you in my arms, and dream without a care.

My broken heart can never mend
So loving memories to you I send
Remember me when you wander near
As I stand in the rain and hide my tears

When the gentle breath of spring, warms the winter air
I'd hold you in my arms, and dream without a care.

Now all I have are memories
And your picture by my bed
I stare at it as I fall asleep
and dream of you, and what we had.

When the gentle breath of spring, warms the winter air
I'll hold you in my arms, and dream without a care.

What if he's the one, can this love last
Will his love fill this cold and empty heart
For if his love is true, the past can fly
And I'll dream again the dreams gone by.

When the gentle breath of spring, warms the winter air
I'll hold you in my arms, and dream without a care.

I stand in the rain and hide my tears. (Nancy's Song, from "The Falcon")
©Alex Willis July 2016

Alex Willis

Alex is the author of the growing and successful detective series about DCI Buchanan, a Glasgow cop relocated to the genteel town of Eastbourne.

Alex also writes stand-alone mystery stories. He lives in the picturesque village of Westham with his lovely wife Nancy. They have three married children and currently three grandchildren.

Alex spends his days writing, giving talks, being a househusband and gregarious grandfather. He enjoys travelling, especially cruising, going for walks with his wife, cycling, and when he gets time, tending the family allotment. You can learn more about him and his writing on his website,

www.alexwillis.me

Lightning Source UK Ltd.
Milton Keynes UK
UKHW020322040921
389836UK00010B/2501